"I find the book to be simply wonderful with the perfect balance of being an accessible read without compromising historical depth and plot complexities. But most importantly the words easily weave a visual image that draws the reader in. When I look for a "good read" it is this factor that makes me not only pick up the book but keep me reading. The characters are believable and come alive on the pages. I will be at the front of the line when the book is published!"

-Lieutenant Colonel Todd Meaker, Canadian Forces

"*Getarix* was an enormously enjoyable read. Mike Allen has combined a thrilling adventure tale with a chariot load full of historic fact and technological detail to make a story that is interesting on two levels at once. The characters and group dynamics were extremely well developed; Mike has obviously taken his experience with modern soldiers and contextualized it within the Army of Ancient Rome in a way that is both believable and accessible. Mike Allen is the Iron Age Tom Clancy."

-Matt McDonald, Hilperton, UK

GETARIX

OUT *of* OBSCURITY

To Duff
A fellow author
+ friend God bless

Michael W Allen
15 Oct 2014

MICHAEL W. ALLEN

WORD ALIVE PRESS
Just Write!

MIX
Paper from
responsible sources
FSC
www.fsc.org   FSC® C016245

For more information visit www.getarix.com.

I dedicate this book to my wife Paula for without whom it would not be.

TABLE OF CONTENTS

Roman Numeral Chart

I=1	V=5	X=10	L=50	
I 1	XI 11	XXI 21	XXXI 31	XLI 41
II 2	XII 12	XXII 22	XXXII 32	XLII 42
III 3	XIII 13	XXIII 23	XXXIII 33	XLIII 43
IV 4	XIV 14	XXIV 24	XXXIV 34	XLIV 44
V 5	XV 15	XXV 25	XXXV 35	XLV 45
VI 6	XVI 16	XXVI 26	XXXVI 36	XLVI 46
VII 7	XVII 17	XXVII 27	XXXVII 37	XLVII 47
VIII 8	XVIII 18	XXVIII 28	XXXVIII 38	XLVIII 48
IX 9	XIX 19	XXIX 29	XXXIX 39	XLIX 49
X 10	XX 20	XXX 30	XL 40	L 50

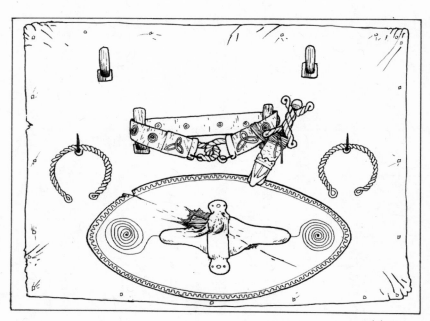

I

OUT OF THE FOG

The bonfire crackled as the people gathered with a sense of anticipation. The sun sank lazily into the horizon, as if nothing unusual was about to happen. The old man felt the stiffness in his knees as he bent to sit on the rocky outcrop overlooking the sacrificial site. The light wind carried the last of the winter cold across the small crowd. As he got comfortable and wrapped the old, worn, heavy woollen cloak around his aging body, he thought this would be a good vantage point to witness the ceremony. *Ceremony indeed. Why don't we call it what it is, a sacrifice, murder if the whole truth were told.*

Every year, the old man had to find a new place to observe the annual sacrifice. Every year, the ceremony moved along the borderland. The sacrifices were performed to protect against invasion from the other tribes. *Little good it seems to do. These ceremonies usually mark the beginning of the raiding season when the tribes of Britain cross these same boundaries to steal cattle and sheep, and occasionally an unlucky soul who ends up in a Roman slave market somewhere.*

He hated these things. *Human sacrifices are barbaric to the extreme. Even the Romans outlawed them. And we call them the barbarians. But who knows, the Druids could be right about the gods. It never pays to anger the gods.* That is why he sat back where he could be part of things without participation. First, the victim would be stabbed in the belly with a dagger as he stood before the priests.

This blow would not kill him, but simply disable him. Next they would torture him mercilessly, cutting off parts of his body until mercy finally stepped in and death arrived to take its prey. They would start with the nipples, and in the end his body would be cut in two. They would push the upper torso under the water of the bog, running hazel rope right through the upper arms of the sometimes-headless torso to hold it in place, anchored down into the deep mud holding its poor victim in place, some say for many generations. *The priests say the gods preserve them for eternity.* It was the old man's job to make the rope by taking two or three green hazel branches about the size of a man's finger and twisting it like a rope into what really became a stake, so when it dried no man could pry them apart.

The thought of being such a victim was unbearable to him, but he need not worry. The subjects of these ceremonies were always from the noble class and always young. He felt safe on both accounts. He would just have to bear watching. He noticed the crowd now standing around the fire soaking up its heat, waiting for something to happen. As the darkness was just settling in and the chanting began, he saw two riders on what looked like the large Roman horses draw near. The two were the last to arrive at the border area where the sacrifice was arranged to take place. As they approached the bonfire the old man could see them clearly through the mist.

Getarix, the taller of the two, was a handsome young man of only sixteen. He had mixed feelings of fear and anxiety. Not fully aware as to why his elder brother was adamant he assist in this year's sacrifice. Cunorix, his brother, had never explained how he was to help. Only that he would come into his own, to fulfil his role as a man of the family and a full member of the community. Getarix had a passionate hate for these things. If it wasn't for his brother he never would have gone near the place. He did not fear the gods; he hated them—that is, if they even existed. He worried they would arrive too late to take part in the ceremony and at the same time was afraid they weren't late enough. As they got closer, they heard the chanting. The tone let them know they were just in time.

When Getarix was a boy of ten, his brother took him to one of these ceremonies. What he saw horrified him. He found a place at the back of the crowd, where all he had to endure were the screams of that year's victim of divine blood lust. He had never been to one since. Getarix hated everything to do with the gods. He always found himself away from the village during the day and evening of the sacrifice, usually dragging Cullen with him.

Getarix estimated the crowd to be about eighty people strong. His companion and closest friend, Cullen, thought almost everyone from the village must have been there. As they dismounted, the crowd opened wide, creating a path leading from their horses to the bonfire. In front of the fire stood the three village priests, and Cunorix to their left. Getarix noticed a great sense of relief on his brother's face upon his arrival. However, he refused to look Getarix in the face, keeping his eyes lowered, peering at the ground.

Getarix knew he was the centre of attention and had a feeling they had delayed the ceremonies on his account. He could not get rid of the nagging thought that he should've followed his uncle's advice to flee.

As he slowly advanced toward the fire, the people turned to face him. Their gaze fixed on him as he moved closer to the centre. Cullen stayed with the horses.

The closer he got the louder the chants echoed, giving him the feeling that he was losing control of his own movements and, for that matter, his mind. The hypnotic sound of the chanting lifted and carried him toward the centre. When he reached the spot where the priests stood he stopped, less than an arm's length away. It was only then that he saw the dagger in the hand of the older frail Prasutagix, senior of the three priests.

Prasutagix stood in the middle, flanked by the other two Druid priests. Cunorix now was looking on with anticipation. When Getarix finally caught his eyes, it all came to light. He could see the hate and blood lust deep in his brother's soul. In that instant Getarix understood why Cunorix had suddenly treated him with so much respect, even camaraderie. He also understood the villagers unexpectedly acting as if he was a long-lost hero, even the beautiful Boudica's unexpected flirting, and most of all, his uncle's warning. It all made sense. Even the feast in his honour fit for a nobleman. But the one thought he fought was where his mother fit in the events of the day. *She could never…*

He saw the glint of light from the fire reflecting off the blade as Prasutagix pulled his dagger arm back, readying to thrust it into their sacrificial victim's belly. As the dagger raced forward, Getarix understood fully he was this year's sacrifice.

24 HOURS EARLIER

Grey…! As far as the eye could see, grey, which was about as far as the tip of a normal man's nose. An all-encompassing grey, leaving no room for anything of value; a choking greyness, erasing the visions of the most optimistic of dreamers.

Getarix could hardly remember what the blue sky looked like or even the feeling of the warm sun on his face. He was dying inside. Or already dead, he could hardly tell any longer. If the grey was not enough, the constant drizzle was soaking everything to the core, a cool soaking able to dampen the fire of any life. When it was not raining, the cold of the ever-present fog felt like it was coming from within the bones of its victims.

Getarix knew he had to get out, the sooner the better. But where? The only way was through Roman lands, and that was the crux of the matter.

The only thing Getarix felt other than the faithful cold was hunger. If only Cunorix would trade with the Romans directly. Then they could afford all the food they could eat, or like his uncle, they too could enjoy a life of wealth. Cunorix, his brother, refused to let go of his soul-eating hatred for all things Roman. It did not make sense to Getarix. *We sell our dogs to other Britons, at a great loss, who in turn sell them to the rich Romans at a great profit, making them rich by our labour.*

Getarix noticed the sky was growing dark; a crowding darkness that told him it was time to get home for the evening meal. If he was lucky they would be having mutton. He hated mutton. Getting up, his knees cracked, and only then did Getarix realize how many hours he had been sitting with his head in the clouds. He looked around to see if Epona, his big bay mare, had stayed with him. Suddenly he felt a painful thud and the loud annoying voice of his younger friend. Cullen's full weight pressed down on him as they both tumbled onto the wet grass.

"Cullen, blast you," Getarix yelled.

"Ha!" Laughed Cullen.

"Now I am truly soaked to the bone. What by the gods is wrong with you?"

"Did I take you from your dreams of warmer places? An army could sneak up to you."

"You would be dreaming of warmer places if you had a half a brain," Getarix said in a tone only a close friend could get away with.

"Oh come now, don't be so dark! It's a beautiful day," Cullen said as he swept his arms broadly.

Getarix gave him a look of utter disgust. "How can you tell? I've yet to 'see' today. Cullen, don't you ever dream about what it's like out there?" Getarix pointed to nowhere in particular. "You know neither of us has traveled more than a half-day's ride from the very spot we were born," he said, once again getting lost in the clouds. "Think of it: cities, great cities, with stone buildings and places where people just sit and learn and debate all the great ideas of the ages. Great ships traveling to all the exotic lands of the world. Great armies marching into new lands."

Cullen once again broke into his daydreaming. "Oh, come on, what do those places have that we don't?"

"Uh, Cullen you dolt, everything!" Getarix got up, swung himself onto Epona, and began to ride off toward the village, with Cullen riding after him on his father's tired old British pony.

"Getarix, I don't know…there's so much unknown out there. I think I'll choose the known."

Getarix pulled the reins, stopping Epona in her tracks, and faced his younger friend. "Let's look at it, shall we? This is what we know. My father died before I was born. He died fighting the Romans, not knowing I was even conceived. My brother, Cunorix, rules me like a slave. His refusal to do business with the Romans, because of my father, keeps us in poverty, even though we are a so-called noble family." Getarix lowered his voice. "Now let's look at you. Your mother died mysteriously under circumstances your father has yet to explain, and you…you will be returning to an empty hut. That's if you're lucky, because if he is home, he will just as likely beat your brains into the dust. If it was not for my mother's cooking, you would have starved to death years ago. So there, that's what we know. Now let's get home or my brother will beat my brains into the dust or, more accurately, the mud."

At that, Getarix whistled for the dogs; he heard their howling get closer as they ran toward him through the fog. Once the dogs arrived, it hit him that he had failed to run them like his brother asked, so he prayed to the gods that his brother would not inquire if he had. He turned Epona toward home. They approached the last hut that stood along the west road just outside the village where Getarix lived. The smell of the cooking fire permeated the air. Smoke was rising from the small hole that surrounded the main support pole for the cone-shaped thatch roof. His eyes followed the roofline down to where it rested on mud walls about waist-high off the ground. His nose caught the smells of the evening meal. *Great, leeks,* Getarix thought. *No meat.* He liked his mother's cooking, but there was never enough to go around. Once again hunger would be his companion for the night—hunger and bedbugs.

Cullen and Getarix secured and fed the dogs. "Cullen, do you know that was more meat than I'll eat in a week, and we just gave it to those dogs?"

"True, but the Romans won't buy skinny dogs, will they?"

"We wouldn't know, would we, Cullen?"

The fog had lifted enough to see the rundown hut that Cullen and his father lived in, about twenty paces down the lane toward the village. It was dark and no smoke came from the thatch. The two lifelong friends stood and talked without a single word spoken between them. "Come on." Getarix motioned to Cullen. "There's always room for one more." As they bent down to enter the hut, the inviting warmth met them. The hut was a clean orderly home, well laid out in spite of the sparseness of their possessions. To the right of the support pole was the fire pit, where all the cooking took place and in the evenings people would sit and talk about the day's events, as long as Cunorix was not there. On the other side was a small wooden table with two benches where all the food preparation took place. The same table would be cleared off and serve as an eating table, later as a games table. Around the low walls were four bed spaces, one for Cullen when escape became necessary. The rest of the wall space was used to keep provisions, not that there was much there nowadays. The only bare wall was found directly across from the door where hung the things of the great warrior, Vercingetorix the Great, great grandfather of Getarix and the man his mother named him after.

The fire in the hut was enough to burn off the humidity in the air, replacing it with the familiar smell of smoke. Smoke mingled with the smells of his mother's cooking that, for Getarix, would always be the smell of home. It registered deeply within his soul. The mother of Getarix and Cunorix, Aigneis still held her beauty in spite of many difficult years when tragedy held sway. At forty-one, she still had the strength of her youth but in her eyes one could not escape seeing the sadness and loss. In the quiet moments of the day, Aigneis would search her memory, seeking images of happier days, days before Getarix was born and Cunorix was just a strapping boy of eleven. She would weep at the memory when Kailen, her husband, left her and Cunorix. The time when the call came out for young Celtic warriors to arm themselves and cross the water to take back Gaul from the Romans. Foolish dream. What could a few hundred untrained Celtic farmers do to the mighty armies of Rome? That did not seem to matter to Kailen, the grandson of the great Celtic warrior Vercingetorix, who was one of the first to answer. He had girded himself with his grandfather's shield, dagger, and sword that hung on the wall. These were the only weapons that the Great Vercingetorix did not lay before the feet of the Roman General Caesar. When called upon, the men left with enough confidence that one would think Vercingetorix himself was leading a column of thousands. Kailen's last words to Aigneis were a boast about being the grandson of Vercingetorix the Great, so how could some weak Romans do him harm? "He beat the mighty Caesar and I will do no less." As is in these situations, he left out the fact that Caesar in his turn eventually beat the great Vercingetorix and later had him strangled. Just before marching off, Kailen turned to his eleven-year-old Cunorix, telling him he was the man of the house and making him promise to take care of his mother. Undue pressure to put on such a serious-minded boy of eleven. Months passed and they heard nothing of their men or of the battle. For all the villagers knew, no battle was fought. Then they started to stumble back. Broken men all of them, some of their injuries obvious yet others deep and unseen. Kailen, along with his sword, was never seen nor heard from again. Astnicx, father of Cullen, reported that Kailen fell in battle. He recovered the shield Kailen had from his grandfather. Astnicx had found it abandoned on the battlefield, and he later recovered the dagger and belt from a dead Roman, probably the Roman who had killed Kailen. The same shield and dagger from two generations before, hung once again on the wall with the golden arm torques. The missing sword's absence stood out on the wall.

In the quiet stillness of the nights, Aigneis would weep, tormented with visions of her husband's unknown, unattended grave on some lonely plain.

A few months after the return of the men who had survived, Getarix was born. By his sixteenth year, he had grown into a vision of his namesake, Vercingetorix the Great. He was tall, strong, and handsome, with his red hair worn in two braids that framed his freckled face. He had also grown into one of the greatest horsemen known to Britain. His only equal was his friend Cullen. Aigneis feared for her younger son, for he possessed the same restless spirit that had afflicted every generation of her husband's family, causing them to wander into history and die young.

Aigneis heard the door open and there was Getarix. From her first glance, she knew he was in one of his moods. She only hoped Cunorix was not in one of his. Cunorix at eleven could never have been more proud of his father than when he stood by his mother with a promise on his lips to take care of her some seventeen summers ago.

Following Getarix through the door was Cullen. Cullen was not as tall or as quick of mind as Getarix, but made up for any slowness by his gentle strength. "As strong as an ox," they would say, "and such a nice boy, too bad about his father." Cullen may not have been the brightest lad in town but his outlook on life was so simple that he was able to see some things more clearly than others who tended to complicate things. His greatest virtue had to be his loyalty, something he never experienced from his father.

"Getarix, my son, you look cold. Come by the fire." Aigneis smiled. "Cullen, come my boy, you too warm yourself. I noticed that your father is away. You will stay here tonight where it's warm."

"I should call this my home, for as much time I spend here. I'm sorry—"

"No reason to feel sorry. Getarix, you're all wet. What have you been doing?"

"Ask Cullen…" Cullen smiled. "Where is Cunorix?" Getarix added nervously. At just the mention of his name, the room tensed. With every inch Getarix grew in height, Cunorix grew in hate of anything Roman. He particularly hated the fact that his younger brother did not share his disdain for Rome.

"He will be late tonight. He told me that he had some business with Priests tonight…he has already eaten—" The sound of horses clopping just outside the door interrupted Aigneis. Everyone tensed up, glancing at the door with fear. The door slammed open, not with the wrath of Cunorix but with the familiar laugh and happy face of Cunhail as he tumbled into the home of his sister.

"Cunhail," Aigneis cried in joy as she ran into the arms of her elder brother. His usual bright shining face never failed to lighten up any room he entered. Getarix, just behind his mother, greeted his uncle with a hug and uncharacteristic joy.

"Uncle, where have you been? What adventures have you been on? Are you still trading horses? Did you see…?"

"Getarix, let him sit and catch his breath." Aigneis turned her attention to Cunhail. "Here, brother, take some food first. Getarix, there will be plenty of time to interrogate your uncle later…"

"Wait, wait, wait…before any interrogation or even food, get your boots on, boy."

Getarix got his boots on. Cullen by his side, his uncle said, "You will be sixteen soon, but alas I will not be here to give your gift."

"Gift?"

"Yes, my son, gift…it's outside." Getarix almost tripped over himself getting out of the door.

"Get your cloak on…" He was gone before his mother could finish. She grabbed his cloak and went for the door after her brother.

Getarix darted out of the hut in the dark of the night headlong into a mountain of horseflesh. As he picked himself up off the ground, he heard the laughter of his uncle. "How do you like him?"

Getarix, still trying to get his bearings, did not quite understand. "How do I like what?"

"Your horse, boy, he's yours…he's a bay like mine."

"But Uncle, I already have one."

"Now you have two, my lad. A man could never have too many horses now, can he?" His uncle became a bit more serious. "Now Getarix, this horse is a full breed Gaulish horse like Epona, but he is of the finest pedigree, unlike our little ponies. A year old he is, with a lifetime of service ahead of him, up to twenty years if you treat him well."

"What's his name?" Getarix was still in a bit of a daze.

"I call him Caballo. Do you remember that word?"

"Of course, Uncle, it's Roman for horse."

"I got him from a Roman in Gaul, so it seems to make sense to call him that. Mind you, the name Caballo in Roman country might not make as much sense."

"Actually it makes perfect sense, just like Epona in Celtic country."

Cunhail chuckled. "You got me there, boy."

"About Epona, she is…" Getarix cut himself off as he looked at Cullen and then at his mother. Aigneis gave him a nod of understanding. "Cullen, you just turned fourteen, yes?"

"I did." Cullen answered, off guard.

"Epona is yours, my friend."

Cullen's eyes grew huge. "What…why, I could not…"

"Too late, she's yours."

"Well, it's getting colder and I for one am going inside," Aigneis said as she handed Getarix his cloak, catching his eyes for a moment. He could see the immense maternal pride in her eyes. Getarix felt good deep within his soul, as if he had done just the right thing.

"Getarix, why don't you take Caballo to the barn, and take care of my bay as well. We have all night to catch up, my boy."

Getarix led Caballo and Cullen led Cunhail's horse to the barn.

Once inside the hut, Aigneis said, "Brother, you spoil him too much."

"Someone should. He's probably one of the best riders in Britain, and don't think I don't know how Cunorix treats him. You know, Aigneis, he's a good lad."

"Oh, by the gods, I know. He is so often sullen, feeling as cloudy as the weather; except for when you are here, brother, he completely changes. It's like you give him his soul back."

"He's the joy of my life. How has Cunorix been to him?"

"Cunorix is a good lad as well…"

"He might be, but it's locked under too many layers of hate and resentment, and that poor lad out in the barn has been destined to take the punishment for

Kailen's death. Imagine…that kid out there was not even born. It's wrong, you know, Aigneis."

"I know, Cunhail, I know. What can I do about it? Cunorix is so filled with rage, even I, his own mother, fear him…maybe you could talk to him."

"You know he would never listen to the likes of me. I deal with his chosen enemies. Romans make me unclean. He won't even sell his dogs to me. Besides, I must be off first thing tomorrow. First to the village and then to western parts. I have neglected my business there. The Romans are screaming for tin to make their bronze, and they pay handsomely these days."

"Something we never will see as long as—"

"I'm sorry, I should not burden you with my problems. You know, you still have not answered my question. How has it been going between them?"

"Um…things are not good and I fear they are getting worse. I'm afraid they might go to blows before it's over. You know…Cunorix blames you for Getarix not taking on his torch of hatred of the Romans. He still dreams of a great war where the Romans will be pushed out of all Celtic lands."

"Never'll happen! The Gauls have become more Roman than the Romans."

"I know. I think my younger boy even looks up to the Romans and wants to leave us. Your teaching Getarix Latin is a real bone of contention. Cunorix blames his brother for our poverty. He says that if Getarix would spend more time helping him with the dogs and not offending the gods, we would be all right. Cunorix believes Getarix has brought the displeasure of the gods so they keep us in poverty. You know he will have to rename that horse. Cunorix will never stand for a Latin name."

"I know." Cunhail chuckled.

"And we keep the scrolls you gave Getarix hidden. If Cunorix ever found them here, he would probably burn the hut down just to be rid of the books."

"What Cunorix does not know is that the ability to read is never a mistake. The Romans have a saying, buyer beware. I can't tell you how many times I have been saved because I was able to read the contracts myself before putting my mark on them. Few expect a mere Celt to be able to read, especially their language, and they try to cheat me on paper. The gods have been good to me, the gods and Roman wealth. And I think Getarix will be similarly blessed. He has a sharp mind."

"I hope so," Aigneis said half in a dream. "So much wealth in the world and we live like slaves. Some days it's so bad I am tempted to sell Vercingetorix's things. They just hang there rusting…a reminder of what we have lost." Aigneis looked at the low wall that only came up to her hip before it met the roofline. There on the wall all covered with soot from sixteen years of neglect hung the damaged shield. The central boss, a round metal cup used to protect the hand of holder of the shield, had been crushed. From the inside the dried blood from Kailen's crushed hand could still be seen. Aigneis could not bear to ever look. With the shield hung the dagger and belt, and on either side of it hung the two arm torques of pure gold. The arm torques were beautifully designed with golden strands twisted into a rope, creating the distinctive Celtic style. She gazed at the place where the missing sword once hung above the shield and a wave of sadness flooded her heart. Visions flashed before her eyes of Kailen cleaning his grandfather's arms. He used to keep them so clean and shining that you would think they were just new from the smith.

Suddenly she broke out of her dream state, went to the wall and bent down onto her knees, taking the dagger and belt from its pegs. The same dagger Cullen's father handed her sadly the day of his return from Roman lands, which was probably the last sober day of his life. She also picked up the gold arm torques, the last of the great wealth the family had once known.

The arm torques of pure gold could bring in a tidy sum. She knew this was not an option; they belonged to her son, their once great owner's namesake. Aigneis got up with purpose and went and set a bowl of warm water on the table. She left the broken shield. She took the arm torques and dagger and submerged them in the water, washing the years away, revealing the intricate twisted Celtic rope designs, so beautifully created at the hand of some long-dead master craftsman. After cleaning the dagger and sheath, she made sure to dry and oil the hard steel blade with extra care, ensuring it would not rust. Cunhail just sat there watching his sister, wondering what this sudden flurry of activity could mean.

By the time Getarix and Cullen returned from feeding, cleaning, and admiring the horses, they found the three items neatly placed on the centre of the table. Getarix looked at them with a question in his eyes. "What's with these, Mother?"

"Well, my son, your sixteenth birthday celebration is not far off, so I thought that today would not be complete without a gift from your father and me. It is only appropriate for you to receive your inheritance now."

For the second time this evening Getarix could not believe his eyes. These items of family history were almost sacred to him. His mother helped him put the arm torques on. "They are a little big, but you will grow into them in no time.

The gold is soft and can easily bend, making them tight upon your arms, and as you grow, so will they."

Later that night after many pleasant hours of stories from Cunhail's adventures, laughter, and a thousand questions, all were soundly asleep except Aigneis. She stayed up to clean, true in all ages that a mother's work is never finished. Just as she was about to turn in, the door opened quietly and in walked Cunorix. As he bent down to enter, Aigneis saw something different about him: calmness. "Cunorix, my son, there you are. I was worried." She looked into his eyes that avoided hers. "My son, are you well?"

"No need to worry. I see my uncle is here. I saw his horse in the barn, but who travels with him?"

"What do you mean?"

"There are two horses with him."

"Oh yes…that." Aigneis hesitated. *Well, he will find out soon enough.* She was struck with the thought of the dagger and arm torques. What had seemed like a good idea earlier in the evening now looked like a foolish act that would only cause a deepening of the injury to her small family. "The second horse is a gift…a gift from your uncle…to your brother…it's for his birthday," she finished sheepishly, expecting a cascade of profanity and exaltations about how Getarix has become spoiled. However, it did not come.

"Well…that's…that's good. That will work out just fine. Yes, I like that very much," Cunorix said as he scanned the room, noticing the sleeping figure of his uncle and the two boys. As he examined the room, Aigneis tensed up. Then he noticed the missing dagger and arm torques. He pointed with an uneasy question on his face.

"Yes…those…I…I, your father and I gave those to Getarix." She stressed 'father' but Cunorix could hardly hear the name of his brother. As Cunorix's face went red with anger his mother added, "For his birthday." Almost in a whisper, she said, "I'm sure he would want it this way."

At that, Cunorix stopped as if struck by a new thought and a calm came over him. "No…yes, I approve…yes, actually that's perfect in fact." With that, he simply went to his bed space and prepared himself for the night's sleep. Just before he laid his head on his bedroll, he said, "Let Getarix sleep in. I'll take care of the dogs in the morning." Saying no more, he rolled over and was asleep within seconds.

Aigneis just sat there, stunned. Had her little family taken a turn for the good? Had the gods finally answered her many prayers? She sat for an hour, simply soaking in the turn of affairs. As the fire died down, she cried tears of joy mixed with tears of sadness until the she found herself in complete darkness before she shuffled off to her bed.

I I

A NEW DAY SHINING

The next day dawned like so many others, with a torrential downpour. Getarix opened his eyes seeing the light of day. As the significance of this became apparent, his mind began to panic. How could his mother do this to him and why had his brother not already extracted him from the warm comfort of his bed with curses and a beating? "Mother!" he gasped, and then with a mix of panic and anger he continued. "Why...?"

"Shh, my son, Cunorix told me to let you sleep in."

"Whaa...?"

"Last night he came home late, all in peace. I told him about your new horse and even your great grandfather's things...and Getarix, he approves...approves completely."

It was Getarix's turn to sit stunned, trying to unravel this new mystery. He thought surely he was dreaming. Maybe he was not fully awake. As he got up and pulled on his checked woollen trousers that the Celts and Germans wore, he could smell the meat cooking...*Meat cooking?* he thought.

"Here Son, take this to your brother. It's his lunch. He's in the barn preparing his horse. He's off to visit the priests. Must be about tonight."

"Oh, yeah, the summer solstice." Getarix hated these things: a great celebration for all except for one poor soul. A celebration to appease the blood lust of hateful angry gods. Gods Getarix seriously doubted even existed. What a waste. Getarix thought about this with distaste. He had only been at one such event and had bad dreams for months after. He had vowed never to be near one again. He did not even know the sequence of events, nor cared to learn. This only heightened his brother's contempt. He would once again forgo this year. Just disappear as he had each year since he was ten. His mother never went. Nobody asked, she just didn't go. "Where is Cullen, mother?"

"His father was screaming for him this morning. I'm surprised you slept through it. That tells me just how tired you are. I'm afraid things did not go well for Cullen this morning. He would be well bruised by now after his father finished with him. Getarix, I was thinking it would be better if he left Epona in our barn so his father does not know who owns her. If his father found out he would exchange the horse for spirits before the day's done."

"I don't doubt that for a moment."

"Okay, here's Cunorix's lunch. Get going. It sounds like the rain has let up. Off with you. Don't keep your brother waiting. We don't want to spoil the good mood he seems to have found." With that, Aigneis opened the door and Getarix bent down into the sunshine.

The rain had truly let up and the sun broke through the clouds just as Getarix emerged from his family home. Life was odd. A day ago, the air was thick and soupy where the cold pierced his body as fear pierced the soul. With his newly received gifts, summer approaching and apparent changes in his brother, it truly looked like his fortune had turned. Not to mention the extra rest he received. He felt better than he could ever remember. Maybe there were gods who listened and cared after all. When the warm sun hit his face, Getarix was almost giddy. As he approached the barn door, he noticed newly twisted hazel rope. *The priests must have asked Cunorix to help prepare for tonight.*

"There you are, brother."

Getarix doubted his ears. Cunorix sounded almost buoyant. "Getarix, due to the fact you are almost sixteen, I have talked to the priests and as a Druid they feel that you are old enough to help in tonight's ceremonies."

Getarix stopped dead. The blood left his face.

"I know, brother, you do not care for such things, but as you know, they are necessary for the survival of our people. I have ensured that you will not have to do anything you find distasteful. It would mean a lot to me. I know…um…I've not always been kind to you. It's just I am stressed and worried about how we will survive."

Getarix could hardly believe what he was hearing. Cunorix was speaking in a tone Getarix did not know he could. He only wished that Cunorix would make eye contact, but Getarix perceived that his brother was feeling a measure of guilt. "Oh yeah," Cunorix continued as he bound the hazel rope to his saddle, "I think you should wear Great Grandfather's dagger and arm torques tonight, okay?"

"Ah yeah…sure Cunorix…if you wish," Getarix said as Cunorix rode off.

Getarix wondered what had come over his life. He did not know whether to rejoice or to fear. Indeed, he felt honoured to be included in tonight's ceremonies, but just the thought of a human sacrifice…and now he must take part in one.

By noon, summer had finally broken through in full force. The landscape screamed green. Forests of oak, elm, beach, and hazel wood boasted every shade of green found in the palettes of the gods. Getarix felt something new. Was it happiness, hope, or even joy? He was almost drunk with it. It was then he smelt something wonderful coming from the thatch of his home. *That must be the meat cooking.* He remembered smelling it as he got dressed. He went to investigate. Their hut was uncommonly dark in contrast to the bright sun outside. Along with the darkness, Getarix felt heat from the roaring fire. As his eyes adjusted he saw his mother preparing a feast like he had never seen in his life. Real meat, beef at that.

"What's going on here, Mother?" he asked in a voice that almost skipped with laughter, catching the words in his throat.

"Your brother sent this meat from the butcher for a feast tonight. Make sure Cullen knows about it," she said as she stuffed garlic cloves into the cuts of the meat. "You know, Cunorix has really changed. Just like that, too. Whatever the priests are telling him has really been working. Maybe it's one of their magic potions. I don't know and I don't care, I'm just so happy."

"I must say I've never seen Cunorix so pleasant, or you so happy for that matter. I am having difficulty believing it," Getarix said quietly.

"Well, I admit I have not felt this feeling since before that horrible day when your father walked into the mist toward his demise." A small cloud of doom crept into her voice but not enough to break the spell. "Oh, when you talk to Cullen, invite his father as well." Getarix thought that his mother must be in a good mood. Aigneis caught the look in his eyes. "I know he probably does not deserve such a meal, but there is plenty and without more help eating it, much of the food will go to waste."

"You know, Mother, he's not a bad man…when he's not haunted with the past."

"Or with drink."

"Or with drink," Getarix agreed. "Cullen tells me that often he wakes screaming, swinging his arms like he's back doing battle with the Romans…he just drinks to chase the memories away."

"Be that as it may, my son, Cullen does not need to be punished for what the Romans did to Astnicx."

"I know, Mother. I'll tell you what, if he is sober enough, I'll let him know."

"Sounds fair. Now off with you."

As Getarix bent down to enter Cullen's home, he saw a small fire in the central pit. Getarix could barely make out the silhouette of Astnicx, father of Cullen, hunched over by the fire. Astnicx, once the pride of the village, was now a shell of the proud warrior he once was. There was a day when all the young girls of his village had dreamed of someday calling him their own. Years of Roman wine and British beer had taken their toll. It only got worse after Vanora, his wife, and mother of Cullen, died suddenly. Cullen was only ten at the time, and since that time Cullen lived more of his days at the house of Getarix than his own. Speculation abounded about Vanora's death. Some, primarily her own family, talked of Astnicx's part in her death and a call of vengeance was even heard. Disaster for Astnicx was averted by the intervention of Marbod, the village chief. Astnicx—not once, but twice—had saved the life of Marbod in battle. In the eyes of Marbod, Astnicx was a hero worthy of protecting. Why he turned to drinking, he could not understand. All he knew was that many of the men who fought with him in Gaul suffered in the dark of the night.

Astnicx was chastising himself. *How could I do that to my own son, my boy so innocent and somehow still trusting?* Astnicx was as much an expert at beating himself up as he was in destroying anything good in his life. Almost audibly he asked himself over and over, *Why, why, why?*

"Good morning, sir." Getarix broke Astnicx's self-destructive meditation, keeping one foot outside, preserving an escape route just in case.

Astnicx slowly looked up, tears in his eyes, and whispered, "Getar…" He could not even finish his name. He took a deep breath. "Cullen's not here, he went to the forest to collect wood. He should be back before the evening meal." He stared at nothing in particular. Again under his breath he continued, "Not that there will be one." Looking directly at Getarix, he finished with, "I'll tell him you called." He then returned to whatever deep thought he was in, figuring the conversation was over.

Getarix could not get over how thin and pale he looked. Every month he became less of the man he once was.

"Ah, sir...my mother is cooking a feast and wishes both you and Cullen to be our guests...that's if you want...sir."

Astnicx didn't turn, but said, "That...would be nice. Let your mother know we will be there."

Back out under the sun, Getarix realized just how depressing life in that hut would be. He could not call it a home. He was lost in thought when he heard the sound of horse's hoofs coming up from the village road.

He turned around to see his uncle. One look in his eyes and Getarix knew something was wrong; it looked like he had seen a ghost.

"Uncle, what's the matter?"

As Cunhail reined in his horse, he said, out of breath, "Getarix...my boy.... um...you have often dreamt about life in other lands, have you not?"

"Yes, bu—"

"And your Latin is passable, yes?"

"I...um...I really would not know...what's...?"

"Well I say it is, this would be a good time...well, you know....to begin your adventure."

Getarix was stunned, wondering if these last two days could get any more bizarre.

"I don't understand, Uncle...?"

"I mean..."

"Look, Uncle," Getarix interrupted. "For the first time, everything is going well. Mother, as we are speaking, is preparing a feast, with beef! I have never seen her so happy."

"Nonetheless, I have taken the liberty of securing a passage on the Black Rose. It's moored on the first wharf, second ship on the left. It leaves tonight at high tide, shortly after dark. They are expecting you, the passage is paid for. When you get to Portius Itius...it's in the land of the Morini in the Roman province of Belgica north of Gaul, there you'll find an inn, the White Swan. Just let them know you're my nephew and here—" Cunhail lobbed a bag of Roman coins at his young nephew. More money than Getarix had ever held or even seen in his life. "Here is some money. It should last you two months if you spend it wisely, time enough to find employment. I'll meet you at the White Swan just after summer harvest and I'll explain all. And my son, did Cunorix take the hazel rope that stood there this morning?"

"Uh…yes…yes, he did, and that's another thing, Uncle, Cunorix has become a new person. He's become kind and now treats me like an equal. He even let us—"

"Yes, just as I thought, mark my word lad, this is it, today is a good day to start the new life you have been dreaming of. Now I must go. I am late."

Cunhail turned his horse and began to ride off, and then he twisted in his saddle and yelled back, "Don't forget to take Caballo with you, I have secured his passage as well and I'll meet you in Gaul as the leaves begin their turning, take care and may the gods protect you. Please do as I have instructed."

Getarix's head was swimming, unable to make any sense of this day. After his uncle's confusing message, he was almost afraid to finish the day. All his life he only wanted respect from his brother and happiness for his mother. The mind has a powerful ability to ignore all else if it wants to.

"Getarix, I need…"

The familiar voice of his mother brought him back to reality.

"What is it, Mother?"

"I need you to go to the market and pick up some herbs for the meal tonight."

As Getarix began to walk, he was trying to mull over the day's events. He was so confused that at first he didn't notice how the villagers were treating him. As he walked through the village, people looked at him differently, only adding to his confusion. They smiled at him and gave way for him in the crowded market. Folks who would not have noticed if he lived or died came up and took him by his hand, almost in gratitude. Even the beautiful Boudica, who until this day had looked upon him as being beneath her contempt, approached him and took his hand, looking him in the eyes telling him how handsome she thought he looked.

That must be it, he thought. *Yes, Grandfather's things must make me look noble and people are finally noticing me as a member of the community. Brother did say that he talked to the priests about me taking a more prominent position in the village. We are of noble blood. It's only right, right?* He argued within himself not fully successful in removing the dark foreboding placed there by his uncle's strange behaviour.

III

THE DAY OF CEREMONY

Later, as Getarix helped his mother prepare the meal, he became torn between heeding his uncle's warning, packing the few possessions he owned, and heading dockside or staying for the evening festivities. Their shabby hut was host to several members of the community, invited by Cunorix, who had not yet shown up.

Cunorix must have told everyone that I am now a man of the village, important and not to be taken for granted.

After most of the guests were present, the door of their hut swung open. There stood Cullen, the bruises from the morning beating showing so much he glowed indigo and his left eye was swollen shut. Both Cullen and his father entered sheepishly, one due to embarrassment, the other due to shame. Astnicx, fully aware that all eyes were upon him, hung his head and almost bolted for the exit but was captivated by the smell of the feast. He could not remember the last time he had such a meal.

Around the fire that afternoon, the feast was truly spectacular. Besides the roasted beef there was lamb, spring vegetables, and even Roman wine. Such a feast neither Getarix nor Cullen had ever seen in their life. Like all young men their age, they worked hard to remove all evidence of the food, almost as hard as Astnicx bruised himself removing all evidence of the wine. Everyone enjoyed themselves, even Cullen's father, who by the end quietly slept in the corner, still embracing an amphora of wine all paid for by Cunorix, whose absence did not go unnoticed, since he had invited all of the guests, save Cullen and his father.

Throughout the meal there were many toasts. The guests from the village were most interested in toasting Getarix. Cunobelin, the village butcher, who sat to his right, put his big burly hands on Getarix's young shoulder whenever anyone toasted their newfound hero. Even old Marbod the grey-bearded village chief who sat across from Getarix looked upon the unofficial guest of honour with a mix of sadness and pride.

Partway through the meal, Getarix leaned over to Cullen on his left and asked if he thought that his sudden popularity was peculiar at all.

Cullen's answer was short and to the point. "No, you should have been toasted long ago."

"Did you hear anything today?"

"No, mind you I have been hiding in the forest collecting wood all day, avoiding any and all eyes. I almost did not come tonight. Well, at any rate, we have enough wood now to last the summer."

"Next time, get me up and I'll help you."

"No, I thank you, but I needed the time away from everyone. Matter of a fact, I will be sliding out of here soon to hide in the quiet of my home to nurse my pride...what's left of it." He glanced over to his father, who sat silently with wine in hand.

"No, Cullen, you can't."

"What?"

"Come with me to the ceremony." His voice almost begged.

"You're not going. You never...I thought you hated these things."

"I do."

"Well that settles it, I'm going home."

"No, please! I need you there. I have been asked to help in tonight's event."

"WHAT!" Cullen could not help himself, but then became aware that all eyes were now upon the pair of them. Cullen leaned closer and in a whisper continued as the din of the table returned. "Have you forgotten your own preaching about these things? Have you forgotten the nightmares you experienced? Have you gone soft in the head?"

Getarix leaned back and threw his arms up. "Cunorix has arranged everything. He has been really nice to me, almost treating me like an equal. I fear that if I do not show up I'll be worse off than before. This is all I have ever wanted. I don't want to go back there and I don't want to go alone tonight…I need you." Getarix was unsuccessful in hiding the desperation in his voice.

"Me…why me?"

"Because you are the only friend I have. Cullen, I'm scared."

"I would be, too."

"No, you don't understand." Getarix explained his whole day to Cullen, including his uncle's strange behaviour.

"Okay, if you insist, I'll go with you. Strange events, maybe it's an Omen."

"Omen indeed, by Ludd, there are no Omens, no gods beyond the green of the forest."

Cullen laughed.

Getarix looked at him. "Why do you laugh?"

"You…you deny the gods by the name of the gods." Cullen chuckled. Cullen had a way to bring humour into even the darkest night.

"Well, if they exist they are not worthy of our worship. It makes me sick to think of the poor soul we will be killing tonight. The only god worthy of worship would be the one who prevents tonight's sacrifice. I wonder what the poor fellow is thinking now. Is he going to the bog willingly, or is he being drugged? Is he happy to sacrifice himself to keep the gods from destroying our village just because they have nothing better to do? As we bury him in the bog on the border of our tribal lands, will he jump up and defend us from Trinobantes? How will he see if we take his head off? After all that, will he defend us? I think not!"

Here Cullen changed the subject before he was overheard and ended up becoming the sacrifice himself. Cullen also knew his friend was about to slip into one of his moods.

After most of the guests left for the bog, Getarix and Cullen got up to go when Aigneis reminded her son that his brother wanted him to wear his grandfather's things. "Here, my son," she added. "Take your cloak. It will be cold tonight, and Cullen, you use this one. It belongs to Cunorix but I am sure he won't mind." Once they had their cloaks on, she asked if they could take Astnicx back to his own hut.

"I'm afraid he feasted mostly on wine tonight," Cullen said, knowing he would most likely be the sacrifice in their hut sometime during the night, once his father sobered up enough to let loose the rage that haunted his innermost parts.

"Mother, are you coming?"

"No, Son, like you they give me haunting dreams."

They were late arriving and the old man began to wonder if Getarix was even going to turn up at all. He had watched as young Getarix grew up under that cruel hand of his brother. He was old enough to have watched their father grow up before them. A good man, if not a bit arrogant. The old man could not wrap his mind around how young Getarix would ever consent to such a thing. He sat up when the two young men finally arrived. Cullen stayed back with the horses as if the two of them would quietly ride off after the sacrifice. *Did they even know?* Getarix slowly walked as in a trance, almost floating toward the fire, where the three village priests stood with Cunorix next to them. Once he stopped and looked into the eyes of his brother, Prasutagix pulled the dagger back to drive it deep into the belly of their scapegoat.

Getarix saw the glint of light off the blade. The spell was not totally broken until he heard the voice of Cullen yelling for him to run. In a flash Getarix woke up and with lighting speed brought his muscular arms down hard, breaking the dagger arm of the feeble Prasutagix. He swung around. His right fist found the ribs of the second priest with a cracking sound and he fell. The third priest thought better and fell back out of Getarix's escape route. Cunorix lunged for his brother but the reflexes of the hunted proved to be quicker than the hunter. Getarix jumped backward, darting through the crowd, leaving nothing to break the fall of Cunorix. As Cunorix landed on his face, Getarix had cleared the crowd. The congregation was so stunned, they froze. By the time Getarix reached the horses, Cullen was already mounted, ready for flight.

When Getarix had knocked the dagger from Prasutagix's hands, the old priest fell to the ground almost into the fire, holding his right arm that appeared to be unnaturally bent. The old man was on his feet. The second priest went to the ground holding his side. The third backed off as Cunorix lunged for his brother. The old man could not help himself. He cheered for the young victim as he made his escape.

As Getarix bolted, he could hear his brother's voice yelling, "Get him you fools, get him!"

Cunorix recovered to pursue his prey. Prasutagix got up, blocking his way though his right arm hung uselessly. "I thought you told me he agreed," he yelled.

"How can I help it if he is weak?"

"Then he is not worthy of sacrifice."

Cunorix, not wanting to hear this, went around Prasutagix in pursuit.

As Getarix cornered the first bend in the trail, he sensed his pursuers closing in on his heels. On the turn he glanced over his shoulder and noticed about twenty men on ponies.

They did not worry him, because he knew Caballo could easily out run them. What concerned him was his brother out in front and gaining. Around the next bend he could not see the ponies at all, however Cunorix was close. Getarix dug into Caballo's sides without mercy as his ears picked up the sound of his brother just off his left side. He brought his knees high on the saddle, flowing with the rhythm of his horse as he lowered his head just behind Caballo's mane, allowing him to open up with more speed. He was encouraged as he crossed the creek. He heard his pursuer splashing three paces back but as he ascended the embankment Cunorix was once again dangerously near. Getarix knew that soon his brother would be able to drive a dagger into his side, bringing him to his end. He realized that he had to face his brother head on, be what may. At the top of the embankment there was an open meadow just before the sacred grove that surrounded the village. The road turned to the left and circled around the grove before entering the village proper. No one ever entered the Sacred Oaks other than for religious reasons, and then only after they removed all iron objects. Just before the bend in the road, Getarix chose to dismount and kill or be killed. This kind of death would be the better option, for it was highly unlikely that the boat his uncle had secured for him would still be there, as high tide was just on its way out.

As they reached the bend, Getarix pulled back on the reins to the left with all his strength, causing his pursuer to run into him, stopping just as suddenly. Cunorix's cloak swung around, covering his face. Getarix thought this was his chance. He leaped from his saddle onto the hunter, knocking both onto the soft green moss of the ground. In his rage he heard not the voice of Cunorix but the voice of his friend Cullen. As Getarix readied his grandfather's dagger to thrust through the cloak into his brother's heart, his purser pulled the cloak from his face. Getarix froze, for he did not come face to face with the Cunorix the hunter, but Cullen.

"Cullen! By all the gods, what the hell are you doing? Go home. You cannot follow me; my road has taken a different turn." Getarix stood and remounted, readying himself to continue on.

"So has mine, Getarix!"

"Go, Cullen, for I no longer have a home to go to."

"I never did!"

"Go, Cullen."

"Just like you, I cannot go back." Cullen's voice softened.

They both saw Cunorix cresting the embankment before the meadow. At that moment they both knew how much time they had lost in arguing. Not wanting to lose any more, Getarix shouted as he turned his horse straight for the Sacred Oaks. "Well then, you'd better keep up!"

They both ducked through the trees as the cheated worshipers arrived at the bend in the road. Cunorix shouted, "Getarix, curse you…Cullen curse… curse you both for disturbing the Dark Mother, may she slay both of you as you trespass her sacred forest!"

Not having enough faith that she would slay them, he kicked his horse and followed the road around the Sacred Grove, praying that if she chose not to strike them dead, he could reach the village docks before them. He guessed they would be heading there to escape by boat—it was their best hope, but not if he could help it.

It was not until they passed the Altar to the Dark Mother that the sacrilege they were committing hit Cullen. Between keeping himself from being cast from his mount, he prayed for forgiveness, hoping he would not be struck dead. Before he knew it they cleared the Oak Grove, coming directly into the edge of the village.

As they navigated the narrow dirt streets of the deserted village, they slowed their pace to keep their horses from losing their footing around the sharp corners.

They could now hear Cunorix in the village with the others closing in behind them. Getarix was trying to remember his uncle's instructions. "First wharf second ship, but was it to the left or the right?" he muttered. "If there are any gods, let the Black Rose still be there." To his horror Getarix noticed the second ship to the right had just slipped out and was under sail. Still in the harbour but by no means reachable. They were now riding on stone and Epona, Cullen's horse, lost his footing. As he went down, Cullen pulled his knees up to his chest, keeping from being pinned under all the weight of the horse or dashing his leg upon the stones. Almost as fast as the horse fell, he was back up with Cullen on his back. Cullen realized that Cunorix had gained on him, only three paces back as his horse found his sure footing on the wooden dock. Getarix quickly scanned the remaining five ships. Seeing the Black Rose, his memory was restored. He spurred Caballo on and leaped over the rails. Cullen noticed Getarix momentarily pause before he darted for the second ship on his left that was just slipping away. Cullen dug in, forcing his horse to jump the span, knocking the railing off with Epona's back hoofs.

Getarix pulled heavily on the reins when Cullen landed behind him. Epona lost his footing and slipped on the wet deck, almost killing some of the crew, and Cullen was thrown hard to the deck. When Cullen got up, one of the crewmembers accosted him. A short wiry man of untold strength built up among the rigging held him ready to throw the both of them overboard, his thick Gaulish accent pronouncing curses of the gods upon him.

As Getarix dismounted, he noticed many of the crew surrounded the two of them, daggers and swords drawn, ready for fight. Over their heads they heard the curses from Cunorix and the villagers left on the docks. A man, evidently the master of the boat, elbowed his way through the clag of sailors to investigate who dared board his ship in such a manner.

"I'm Eppillius and this is my ship you just stowed away on. I have the authority to have the two of you executed and keep your horses, or even sell the two of you in the slave market." When he finished, everyone noticed Cunorix yelling from the dock.

"Master of the ship, send back those criminals and you may keep the horses."

"Criminals, eh?" Eppillius yelled back.

"Yes, criminals of a grievous crime." This time it was the voice of Marbod, the village chief. "I am Marbod the chief, and as such I demand the return of the criminals. They have offended the gods and must be punished or the sky will fall in."

Turning to the two alleged guilty parties, Eppillius raised his eyebrows. "Offended the gods, have we?"

Marbod broke in, now at a ship's length distance and growing. "Keep the short one. He will fetch a very good price at the market, but throw the tall one into the sea. He must be put to death."

"Well, they must really want you. I see it does not always pay to be so popular. So what grievous crime did you commit that merits death?"

"Without my knowledge, nor consent, they were to sacrifice me to the gods this very night."

"Human sacrifice, eh?" His face hardened. "The Romans have outlawed it, you know."

"Send back the tall one to be sacrificed or we will bring the curse of the gods upon you!"

Eppillius laughed at the threat. "You may keep your curses to yourself."

Marbod began to yelling hysterically. "Send back the tall one or you will never enter this port again."

"Now that is a heavy blow, but I must say there are few things I hate more than the old superstitions; especially when they take the life of the best and brightest away from us." He turned to Getarix. "To be chosen for such a dubious honour must mean you are of noble blood. Who are you, my son?"

I am Vercingetorix, grandson of Vercingetorix the Great, nephew of Cunhail the merchant—"

"Uh, so, you do exist. You are the reason we barely made the tide. Now I understand your uncle's insistence that I wait until the very last moment before sailing. We almost did not make it. Fear not, I will not turn you over to those savages." Turning, he yelled back, "I will not send this innocent man to his death. His passage is paid for and I am satisfied."

Marbod screamed back. "How dare you declare him innocent. You have no authority!"

"On my ship I am all authority!" With that he turned and ignored any further comments from the village, either their pleading or finally their curses, which by then the ears could hardly pick up the distance being too great.

When Marbod finally gave up, he shot Cunorix a look of intolerant hate and spat out, "You have brought this curse upon the village." With that, the crowd dispersed, not knowing exactly where to go from there.

Back on board, Eppillius turned his attention to Cullen, continuing his trial. "You, my son, however are guilty of being a stowaway and causing damages to my ship, not to mention almost murdering members of my crew. You might make up for it all at the slave market. I see by your face you have already been punished." Eppillius had his good qualities, but he was not a man to ever lose a profit. Saving Getarix was motivated more from his own hate of the old ways than any sense of duty to his fellow man. If Cunhail had not paid the passage for Getarix, they both would be heading to the market.

Cullen looked over to his friend with panic in his eyes, almost wishing he had not followed Getarix on this day.

"How much?" Getarix demanded, pulling out the bag of coins given to him that morning from his uncle's hands.

When Eppillius saw the bag, he simply grabbed it, dumping the contents into the palm of his hand, knowing in an instant it would be more than he would get at the slave market. "This would just about do." He put the coins back into the bag, tucking it neatly into his belt.

Getarix sensed that they had just been taken, but chose not to fight it, given the alternative. Getarix felt more relaxed knowing they were secure. Without thinking, he pulled off his cloak, exposing his grandfather's arm torques and dagger. He noticed Eppillius' eyes grow with greed.

Getarix stood his full height, hand on the hilt of his dagger, and said sternly, "I believe we have paid in full and then some."

"Yes, yes, of course." Not letting his greed get the better of him, Eppillius realized he had already made a handsome profit on their misfortune and he could not be sure who these two young men might know in Gaul. The young man's uncle had connections that could put the Black Rose on the black list. It was not worth the risk.

With that, his attitude changed toward his new passengers. "The crew will show you to my cabin, which will be yours for the voyage. I will send a meal down to you. It appears the passage will be calm, so even you should be able to take some food in, and wine, of course."

"You have all my money. I cannot pay for these things," Getarix said with irritation.

"No need, it comes with the cabin." Eppillius smiled.

Getarix lowered his head to enter the Spartan wood-paneled cabin that smelt like it could use a good cleaning and some fresh air. He was filled with so many emotions that his chest hurt and he found breathing difficult.

Eppillius followed them, making sure everything was to their satisfaction, not wanting to offend them anymore. It seldom paid to offend the rich and powerful.

"Word of advice. I don't know what's gotten into me, I guess I simply like you. Hide those things," he said, pointing to the heirlooms of the Great Vercingetorix. "It would not pay to escape a sacrifice to be simply killed on dockside over some gold. Put them in your pack now, even that dagger. It's more pretty than useful and I recommend not taking them out again until you are truly safe." Eppillius ducked under the door, yelling orders to his crew, knowing that he would have to stay up all night to keep his own crew from killing the two of them just to get to the gold.

Later that night, Getarix and Cullen finished the wine, drinking themselves out of their present predicament. Cullen had to continually reassure Getarix that his mother would not have condoned what happened to them, let alone be party to it. Cullen knew his words landed empty and un-received. Getarix rehearsed over and again how credulous and stupid he was to fall for his brother's scheme. Getarix never stopped mentioning it that night until the wine took effect, pulling him into a fitful sleep. After that night, Cullen never heard Getarix ever bring the subject up again.

IV

DESTRUCTION IN HIS WAKE

"Where in all Hades is this place?"

"It should be just over the next hill, sir," Antonio answered quietly, somehow hoping a soft reply would produce a gentler rebuff from his master.

"You said that two hills ago, it's getting late, and this cursed forest is closing in on me. If we are not there by the sun's setting I'll have you flogged!" Damianus Aurelia Marius Gius, Senator of Rome, bellowed.

"Yes, sir." Antonio accepted his fate.

"Mark my word, never trust a German. Barbarians all of them…pigs."

"I was not sure of all his words, sir."

"I thought you spoke that pig's language?"

"Yes sir…I speak a variation of their language. Some parts are identical. Other parts…"

"Then why do I keep you?"

Why indeed? Antonio asked himself under his breath.

"All I can hope is that your backside pains you as much as mine pains me," concluded his portly master.

That is highly unlikely. First I carry one-third your weight, not to mention the fact that I was practically born in the saddle. Antonio's mind began to search the memories of his early years, now faded. At times he could not be sure what remained as memory and what was fancy. His early days seemed more dream than real. Now reaching his middle years, Antonio had settled into his life as a slave. *It helps if you stop fighting it*, Antonio thought. Years ago he learned that only death could free him now. *It's more likely that Mount Vesuvius will suck back its ash than the great Damianus Aurelia Marius Gius would ever free a slave.* Antonio even heard it from the senator's lead optie that his master had it in his will that upon his death his legions of slaves were not to be freed. They were to be sold to the great mine works on the Island of Cyprus. Even the women, children, and the infirm, no exceptions. The will also stipulated that the mine could not sell any of his slaves out of the pits, instead they were to spend their days toiling until they were rescued by death.

Antonio had found only two places in the senator's sweeping estate where he could feel a measure of happiness: the garden where he found peace and the grand weapons room where he fantasized killing his owner. He would sit and stare at a long Gaulish sword mounted high on the far wall. It was mounted too high and too secure to easily grab. The senator was not taking any chances that in the heat of the moment some angry slave might grab it and exact revenge.

As much as Antonio hated the senator and dreamt of slipping that sword between his fat ribs right into that stone cold heart, he would protect his master's life with his own. The lives of all the slaves depended upon it. *A brilliant, if not evil, way to protect yourself. Not even the elite Praetorian Guards are as vigilant in protecting the life of the emperor than the servants of Damianus are in protecting the life of their master. No matter how cruel he is to us. The mines are a fate worse than death if any of the reports are to be believed.*

Antonio looked around from his mount, seeing the sun hitting the tops of the trees and descending fast. He fixed his eyes to where the Roman road crested the hill, knowing the eyes of his master were boring a hole right through the back of his head. Antonio prayed to the gods to miraculously produce the Boar's Head Inn they were seeking.

Next to Antonio, Cornelius rode silently, keeping all comment to himself. The centurion looked the part of a war hero, proudly mounted on his steed, resplendent in his uniform with its banded armour. Six strips of shining iron ran across his chest held up by additional iron strips that went over his shoulder. Very little of this could be made out due to the many phalera. The large round disks mounted on leather straps awarded for bravery virtually covered his breastplate. He had three bronze phalera, two silver, and even a gold one. Each disk represented a medal of honour earned in the heat of battle. He sported the distinctive helmet of a Centurion, with its red plume forming a half-circle over his head running almost from ear to ear. The effect was completed with his wool cape died bright red that flowed off his shoulders covering the back end of his horse. He might have looked the part of a powerful warrior, but after almost two years of unmitigated cruelty at the hands of the noble Senator, Centurion Cornelius found silence his best defence. The mighty warrior Cornelius Faustus Aeolos Pricus had been reduced to almost the level of a whipped slave boy. Taken down by a fat politician equipped with a foul mind and a black heart. In his earlier days, he had fought to pacify these very forests. His own cohort built the road under their feet. Rome consolidated her empire through her soldiers. When they were not fighting the enemy, they built. *Between the many battles we fought we built forts and the roads to connect them. We, the soldiers of Rome, are the only reason the Empire exists.* Not far from this very spot he faced down Lothair, the powerful German warrior, beating him in the fight of his life. It was there Cornelius earned his place in the ranks of the centurionent and another medal of valour. He became a man in these woods only to be reduced to less than a child again. Cornelius could not help but sense the spirit of these trees were laughing at his present humiliation. This forest which once was firmly in the hands of the Roman Empire now ruled by the Germans again. Lost by Varus, brother-in-law to the senator. Yet all hope was not gone. Only a few more months and he would be granted his freedom, and hopefully a promotion to go with it. A promotion truly earned. Yet upon reflection he would settle just for his freedom. Few officers assigned to Senator Damianus made it past the six-month mark of the ascribed two-year appointment. Many a career had been destroyed doing this job, not to mention a few rumoured to have made their escape though suicide. Yet here he was, injured but not dead. It appeared he would survive. *Only two more months, only two more,* he could not stop telling himself.

Next to him, Antonio strained his eyes trying to see through the crest of the hill, knowing his master was not known for keeping his word unless it involved the whipping of a slave or some such sadistic joy he seemed to get from the suffering of others. Antonio could not reconcile why the gods seem to continue to bless this monster.

Smoke is difficult to see at dusk, but Antonio was sure he saw something.

"Centurion, do you see the smoke?"

"No...but I can smell it...oak, yes, an oak fire," Cornelius said with some excitement. Oak burns hot and steady and is used for cooking, giving him cause for hope.

As Antonio sent up another desperate prayer he caught sight of the roofline where everyone could clearly see the smoke billowing from the thatch.

"Antonio, is that the place?" the senator asked with mixed emotions. He wanted to get out of this infernal saddle, however he was looking forward to working out his frustration on the back of his slave.

Just then Antonio caught sight of the road wrapping itself around on either side of the little thatch roof Inn. A few more steps and all in their company could make out a crudely painted sign of a Boar's head. No words, just the picture, more useful to an illiterate population.

"Yes sir, it is."

Upon their arrival outside the tidy little Inn, Günter came out to greet them. Seeing the wide purple strip that lined the senator's toga hanging below his traveling cloak, he bellowed for his son. "Fritz, get the horses." A young man in his mid teens came running out of the barn like a beaten dog, holding his head down.

"No, do not trouble your slave. Mine need to earn their keep."

Fritz gave the senator a glaring look that did not escape the notice of his father. Günter picked up a willow switch he kept by the door and gave Fritz a mighty whip across the back of his head. The end of it swung around and cut Fritz in the face. "Go get the feed ready!" Günter bellowed angrily. "Or I'll give you more of this!" He held the willow branch above his head and ready to strike.

Antonio jumped down to help the senator off the poor suffering animal, fearing that if he lost his grip he would be crushed to death. This was neither the place nor the means by which he wished to die. Once down, the senator said with a look of approval, "A man who knows how to treat a slave. That's the problem today, slaves who do not know their place, with masters who do not know how to show them it." He finished his discourse with a half smile toward the innkeeper. "Nothing a stout whip in a sturdy hand could not solve, eh?"

Günter answered with a nervous laugh. "He is not a slave, noble sir, rather he is my son..." he trailed off, not sure what reception this news would receive.

"Oh...is that so. Even better. A man who knows the order of things. Centurion, mark this and take heed."

"Yes, sir."

As Damianus was saying this, the innkeeper was counting to himself. *Six, no seven guests, a full house tonight. With all the trouble of late it has been difficult... this will help.*

"Sir, I will have four rooms prepared. One for you and—"

"You will do no such thing. Two will do: one for me of course and the other for the centurion. The slaves will stay in the barn with the other animals, and so will the soldiers."

"As you wish, sir." Günter tried to hide his disappointment. *This means fewer profits, but better than nothing.*

The inn was warm and clean if not richly decorated. Across from the large central door stood a big stone fire pit. The main floor consisted of only three rooms. The kitchen shared the north end with the storage room. On the south wall ran a staircase that led to two rooms at that end of the building. There were another two rooms on the north end of the second floor. A balcony ran the distance between, joining the north and south end upper rooms. These two were situated above the kitchen and storeroom. The largest room on the ground floor was the great room, big enough to hold six tables wrapped with benches. On a busy day, thirty-two people could comfortably sit around the four small and two large tables. A few short years earlier, the inn had usually been full. In addition, many locals had taken their meals in the great hall. But, ever since the trouble of Teutoburger Wald some years back, business fell off. The Germans had soundly beaten the Roman Army, destroying three whole legions. The borders changed and with them so did the travel routes, taking travelers away from the Boar's Head Inn. It did not help that many of the German nationalists chose not to patronize one of Rome's 'loyal' subjects.

Entering the inn, the noble visitors scanned the plain wood plank walls decorated only with shelves holding square wood boards that served as plates for the more common guests who frequented these parts.

They saw the innkeeper's wife, a fine-looking woman of fading beauty. Her golden hair still held its shine, however on her face anyone could see the heavy years of abuse. Instantly Centurion Cornelius' heart went out to her, recognizing a comrade of mistreatment. Two years ago he would not have noticed nor cared about her plight.

As she served them mead, a popular drink in the province of Germania Minor, she broke in tentatively. "Sir, there is a late spring storm brewing, which can be extremely cold. We have a small garden shed where your slaves could bed down out of the drafty barn, it—"

"No, they will stay where they are and know their place, otherwise they will become soft and lazy," Damianus growled. "And furthermore, you will feed them only after we are done. Understand?"

She looked down. "Yes, sir."

"And I better not catch you feeding them anything better than gruel, if it's good enough for pigs. Now go and get our supper, we're hungry."

"Yes sir…right away, sir." She departed head down, as if life had just defeated her again.

Cornelius burned with shame having to be associated with the great senator. *Why would Augustus send this man to negotiate peace…does he wish for war? There are rumours that the old emperor is losing his senses in his failing years.* Cornelius broke off his musing by Freya's voice instructing her young daughter.

"Isolde, go get bread for the masters."

The young, beautiful daughter of the innkeepers attended to her tasks without hesitation. The eleven-year-old was still a child in many ways, but men already noticed her beauty. Her hair was a brilliant golden like her mother's. It differed in that when you gazed upon it you swore that the light shone from within. Unlike her mother, she was not required to pull it back in a braid. It fell freely upon her shoulders, accentuating the beauty of her innocent face, where the observer could not miss her eyes. Her eyes were the colour of ocean blue. Eyes you could drown in. It was easy to see that in a few short years her beauty would be unstoppable.

In spite of her petite frame, she could work harder than girls twice her age. This did not seem to matter to her father, for he never noticed her. She often thought that if she would fall off the end of the earth he would not even notice. All he would care about would be the work left undone. The one advantage to this was that she was spared the hitting and yelling her brother Fritz had to endure. Yet she was still expected to earn her keep working up to twelve hours a day.

Somehow, nothing could crush the indomitable spirit that shone through her eyes, only intensifying her beauty. It could even be said she was a happy child, her mother being the centre of that happiness.

As Isolde approached the table, Senator Damianus looked up, catching sight of her. Lost for words, he only stared. Centurion Cornelius prayed, *if there are any gods at all, do not allow this to happen.* Cornelius could not look at the girl, fearing her fate. Isolde noticed the senator's stares. Feeling uncomfortable, she dropped the bread on the table and beat a hasty retreat.

After the meal and many uncomfortable stares from the senator, Centurion Cornelius wearily got up, looking forward to spending at least eight hours out of the senator's presence.

"Cornelius, you go on. I need to talk to the innkeeper about his little slave girl." He cast his eyes upon the girl taking the remains of the meal back to the kitchen.

"Sir…maybe…"

Senator Damianus Gius shot a glance to his military aid that screamed silence, not another word from you lest you find yourself on some outpost left to rot.

Without any further comment, Cornelius slinked away. Once again he was totally beaten, feeling the part of a slave boy not a Roman officer.

"Innkeeper!" the senator bellowed.

"Yes, my Lord." The Inn Keeper rushed into the main dining room. "I have the food for the slav—"

"Yes, yes, that does not concern me," Damianus interrupted with a small measure of frustration. "I wish to talk to you about the girl."

"What, was she rude or did she…?"

"No, no, she was fine…matter of a fact, she was better than fine. Her beauty is simply radiant."

Standing to his full height, Gunter, not understanding the nuance, boasted with no small measure of pride, "Why thank you, sir, she has her—"

"Enough of that." He looked the innkeeper straight in the eyes, becoming impatient, and shot right to the point. "I wish to rent her for the night. It looks cold out and I…need something to keep me warm." His words slithered out, finishing with a smile. "I'm sure you understand, eh Gunter?" he asked, using the familiar to win favour. "She has probably kept you warm yourself, eh?"

"She is beautiful, sir," Gunter said sheepishly. "That's because she has her mother's beauty, but…sir…as you can plainly see, she is not yet developed into womanhood. Her mother…"

"I'm not interested in her mother. I'm interested in her, besides the less development the better!" Damianus began to get angry. "So why is this slave so valuable to—oh, now I understand, you want to keep her for yourself, eh?"

"No sir, absolutely not," Gunter said with an edge that bordered on courage. "She is not a slave. Rather she is my own daughter."

"Oh, so this is going to cost me, eh?"

"Well sir…her mother would never agree."

"Her mother, her mother, her mother, that's all I hear around here. Who is the master of this household? I thought it was you, but I'm seeing who rules this domain."

Gunter found himself cornered. He was a cruel man but the girl was the special domain of Freya, his wife. She protected that child with her life and became unreasonable if her husband demanded too much. So for the peace of their household and the entire inn, he ignored the girl, placing all his attention on the unfortunate Fritz.

"Look here, you!" the senator continued. "I am tired and will not be trifled with." He placed a small bag of coins upon the table. Gunter just stood there and stared at it. Damianus Gius knew he had his mark. He could tell who the innkeeper's master was: the mighty coin.

"Sir, her mother will never…"

"Well, let me make it worth it." He pulled another bag of coins from the many folds of his tunic.

Gunter began to perspire, shifting his weight from one foot to the other, indicating the war waging within. He cared little about the suffering of others, even his own children, but his wife had ways to make his life hell. He looked like he was about to hesitate when the senator quickly hammered another bag on the table, looked Gunter straight in the eyes and hissed, "This is more than I would pay to buy her as a slave!"

"Indeed sir…" Gunter could barely get it out, consumed with greed. "I'll bring her to your room."

"Good!" The senator began to get up.

"It's just her moth—"

"Who is the master of this inn?" Damianus bellowed.

"I am," Gunter muttered.

"Well I suggest you begin acting like one. I'll be in my room. Good night, and don't forget we have a legal contract." The threat was obvious in the great senator's last comment.

Centurion Cornelius felt as if he could bring up his supper meal, thinking of the deal with the devil being made one floor below. His nightmare was broken by an argument in the room below. He remembered seeing a storeroom next to the kitchen. The floorboards were still green when the building was built. As they dried, the shrinkage opened gaps between the boards, allowing Cornelius to hear every word spoken. Not that he understood all, but his German was not so rusty that he could not get the details of the argument.

"No!" a female bloodcurdling scream screeched through the floor.

"Freya, look at these bags of gold. There must be more money here than we have ever had or ever will!"

"No!" she screamed again, this time in hysterics. "Never! Not as long as I live."

"This is more money than—" Gunter began to get angry. Standing to his full height, he concluded, "And besides, the deal is done and we cannot go back on it."

"We…did not make a deal. He can keep his Roman gold."

"What is your problem? It's just one night. She will forget it by season's end, but the money will last."

"No!" Now she seemed to have lost all control, taking on the sound of panic. "Those memories will last longer than all the money in Rome!"

Cornelius saw movement through the floorboards as Freya rushed Gunter, blocking the door.

"Ack, how would you know?" Gunter shot back, raising his hand and backhanding her across the face. She fell to the floor violently. He stopped suddenly, looking at her stunned, knowing he had just crossed a barrier. As violent has he could be, he had never raised a hand to his wife. This thought however did not stop his pursuit of the senator's gold. As she lay on the floor, he repeated, "What do you know?"

At this point she lost the last threads of control. "I know…because it happened to me." She was crying uncontrollably, spitting out blood that ran from her nose. Through the sobs and blood she got out, "A Roman soldier… when they took this land. I was Isolde's age…" Freya felt spent and broke into long howls of crying, curled up on the cold stone floor.

"Ack…you make no sense at all whatsoever. Besides, you're doing fine and I'm the master of this inn and my word stands." He turned on his heels and stormed out of the storeroom, slamming the door behind him.

Hearing her weak sobs, Cornelius was ashamed to wear the uniform of Rome after that narrative. He was sure Senator Damianus could clearly hear the argument. He would not have understood the words, but the intensity could not be missed. Over Freya's sobs he heard a few doors slam and then it was time for the little girl to scream. He heard Freya get up partway through, perhaps thinking she would confront the senator, but all he heard was the inn door slam shut. That night he could not sleep at all. Even when the screaming stopped, his soul tortured him, robbing all hope of sleep.

As they rode off in fresh snow, the only person they saw from the innkeeper's family was young Fritz. He looked like he, too, had not slept one minute the night before. When Cornelius caught his eye there was a burning hate that cut the soldier to the core.

Once on the road and away from the senators' hearing, Antonio spoke. "What the hell happened in there last night?"

"I don't want to talk about it. Ever. Just be thankful you were freezing in the barn."

Cornelius looked over to Antonio, just then noticing a look of horror on his face, and asked, "What happened to you, Antonio? You look like you saw a ghost."

"We did. In the middle of the night we were so cold we sought a warmer place to sleep. Marcus remembered seeing a shed. So we trudged through the snow and wind only to discover the lady of the inn."

"What did she say?"

"Nothing. She was dead. Poison, it looked like to us. The bottle was still in her hand. It also looked like she had taken a beating."

Cornelius could not take any more. "In the wake of some, only destruction. What I would give to put a dagger into his chest!" the centurion hissed under his breath.

"And condemn us to the mine. Don't forget you will be free soon, but for those of us he owns we've only one fate."

"My apologies."

That's the only thing keeping me alive. Two more months…two more months.

V

THE LANDING

Thud.

"What was that?" Almost thrown from his bunk, Cullen awoke with quite a start. At first he didn't know if it was his father, and braced himself for the blows that never seemed to fail. Years of training had taught him to be on his guard. His body, a deep blue, and stiff, now gave clear witness to his most recent lesson. As his head cleared, he remembered where he was. For a second, a wave of excitement rushed over him as he realized he would never be victim to another beating. He lifted his hand and gently examined his face. His left eye had swollen completely shut. His face was so bruised it hurt whenever he moved his mouth. Looking over to Getarix, he noticed his lifelong friend blissfully asleep.

"Getarix. Getarix, wake up. Something's happening," Cullen cried out, enveloped in fear, not knowing what was going on.

Getarix lifted his head from his leather bag that served as a pillow. He listened to the yelling from the upper deck.

"It sounds like we have landed."

"We're there?"

"We're somewhere."

The sudden feeling of 'what now?' rippled through Cullen. He looked over at Getarix for reassurance, but he was busy getting dressed, seemingly unaffected by it all.

The morning sun was hot enough to be uncomfortable. As the two refugees climbed out of the hold, they had to stop on the top step. They closed their eyes and then squinted until they adjusted to the bright morning light. When the world came into focus they beheld the grandeur of a Roman city. A sight they could never have imagined.

Getarix looked at the ship's captain and asked, "Why have you brought us to Rome?"

"We only wanted to go to Gaul!" Cullen added.

Eppillius just stood there for a moment, trying to grasp the question.

"Rome! You little idiots, this is Portius Itius…that would be in Gaul, Belgica to be exact."

The crew broke into laughter, mocking the pair.

"This is where you wanted to go. Exactly where you asked to go. Exactly where your uncle paid me to take you!" Eppillius turned around in disbelief of their naivety.

Cullen and Getarix hung their heads in shame, feeling truly stupid. Getarix held his leather-bound treasure tight to his chest and pushed through the crew to the gangplank, in a hurry to be out from under the cloud of ridicule. Cullen followed closely. They hit the stone of the quay eager to leave the laughter and mocking of the crew behind. As they began to walk down the quay, a voice yelled from the ship.

"Hey you fools, do you want these or are you donating them to the crew?" More laughter exploded from the crew.

When Getarix and Cullen looked back they saw a brawny crewmember sporting a toothless smile. In his hands he held their horses' reins.

"Could this get any worse?" Getarix muttered. "Cullen, go get them please!"

Cullen ran back up the big gangplank. He led the horses under a storm of mockery from the crew.

Eppillius watched the comedy unfold from his open bridge. He wondered just how long the two of them would last there in Belgica. *Maybe I should have liberated them of their gold and possibly their lives?* It seemed evident that both would be taken away, before the sun set.

The two lost noblemen walked down the quay, horses in tow and their own tails firmly between their legs. Back on deck, Pathius backhanded the big African on the arm. He leaned over on his rope and said, "Duka, would it be fair to say that the gold in that kid's bag is far too great a burden for these two fools?"

Duka smiled broadly, showing the brilliant white of his teeth. "I think it would be our duty to the public to free them of such a burden."

"Get to work, you lot, or I'll have your skin tanned for my new captain's chair!" Eppillius bellowed at them. Without hesitation they got to work, looking busy while whispering their plan between them. Pathius kept an eye on his prey as they moved slowly down the quay. Even without the horses the two of them would stand out in the crowd with their brightly coloured checked cloths tightly wrapped around their legs and their long hair hanging prominently in braids down their backs.

Eppillius disappeared down the hold to his cabin, reappearing in his finest robes. This gave hope to Pathius. The old man only dressed in his finer robes when he was heading for the market to find buyers for his wares. Leaving the ship, he yelled his expectation to the crew, placing his second in charge. As soon as he disappeared down an ally leading away from the quay, Pathius and Duka tied up their ropes and descended the gangplank so fast no one noticed their departure.

They ran for all their might, attempting to keep the oddly dressed youths in sight. Losing sight of them in a crowd, they ran even faster. Darting left and then right, pulling out all the stops, working their way through the morning throng. As they broke through the crowd they found themselves before the back end of two horses. They almost ran right into one of the big bays. The two Britons had stopped, preoccupied deep in conversation. Then Getarix swung around, the hairs standing on the back of his neck. Pathius grabbed Duka and threw both of them behind a pile of red clay amphorae piled next to a warehouse. The red clay pointy-ended jars, half the size of a grown man, used to transport wine, oils, and other liquids were piled on their sides high enough to hide both men. Both men could easily take cover from any searching eyes. As Duka placed his hand on one of the jars and felt the oily residue seeping through the clay, he instantly knew it was filled with olive oil destined for the rich of the area.

Getarix was sure he had seen something just behind his horse. He searched the crowd behind him, seeing only Romans going about their daily business and slaves making sure that business was profitable. Thinking nothing more of it, he turned again and continued on his journey. Getarix nonetheless nervously held his leather bag a bit tighter to his chest. The two Britons continued on in awe of what they saw. Walls standing the height of seven or eight men, big, flat, square stones neatly lay underfoot. Walls painted white or yellow trimmed in red, some with scenes of birds and animals painted on them. The tops of the building were covered with what looked like clay pots bright red in the morning sun.

"Look, Getarix, they use their dishes for a roof." They both laughed, Cullen doing so in pain. Under the roofs were windows and doors suspended way above the ground with people reaching out, talking to their neighbours.

"How do they get up there?"

"Uncle Cunhail told me about such things. They build one house on top of another. They build steps, like the stone ones we have coming up from the village creek. They make them out of wood and they are inside their houses. I could never have imagined…" Getarix finished quietly.

"I never tried," answered Cullen.

As they walked alone, people stopped and stared at them.

"Cullen, I think your face is drawing a crowd. Look at the people." Getarix turned his attention to the crowd.

"Yeah, they're all rich."

"Of course they are. They are all Roman—look at their dress. The Gaulish village is probably somewhere the Romans don't want to live, likely in poverty." Getarix spoke with a touch of bitterness.

Cullen looked at him in surprise. "For a second I thought I just heard Cunorix."

Getarix shot him a hostile look. Cullen shrank back a bit.

Getarix was hit by the fact that Cullen was right. "Sorry Cullen, I don't know what to…I'm not blind to the faults of the Romans."

"Getarix, listen…do you notice…?"

"Yes, they are speaking Celtic. Why?" *Could it be that they are Gauls dressing as Romans?* Getarix remembered his uncle had mentioned something of this. "They are Celts, Cullen."

"I can imagine what your brother would think of this."

"He might know. That would explain some of his anger."

"Where to, now?" Cullen wanted to change the subject before his friend slipped in to a nasty mood. "Getarix look, up there is the main village." Peering down the street that inclined from the dockside, they could see bigger buildings and what looked like a town square.

"Well, my uncle told me that once in Portius Itius we were to seek out the White Swan Inn, but I haven't the slightest idea—"

Cullen cut him off with a wave of his hand, simply pointing down the quay toward a hanging sign in the shape of a swan painted white.

"That would be it," Getarix said.

"And to think I did it with only one eye." Cullen tried to smile.

"Yeah, you're good."

As they headed to the inn, Getarix explained the arrangement he had with his uncle. He also explained about the funds given him to hold him over until the harvest season when Cunhail returned to Portius Itius and the White Swan, where he was to stay. Getarix would then join his uncle in business.

"Is there enough money for both of us? Where did you get the money for my passage on the boat?" Cullen asked, fearing the answer.

"That's the problem."

"What's the problem?"

"That was the money. It was all we had."

Pathius peered around their blind and noticed that the two had moved off toward the White Swan, away from the crowd. The inn's door opened and two Romans dressed richly in togas began down the quay.

"Look at them. They look like barbarians on their first day in the city," Pathius said.

"They are, ha ha," Duka added.

"It will be like taking a bowl of cereal from a baby." Both laughed.

"Duka, they are heading for the White Swan. They just tied up their mounts. Remember, you grab the short one. It should be easy; he's already half-beaten. If our plan is going to work it's now or never."

"Why?"

"That's where off-duty soldiers go. Let's go."

With that they sprang from their perch at full tilt toward their prize just as the Celts reached the door deep in conversation.

"Get the little one, Duka!" Duka went left, grabbing Cullen, knocking him to the ground. Pathius deflected right, straight for the leather bag.

Hearing his assailant, Getarix swung left, putting his back between his treasure and Pathius.

Cullen did not know what had hit him, but as he hit the ground hard he instinctively knew that if he did not fight it would cost him his life. In a flash all the years of suppressed rage held in gave way. All the humiliation endured, all the abuse suffered, exploded in a volcano of anger he could not have called back if he had wanted to. Duka had no idea what he had ignited. Cullen was taught that it was wrong to strike his father. This was not his father. Duka went to jump on Cullen. Cullen brought his knee up and planted it firmly in Duka's vulnerability. The giant African reeled in pain, temporarily losing his ability to breathe. Cullen saw his opportunity, jumping to his feet before Duka landed on his knees. With the tables turned Cullen gave Duka two solid boots to the stomach just above where he held his hands, which were holding his loins. Duka rolled onto his side, curled up in an effort to protect himself. On his indignant landing he lost his breakfast and Cullen dropped all his weight on his now-exposed side, driving his knee into his ribs with an audible crack. Duka screamed. Cullen continued his work using his fists and boots to Duka's head, face, and ribs for good measure.

Pathius could not get a hold of the bag, and his momentum caused him to run right into the door of the inn with a loud crash. Turning face to face with Getarix he lunged for the leather-bound treasure. Using all his strength, Getarix swung around away from the building with Pathius firmly holding onto the bag. As Pathius fell back, the bag's leather flap, unable to support the weight of the swinging thief, gave way and tore. He fell back toward the quayside. Stopping himself, he gave one more desperate lunge only to be met by the big Celt's boot to his chest. This time he fell on his backside, winded. Glancing over to Duka he saw the shorter stout Celt coming firmly down on his ribs, obviously breaking them with a loud crack. It became obvious that Duka was on the losing end of his battle. The plan was for Duka to take out the little one with one blow and the two of them would finish off the bigger one. He noticed the bigger one bending to pick up a loose paving stone. With lightning conviction, Pathius gave up his mission. He rolled over to his feet, running into the crowd, becoming lost, but not before the paving stone found its target. He continued to run despite the crushing pain. He turned into town knowing that he could never return to the ship. He became lost to all.

Just as Pathius disappeared into the crowd, the doors of the inn swung open violently. Out thundered three Roman soldiers in full chain mail armour over light green tunics, swords in hand ready to fight.

"What in the name of Mars is going on here?" the largest of the three bellowed. Pointing to Cullen and Duka, he added, "Get that man off him." He placed the tip of his sword at Getarix's belly, poised to thrust. His two junior companions separated Duka and Cullen. Duka, not knowing quite what was happening, just sat there preoccupied with his wounds. Cullen on the other hand had to be restrained before he returned to sanity.

"Would someone tell me what in Hades is going on here?" Gallus repeated slowly. Getarix stood to his full height, looking the senior Roman in the eyes, and spoke broken but passable Latin.

"We were minding our own business when this big African—" he gestured to Duka on the ground "—and a smaller Greek attacked us."

"Why would they want to attack two pathetic Gauls like you?"

"We are from Britannia, not Gaul, and they did attack us."

"Can you prove it?"

The two Romans who had just left the inn spoke up with a patrician air.

"Duplicarius," the first one began, using his senior non-commissioned officer rank, "we are witnesses to the entire event and it is as the Gauls, or should I say the Britons, speak. Just after we left the inn, they approached the door but before they could enter this one and a skinny Greek attacked. The Greek was grabbing for that bag he holds."

"Noble sirs, how can you be so sure you saw it all?"

"We were amusing ourselves at their expense. They look like they just got off the boat and were walking around like this is the first time they laid eyes on a civilized nation." He directed his next comment to the displaced Celts. "Is that not so?"

"Yes, we arrived this very morning on the Black Rose. I recognize this one as a member of her crew," Getarix said as Cullen looked on in pain, not knowing any Latin.

Duplicarius Gallus, still unsure about these two, took a step closer to Getarix and looked him square in the eyes. "Why did these two take such a keen interest in an old leather bag?"

Having no choice, Getarix resigned himself to losing his inheritance after all. He was sure the duplicarius would seize the contents. He opened the bag so only the senior Roman soldier could look in. When Getarix pulled out his winter woollen, Gallus saw clearly the Celtic design decorating the last of Vercingetorix's treasure.

Closing the bag, Gallus asked, "Where in all heaven would poor immigrants like the two of you ever get these?"

"They were my grandfather's." Getarix left out his famous forefather's name, not sure what reaction he would receive.

"Well, they are old enough and they are definitely not Roman nor, for that matter, African or Greek." The duplicarius addressed his subordinates by rank. "Miles Aquilla and Cassius, take this man." He pointed his sword to Duka still on the ground. "We will see if Rome can redeem something from his sorry life at the slave market." There ended the trial that determined Duka's fate. If he had been a Roman citizen, he would have stood before the magistrate.

Aquilla and Cassius lifted Duka to his feet and led him away.

"How about you two stay out of trouble?" Gallus ended their meeting by turning on his heels. He returned alone into the inn, leaving the two Celts alone but vindicated.

VI

A NEW IDEA INTRODUCED

"Getarix, what just happened?"

"Well, Cullen, it looks like we passed our first test. Not our last, I expect."

Getarix opened the inn doors and followed Gullis into the darkness, Cullen on his heels. The inn was full of diners enjoying their morning meals. The mix of smells made Cullen and Getarix notice their hunger.

"Getarix, what do you mean, what did they decide?"

Ahead of them, Gullis turned and answered in perfect Celtic. "The big African will be sent to the slave market and you two are free to go. However, I'm afraid the two of you will not last long in our world."

Both Getarix and Cullen stood speechless, giving Gullis a look of astonishment.

Cullen, finding his voice, said, "How did you learn our language so perfectly?"

"Your language? You Britons are not the only Celts around, you know. I learned it on my mother's lap as she did hers, and so on." Turning on his hobnail sandals, he went to his table and sat back down to his breakfast. To his dismay his tiropatinam had arrived but now was cold. Gullis ordered the sweet egg soufflé every week. He needed the break from army porridge. It amazed him that Rome had built the largest Empire ever on wheat porridge—that and wine. Barley porridge if you were a slave. He at least had his honey-soaked fruit to enjoy. As he ate he tried to forget the morning's events. He got precious little time off as it was. With his recent promotion he was able to afford a weekly meal off base. Once a week he would treat himself with this meal at the inn. "Looks like today is ruined," he grumbled to himself.

Just as he was settling down to enjoy what was left of his meal, he saw the shadow of his two new acquaintances standing at his table. "How can I help?" *This soft heart of mine is going to kill me.*

"Sorry to be a bother. Um, we were to meet my uncle here…" Getarix trailed off.

"Well, you might as well sit here to wait. It looks like the only bench left in the place, anyway." Gullis gestured with his hands to the empty bench across from him.

"Is this uncle of yours staying at the inn?"

"Um…no," Getarix answered sheepishly. Once again, Gullis began to wonder about these two.

"And when is this meeting supposed to happen?"

"After…um…the harvest…before the winter rains."

"You're a little early, seeing that it just turned summer. Not only are you two lost in the land, you're lost in time as well. You are aware that two days ago was the last day of spring, eh? The harvest is not yet planted."

"Yes, we're perfectly aware of the time." Cullen put in.

Just then the inn doors swung open and the two junior soldiers approached their table, stopping smartly before their superior to give their report.

"Duplicarius Gullis, the large thief has been delivered to the slave merchant, where we met the Captain of the Black Rose, a Greek named Eppillius. He confirmed the story we heard from these two. The little one got away but we told the captain of the Black Rose to turn him over to us if he shows up."

"If he shows up we could arrest him for stupidity. Okay, very good, is that all?"

"Yes, Duplicarius."

"Very well, keep searching and I'll see you back at the fort."

Before leaving, the two soldiers glared at both Cullen and Getarix. They had just secured a table by the window when the uproar began. Having abandoned their table to deal with the crisis, there was no chance of getting another, ruining their only day off in weeks.

After they left, Cullen asked, "Them too?"

"Them what?" Gullis asked, then it hit him that they had been speaking in Celtic. "Yes, them too. As a matter of fact, our entire unit is Celtic."

"How many Celts are there in the Roman army?" Getarix asked.

"Thousands, probably more."

"How can the Romans trust the Celts not to rise up arms here and take Gaul back?" Cullen asked.

"There are very few Celtic troops here. Most of the troops stationed in Gaul and Belgica are German, Greek, Syrian, and such. The Celts are sent to other parts of the Empire. Besides, Rome has brought a great improvement to our lives. We lived in poverty before and now we live in plenty."

"If Celts are sent to other parts, what are you doing here?" Getarix still did not believe his ears.

"They need us here for our language. We train Celtic soldiers. Our unit, four hundred strong, is a training unit."

"A what?" Cullen asked, not understanding the concept of a standing professional army. "A man should just know how to fight, right?"

"Most people can fight, but can they fight smart...smart and disciplined? That's how our forefathers lost Gaul to the Romans.

"Vercingetorix gathered most of Gaul to the cause, but still lost the initiative due to his undisciplined cavalry fleeing the battle when they became scared. He had no choice but to retreat to a hilltop village at Alesia, where Caesar laid siege. He lost the battle to hold the area around the fort when his troops again fled in fear. Many were killed as they jammed the laneways in flight. This happened again and again until the defenders of Alesia were exhausted and Vercingetorix was forced to surrender, placing all his weapons and shields at the feet of the victorious Caesar. Some say he even stripped naked before the great Roman. That was a long time ago, but I saw that same thing myself here fifteen years ago."

Getarix and Cullen sat up and took notice. "You were there?" Getarix asked.

"Yes, but it did not amount to much. A band of unorganized Britons came over and tried to take the fort. In those days it was all wood, no stone anywhere. After the raid the authorities decided to rebuild the fort in stone."

"Tell us more about the raid." Cullen peered intently through his one good eye.

"Like I said, there's not much to tell. About one thousand Britons came over by boat and tried to lay siege to the old fort. I found out later that the grandson of Vercingetorix led the raid. He may have led the raid, but he did not posses his grandfather's abilities. After the battle of Alesia some of Vercingetorix's family fled to Britannia, rather than be caught and turned into slaves, so goes the rumour. As far as our little battle went, we assembled the training staff in front and the trainees behind us and confronted them. When they could not break the line they became scattered and ran. Some fought very valiantly but to no avail. Most were killed or captured, the others escaped."

"Whatever happened to their leader?" Getarix asked.

"No idea."

"So you fought in the battle?" Cullen asked.

"No, I was sent to help the physician as his aid. That's how I got interested in medical care. Anyway, I worked with the injured from the battle. Actually, I remember working on the hand of one they said was their leader. It got crushed in the handle of his shield. But I don't remember what happened to him. We lost the location where their injured were and later when we regained it they were gone. I imagine he escaped along with the rest of them, or died later in the battle. But enough of that. What about you two? Where will you go from here?"

The innkeeper interrupted them to inquire if the two new guests would be buying breakfast. "You can't be sitting here and not buy something. We're not a charity, ya know."

Remembering his uncle's instruction, Getarix introduced himself to the innkeeper. "I'm Getarix, nephew of Cunhail the merchant."

On hearing his young guest's name, Gullis took notice as the pieces of this mystery started to fall into place.

"Cunhail, yes, any relative of his is welcome here. What can I get you two?"

Getarix looked to Cullen with the unspoken question.

Cullen pulled out a small bag of coins and asked, "What would this buy?"

Those, ha—those are not Roman coins...well, you're serious. Um, for Cunhail's sake, let me see." Marcus took the coins and examined them carefully. "They are virtually worthless, but I could see to two bowls of barley porridge."

"That would be fine," Cullen answered like he had just closed a deal of a lifetime. The fact was he had just spent his entire life savings. Cullen tried to smile but his face would not respond.

Once Marcus left on his errand, Getarix noticed Gullis staring at him. "What is it?"

"Not all his things were dropped at Caesar's feet, were they?"

"What do you mean?" Getarix asked, not without a touch of fear as he clutched the leather bag tighter to himself.

"Those things in that bag were his, am I not right?" Leaning back, he continued. "And that was your father I treated some fifteen years ago on the battle field. I take it he never arrived home. Again I am right...am I not?"

Getarix just looked down.

"And here is, I would say, the only living descendant of the Great Chief, his namesake, penniless and poor."

"No, I have an older brother."

"And he is as penniless as you?"

"No, but he is not good at earning it."

"Drink, eh, he likes his wine."

Cullen cut in. "No, that would be my father."

"Ah, so the mystery of the bruises is solved as well. Those bruises were not issued today. Yesterday, I would say. I treat enough soldiers who acquire them. Now, a brother you say."

"It's a long story," Getarix said, slightly irritated having been found out. He tightened up, ready to flee in case there was a price on the descendants of Vercingetorix.

"Relax. I won't hurt you, and as it happens I have all day and I am suddenly interested in your story. So much of what I already know makes little sense."

Gullis was a very likable person able to put both young men at ease. Getarix and Cullen told their whole life stories from before birth to the landing in Portius Itilius that very morning. As their stories progressed their porridge came and went, leaving two empty bowls and two hungry lost friends.

Gallus looked at them with a bit of wonder. "That's quite a tale, but—"

"It's true, every word of it," Getarix cut in.

"Oh I believe you, every word of it. But what now? No money, no employment, no skills, and worst of all no means of survival. You can't go home."

"Well, we will just hire ourselves out to earn enough until harvest," Cullen said.

"Won't happen," Gullis said. "All the unskilled jobs are done by slaves. Who would hire freemen at cost when all one has to do is feed his slaves? Something he would be doing anyway. And those who own no slaves would use someone else's slave at minimal cost. On top of that, many of the skilled jobs are done by slaves. Even some physicians are slaves. All that to say, I don't think your plan will work."

"We can make it. We have no choice," Getarix said.

"You have three choices, as I see it. Your first would be to sell those treasures, and hope you don't get cheated so badly that the two of you can't pay your way until fall. If for whatever reason your uncle does not appear, you would be forced into the second option. With your great family heirlooms now gone for good, you would be forced into selling yourselves as slaves just for food and shelter. This option is permanent, and here in the rural areas without any skills you would end up on a farm where the animals are treated better. City slaves have it good in comparison; however, they are unpaid slaves, the possessions of another man, no freedom."

"The future looks bleak," Cullen said to Getarix.

"There is a third option."

"Third option?" Getarix asked.

"The army."

"The army?" both asked.

"Why not?"

Getarix answered. "We are Britons. You know, the enemy! They would not even think of taking us."

"That was over seventy years ago. The war is over. My grandfather died in Alesia. He fought beside yours and here I am. There are special Celtic units... ours is called the Fifth Legion, the Alaudea."

"The Larks," Getarix translated.

"Your Latin is good. Anyway, you sign on for twenty years, the last four on light duties. You get paid and if you do well and don't step on it, you get promoted, and at the end of it all a grateful Rome will give you land and citizenship to pass on to your children. Not a bad deal, contrasted to the alternative. Oh yeah, and with this option you can keep you family treasure—something more to pass on to your children."

"I...I don't know," Getarix said.

"Well, hunger will help make up your mind. I must return to the fort and make my report. I'll tell them to expect you two. They begin training a new group first thing tomorrow. For once your timing is perfect. You'll find the fort by following the quay north where it turns into the way of the sea and leads you straight there. Good day, gentlemen." Gullis got up but then stopped. "Word of advice: keep the contents of that bag and your connection to the great chief a secret. I see no advantage to anyone else knowing about such things. See you tomorrow." Gullis left feeling satisfied that he at least had given the two lost souls a means of survival.

"Well, Getarix, what do you think?"

"I...I really don't know, Cullen. It's one thing to come here, it's quite another to join the Roman Army."

"You know who that sounds like."

"I know, Cullen, but it's different. My grandfather—"

"Fought beside Duplicarius Gullis' grandfather."

"The Gauls don't seem to be oppressed like I thought."

"And if I heard right we would never be asked to fight our own," Cullen added. They looked around and noticed that the noon crowd was filling the room and some were waiting for their table. Cullen and Getarix took this as their cue to move on.

"Well Cullen, we wait until tomorrow, eh?"

"Until tomorrow."

VII

BATTLES LOST

Cool mist covered the ground. The icy breeze cut through their cloaks. Moisture built up on their armour, dripping from their helmets into their eyes. In the cool morning they stood in the midst of the Teutoburg Forest, stunned. Before their very eyes lay the carnage of the battle that had raged years ago. Three whole Legions: the XVII, the XVIII, and the XIX, not to mention three Cavalry units, had been destroyed. An entire army died that September day, left unattended where they fell. Their bones now bleached white from the sun and long cleaned bare. Rusting swords, some still gripped in bony hands, littered the ground. The forest floor boasted gigantic red blossoms. Capes that once protected the backs of the soldiers from the sun and rain became their only grave-markers. As far as the eye could make out, amongst the capes, was armour tarnished and rusting, breastplates, shin-guards, spears, and helmets all mingled with the bones of the flower of Rome.

The bones now wet from the early morning dew mocked the beauty of the spring day. The small delegation of Romans could almost hear the battle in the cool damp wind as it worked its way through the trees. It blew first to the left around an ancient pine, then down under a bush, picking up the death cries and sweeping them loudly to the ears of the living.

"This place is haunted," one of the soldiers said, wanting to flee.

Four years prior, this was Augustan's proud army entrusted to the Governor, Publius Quinctilius Varus. Varus was Governor of Germania and brother-in-law to Damianus Aurelia Marius Gius, Senator of Rome. On that fateful day when Varus saw all was lost, he fell on his sword and now lay with his lost legions.

Centurion Cornelius, aid to the senator, felt pity for his master for the first time as he searched the bones carefully.

"What does he seek?" Antonio whispered to Cornelius.

In a low voice Cornelius answered the slave. "His brother-in-law...Varus."

"How does he expect to recognize him?"

"The German leader Arminius had his head removed and sent to Marbod, king of the Marcomanni, a neutral German kingdom."

"What did Marbod do?"

"He sent it to Rome for proper burial. I take it he's looking for the rest of him, a hopeless endeavour. You are looking at twenty-thousand sets of bones."

"That many!" Antonio gasped.

"I was with the XIXth and almost ended here with my brothers, but a month before this battle I, along with another, was called back to Rome. We had been selected to join the Praetorian Guard, a rare honour indeed. Very few get selected to be part of this elite unit. I was with them only a few years when suddenly I got this posting. I was selected on the recommendation of Governor Varus. If not for this assignment, I guess, you would be looking upon my bones."

"You must feel like this assignment saved your life."

"No. Getting posted to the Praetorian Guard saved my life. This assignment might kill me yet. Some days I wish I would have stayed with the XIXth." Cornelius saw something out of the corner of his eyes. "Did you see that, Antonio?"

"No, but I heard something."

"There it is again, and over there. We are surrounded. We have been shadowed since we crossed the Rhine. But something is wrong. They are getting nervous. One false move and I fear we will join these bones. Senator—" Cornelius tried to warn the senator, but one of the young soldiers cut him off. Thirty soldiers had been added to their delegation once they crossed the Rhine River into German territory.

"Sir...Sir." The soldier ran toward the small group, examining the ground.

"What is it, you fool? Stop your yelling."

"But sir..." The soldier was catching his breath. "Sir, the standards, I found the standards, the Eagle Standards, sir. They are all together leaning against a great stone," The soldier gasped, pointing up the trail he just descended. Suddenly everyone stopped their search and took note.

Senator Damianus began to think. *If I'm able to return the standards, I would be a hero.* "Soldier, show us!"

"Senator Damianus, sir—" Cornelius began.

"Not now, Centurion. We have work here to do."

Before Cornelius could say another word they took off following the young soldier a half mile through the mist. Upon arrival they could see the standards leaning right where he said they would be found. The three Eagle Standards that represented the lost legions stood higher and loomed larger than the many others representing the sub-units that made up the three legions. Their bronze wings now tarnished black stretched proudly above their pennants. The red pennants with their golden letters signifying the unit they represented were now faded. One was torn and the gold letters were hanging, ready to fall at any time.

As they stood there looking, Cornelius noticed something on the trees that surrounded the stone outcrop. Mounted on them with large spikes were skulls of the dead left as a warning to any visitors.

"Soldier, you there, go get the Eagle Standards. Antonio, go help him with—"

"Sir!" Cornelius said.

Damianus pointed to Cornelius with his finger. "Silence!"

"But sir, the forest is—"

"Silence you, or you will spend the rest of your miserable life with these bones. Never, ever, interrupt me again. Do you hear me, Centurion Cornelius?"

Cornelius just stood there, silenced and humiliated.

The senator turned his wrath on the soldier and Antonio. He picked up a long leg bone and began to strike Antonio fiercely on the back, yelling, "Now get to it and remember who owns you, you worthless piece of garbage." Without hesitation, Antonio began to move toward the standards where the first soldier was already about to pick up the first, when an arrow landed just shy of his head, bouncing off the granite with a spark. The soldier stopped dead in his sandals.

"What are you waiting for, get them!" the senator raged.

"But sir—"

"Sir, they will be killed instantly. I promised his commander to bring all of his soldiers back alive." Cornelius had found his courage for the first time working with the senator. Cornelius addressed the soldier on the ledge. "Soldier, I order you to come down from there this instant." With relief, the soldier made a move to step down off the ledge where the standards remained.

"You will stand your ground or I will flog you myself! I outrank this pathetic excuse for an officer. Do you hear me?" Such was his rage that foam flew from his mouth. The soldier, thoroughly confused, stopped. A second arrow came his way. This one found the centre of his chest, killing him instantly. Antonio jumped to the ground, landing on his belly.

"Get up you, coward—" Senator Damianus began.

"The centurion is right," a thick German-accented voice announced from behind the tree line. "You have worn out the great leader's welcome here. The next arrow will be embedded in the fat one."

There was a silent standoff for a few long moments until Senator Damianus loudly proclaimed, "Do you know whom you are addressing?"

"Yes, an overstuffed swine about to die."

The senator paused for a moment. "Okay, gentlemen, let's be on our way. We have to meet with the great German leader Arminius." Under his breath he muttered, "Another day, we will get them back." Looking to Cornelius, he spat out, "And you will get yours! Your career is over, mark my words."

When Cornelius moved toward the body of his soldier, the German voice bellowed, "Leave him; he now belongs to Woden, our god of war."

Not wanting to cause any more trouble, Cornelius backed off, muttering under his voice. "Someday we will honour you, Son."

As their company continued on, Antonio asked Cornelius, "Why are those standards so important?"

"They represent the unit you belong to. Great victories are displayed upon them. Great victories that cost many good men their lives. So in a way they represent all the men who died in battle. As you know, they are tall and can be seen from far away. If a soldier gets lost in the confusion of battle—and trust me battle, is confusing—he simply looks up and when he sees the standard of his unit, he knows where to go. To the soldier they are sacred. To Rome those standards back there represent a great defeat and humiliation."

"And to the senator?"

"Nothing more than feathering his political nest." They walked in silence through the rolling mist. They noticed what looked like altars where the tribunes were sacrificed to Woden. Their gold-plated armour strewn about still reflected the weak sunlight.

Cornelius broke the silence. "Well Antonio, I think we now know why Arminius insisted on seeing us so deep in German territory. He wanted to make a point."

"He made his point with me, but not as firm of an impression as on Miles Crassus back there. Do you think the senator got the point?"

"I doubt it. Mind you I think he left a pile where he stood." They both laughed quietly. "I'm afraid he is going to get us killed or into another war."

"Do you think he cares?" Antonio asked.

"He won't have to fight it and, as I have discovered, he would stand to make a tidy profit off any war Rome engages in. Tiberius wants to re-establish Rome, east of the Rhine. Augustus wants to negotiate for the land. But more than anything he wants his standards back. They say he wakes up in the night, yelling, 'Varus, where are my Legions?'"

Later that night they were guests of the great German general, Arminius. Arminius, the same general who placed those bones on the forest floor, the same general whose orders kept them there.

"There you go, sir." Antonio handed Cornelius his breastplate and held the back plate in place.

"Thank you, Antonio."

"I hear Arminius was once a Roman centurion himself. Did you ever know Arminius?"

"No, never met him. Only know about him. He was one of the brightest military minds of his day. He joined the Roman army and within five years rose to centurion. He earned Roman citizenship and then the title of Knight. Upon the death of his father he returned here to his homeland, which was Roman. He was twenty-five years old when he left the army. When he arrived he found his people suffering under the inept, cruel governorship of our senator's brother-in-law, Varus. Indignant by what he saw, Arminius gathered together many German tribes in an alliance. After training them using Roman military techniques, he took on his onetime employer and won back the lands east of the Rhine River."

"So you must have fought him?"

"Well, not him directly, but yes. Mind you I fought in these forests long before that. It seems it's where I am destined to fight."

"Destinies can change."

"I hope so." Both men prayed the last statement would come about, their minds preoccupied with the senator's threats, which were never idle.

Still a very young man in his thirties, Cornelius knew he was in the presence of true leadership. He could not help contrasting him with Senator Damianus.

Across the table next to the handsome Arminius sat his treasonous father-in-law Segestes, the chief of the Cherusci, a Teutonic tribe. Cornelius could not help noticing that when Segestes and the senator's eyes met there was recognition, that they were somehow in league.

Arminius opened. "Senator Damianus, it has been a long time. I believe the last time we talked was at your villa on the slope of Vesuvius outside Pompeii."

"Arminius, I believe it was."

"I am now called Irman. I hear you found your lost standards. You know they now belong to our god of war, Woden. They were won in battle and all that."

"Yes, well…the emperor wishes to have them back," Damianus said. It never ceased to astonish Cornelius how strong and powerful the senator was in the face of slaves and how he began to crumble when met with a character of greater stature.

"Very foolish of you," Arminius said.

"You must forgive my aide. Centurion Cornelius here can be impetuous. I tried to stop him." The senator glared in the direction of his aide. Cornelius could not believe his ears. *So that's how he's going to get out of this one. I should have known I would take the fall.* Cornelius looked straight into Arminius' eyes. The two warriors connected.

"Ho, is that how it happened, eh?" He left no doubt he knew where the blame lay. "You know, your brother-in-law and I fought together in the Pannonian Wars. I even thought of offering my services to him when I arrived back home. That was until I saw what he was doing to my people. I trust you are cut from a different cloth, eh?"

"He was my brother through marriage only. His weaknesses were well known to the family. I even advised the emperor not to send him, but alas, good counsel is seldom listened to." The mighty senator was reduced to grovelling and lies, worried only about his own hide.

The negotiation went nowhere. Arminius would not give up any of the land he had gained east of the Rhine. Nor would he allow the Romans to venture into Teutoburg Forest to bury their dead or retrieve the standards. "The dead and the standards are to remain where they are until the gods themselves take them," Arminius declared. Between the stubbornness of Arminius and the spinelessness of Damianus, the negotiations were destined to failure. To the senator, everything was someone else's fault. Even his ally Segestes looked upon him with disgust.

The senator took out his anger with his failure and humiliation on his military aide. Cornelius was treated like one of the slaves on their return trip to Rome. He was even forced to sleep in the barns amongst the slaves and common soldiers at the various inns along the way. When they arrived at the Boar's Head

Inn, Cornelius did not see the pretty little daughter of the innkeeper. He only saw the hateful glares of Fritz. Cornelius had never been so thankful he was sleeping in a barn. However, the air was warm and through the open window all could hear the muted cries from an upstairs room. When Antonio heard this he, for the first time, fully understood the depravity of his master and he felt sick he had ever protected the senator's life. He prayed he could somehow make it up to the poor hapless victim.

Centurion Cornelius knew he would feel the full wrath of his master's blame upon their return to Rome. A foreboding came over him. *Maybe I did not survive the hateful touch of my master after all. Now I, too, will be finished. Taking my own life is an option. No, I will not give such a gift to that fat swine.* Cornelius rode home in silence, desperately trying to work out how he was going to survive. He could not get out of his head the idea that after so many sacrifices, so many risks and so much discomfort, so much of his life given for Rome, this was to be his reward. As they crested the hill where the city of Rome came into full view, his heart sunk. A bitter taste came into his mouth and thoughts of just running and disappearing into the borderlands filled his mind.

VIII
ENLISTMENT

The road that led to the fort ran south to north, following the coastline. It was a typical Roman road built by the soldiers. The surface was paved with local stones and ran straight as an arrow. Water had collected in the cracks between the paving stones. The rhythm of the horse's hooves splashing in the puddles almost put Getarix to sleep. He struggled to stay awake atop Caballo. It rained all night, soaking both Getarix and Cullen to the skin as they slept on the stone of the town square. Cullen had slept like he was in a dry, comfortable bed. Getarix looked at him during the night in wonder. The cold rain that accompanied the pain of hunger kept sleep an elusive goal for Getarix. The rain had let up, the hunger hadn't. They rode in silence, hardly a word since sunrise.

"You're awfully quiet. Hardly a word from you since you woke up," Cullen said.

Getarix tried in vain to adjust his rain-soaked clothing. He answered in a sour mood. "I'm too busy shivering. You're awfully chipper for someone who spent the night on paving stones in a rain storm, with a face that looks like it was just sent through the grain mill."

"Practice."

Getarix shot him a puzzled look.

Cullen smiled. "Practice. All my life I slept in a cold wet hut, except when I slept at yours. Besides, I can see out of my right eye again!"

"You're smiling."

"Why not?" Cullen smiled again, despite Getarix's sour mood.

"How about not eating for almost two days?"

"Again, practice. Besides, there was that porridge yesterday."

"That was not food. That was feed."

"Well, I'm sure army food will be quite good. It has to be."

"You're actually happy."

"Of course I am. Why wouldn't I be?"

"Why not…why do I even talk to you? We're about to join the Roman army, you fool."

"You're the one who wanted to leave home and live a life of excitement. Yesterday at this time we did not know how we were going to survive."

"I wish it was as simple as—"

"It is."

Getarix grunted in disgust, ending the conversation. They were approaching a small village that had grown up just outside the fort's south gate. The road cut straight through the village and the fort connecting the north and south gates. At night the soldiers would close the gates securely, essentially cutting off the road. This made sense, since the roads were built to accommodate the coming and goings of the fort. The new trade route that had developed was not even considered. The traders who used the road did not like it. The innkeepers did. Both gates were now open and the fort was a hive of activity.

The village, in contrast to the well-ordered fort, was a scattered mess. The buildings were built in places that made no sense at all. Only a few of them lined the road. Others were set about, creating many tiny squares but few streets. Not a right angle amongst them. For Getarix and Cullen it had a feeling of home. To the Romans it felt like chaos. The structures were built in the Roman manner, same as the town of Portius Itius, but on a much smaller scale. Most were no more than two stories and making the corners square did not seem to have mattered. In many of them the merchant's family would live in the upstairs, leaving the bottom floor for their shop. The shops opened into the road with the merchants' wares spilling onto the cobblestone. The Roman army put up with this because of what the village brought them—services the army needed but could or would not provide itself. Soldiers kept their unofficial families in the apartments. Single soldiers could also find services at the inn, which not only housed the oldest profession known to man but also provided what passed for fine dining. Aside from providing hot meals and company, the inn produced accommodations for visitors to the fort. The market provided not only for the village but many essentials for the fort itself. The butcher supplied fresh meat to augment the issued rations. The fort cooks had their pots made and repaired by the smith. When he was not repairing pots, he would work for the armoury, mending and occasionally making weapons. Without the village, life in the army would have been much more difficult, and without the army the village would have been much poorer.

As they were about to enter the village, Getarix broke his silence. "Cullen, I don't think we should take the horses into the fort. Who knows what they would do with them?"

"You surely have a problem trusting."

Getarix ignored his comment. "When we are sure, we can easily come and get them. Better that than sorry."

"I guess you're right."

"Look over there, behind what looks like the stable. There is a post with plenty of fresh grass and water."

After making arrangements with the stable keeper, they continued on foot.

"Getarix, how are we going to pay him?"

"Ask me tomorrow," Getarix said quietly, not wanting anyone within earshot to hear about their predicament.

As they walked toward the south gate they were struck by the size and grandeur of the fort. The walls of stone shot straight up two stories, and the gate towers raised themselves three stories. Getarix and Cullen just stood there in the narrow street, slightly stunned. The shops were just opening up. The village was coming to life all around them.

"Centurion Calyx, look, it came last night just before closing. That's the Egyptian cotton you were asking about," the merchant said, showing a small bolt of white cloth to a Roman centurion.

"Excellent, bundle it up. Livia will be pleased. What is that?" The centurion pointed to some brightly coloured cloth that shone in the sunlight.

"Oh! Excellent taste I see you have. That's called silk and it comes from the east, the other edge of the earth. It is extremely dear…"

"Then hide it when Livia comes by."

"Ha ha, for you I will."

The meat cleaver of the butcher suddenly stopped when a group of soldiers arrived with two boars and a deer.

"...by tonight? Yes, yes it can be done." The red-haired butcher resigned himself to a long, hard day's work.

Across the way, a Roman soldier was declaring angrily, "We need them now, this morning."

"I have thirty-three pairs ready; the other two will be done within the hour," the cobbler said, defending himself.

"I'll take the thirty-three now and I expect the last two in my supply room before midmorning, or I will dock it from your pay." The soldier bent and picked up a bundle of hobnailed sandals, taking them straight into the fort. The cobbler was left in a frenzy, calculating to himself how he was going to accomplish his task.

Getarix and Cullen were so engrossed in the goings-on of the village they did not even notice their hunger until they were standing beside the little village inn. Above the door was a carved wooden sign of a Roman helmet adorned with white wings. On the little stone-paved covered porch sat two tables leaden with all manner of food. The enticing aroma grabbed their attention and reminded them just how hungry they were. They stopped walking and faced the diners. Off-duty soldiers were devouring hot egg dishes, washing them down with honey-soaked delights. One of the soldiers noticed them and barked.

"What are you looking at? Carve a statue, it lasts longer!" The other soldiers broke out in laughter.

Getarix and Cullen quickly turned back toward the fort gates, approaching the guards on sentry.

"Halt you two. Where do you think you're going?"

"To the fort. We—"

"You think you could just wander in like that, eh? Like it's your own little village, eh?" The other guard gave them a hard look and said, "You are Britons, aren't you?"

"Yes…how…?"

"Your accent, your clothes. What's your business here?"

"We, we have come…" Getarix wasn't quite sure how to ask.

"Come on out with it before I'm pensioned off."

Getarix began to question their decision about coming and was about to say 'no business' and turn around when Cullen found his voice.

"We have come to join the Roman army!"

Getarix gave him a look as if he wanted to strangle him.

"Well why didn't you say so?" Looking at Getarix, the second guard pointed to Cullen and said, "Looks like your friend has all the brains, eh?" They both laughed.

The first one pointed into the fort to a large central building, addressing Cullen. "That there is Fort Headquarters. Tell the guard you want to join and he will take care of you. Mind you, don't let your friend talk. He will just confuse things." Getarix was getting a little angry, but felt it better to keep silent.

Walking on, he addressed Cullen under his breath. "Cullen, what the hell are you doing?"

"Something you seemed not able to do."

"Oh shut up, I was about to change plans before you—"

"It was a good thing I spoke up. All you needed to do was say we have come to join the army."

"It's not as simple as that—"

"Apparently it is."

"Well, here we are. Our fate is about to be made."

The building they stood before was a classic one-story Roman building—white plaster over red bricks. The bricks showed through where the plaster had been knocked off. They could not see any roof. All the buildings in the fort were built the same way and were identical except for shape and size. The headquarters building was the largest and most impressive of all. It was built right in the centre of the fort, where all roads led to it. The west wall faced the north-south road that ran through the centre of the fort connected the two gates. The wall was over one hundred feet long. The only access to the building was a single door found at the halfway point. It was plastered a brilliant white and neatly trimmed in red. At this door stood another guard who asked them their business upon their arrival. This time Getarix found his voice. "We have come to join the Roman army."

"You're late."

"Late?"

"Yes, the training is about to begin. You should have reported yesterday. Were you not told?"

They gave him a blank stare in stereo.

The guard looked them up and down and quickly assessed the situation. Well, okay, it should not be a problem."

"Optie Servius, I have two more," the guard hollered through the door.

A voice from inside yelled back, "They were supposed to report yesterday. Wait a minute, everyone did report."

"These two are from out of town. Way out, I would say."

A few seconds later another soldier appeared through the door into the sunshine. The small young soldier, who looked like he did not get out into the sun that often, looked at them with an irritated snarl. "Too late. You should have showed up yesterday."

"We only just arrived yesterday from—"

"Britannia, right?"

"Yes."

"Yes, I remember. I was told of you. Come this way and we will fill out the appropriate contract and get those braids cut," he grumbled. Getarix tenderly ran his fingers along his soon-to-disappear hair.

When they entered the building they found themselves back outside. The entire building surrounded a central courtyard that gave light to all the rooms. The courtyard was paved in the same stone as the road. It was void of everything except about twenty pillars that supported a roof that sloped into the courtyard. They were led across the courtyard to a large door that entered midway into a very large hall. The hall had a very high roof. It was lined with small windows at the second-story level that let in a surprising amount of light for their size. Crossing the hall, they entered a small room lined with shelves filled with scrolls. Below stood two small, unadorned desks. The optie sat behind the desk in the centre of the room and began to explain what was expected if they joined the army.

"The agreement is for twenty years of service, the last four on light duties, which means the first sixteen you will fight and you will work. You will surely be sent to other parts of the Empire. If you do not know Latin, expect to learn it, and if you get posted out east, expect to learn Greek besides, and a bit of the local language. Now as to your pay, you will be paid two hundred and fifty *denarii* per annum. You will be paid three times a year, so when you get it leave it with us and we will secure it. As thanks for showing up, here is seventy-five *denarii*. This is one third of a year's pay. It will be secured with your belongings. I dare say you will have little use for it for the next eight months. And if you survive the twenty years, you will be granted land and a pension. Pretty generous, if you ask me. Now, what names do you two go by?"

After they gave the required information, the optie opened the contents of their bags. Finishing with Cullen, he turned his attention to the torn bag Getarix still held firmly. He reluctantly handed it over. Upon seeing the golden treasure, the optie gave out a whistle. "A man of means, I see." He looked up and saw the fear in the eyes of Getarix. "I also see that they are important to you. Do not worry, this is the Roman army. We are not thieves. Do you know how many lashes my back would see if I stole your things? Not worth it. Now I need you to place your mark here indicating that you have entrusted the items with me."

With the administration completed, they were quickly taken to the quartermaster for all their issued supplies, everything needed to begin their training. Everything, that is, except hobnailed sandals. The quartermaster went red when he saw the number now being raised to thirty-seven recruits.

They were rushed to their barracks wearing nothing but light-green tunics and brown short pants that came down just below their knees. They were allowed to wear their old shoes until sandals could be procured. They had nothing else to their names. Everything else was taken and locked up securely, including the treasures that almost cost them their lives.

The quartermaster told them to hurry back to the headquarters great hall for the swearing in ceremony with the base commander. As they crossed the square, Cullen asked about the gold. "Getarix, do you ever expect to see those things again?"

Getarix muttered his answer quietly as they entered the hall noticing all eyes upon them. "I don't know. I seem destined to lose them."

IX

TRAINING BEGINS

Aquilla was tall and handsome in a rugged sense. His uniform was immaculate without a thread out of place. As soon as Getarix and Cullen entered the great hall, Aquilla recognized them. Placing his eyes upon the two of them, he stopped what he was saying to the new soldiers and exclaimed, "Well, well, what do we have here? It looks like two lost swine seeking a home. I don't take it that you remember me…now do you?"

"Hum…no…"

"Well you should," Aquilla bellowed. "The two of you ruined my day off yesterday. Miles Cassius and I get very few days off and with this course starting today it was the last day off in months, but no! We had to spend it looking after your affairs. That stupid little Greek should have ended your miserable little lives. But fear not, my friends, Cassius and I have almost a year to exact a little payback out of your sorry hides.

"Miles Cassius!" he called into a small room off the hall. "Look who's here?"

As Miles Cassius entered, he said, "Oh my, my, look at these two…and improperly dressed. I see you're still black and blue," he said to Cullen. "And what is this? So you two think you're special, eh? You're too good to join the rest of us. Do you?"

Cullen and Getarix were confused and a little scared.

Cassius bellowed, "Where's your proper footwear?"

"Um…we?"

"Don't talk to me, you!"

"Miles Cassius, stand down. The quartermaster says he ran out," Centurion Martialis said as he entered the hall. He addressed the group of recruits. "My name is Centurion Secundus Lucius Martialis. You do not speak to me unless you are answering my question. Do we have an agreement?" Not giving anyone a chance to respond, he continued. "Very good. It is my job to turn you into the best soldiers this world has ever seen or will ever see. If you fail I will take it personally." Martialis turned as another Centurion entered the hall. He stopped his speech and gestured toward his superior officer, still addressing the new recruits. "This is Centurion Appius Valerius Domitus, the base commander. While you are here, he has the power to end your sorry little lives. You will repeat after him the oath that you will carry to the grave, the oath you will be true to, barring all else." After Centurion Martialis handed the parade over to the commander, the soldiers repeated their oath.

"I swear to follow the emperor to whatever wars I may be called to.
I swear to perform with enthusiasm whatever the emperor commands,
never to desert the colours nor do anything contrary to law, and not to
shrink from death on behalf of the Roman state."

Once the oath was completed, they were formed up outside in the hot morning sun. Centurion Martialis addressed them. "You now are truly in the Roman army, which means Rome now owns you. You, however, will not be soldiers until you have successfully completed your training here. Once you have completed your training, you will then go and join the rest of our Legion stationed at Oppidum Batavorum. Until then, Rome has entrusted your sorry hides to my loving tender care. Let's make one thing clear here: Rome does not care who your father is…or your mother for that matter. If you serve Rome, she does not care if you are the son of a slave or even were once a slave yourself or some displaced prince. You will be granted citizenship equally, and land to raise your scrawny little prodigies, if you so choose to reproduce yourselves. Let me warn you now, though: if you choose not to comply, if you choose not to live up to what is expected of you—" He raised a wooden staff the length of his arm in the air. "I will beat you with this until you beg to be terminated. Is that understood?"

"Yes sir!" the troops said.

"What did I hear, a whisper?" Centurion Martialis roared, raising his staff again, ready to come down on anyone who would not comply.

"Yes sir!" the troops bellowed as one.

"Okay, that understood, no excuses right?"

"Yes sir!"

"Now I will leave you in the loving embrace of Miles Cassius and Aquilla for your little morning walk. But before that, you will enjoy a hearty Roman army breakfast."

"Okay you lot, back to the barracks where your breakfast will be served."

As they left the hall into the bright sun heading toward the barrack blocs, Getarix muttered to Cullen, "This breakfast better be worth it, Cullen. I tell—" He was cut off by Cassius' caustic scream.

"Where in the name of Mithras do you two think you're going? Get over here, you foul maggot. Stand to attention up against that wall and stay there until we return." They looked bewildered, and hesitated. "Get moving! You two had better contemplate why you find it appropriate to wear whatever you choose."

Getarix broke in. "The centurion said the quartermaster—"

Cassius quickly took a step forward, landing his powerful fist deep into Getarix's gut. He bent over. If he'd had anything in his stomach he would have lost it.

Cassius hissed into his ear with all the hate he could muster. "Understand this: Aquilla and I hate the two of you and we will break you."

Getarix glared at him. *Come on, hit me, just try it.* Thinking better of it, Getarix looked down. Cullen stood to attention, fearing to move at all.

Cassius continued. "Haven't the guts, have you?" He turned away and moved toward the three-barrack blocs assigned to their course. Just before entering he turn back to them. "Not one muscle until I came back and relieve you!" Getarix straighten up, coming to attention beside Cullen.

"Well, one thing," Getarix whispered through the pain.

"What?" Cullen said, not looking at him.

"Now I don't feel the need for breakfast." At this, Cullen smiled.

There they stood in the hot sun. Before they knew it, the rest of the troops had returned from the morning meal.

Aquilla ordered Getarix and Cullen to fall in with the course. He addressed the group. "Now, two of your number seem to think they are special and see themselves as better than the rest of you. They want to rewrite the orders from our divine Emperor, so they stand amongst you but refuse to be part of you. So they stand here wearing their own footwear." He drew his attention directly to the latest recruits. "Now get those thing off!"

Cullen moved instantly, removing his footwear, and his older friend quickly followed. Once barefoot, they marched at a fast pace five miles up the coast and returned without a rest. As they returned to the fort, hunger raged in Getarix's stomach. He looked up and noticed the sun at its height, indicating they were close to the noon hour.

Cullen broke into Getarix's private thoughts. "That was easy."

"I'm sure there's more to come. By the gods I am hungry. How are your feet?"

"Only a few cuts. Yours?"

"Same."

Once they came to a halt in front of their barrack bloc, Aquilla addressed them. "Well girls, how does that feel? When you're done your training, you will be able to walk twice that distance with full kit, all sixty-five pounds of it. And you will do it in the same time it took you ladies this morning. That will be the standard you will maintain for the next twenty years, and to be sure you maintain the standard you will do it each and every month. Now go and get lunch inside." Once again he called out Getarix and Cullen. "Not you two. Because we care so much for you, we put in a special order for hobnail sandals, the way you like them. Now get over to the quartermaster and get 'em."

Getarix hesitated, fighting anger. This did not escape the notice of Aquilla, who stepped forward to land a blow where Cassius had landed his earlier that morning. Without hesitation, the two of them flew off to the quartermaster's stores with the words of Aquilla bouncing off their backs: "You better move or you will wish that the big African had his wicked way with you." As Getarix ran, he held his stomach in pain, wondering if slavehood would have been the better option.

When they arrived at the quartermaster's stores, they found it locked so they waited by the door. The ground was too hot to stand barefoot, so they replaced their leather shoes. They waited until they noticed that their course was forming back up for the afternoon training. They began to panic, unsure what to do. *Do we go back, risking a beating for having the wrong footwear or a real beating for being absent?* Just then the quartermaster arrived, asking what they wanted. "Ah, they're here." He barely had them on the counter when the two of them snapped the sandals out of his hands and were gone. After their quick departure, the quartermaster quibbled. "Not even a thank you." Having worked at the fort for years, he had an understanding as to what these young soldiers went through. It was his policy never to add to their stress.

When the two of them rejoined their group, they had just enough time to change over to the new, stiff, hastily thus poorly constructed sandals. They had nowhere to put their old shoes. As the two instructors approached the formation, Getarix and Cullen stuffed their old soft shoes up their tunics, held in place between their legs. Aquilla and Cassius approached them looking for some deficiency, but found none. They sneered at them. Aquilla spat. "You will fail. And when you do, we will be there to celebrate." When the instructors turned their backs, Getarix gave Cullen a look of frustration. Before he knew it, Aquilla turned and landed his fist with all his force into Getarix's gut. "I told you I would be there for you. I can see through the back of my head, fagot." Through the pain, Getarix's only thought was not to drop his shoes. With all his might he stood back up.

Their centurion arrived, dismissing Aquilla and Cassis to warn the quartermaster of their imminent arrival. "Okay, now that you have been loosened up with a gentle little walk and fortified with good Roman army food, we are going to pick up the pace. From here you will be issued your training shield and sword. This afternoon we shall retrace our steps, only faster, and you shall carry both shield and sword. As the centurion led the men off to the quartermaster, Cullen slapped Getarix on the shoulder, indicating for him to hand over his old shoes. Cullen quickly darted into their barrack bloc, returning just before the centurion glanced back. Seeing nothing out of order, he turned and continued toward the quartermaster's stores.

When the group of thirty-odd recruits arrived, they laughed at the sight of their new arms. One of the recruits, now badly sunburned around his freshly cut blond hair asked, "What are we to fight, old ladies and children?" The crowd laughed at his joke as they looked upon the wicker shields and wooden swords.

Centurion Martialis shot him a look. "What's your name?"

Coming sharply to attention, he answered, "Ansgar, sir."

"Well, you think you can carry four of each?"

Ansgar answered with all the confidence in the world. "Yes sir."

"You're fully confident for a young sapling."

"Yes sir." This time there was a noticeable lack of confidence.

"What was your employment before coming to join our happy band?"

"My father was a stone-layer, sir. I helped."

"A stone-layer, you say. So you think you're strong, eh?"

"Yes sir."

"Strong enough to carry some wicker and four little pieces of wood?"

"Absolutely, sir," Ansgar said without conviction, wondering what Centurion Martialis was up to. It was too late to back down.

"Aquilla, lash four shields together and do the same with the swords." With an evil grin, Aquilla followed the order. Once done, Centurion Martialis addressed Ansgar. "Alright, go get your kit, boy."

Ansgar slowly approached, misjudged their weight and almost fell over trying to lift the shields off the ground. He finally stood there proudly but realizing he had been outwitted and vowed to keep his porridge hole closed from now on.

"That's right, gentlemen, you will notice that they are heavier than they look. We have kindly placed lead into the hollow spaces. Actually they are two times as heavy as the real ones. As for Ansgar, that would be eight times as heavy. But that should not be a problem for him, son of a stonemason, eh Ansgar?"

"No problem sir!" he bellowed, determined not to show weakness.

As they marched out of the fort, Getarix and Cullen noticed their feet beginning to hurt. Even before they reached the gate they felt it. Before long the new sandals were cutting deeply into their flesh, promising to make this route march a most painful one. By the halfway point, both their feet were bleeding from the top and blistered from the bottom. They stopped at a creek where they were told to drink up. Getarix and Cullen had never been so thankful for a rest. They placed their burning hot painful feet into the cold stream, gaining temporary relief. They were thankful for the rest, until they were back on the road again. The rest seemed to have woken their feet to the pain of their multiple cuts and blisters. On the way back the recruits were feeling the day's exertions and began to slow. Aquilla and Cassius ran around them like sheep dogs, keeping them motivated and in perfect rank and file, telling them that if they broke ranks when the enemy was attacking they would certainly be killed. Ansgar, Cullen, and Getarix marched in the same file beside each other. Ansgar noticed their feet now caked with mud, dirt, and blood. He shot them a look of understanding and camaraderie. All three were determined not to show weakness in front of their sheep dogs. They silently and stoically marched on, losing sight of everything else except the next step and the one after. By the end of the march, they were vaguely aware that some had fallen out. When they were halted outside their barracks, it took all their effort not to fall over. Their centurion addressed them, but none of the three could make out a word. All they remembered was he had not even broken a sweat.

They formed up in rank and file on the main road that led through the fort. They stood in front of the narrow ends of their three-barrack blocs. Ten men were assigned to each. Getarix, Cullen, and Ansgar were all assigned to the centre bloc.

Upon dismissal, they went to their assigned bunk space to try to regain their composure. The barrack bloc was comprised of two rooms. The building was twenty feet by forty feet, two thirds of which was the bunkhouse. The other room was a small common room where the soldiers took turns cooking the section's food. As Getarix and Cullen sat on their lower bunks, Ansgar took a studied look at their feet, declaring that something was wrong with their sandals. When he pointed this out to Cassius, the instructor only muttered something about them being weak and soft. "Some simply do not have the right equipment to be part of the Roman army." This would not have been so hard to take if he had not said it with such obvious glee.

Shortly after Cassius left the building, the troops were told that the detail assigned to prepare their supper was now ready and they were to come to the common room to get their evening meal. Getarix could not help himself. "About blasted time." He gave Cullen a friendly punch and said, "Let's get some of that great Roman food you've been talking about."

As they hobbled barefoot into the common room where the other soldiers had already gathered, Ansgar asked Cullen, "What is he talking about?"

Cullen explained their understanding about army food. Getarix then saw the cauldron of barley porridge that passed as the evening meal. He frantically looked around for the other courses. "The meat, the fruit, a vegetable, a piece of stale bread, anything." He looked at Cullen and declared in astonished anger, delivering each word slowly and carefully, "Cullen...what...the...hell did you get me into?"

"How should I have known, you're the expert in all things Roman."

Getarix stopped short, knowing he had no answer to Cullen's logic.

Ansgar interjected. "Well, the good news is that even if you do not like it, you at least can eat all you want...there's no limit." With this comment the other solders laughed and the spell was broken over Getarix. He joined them in their laughter as each man in his section came over to inspect their feet and Cullen's face. They introduced themselves to the two newcomers, welcoming them into their small group. It looked like they had found acceptance and a new home. Getarix even joined them in a meal of porridge. Five bowls to be exact.

X

THEY GET WORSE

Exhaustion took both Getarix and Cullen. Before the sun set they became lost to the world in sweet sleep. A luxury they would not be able to afford later, when they would have armour issued to them. Armour they would be required to keep clean and shiny. One moment they were slipping into oblivion with the animated talk of their newfound friends about them and the next they were awoken by Miles Cassius screaming in their ears.

"Well girls, don't you think it's time to get you sorry hides out of bed!" As he walked out to the next barrack bloc, the waking troops could hear him mutter, "How are we expected to build an empire with such trash?"

Ortwin, a slightly built recruit just waking up, quipped, "Well there's the master sunshine himself, what an arse hole." The whole barrack bloc broke out in laughter. His major misjudgement was he hadn't waited until Cassius was out of earshot.

Miles Cassius pivoted on his heels, bolting back into the building, red-faced with veins popping in his neck. "Who wants to die today? Who said that!? I will kill the son of thunders who said that!" He looked frantically for a victim but could not identify the culprit. Ortwin busied himself getting dressed, trying not to draw any attention. Cassius' eyes settled on Getarix, who was sitting on his bed looking at his feet now red and all crusted over beginning to grow white puss.

Without hesitation, Cassius grabbed Getarix by his short-cropped hair, pulling him to his feet. As Getarix put weight on his injured foot, he winced in pain. Cassius took this as a confession. "So it was you, eh?" He punctuated his remark with a wicked punch to Getarix's stomach. "I will see you outside in two minutes to have a little chat with the centurion. Now get your cloths and sandals on!" Cassius bolted out of their barrack bloc to wake up the rest of the course and then find Centurion Martialis.

As soon as Cassius was out of earshot, Ortwin spoke up. "I'm sorry, Getarix. When the centurion comes I'll let him know—"

"No you will not. They are just looking for an excuse to beat on Cullen and me. I'm afraid it would not change things at all. Kinda like what we just left, eh Cullen?" Cullen smiled.

Getarix bent over, carefully strapping on his sandals that were still as stiff as when they had been issued.

"Cullen, there has got to be something wrong with these sandals." Cullen looked at his feet and then over to the feet of his friend, which looked to be in the same shape.

He bent over to him and whispered, "Getarix, why don't you let Ortwin confess?"

"If you didn't notice yesterday, Ortwin was one of the ones who fell out of the march. I fear that if those two wolves ever targeted Ortwin he would not last two days. And I am convinced that, whatever we do, it will always end the same, with a punch in the stomach, so if Ortwin confesses the only difference would be nothing more than the end of Ortwin. Now help me up, but not by my hair."

As he limped slowly out of the barrack bloc, Getarix could barley move. The muscle stiffness was the least of his concerns. He felt the blood trickle between his toes. The puss made the sandals sticky.

Cassius found the centurion at the base headquarters submitting his plan for the day's training. Marching up to him smartly saluting, he addressed his superior. "Sir, we have a discipline problem in barrack bloc two. It's one of those latecomers."

Martialis listened carefully to the offence according to Miles Cassius.

When Cassius was finished, Martialis returned to the optie he was dealing with. "Are we okay here?"

"Yes sir, the CO will review your training plan this morning and get back to you if he has any concerns."

"Good enough. Miles Cassius, show me this court jester and I'll beat the laughter so far out of him he'll have to take a boat in order to find it again." On their way back to barrack bloc two, Centurion Martialis was warming his wooden mace in his hand, eager to employ it.

Once Getarix found his place outside the building, at attention against the wall. Cullen hobbled back. Unencumbered by ill-fitting sandals, he was able to move a bit faster.

When Cassius and Centurion Martialis arrived, Getarix was standing as straight as he could, which was not very straight at all.

"Stand straight you waste of barley," bellowed Centurion Martialis as he raised his mace, bringing it down hard on Getarix's shoulder. Cassius could not restrain himself. He was grinning ear to ear in obvious glee. Getarix tried as hard as he could to put all his weight on his torn, infected feet. "What in Hades is wrong with you, legionnaire? Are you some kind of gimp?" Martialis inspected his delinquent soldier. When he looked down to see what was so difficult about standing straight, his eyes landed on Getarix's feet.

"What in the hell are those, legionnaire?" Getarix looked down to see what he was looking at.

Cassius jumped on that in a second. "Get your head up when you're addressing the centurion, you bag of dirt."

Martialis gave a look of frustration being interrupted by his overeager subordinate.

Nonetheless, this snapped Getarix back to attention and he answered. "My feet, sir."

When Cassius stood back, Martialis continued. "What did you do to them?"

"These sandals, sir…there seems to be something wrong with—"

Again Cassius interjected, moving right up to his face. "How dare you question Roman equipment?" Again he punctuated his reprimand with a punch in the stomach.

"That will be all, Miles Cassius." Martialis found it difficult to hide his frustration. "I can carry on here. Get the rest of the troops ready, will you? I want them formed up on the parade square in one hour for drill."

"Yes, sir," Cassius said with some reluctance. He realized he had become a bit overzealous.

Once Cassius had moved off, Martialis addressed Getarix in a much softer tone. "Take those things off and let me see." Getarix did not hesitate. Still smarting from the blow to the shoulder and the midsection punch, he managed to pull both sandals off but not without tearing open his cut feet again. Once in his hands, the centurion began to bend the sandals in various ways.

"There were two of you who came late. Is that not true?"

"Yes, sir. Legionnaire Cullen also was issued a pair at the same time."

"And how have his feet fared?"

"About the same, sir."

"You don't say? Well, there is definitely something wrong with these. Now, you seem to be a quiet type. It has not escaped my notice."

"Sir?"

"Do not lie to me. You did not make that comment Miles Cassius took offence to earlier today, did you?"

Getarix hesitated. "No, no sir."

"Protecting someone, are you?"

Getarix did not answer, already ashamed he had betrayed his trust thus far.

"Well, I'll inquirer no more. You have been struck twice since you have stood here. Two blows for something you did not do. I consider that matter closed." He looked down at the sandals in his hands. "But I consider this matter still open. Go inside and get me the other legionnaire's sandals, and the two of you report to the surgeon so he can have a good look at those feet of yours. Your feet, next to your sword, are your life."

Armed with the uncompromising sandals, Martialis sought the quartermaster for a stormy exchange.

Getarix and Cullen slowly worked their way up the main road to the gate which opened to the village. The hospital sat just inside the gate next to the stables. Just as they were about to enter the building, Miles Cassius caught sight of them. Unaware that the centurion had ordered them to the doctor, he exploded. The cascade of profanity that flowed down the road could be heard throughout the camp.

"Cullen, hurry up, get in the building."

"He will kill us—"

"He's going to do that anyway. Besides, we can claim we were unaware he was talking to us."

They proceeded into the building, leaving behind Cassius in a state of uncontrolled rage.

"Well, look at the two of you."

When they looked up they saw the camp's medical assistant, Duplicarius Gullis. He was no longer in his armour, nor any of his fineries. Today he was in his work clothes, which amounted to the auxiliary soldier's green tunic covered in the front with a dirty white apron. "I see you made the right choice and joined the army."

"We'll get back to you on that one," Getarix said.

Gullis gave them a funny look. He could not escape noticing that their feet were in a bad way. "I never took the two of you to be so tender of foot."

"We're not, or weren't so tender of foot. Those great Roman sandals we were given were made of rawhide and cut the life out of our fe—"

Getarix could not finish because a raging storm entered the building in the form of Cassius. "I…will…personally…take pleasure…in flogging you two until I die of exhaustion."

Getarix and Cullen saw their life flash before their eyes.

"Now the two of—" Cassius began when Gullis put up his hand, stopping him cold.

"Hold up there, Miles Cassius," Gullis said, emphasizing his rank. "I'll remind you that you are in my hospital and these two are my patients."

"Yes, Duplicarius." Cassius struggled to gain control. "They are in my course and they came here without authority and it is my job to maintain discipline. And I will personally flog the both of them for this offence!"

Gullis addressed the two junior soldiers. "Well…you two, is this true?"

"No, Duplicarius. Centurion Martialis himself told us to come here," Getarix answered.

Gullis addressed Cullen. "Is this true?"

"I was not there."

"He was in the barracks when Centurion Martialis instructed me to get him and get down here."

"Okay, this is what we are going to do. Miles Cassius, you are to go to the centurion and confirm with him if they are telling the truth."

"Yes, Duplicarius."

"And Miles Cassius, I too will talk to the centurion about his orders. If you are right, you certainly may flog them. Until then they are in my care. Is that understood?"

Cassius tightened up, retraining his anger. "Yes, Duplicarius." With that he turned and left without being dismissed.

Gullis gave the two sorry specimens of soldiers a long, thoughtful look. "How is it that every time I see you two I end up doing an investigation?" He chuckled to himself, noticing the obvious stress the two of them were under. He assured them that if they told the truth there would be nothing to worry about. As he inspected and cleaned their feet, he heard from them their story of woe since they had joined the army one day ago. Halfway through their discourse, Gullis put up his hand as if a thought had just hit him. Cullen, who had been talking just then, went silent, waiting for Gullis to continue. "Who did you say your Centurion is?"

"It is Centurion Martialis. Why?"

"He's infantry. So is Cassius. Is Miles Aquilla one of your instructors?"

"Yes," Getarix answered. "He is the other half of that evil act."

"You two have managed to get on the wrong side of Cassius and Aquilla?"

They nodded affirmative.

"And in less than a day, well done you. Now, why are you in the infantry?"

"Why shouldn't we be?"

"Your…where are your horses?"

"At the stables."

"You mean the ones here in the fort? Why would they put you in the infantry if you have horses?"

"No one knows we have horses," Cullen said.

"How did you get them into our stables?"

"Army stables?" Getarix asked. "No, we put them in the stables in the village."

"Not the ones at the edge of the village? How much did he want to keep them there?"

"He said we could settle it after our training. He assured we would make enough to pay," Getarix said, beginning to worry.

"The thief has probably already sold them both, to 'cover costs' he will claim."

Cullen gave Getarix a sidelong glance. "Well I guess we lost them after all."

"You have lost more than just that. Those horses are your way out from under Cassius and Aquilla. Besides, why carry your kit when your kit can carry you?"

"What do you mean?" Getarix asked.

"There is more to the army than just the infantry. The cavalry fight from horseback. And the majority of Roman cavalry are Celts. How is your riding?"

"I was born on the back of a horse," Getarix said, and gestured to Cullen. "And he is better than I."

"Do you two know what bad luck is? Well, you should get to know her because it appears you're married to her." Gullis looked into the next room that served as the hospital ward. Seeing two empty beds, he immediately admitted his new patients. He figured that since Cassius had not returned for his prey that they had told the truth and for the time being they were safe.

As he replaced his doctor's apron with soldier's armour, he ordered the two of them into bed.

About an hour later, Centurion Martialis walked into the ward followed by Miles Cassius. Cullen and Getarix stiffened up, waiting for it. Centurion Martialis handed them both new sandals and addressed them in a formal tone. "Where has Duplicarius Gullis gone?"

"He didn't say, sir."

"Well that's quite a way to run a unit. When did he say he was coming back?"

"Didn't say, sir."

"Did you or did you not inform Miles Cassius that I sent the two of you to the physician?"

"We did not, sir," Getarix said.

"Did it not occur to you to do such?"

"No, sir."

"Well, when you get out of here we will deal with it then. Is that understood?"

"Yes sir." They could see Cassius almost exploding with glee behind the centurion. When they were alone, Cullen said, "When will this end?"

It was Getarix this time with the words of encouragement. "You have survived worse."

XI

THE SENATOR'S FIRST DEFEAT

"Cornelius, where are you! Antonio, do you know where the centurion is?"
"No, sir." Strictly speaking, that was the truth. Antonio did not know where he was, even though he knew where had gone.

The senator picked up a small switch Antonio was using to secure the plants in the garden and whipped him across the face. "Don't trifle with me, boy." The senator looked straight into Antonio's eyes. Antonio knew that the truth would be known and saw little reason to keep from the senator what happened earlier.

Though the pain, he said, "Well, sir, a messenger from the palace...came first thing and summoned the centurion."

"Summoned him? What do you mean, 'summoned him?'"

"All I heard was he was too see the emperor today." Antonio prayed he had not given too much information. Centurion Cornelius had asked him to tell the senator as little as possible.

The senator pointed to a female slave. "You, whatever your name is, get my toga ready." He looked to Antonio. "And you get me my horse. When I get back, the whip for you, slave." As he walked away toward his changing room, he muttered to himself, "Who knows what lies he is telling the emperor."

Antonio thought, in this house, lies are truth and the truth is a lie.

The day before, the senator had petitioned the emperor to have Centurion Cornelius cast from the army, thus blackening his name and closing all political doors forever. The senator saw it as his right of rank to destroy anyone, even to gain a minor benefit for himself or to hide his own failure. The bungled diplomatic trip was no minor failure and it was his intent to have the centurion take the fall. He was expendable, after all.

Augustus was not unaware of his senator's own weaknesses, and had Centurion Cornelius sent for after the senator gave his full report.

Cornelius was summoned to the emperor's villa outside Rome, where he now spent most of his days, letting Tiberius, his stepson, run the day-to-day business of government. As Cornelius entered the beautiful, spacious receiving room, he saw the emperor bending over some papers on his ornate, oversized marble desk. The room was three stories tall, flanked with streaked red marble pillars. The red pillars contrasted with the white marble of the walls. The floor boasted every colour the empire's marble could supply. The design was simple squares of highly polished stone. Centurion Cornelius came sharply to attention, hitting his chest with his right hand and bringing it out straight in salute. "Hail Caesar, I am Centurion Cornelius Faustus Aeolos Pricus. You sent for me, sir."

"Centurion Cornelius, come closer, my eyes are losing their loyalty." Augustus waited in silence until Cornelius was only a few feet away. He saluted again before Augustus began. "So, you worked these last two years for the noble Senator Damianus, did you not?"

"Yes, sir."

After a protracted moment of silence, the emperor continued. "I can only imagine that working for the senator could be a tiring experience."

Cornelius felt no need to protect the senator anymore. "He does present a challenge at times, sire."

"Mmm, mildly put. I have ruined many a good career on his recommendations. I know of one of your predecessors who took his own life because of it. Am I safe to assume you are innocent of the charges brought to me by Senator Damianus? As were the others, probably. The guilt lies with your accuser...am I not right?"

Cornelius' eyes betrayed him, asking, *If you know, why not...?* He simply said, "Yes, sir."

"Even the emperor of mighty Rome is not all-powerful. I still need the support of the citizens, especially the nobility. When I became Emperor, I thought I would have the power to do good. Some days the best I can manage is to do the least amount of damage." After a moment of reflection, Augustus continued. "The senator would have you driven out of the army and disgraced politically. I am not prepared to do that. I am sending you to Judea, as far away from the senator as I can. I need good officers there. As it turns out, we now seem to be a few centurions short. It will look simply like a next assignment. Do well and you will return to Rome fully recovered. The senator does not look too healthy. Maybe when you return your problem will be gone. I do not understand one thing. Why one of his slaves does not end his master's life? His treatment of them is legendary."

"He has ways of ensuring loyalty, if not affection, sir."

"Mmm…well, he is no longer your problem. As of now you are on your new assignment. I was signing it when you arrived. Here is your copy. The other will be delivered to the senator this afternoon. Your ship sails today. It's all in there. That is all."

Cornelius took his cue that the interview was over. He hesitated a bit as his mind was processing this unbelievable news. Gathering himself up, he came sharply to attention and saluted, declaring, "Hail Caesar." With that he turned around, heading for the large oak double doors framed in streaked red marble. The guard opened the door. Cornelius took one step out, stopped, turned and asked, "Sir, why?"

"Why bother to call you up here and explain? Chalk it up to the sentimentalities of an old man. I simply felt a need to explain myself. Odd what age can do to a man."

It was only then that Cornelius saw just how old and tired the emperor looked. "Thank you, sir." He slipped out of the emperor's villa a new man with a new start. "Cornelius, it looks like you did survive after all." He laughed bent down and impetuously hugged his horse by the neck. Giving him the spurs, he began to formulate a plan to get his belonging and be at the dockside by evening sailing.

As he rode down the narrow road from the emperor's summer Villa, he saw what could be none other than the senator mounted on some poor, long-suffering beast. He looked more like an enormous toga-clad egg precariously perched, ready to fall at the slightest breeze. As Cornelius got closer he could see that the poor horse was spent. He must have ridden him hard until it was ready to fall. Cornelius also realized that the senator was in a hurry, because he did not have his usual gaggle of slaves to do his bidding.

"Centurion, what is the meaning of this?"

"I do not know what you mean, sir." Cornelius was determined to keep his composure while staying in the realms of respect.

Damianus turned red, looking like his head was about to explode. "How dare you...how dare you speak to me like that? Now get off your mount and give him to me for the completion of my journey. The emperor and I have to discuss the details of your career and the incompetence you showed of late. He is less than impressed by you."

Holding up the copy of the emperor's orders, Cornelius smiled. "The emperor and I have already discussed it."

"What gives you the right to discuss your career or anything with the emperor?"

"What gives you the right? It is my career and my life." No subordinate had ever spoken to the senator in such a way before. His anger was such that he had trouble breathing. Before he could catch his breath, Cornelius dismissed himself.

"Now if you excuse me, sir, I have business to attend to. Good day and goodbye." Spurring his ride down the hill, he rode for all his worth, leaving a very confused and angry senator behind.

He figured he had enough time to get to the senator's grand house to retrieve his possessions and say his goodbyes on Palatine hill. Then on to Ostia, the seaport at the mouth of the Tigris used by Rome as its main port. If his calculations were correct, he should make port just before sailing. It was only then that it clicked why the emperor had waited to send the orders to the senator's house until the afternoon. This made it impossible for Cornelius' disgruntled boss to reach the coast in time to disrupt the smooth sailing of Centurion Cornelius. From the looks of things, unless the emperor would lend Senator Damianus one of his horses, highly unlikely, the noble senator would have to walk to the coast—even more unlikely. Centurion Cornelius had made his escape.

XII

STEP IN THE MEDIC

The door opened and Gullis arrived with a smile on his face. He pointed to the pair of them. "You owe me, boys, you owe me big." He was almost bouncing. "Almost a year's pay, but I got your horses back. How're your feet?" They looked puzzled, but before they could answer, he thundered on. "Can you ride on them?"

"I guess," Getarix said.

"I know I can." Cullen began to get out of bed. "Come on, Getarix, let's join the cavalry."

"Not so fast," Gullis cut in. "We now need to convince the fort commander. He could still say no. Chances are he will. Now stay here while I take this to the physician."

As Gullis stroked Epona, admiring the fine horse, he argued with his boss.

"Are you sure they can ride these beasts? Have you witnessed it yourself, Duplicarius?" Antonius, the fort physician, asked Gullis.

"I am confident they can handle them well."

"So you're not sure, eh?"

"No, sir."

"Then I am not convinced that I should waste my time on this. I see no benefit to me besides—"

Not willing to call defeat after paying so much to get the horses back, Gullis interrupted his superior. "Doctor, think of it, look at these beautiful animals. It makes sense to me. To own such fine mounts, they must have a measure of knowledge about horses."

Antonius turned to Caballo and Epona. "Are you sure they did not simply liberate them from somewhere?"

"That I can assure you. I know they own both animals."

"How can you be sure, Duplicarius?"

Gullis proceeded to recount his investigation of the previous day, not leaving out the testimony of the captain of the Black Rose, particularly the captain's testimony of their arrival on board.

The physician looked at Gullis for a moment and finally said, "Keep those two in bed until I return." He headed for the door but turned back and added, "And keep those jackals off their backs, will you?" The Doctor never had liked the way Cassius and Aquilla treated some of the soldiers, particularly if they took a disliking to them. "I have to take lunch with the commanding officer, so I'll present it to him there."

The office of the commanding officer was large enough for a small meeting. When there were more than four officers in the room, it felt crowded. Centurion Domitus, the base commander, sat behind his desk that resembled a very large table with sweeping legs ending in lion paws. On either end of the desk stood the two centurions whose courses would be affected by the changes proposed by the physician. On his right was Centurion Martialis, who was presently the course officer for Getarix and Cullen. On the left was Centurion Sergius Vincens Faustus, the cavalry course officer. Gullis stood next to the physician, smartly at attention in front of the desk.

"Well Faustus, what do you think?" the fort commander asked his cavalry officer.

"Sir, we do not have enough instructors as it is. If these two don't know how to ride and ride good, I can't take them on. Not to mention they will now be two weeks behind in training."

"Did you see the horses?" the base commander asked.

"Yes sir, they are fine horses for sure, but they are of no use to us if those two cannot ride them. The best I could recommend is for the fort to buy them for the use in the army."

Gullis felt a sense of relief at the thought that at least he would get some of his money back.

"Centurion Martialis, what are your thoughts. How are they doing?"

"Well sir, um, not so well."

"In that case I don't want them. Let the infantry keep their problems, I have enough of my own," Faustus said, feeling that the issue was finished.

Antonius the doctor interjected. "The problem may not lay with the recruits."

"That's being sorted out," Martialis said, a little irritated that problems with his staff were mentioned in front of the base commander.

The base commander said, "It better be." As base commander of such a small fort, Centurion Domitus was well aware of what went on and who was responsible. He continued. "Well, it appears to me that all that's left to do is see them ride, eh? Faustus, prepare a route to test their skills. Where are they now?"

"They are admitted into the hospital at the present time, sir," the Doctor said.

"Why are they there?" asked the commander.

"You have got to be kidding me. If they are broken, forget it," Faustus said.

"There was a problem with their footwear, and that has been sorted out with the QM, sir," Martialis said.

Looking at Martialis, Centurion Domitus said, "There seems to be some problems with your course, centurion." Looking to the doctor, he continued. "Doctor, can they ride today?" The doctor gave a blank stare as it hit him that he had never set eyes on either of them. He was going only on the words of Duplicarius Gullis.

Gullis spoke for the first time. "Sir, they are both capable of riding."

The Fort Commander never took his eyes off the Doctor. "Well, Doctor?"

"Yes sir, I assure you they can," the Physician said.

"Good. Faustus, prepare a test route, somewhere where we can observe." Faustus gave a nod of consent even though he thought it was a waste of time. "Doctor, I want them to be mounted and at the North gate in one hour."

"Yes sir, they will be there."

As the room was emptying out, Domitus addressed his infantry officer. "Centurion Martialis, please stay behind." Once the room emptied, the base commander and Martialis had a frank conversation about the treatment of his soldiers. "Let me make one thing clear, Martialis. I will not put up with unjustified abuse of the recruits. I fired Centurion Lucilius for the same thing. Am I right in guessing that Cassius and Aquilla are behind this?"

"Yes, sir."

"It only makes sense. Lucilius trained them."

"Is that 'fetch another' Lucilius, sir?"

"Yes, do you know why they call him that?"

"He would break his vine stick on the back of a soldier and yell 'fetch another' and then continue with the beating."

"He is a cruel man who gets perverse pleasure from inflicting pain on anyone within his power. I still have three soldiers whose brains he beat out with that damn stick of his. One can't even remember his name and it has been three months. That's why I sent Lucilius to the Rhine and out of our legion. We can never forget these are soldiers not slaves. This will catch up to him one day in battle when he will meet his end, likely from a Roman blade. Soldiers have ways of sorting these things out. Now those two will be reined in, do you understand?"

"Yes, sir. However, the recruits we are getting these days—"

"I don't care about that. We have to fill the ranks after the loss at Teutoburg. It does not help if we kill them in the process, understood?"

"Yes s—"

"Good then that's all." Martialis knew that the subject was closed. He left irritated with his two junior instructors and vowed to make their life uncomfortable.

Outside he saw Antonius the doctor talking to Gullis irritably. "You had better be right. I am on one hell of a limb out here. You're so close to receiving your authority to be a physician, I would hate to see you lose it over those two."

"I feel there is more to them, and besides, they have had so much going against them, maybe something should go for them on occasion."

"Don't sacrifice yourself for it, though."

"Yes, sir."

The route selected by Faustus was designed to fail those being tested. Faustus was convinced that the problem would not be his in the morning.

XIII

THE RACE

Sweat poured from under their tunics. The early summer sun was intense. Their bodies were still acclimatized to the cold mist of home. It did not help that they were issued chain mail armour to wear during the race. This added significantly to their weight and discomfort. By the time all had arrived at the north gate of the fort, the sun was at its height. Without a cloud to be seen, the full intensity of the heat could not be avoided. Despite the sweat and extra weight, Getarix enjoyed feeling the early summer sun on his face. Mounted upon Caballo, he felt on top of the world. He gazed down the road, noticing his own infantry course on their afternoon march. He gestured to Cullen next to him on Epona, pointing. About two miles down the road they could see the dust kicked up by their newfound friends. Ansgar was in the lead and still had two shields to bear. They gave each other a look of understanding. They must not fail the test, no matter the cost.

Centurion Faustus arrived looking a bit sweaty and irritated because of this interruption in his course schedule. An interruption he could ill afford.

"Okay you two, I have a route set out. I have markers placed showing the way. They are white banner like this one." He held up a torn piece of white cloth, a bit wider than what a doctor would use to bandage a wound. "At each turn I have stationed cavalry recruits like these ones here." He gestured to the three soldiers who had escorted them to the north gate. "They will report if you dismount or if you repeat any of the course. Understood? The chain mail is some added reality for the ride." He waited for any reaction. None were given. He continued.

"Now, we will follow this road north until the first crossroads, where we will turn right at full speed onto the first road. Follow it inland for about a mile. At that marker, make another right across the field. Be aware there are many boulders in the fields. We will continue south through the trees. Take note there are no trails through those trees. We will come to a little embankment. Go down the embankment across the river up the opposite embankment and carry on. The next marker is where you enter the east-west road leading into town from inland. Go west, which is to the right heading into town. At the town square, take yet another right onto the coastal road, the one you used to get here your first day. We are now heading north. Or should I say, I will be heading north. If you have somehow made it thus far, do not use the bridge. You will ford the river to the right of the bridge. Just after the bridge take a sharp left. Cross the road and go down the embankment to the ocean. Take another right at the water. On the beach you will ride in about two feet of water. Just before the fort we will turn inland and finish on that high feature there." He pointed to a hill south and east of the fort where Getarix and Cullen could see a small group of observers. "You will notice that our route circles around them. They will have eyes on us most of the time. Cheating will not be possible, and you will be racing me! Try to keep up, and you better hope this is not a waste of my time, otherwise your life will be a waste of time. Now let's get going."

With no further ado, he kicked his horse and darted north on the road at full gallop. Without regard for the other soldiers at the gate, Getarix and Cullen kicked their mounts so suddenly that the soldiers had to jump out of the way to avoid being trampled. In spite of their quick departure, Faustus had gained a significant lead. Getarix could not help but marvel over this Roman's ability to ride. Romans had a reputation of being great builders and rulers, but they were not known for their prowess on a horse.

With the infantry, Ansgar was too busy keeping pace, still carrying the great weight of his wicker shields. He did not hear the sound of hooves clacking along the stones of the Roman road behind his course. Suddenly the formation disintegrated because of the intrusion of a centurion flying down the centre of the road at full speed. It almost caused his heart to stop as he darted to the side just as the rider flew past. Ansgar did not know what had happened until

Miles Aquilla blurted out some profanity about officers being irresponsible and self-absorbed. Before he could finish his speech, two more riders came roaring by in pursuit. Instantly they were recognized and a loud cheer was raised by the course. Aquilla and Cassius lost their minds trying in vain to have their voices silenced.

Getarix, now second in order of march, noticed the first white banner at the intersection. A mounted soldier held it. Next to him was a small group of dismounted troops with what looked like three or four amphora. As soon as Faustus made the corner, the soldiers advanced into the intersection and poured the contents onto the stones. The light of the sun shone off it, alerting both Getarix and Cullen. As they approached the intersection they noticed what looked like oil on the stones. Knowing that there would be no way to keep the horses on their feet even at a slow canter, Getarix made the flash decision to take the corner to the right of the intersection on dry ground. Cullen, back only by a head, followed suit. As they continued east along the new road, they could hear the soldier yelling at them saying that they had cheated by riding off the road. Getarix glanced back to see if Cullen had followed him and made the corner. He noticed beyond Cullen their old infantry course was on all fours pumping out push-ups at a fast rate, Aquilla and Cassius standing amongst them. When he turned around again he noted that Faustus was half a mile ahead. They pulled their knees high and felt the rhythm of the horses, trying in vain to catch Faustus. As he turned right off of the road, they noticed that the gap had actually become larger. Once in the field, Faustus slowed considerably as he manoeuvred his ride around the boulders. Cullen looked up and noticed that just after their turnoff there was somewhat of a trail. He kicked his horse and passed Getarix, blowing right by the flag about twenty feet. Getarix, not sure what he was up to but trusting his ability to ride, followed. As they turned right into the field, they could hear the soldiers yelling profanities at them. Winding their way along the path, they were gaining on Faustus. The path angled slightly back to the original route and they were heading straight for Faustus. Just as Faustus was about to enter the little trail, all three arrived at the same point. Cullen quickly assessed the situation, realizing they were about have a three-horse collision. One small trail and three large horses would not fit. Coming in from the left of Faustus, who was completely blocking the path, Cullen determined that the only way through was overtop a four-foot boulder sitting to the left of the path. With conviction, Cullen pointed Epona toward the boulder, kicking him in his sides. Epona leaped over the boulder with ease, having done this many times over his years with

Getarix. Caballo on the other hand could not quite clear the boulder, having had no opportunity to see it until Epona had cleared the obstacle. As Getarix and Caballo leaped over the granite monster, Caballo's legs drug on the rough rock, scraping the skin open. Caballo gave out a great cry and landed awkwardly, almost dumping Getarix. Before he hit the ground, in a reflex he reached out and grabbed Caballo by his mane. He almost restored his place on Cabello, but the weight of the chain mail threw him off balance. With great effort he righted himself, pulling a handful of Caballo's mane out in the process. Faustus, unaware of their presence until Cullen was halfway over the boulder, instinctively pulled back, slowing his horse almost to a stop. Just as he was about to kick his mount back into action, Getarix went scraping over the same boulder.

"Blast you two, how did you...?"

But before Faustus could push his mount forward, the both of them were bolting down the trail toward the trees. Infuriated, Faustus spurred his ride on recklessly into the trees. He entered to their left almost head to head with Cullen, who slowed to manoeuvre Epona safely through the virgin forest. Faustus pulled his knees high and increased his speed. He put his head behind his horse's for protection. It successfully protected him but at the expense of a clear line of vision. The trick appeared to be working. As he was about to clear the woods, he was ahead by many lengths. Then he heard a loud cracking of branches in the low ground behind him. He almost laughed, knowing his competitors were meeting failure. The race had become personal.

Cullen felt the broken dead pine branches cut into his legs as he broke trail. Getarix fared only a little better. The chain mail served its purpose as branches scraped harmlessly off their upper bodies. Cullen struggled to keep his head down, rising only to catch sight of the best path. The ground dropped steeply into a little ravine. Cullen exposed his head. As Epona dropped down the ravine, Cullen lifted right off the saddle. His eyes caught sight of a four-inch branch heading square into his chest. What scared Cullen the most was having the branch embed deep into his chest, ending his day in a foreign forest. With a tremendous thud, Cullen landed hard on the branch and remained suspended long enough for Epona to clear and run for all his might. The branch gave up the fight and broke in a loud explosion. Epona continued through the ravine. Getarix had to pull hard on Caballo to avoid trampling Cullen, now sprawled out on his back holding his chest, desperately seeking his next breath. Getarix noticed Epona racing away. He gave a loud whistle, the same whistle he used to call Epona in the days of old. Epona stopped and returned to his old owner.

On hearing the loud cracking, Faustus saw his way clear to victory. Then he heard the sharp whistle. He turned to look but in doing so he raised his head and a branch about the size that took Cullen out crowned him, landing him solidly on his back. His mount darted out of the trees, heading for the stables at the fort.

On the hill, the Fort commander mentioned to the doctor that it was a valiant try but his Celts had failed the test.

Back in the woods, Getarix jumped down beside his friend, who managed to regain his wind. He helped him up and before long they had cleared the woods and were in the river. The cool water was a welcome refresher for both horse and rider. The remainder of the race was anticlimactic, as both Cullen and Getarix knew they had won the day. Upon their arrival at the finish line, Faustus was still peacefully asleep under the trees.

Before Faustus was even found, the fort commander was declaring Getarix and Cullen's success when he was interrupted by Faustus' marker-bearers. "Sir, these two riders cheated. I was witness to the offence."

"Speak on, soldier."

"Sir, they cut the first corner. They were instructed to make the turn on the road but they chose to cut the corner and—"

Centurion Domitus held his hand up to silence the junior soldier. "Tell me the truth. What did you pour on the intersection, eh? Did it not occur that we could see it from this vantage point?"

"Um…well…sir."

"The liquid you poured on, only after Centurion Faustus passed through—I am sure the infantry course would be interested as well because we watched as they, almost to the last man, fell crossing that cursed point."

"Sir, it was oil, sir. We were under orders, sir—"

"I don't blame you, son."

The other mounted soldier piped in. "Sir, they also missed the second turn."

"I saw that, soldier. Not only was it a longer route they took, but also the smarter route. I would rather have soldiers who can think in the saddle. Besides, if you have not noticed, your own centurion did not even finish the course. A course he designed himself. Now the matter is closed. That was some of the best riding I have ever seen. Go and collect your centurion. You will find him in that wood there." He turned his attention to Getarix and Cullen. "You two report to your new barracks. Welcome to the cavalry."

XIV

THE END OF AN AGE

Rome was not only the centre of the world. It was the axis on which the world rotated. The empire had grown to such an extent it turned an international sea into an inland lake. The Romans called the Mediterranean Sea Mare Nostrum, Our Sea. Emissaries from all over the known world found their way to Rome, seeking an audience with the emperor. On occasion there were delegations from the unknown world as far away as Sri Lanka. Roman goods even found their way to China. The city of Rome had the size to match. Over one million souls occupied her seven hills, and more than fifty-five million her empire. There were more people than employment. The emperor was forced to feed almost 300,000 of Rome's poorest or risk riots. In spite of the unemployment and crowded conditions, crime was no great problem. The army made sure of that.

Rome was a living city that never slept. No transport carts were allowed in the city streets during the daylight hours. The daily needs of the market were so great that trade carts would clog her streets, leaving no room for citizen or soldier alike. The emperor declared that the carts were only allowed in the city during the night hours. As the sun set in the west, Rome began to groan and rumble loudly as thousands of wooden wheels bounced over the paving stones of city streets. These nightly earthquakes acted like a mother's lullabies putting many of her citizens to sleep, sure in the knowledge that morning would find their markets full of goods. This was true as long as the drivers kept their cursing to a minimum. Yet for a few citizens, the infernal noise robbed all hope of sleep this side of the grave.

In spite of the early hour, the late summer sun felt uncomfortably hot to Antonio. It looked like another sultry day. Antonio was on his weekly run to the wine market. It was a short distance from the estate of Senator Damianus next to the Thermal Trainee bathhouse on Esquiline Hill. He walked down the steep winding road of Clivus Pullius, descending Esquiline Hill. A part of Antonio hated going into Subura, the forgotten part of Rome, in the Vertus Creek Valley. However, it was one of the few times he felt a sense of freedom being out of the sight of his cruel master. The part of Subura Antonio was heading for had two chief commodities. Prostitution and wine. Antonio was after the latter. The poor community of Subura was wedged between the southern end of the Viminal hill and the western end of Esquiline. From anywhere in the valley, the lifestyle of the rich and famous could easily be seen, a continual reminder of their servitude and humiliating poverty.

The hour was early, too early for the prostitutes to be stirring. Most of them slept until the noon heat drove them from their beds. Antonio noted a few drunks still sleeping in the streets. *They will soon be cleaned up by the morning patrol of the local detachment of soldiers assigned to Subura.*

As chief household slave, he could easily have sent a lower-ranking slave to do the wine shopping for the estate. He would never take the chance again after Marcus (the young Jewish slave) brought inferior wine to be served at Senator Damianus' table. It took Antonio two weeks before he could bend over again, the whipping had been so great. What was worse was the senator had held the whip himself. He whipped Antonio in the garden as the 'after-dinner entertainment' for his guests. Antonio not only had to endure the whipping, but he was subjected to the catcalls and cheering of some of Rome's finest citizens. After that Antonio never trusted the welfare of his back to anyone.

Marcus had felt so bad as he nursed him back to health. He could not hold the young man responsible for simply trying to save the senator a few *sestorii*.

Antonio's first stop would be Julius at his tavern. It was a typical drinking hole found in Rome. The front of his shop was completely open. A thick oaken counter went almost the length of the opening. The counter took a sharp left turn into the tavern, following the wall halfway into the place. Both sections of the counter could accommodate ten patrons, each provided with a stool. The counter had large holes cut in it throughout its length, large enough that an outstretched hand could not cover them. They were there to house the pointy ends of the large amphora. These large terra cotta jugs, used to store and transport wine, littered the Tavern. A few were set in the holes on the counter, their bottoms sticking below the thick oak counter top. The walls were a dirty white with crudely painted four-foot panels framed in red. They sported images of Bacchus, the god of wine and wine makers, dancing and drinking. Above each image of Bacchus were poorly painted swags of grape vines, each with two or three bunches of grapes hanging from them. Antonio often teased the owner Julius that his painter was inspired by too much wine himself when he had painted them. When Antonio arrived at the tavern, he noticed that Julius was tired and had only just stowed away his new stock. Julius held a special stock of the finest wine in Rome. Rumours abounded how he got his hands on it, but no hint would he ever give.

"Julius, you look tired."

"Antonio, my friend, I am. My shipments came in two separate carts and they were separated just before they entered the city. The first arrived at midnight, the other just left. I have had absolutely no sleep last night. The cost of business, I guess."

Antonio chuckled in sympathy.

Julius looked at him, realizing Antonio would give anything to switch places with him. "Well I guess I have it good, eh? At least I do not work for your—" he dared not finish what was running through his mind.

Antonio said nothing, just smiled. Years ago he had learnt not to trust anyone, because word had a habit of finding its way back to the senator.

"I take it you have come for your master's fine wine," Julius said sarcastically. "I've just stowed it in the cellar. That way it keeps better out of this damnable heat." He gave Antonio a wink. "It also keeps the questions to a minimum."

As Julius descended to the cellar, Antonio sat at the inside counter so he could see down the street. By the time Julius returned, manhandling a midsize amphora, the market had miraculously come alive. Most of the stalls were now open, many serving the morning meals to their patrons. Only the wealthy could afford houses grand enough to eat in, houses with space enough to accommodate a kitchen. Nearly everyone in Rome, including all her poor, lived in small apartments known as insulas. They were mostly wood structures, some as high as six stories tall, where few had room for kitchens. Fire was also a concern. To cook one needed fire, and wooden insulas were prone to burn. It would not have been so bad if only one insula burned to the ground. The problem was they butted up to each other, so the entire city was at risk. Most Romans ate at street stalls, taverns, and restaurants. The wealthy also ate at the bathhouses. Antonio noticed that the crowd in the street had grown a great deal. He did not look forward to carting two amphora of wine through the throng. Not to mention the danger of being mugged. The only thing keeping him safe was the hour. Few thugs would be up and about so early. Antonio kept his eyes on the stairs leading down, wishing Julius would hurry up.

When he finally returned, Julius looked out over the crowd and just stared. "Antonio, look." He pointed to the end of the street. "Something is going on." They both stood on stools to look over the heads of those just outside the tavern. It looked like a wave cresting over the crowd, an invisible wave that affected everyone it touched. They could hear crying at the far end. As people heard the news, they turned and passed it to the person next in line. Before long a man in his fifties (obviously a slave) yelled above the din. "The emperor has died! Augustus is no more!"

At this news, Antonio just sat down in shock. Soon some of Julius' regulars arrived and were discussing the news. A tall balding man declared, "I think it's the perfect time to restore the old ways where we were governed by two elected pro-councils and only the elected pro-councils."

"What, and go back to civil war?" a short, fat, young man retorted. "Augustus should be declared a god. I would worship him."

"What are you talking about?"

The younger fellow answered back. "Look here, like he himself said, 'I found Rome a city of brick and left it a city of marble.'"

"Marble, where?" The taller man held his hands out and looked around in an exaggerated gesture. "He must have forgotten Subura. Our main streets are not paved with stone, not even gravel. They are paved by last night's barf; the Subura, where Julius Caesar was born and raised. His palaces are marble, maybe. Marble for the rich, mud for the poor."

"He feeds the poor. Where is your loyalty? Again I say I would worship him if ever he was made a god."

"Worship him? Look at the way he treated his own daughter. His only real child, Julia didn't do anything wrong—"

"Julius, have you been feeding him wine at this hour?" The shorter one addressed his taller debater. "All he was trying to do was pound some morals into her. She—"

"There is nothing wrong with her morals—"

"Have you lost your mind, my old friend? The emperor declared adultery a crime while she indulged in revels and drinking parties by night in the Forum and even upon the Rostra. The Rostra, the very spot where her father declared adultery a crime. She got what she deserved. Don't forget, Augustus' family is expected to be paragons of Roman virtue."

"Julius, what do you think?" the tall one asked. "Don't forget that her father, this worshipable emperor, divorced her mother the day she was born."

Julius, who thus far had kept out of the debate, simply said, "She is a good-hearted and kind woman, who never intended to hurt anyone."

"Ach, what do you know?" the short young man declared. He then addressed Antonio. "What do you think of the emperor? What is your opinion?"

"I am sorry, but I have no opinion. Besides, Tiberius is now the new Emperor, not Augustus nor Julia."

"Tiberius, now there's a force of joy. I bet you he hasn't smiled in the last ten years. And he is not known for forgiving. If I were Julia I would be watching out."

"She will only get what's coming after dishonouring her marriage to Tiberius. Besides, Germanicus should be next, he is the be—"

"Luscious, that will be all. None of that talk in my place, even if you do not...please." Julius pointed to the street in a gesture to leave. He feared the soldiers, who kept a keen ear for words of rebellion.

As they were talking, Antonio noticed that the army was moving into the market in force. A precaution to prevent any attempt at rebellion.

Antonio clumsily picked up his two amphora and headed for the steep winding road to his master's grand house, happy to be leaving the debate behind.

XV
WARNING ORDER

"Close the gate, Marcellus. Marcellus, did you hear me? Close the gate!" Centurion Martialis, the infantry chief instructor, was pulling duty. The day had been long and hot. His course was going okay as courses go, but they were in the intense part of their training. The incident with the two Britons had not calmed Aquilla and Cassius. Martialis had to be vigilant with those two. After Centurion Domitus' heart-to-heart about overzealous instructors, Martialis could not afford another episode. The late summer heat was getting to him and he just wanted the gate closed so he could get his evening meal and maybe an hour at the fort bath before his course began their night training. "What's the problem, Marcellus?"

Marcellus was the junior centurion in charge of security for the evening. He stood on top of the wall next to the south gate that opened up to the little village.

"Sir, it looks like a rider, coming at full tilt."

"Is he a friendly?"

"He's Roman."

"That does not mean much," Martialis muttered to himself. "What in the name of Mars is it?" *It would just be typical for something to steal away my few precious hours of rest.* As soon as the rider bolted through the gate, Marcellus ordered the guards to close the gate for the night. It would only be opened when his infantry course left for their all-night patrolling exercise.

Martialis did not hesitate and grabbed a quick supper, forgetting his bath. A dispatch rider moving at that speed could only be a bad omen. Martialis had finished off two bowls of porridge supplemented with some wild boar (a few off-duty centurions had hunted) when Marcellus informed him that they were summoned to the headquarters.

As they entered the courtyard, they noticed that something big was afoot. Every officer at the fort had gathered in the main hall where the recruits first met the base commander to swear their allegiance to Rome. No one knew what had caused such a gathering. Suspense was in the air along with the standard-issue rumours. "It's probably the Germans again." "It can't be, the rider arrived from the wrong direction." "Maybe it's Gaul in rebellion or the Britons have landed nearby again." Everyone went silent with the entry of Centurion Domitus.

"Gentlemen I have some sad and shocking news that just arrived. I have in my hands a document signed by Tiberius himself informing us of the sad news. Our beloved Emperor of forty-one years has ascended to the gods. Gentlemen... Augustus has died." There was stunned silence as he paused for the news to settle in. "According to this document, he died three days ago. All training will be suspended tonight and tomorrow, but will be picked up in earnest the day after. Have all members of the fort formed up so I can inform them of this terrible news. That is all."

One of the senior officers asked, "Who is the emperor? Tiberius or Germanicus?"

"Tiberius!"

A general murmur of discontent went over the crowd of officers. "Germanicus has won the loyalty of the soldiers." "Germanicus has earned—"

"Gentlemen, that will be enough! Tiberius is the new emperor as stipulated by Augustus himself. Any further talk like this will be treason. Do not trifle with me. Anyone found guilty of treason amongst my officers will be executed! Is that understood?"

"Yes, sir," came the weak response. The officers knew that the base commander was serious about his threat. Regardless of their political leanings, they kept their peace with reference to the new Emperor.

The next day was cool with a northwest wind coming off the sea, bringing welcome relief from the summer heat. Centurion Domitus called a meeting with all his chief instructors to discuss what was next.

His office was too small to accommodate the chief instructors of the seven courses presently being held at the fort. They met in the courtyard of the base headquarters. There was still a sense of expectation when the Base Commander arrived.

"Gentlemen, I have called you here because we have to be ready for what Tiberius might require of us. My last posting was Rome, and I can tell you that it was Augustus who held us back from going into Germany and seeking revenge for Teutoburg Forest some six years ago. If I know Tiberius, it won't take long before he wants to move over the Rhine. There was also a note from a contact of mine. Rumour has it that the Senate is considering appointing Germanicus as the new Governor to Germania Minor. Germanicus, as you know, is the emperor's nephew and adopted son and heir. I am told he has sworn allegiance to Tiberius. That should put to bed any concerns expressed last night. With this in mind, I expect Rome will soon be calling on us to provide as many soldiers as we can spare. I want you to look at your recruits and identify ones who can be advanced early. Faustus, how are our two Britons doing?"

"Well sir, they have surprised me. There is nothing we can teach them about riding."

Martialis cut in. "It looks like that lesson was administered to you by a tree branch."

Everyone laughed at the expense of Faustus. Faustus just smiled, having reconciled himself to a life of being ribbed about the race he lost to the two Britons.

"Their fitness level?" Domitus brought the meeting back on line.

Faustus happily continued. "Their fitness level is better than their instructors. Matter of fact, they say their fitness level has gone down since they joined my course."

"What about their fighting ability?"

"They are taking to it like an Egyptian to the desert."

"How do you think they will fare in the regular legion?"

"They're not there yet."

"Well, get them there, and anyone else you think can keep up. Change your training to only the essentials and intensify the schedule. No days off, train late each day, do what you must but get it done. When Rome comes calling, I want to be ready."

The soldiers of Portius Itius never knew what hit them. Training took on a seriousness seldom seen. Rumours abounded amongst the recruits as to what was afoot. News from the German frontier talked of whole legions rebelling. There was talk of soldiers wanting to march on Rome in order to place their beloved Germanicus on the throne. Some even suggested that Germanicus was preparing himself to march on Rome. This was countered by the argument that Germanicus was Tiberius' nephew and adopted son and heir, so why would he need to take it by force. Patience would pay off with less risk.

"Getarix, what do you think?" Cullen asked one day when they were busy digging the long trench that was nightly placed around Roman encampments. These training exercises never seemed to end. By now they were building three camps a day, making sure each one had a deep trench dug around it. The dirt from the trench would be piled high on the camp side of the trench, where other soldiers were busy planting a wooden wall.

"I don't know what is going on, but if we wanted adventure…something tells me we will be getting it."

"You wanted adventure. I just went for a boat ride."

"I believe you were escaping your father—"

"That's enough talking, you two. Now get your backs into it or you will hear from this." They saw the figure of Centurion Faustus holding his staff high, ready to strike. Without hesitation they shut up and dug deeper and faster. Once Faustus had moved on, Cullen whispered to Getarix without losing stride, "Do you think he is still sore about us leaving him in that forest?"

Getarix gave out a little laugh. "We won, even with the game rigged against us. No, I'm sure he could have gotten us back if he had wanted to."

Their conversation was interrupted when they heard the voice of Faustus down the line. The victim was a fellow cavalry recruit whom Faustus named Rufus because of his scarlet red hair. If the truth were told, Faustus simply could not pronounce his name, Gwalchmai, meaning May Hawk, the Celtic mythological sun god. He was neither hawk-like nor god-like. Rufus was one of the most insecure men Getarix had ever met. He was an excellent horseman in spite of his portly shape. His major problem was he always pulled back when he should strike. Getarix liked him but had little respect for his fighting ability and hoped that he would never have to depend upon him in battle. His present problem was his laziness, which was wearing deeply on the patience of Faustus.

"Rufus! You better put your back into it before those barbarians plant your fat carcass on a stack, leaving your bones to be plucked clean by scavengers."

"Sorry, sir, but my back is killing me."

"You're right there, your back will surely kill you some day, that I guarantee you. I don't give a blast about that. What I do care about are the others you will take down with you."

"Yes, sir."

"Do you know what your problem is, Rufus? You have an eighteen-pound belly with a two-pound spine. Now get to it." Faustus punctuated his comments with a sound planting of his mace across the two-pound spine of the hapless Rufus.

Everyone up and down the line suddenly dug deeper, inspired to turn aside from their own pain, concentrating only on the dirt at hand.

They trained all summer and into the fall. The cavalry did not have it easier than the infantry. They still had to do their daily marches, and learn to fight on the ground as well as from their mounts. Once, Jodoc, one of the recruits, complained about having to learn infantry skills. "We are cavalry. We fight from our mounts." Faustus quickly dismounted and before anyone knew it had pulled the offending soldier off his horse.

"Alright, master of all knowledge, defend yourself." Before Faustus finished saying this, he charged Jodoc with his wooden sword. The attack was so furious that the young recruit did not know how to react. Had their course officer lost it? Jodoc fell back, stumbling over a rock as Faustus violently beat upon his shield. To break his fall, Jodoc had to place both of his hands behind him, exposing his midriff. Before he hit the ground the wooden sword of Faustus was uncomfortably planted in his belly. Faustus stared into his shocked eyes.

"Now, Jodoc, tell me if you can, how do you plan to fight when you get knocked off you horse or if the poor beast takes a spear deep into his chest?" Faustus stood his full height and addressed the surprised crowd of recruits and continued with his lesson.

"I have bad news for you lot. In battle, we the cavalry have more casualties amongst our horses than amongst our men. I cannot grantee you will survive battle, but I can almost grantee that one day you will find yourself on foot fighting well-trained infantry. You have to be better than they are at their own game. Any questions?" No one said a word. "Good. Now stand up, Jodoc, and the rest of you dismount."

By late harvest, the troops were working together like a ship's crew. Faustus looked upon them with a justified amount of pride. He knew that his time with these troops was coming to an end. Germanicus was screaming for troops to be sent to Xanten, his large base on the lower Rhine.

The Legions of Germanicus were angry about the appointment of Tiberius as Emperor. Their leaders were not successful in controlling that anger, and it broke out in rebellion. The appointment of Tiberius was not the only concern. Soldiers up and down the Rhine were rebelling over pay and the length of their contracts. Word was that soldiers had murdered some of their own centurions, including Centurion Lucilius. The ever-loyal Germanicus brutally put down the rebellion that would have seen him as the new head of the Roman Empire. Now with his frontier secure, Germanicus needed to keep his troops busy. With the blessing of Tiberius, he planned to invade Germania immediately. For that he needed troops to build up his army. The rebellion had given the training cadre enough time to properly train their recruits.

"Some are better than others, sir," Faustus reported to the Base Commander.

"But you say they are ready to be transferred to the frontier?"

"Yes sir, I would say that they are better prepared than normal."

"And the infantry, Martialis? Are they ready?"

"Yes sir, I would say they are."

"Nothing like the threat of war to put a little seriousness into their step, eh?" Centurion Domitus said. He paused and thought for a bit and then concluded. "Alright, set it up. I will observe their training this afternoon. Germanicus is demanding new troops. He has to keep his unsettled legions busy killing Germans. Maybe this will stop them from killing any more of his officers."

All went well, and at the end of the mandatory demonstration for the base commander, he declared that their training was complete and successful.

The troop of newly trained cavalry soldiers was now dressed in full battle order as they stood on parade next to their infantry brothers. Their green tunics could be seen under their chain-mail armour that covered their upper bodies. Their new helmets looked just like the ones worn by their training staff. They sported two lark wings on either side just above their ears. The white wings could easily be seen from a great distance. The cavalry were mounted in rank and file two deep, and next to them stood the infantry formed up three deep. They all faced a small dais where Centurion Domitus stood and addressed them.

"You have all worked hard. You have all been tested, and all of you have met the standard. A few have even exceeded it. You are now Roman soldiers. The best soldiers the world has seen ever or ever will see. You are now full members of the great Fifth Legion, The Larks. Raised by Julius Caesar sixty-six years ago, the first Gaulish Legion ever raised. This Legion…your Legion…first saw battle fighting the great Gaulish King, Vercingetorix."

Cullen leaned over to Getarix. "Did you know that?"

"No, now shut up!"

Cullen smiled at his friend's discomfort. "A king, eh, does that make you a prince?"

Getarix looked over to his friend with a look of disgust. "Yes, do you remember that shut-up part? I was serious."

Cullen knew that he had pushed his luck to its limit.

Centurion Domitus continued. "That great battle was won, and the Larks… you…have never lost a battle since. Even against Elephants during the civil wars, the Larks prevailed. That is why we and we alone have the elephant as our mark of distinction. Those who went before you distinguished themselves in battle, as I know you will in your time.

"Thirty-three years ago, our legion returned to Gaul, where we temporarily lent our eagle standard to the Germans."

Every one laughed at the little joke referring to the battle against the Germanic tribe of Sugambri, where their colours were lost to the Germans for a while. They had almost lost the battle along with their standard. But the tide had turned and the Larks had regained the battle and their eagle standard all in one.

On that sunny afternoon, they became soldiers of Rome. No longer were they referred to as recruits. At the conclusion of the parade they were all promoted to the next rank. The infantry were now called Miles, and the cavalry soldiers became Alaris.

XVI

BATTLE PREP

The autumn days were cooling off when their training had concluded. As a reward for their hard work during their course, the soldiers were allowed to spend the evening in the small village outside the south gate. They were confined to the village in order to keep a close eye on them. It would not do to have their freshly minted soldiers arrested by the town's magistrate the night before they were to head out to the frontier, nor was it worth risking the good will of the local citizens. Wine-induced decompression of soldiers seldom turned out well. The fort village had long ago learned to live with the antics inspired by spirits of Bacchus. Jodoc, Getarix, and Cullen quickly secured their horses in the unit stables and were heading out of the main gate when Rufus called them, wanting to join their little party. Getarix was about to send him on his way when Cullen invited him to join. Both Jodoc and Getarix gave a look of death as Rufus caught up to them. They decided to drop the issue, as Rufus was not a bad fellow, just a weak soldier. The four of them strutted out of the fort in full armour, wearing their *spatha*, the longer cavalry sword, off their hips. Rufus looked the most uncomfortable (and the least military) suffering under his armour. He looked like he was going to burst if his chain mail ever gave way. The four of them made a beeline for the Winged Helmet Inn. Getarix told the proprietor that they wanted to sit on the patio and demanded a feast. The scene they had encountered the day they had arrived never left his mind. Many times as he had been about to give up and quit, the vision of having a feast on the patio of the inn had kept him going. Once they were seated and the wine served, Getarix signalled Jodoc and they both got up and stepped out into the street.

"Where are you two going?" Cullen asked.

"I'll come with—" Rufus said, starting to get up.

"No!" Getarix held up his hand, leaving to room for argument. "We will be right back."

They walked through the market and headed south out of town where the village stables were. Cullen could only wonder what they were up to. Upon their return, it was obvious that they had been in a scrap. Their knuckles were bruised and cut. Both of them looked like they had after one of Faustus' infamous full-armour runs. As they stepped up onto the patio, Cullen's eyes narrowed looking straight at Getarix, who avoided any direct eye contact.

"Getarix, what in the hell were you up to?"

"Nothing," Getarix answered with a bit of a nervous chuckle. He then threw a bag of coins on the table. "Do you remember the money we had to pay Gullis for our horses?" He did not wait for an answer. "The nice man at the stable insisted on returning it."

Jodoc said with a half-cocked smile, "He even insisted on returning the money for keeping your horse at the stable."

"Rufus, you had better get out of here, because when he reports this you do not want to be part of it. Apparently I have no choice," Cullen concluded.

"Oh no, he won't report this. What do you think, Jodoc?"

"Oh no, he went straight to bed. Rufus, what time did they say we were off tomorrow?"

"Two hours before sunlight."

Both Getarix and Jodoc looked at each other, declaring in unison, "Oh no, no, he won't be up by then." Getarix and Jodoc laughed.

Getarix then bellowed for the beautiful smith's daughter, Beaudin. Her flaxen hair blew in the wind and contrasted with her clear alabaster skin. "Wine, and lots of it." When she turned to go back inside to fulfill his order, all three could not help but notice her full womanly figure. Getarix pulled himself out of the spell and yelled like he had forgot something. "And food, and there better not be any porridge in it or I will put you over my knee."

Beaudin simply looked over her shoulder and said with a smile as she disappeared through the doors, "You wish."

"I do."

All laughed, including Cullen, who concluded that if they were going to die tomorrow he might as well eat drink and be merry. *Besides,* he thought, *what are they going to do to me? Make me join the army and send me to war?*

Their small table sat to the left of the inn doors as seen from the street. There was a small Roman-style railing separating them from the street. Jodoc sat with his back to the inn wall next to the doors. Getarix sat across from him with his back to the street. Rufus, the quiet one of the group, sat between Jodoc and Getarix with his back to the street at the end of the patio. Cullen sat across from him with his back to the remainder of the patio. The inn began to fill with other course members out to blow off some steam.

As the night wore on and the wine flowed freely, they heard the familiar voice that once shot fear through their soul. "Well, well, what have we here?" sneered the voice. Cullen swung around on one leg of his stool, not getting up. He did a quick one-eighty and came face to face with the drunk Miles Aquilla and Cassius. No one stood for the two of them. The handsome Aquilla bent down, placing his face closer to Cullen's, and began to yell like the days of old. "How about some respect, you British pig's sweat?" Cullen began to rise, to the satisfaction of their old instructors and the dismay of his friends. Abruptly and with lighting speed, Cullen brought his mighty right arm up as fast as he could, cold-cocking Aquilla. He dropped like sack of wheat. For a second everyone just stood there in shock.

Then Cullen broke the ice as he pivoted, showing Getarix his fist, yelling triumphantly. "Look Getarix, Jodoc, my fist is cut just like yours!" He jumped up for joy.

Miles Cassius was shaking with fear and anger. All he could squeak out was, "You...you are...going to get it—" That was all Getarix allowed him to say before he stood and landed his fist on Cassius' left cheek, hard. He began to teeter toward the building in what looked like slow motion. Before anyone knew what had happened, Jodoc was on his feet planting his fist firmly on Cassius' right cheek. Cassius dropped next to his friend in the same fashion. Everyone just stood there with Rufus still sitting and wondering how the evening was going to end for him. They all had their eyes on Jodoc.

He shrugged. "What? It seemed like the right thing to do."

They all laughed in hysterics when they heard another familiar voice. Getarix and Cullen looked up and with joy and embraced Ansgar, their old infantry mate. Ansgar pointed to the floor of the patio with a questioning look in his eyes.

Cullen answered. "Oh, those two. They were tired and wanted to sleep. You guys must have tired them out."

Ansgar laughed, fully understanding the message. "They are such a beautiful sight." After introductions were made, they procured an additional chair and the party began in earnest. All night their friends from both the infantry and cavalry courses stepped over the two peaceful instructors, making and remaking the same jokes at their expense. For many in the infantry, the sight of Aquilla and Cassius had a healing effect on them. It also gave them one more thing to celebrate as they swapped stories about their respective course adventures deep into the night.

Beaudin kept their table full of wine and the best food from their kitchen. Getarix seemed bound and determined to lose the money he had just recovered. Every time Beaudin restocked their table, she rubbed up against Getarix and they would whisper things to each other. No one moved from their appointed stools other than to visit the little house in the back.

Suddenly Cullen noticed that the place had cleared out and they were back down to the four of them—no, the three of them.

"Where did Getarix go?" Cullen asked.

Rufus looked at Cullen. "Is he gone?"

Both Cullen and Jodoc laughed themselves silly. Then Cullen became serious. "Where did everyone go?"

Jodoc answered. "Don't know. What time were we to be back?"

"I don't know," Cullen said weakly, and looked to Rufus who simply shrugged. It hit Cullen then that they had not even stayed for the final brief to find out when they were due back, which he figured had come and gone and the gate would be secured tightly for the night.

"But what of Getarix?"

They heard the drunken laughter and voice of Beaudin from the bedroom window above the patio. Cullen gave Jodoc one look. Both had solved the mystery of the disappearing Getarix. They bolted up in a second and were through the door of the inn before Rufus could utter a word. He wanted to follow them, but being lazy by nature he simply stayed put. Five minutes later, they burst through the doors with the obviously satisfied Getarix secured between them.

"Come on, Rufus, or we will be scaling the fort walls," Jodoc yelled, not stopping for him. As they ran for the gate they could hear the protests of Beaudin yelling from the window. "Hey, come back, he's not finished!"

When they arrived at the gate, it was closed for the night.

"You up there, open the gate," Jodoc hollered.

"The gates are closed for the night," came the reply from the ramparts. "They will be open by first light. Now go, you can stay at the inn."

"That sounds good to me," Getarix said.

Ignoring him, Cullen simply grabbed the last of the money Getarix had secured on his belt and lobbed it up on the ramparts. They heard it land and they froze, waiting to see if it had any effect. Getarix was beyond understanding what had transpired. About a minute later a head looked down upon them for the first time.

"Who goes there?"

They identified themselves.

"Are Miles Aquilla and Miles Cassius with you?"

"Umm, no," Cullen returned.

"They needed to sleep," Rufus said, wobbling slightly from his drink. They could hear some laughing from the top of the wall.

"Yeah, sure, I heard."

The head disappeared behind the ramparts. The three semi-conscious ones began to worry what would happen. Quietly, one gate opened. Just as they were about to enter the small opening, the bag of money landed at their feet. When Rufus picked it up and handed it to Cullen, he noticed that all the money was still there. The head returned. "Quickly." They did not have to be told twice.

When they entered the fort it was a hive of activity. They noticed that it was centred on the barracks and the stables.

Centurion Faustus almost ran into them as he left the base headquarters. "I'm glad to see you could make it," he said sarcastically. "You better get to the stables and get your horses ready. We are leaving within the hour." He stopped and gave them a look. Pointing to Getarix, he added, "And throw his sorry hide in the trough to wake him up." As he left to go about his business they could hear him mutter, "You four better not have gotten yourself into trouble tonight."

They kept silent, that way they kept themselves from lying.

After the prescribed bath, which Getarix failed to appreciate, they gathered their kit and personal items from lock-up and were mounted and headed out the north gate for the Rhine frontier and Germanicus' war.

XVII

ESCAPE TO WAR

"Cullen," Getarix called out weakly. Cullen looked over to him and noticed he could not even open his eyes.

"What in the name of Jud happened to me last night?"

"You don't remember?"

"Remember what?"

"Last night, you dolt."

"Oh, by the gods, do not make me think. Aquilla and Cassius I remember, that was good. How did we get back?"

"You mean you do not remember Beaudin?"

"Beaudin?" Getarix thought through the pain that hammered inside his skull. "You mean the bar wench? Oh please don't tell me that I—" He painfully forced his eyes open and looked over to his friend, who was sporting the biggest grin possible. He did not notice that every rider within earshot was snickering.

"Oh no, I didn't…?"

"Not very well, by all accounts." Cullen's laughter was drowned out by the chorus of chuckles that came from all their friends riding in formation. Getarix looked around and pleaded in desperation. "Please tell me that it was not in public."

Rufus piped up. "There was hardly anything in private."

The whole troop of cavalry broke into uncontrolled laughter. Getarix decided to keep any more questions to himself. For the rest of the day he concentrated on keeping himself from painting his horse with last night's supper. In that he was not alone.

At the end of a long painful day's ride, they were housed in a semi-permanent camp used as a staging point for troops heading to the frontiers for the upcoming battles. The next day dawned cold and wet, only getting colder and wetter.

Wet. That's the best way to describe the mouth of the Rhine in late autumn. The newly promoted Alaris Getarix felt he was back home. The ever-present bone-chilling wet cold dug deep into Getarix's body and memory. After Getarix sobered up, he slid into one of his moods brought on by the weather. Once again he looked at his friend in wonder at how he seemed to thrive on suffering. Cullen was just happy to be finished his training with success.

The cavalry led the procession, followed by the infantry. Centurion Martialis came bounding up on his horse to talk to Faustus.

"I'm telling you, Faustus, I've had it."

"What's wrong, my friend?"

"Those two."

"What two?"

"Aquilla and Cassius. The blighters went to town and apparently they got so drunk they passed out on the patio of the inn and are still there for all I know. I needed them for this march. When I get back…" He paused for a second before continuing. "How did you get transferred to the frontier?"

"I don't know, I just asked. Did you hear that Lucilius was killed in the mutiny?"

"Yes, he brought it on himself. Would not surprise me if he was responsible for the mutiny itself."

Faustus paused to reflect. "You know there's a lot of grievance. Maybe they killed some cavalry officers as well, creating an opening which I now go to fill."

Before returning to his infantry troop, Martialis declared, "When I get back I'm going for a transfer."

Xanten was a major military city on the Rhine. The military was its only industry and reason to exist. It was here that Germanicus made his headquarters. Xanten was also the home of The Fifth Legion, the Larks. When they crested the final hill before descending into the Rhine valley, one of the soldiers in front yelled back. "There she is, boys, our new home…look at the size of her."

"Getarix, look at it. It must be ten times the size of Portius Itius," Cullen gasped.

"It's big, that's for sure. And the home of the fifth," Getarix said.

Xanten was built on the western bank of the Rhine River where the river runs west to east before continuing its journey south. It was completely surrounded by walls of stone. Even the riverside was walled. The city was so big that there were three gates per landlocked side. Each gate had a road leading to and fro. Hundreds of carts clogged the roads, arriving full and leaving the city empty. The town was five big Roman city blocks wide and five deep, a very large military city indeed. The river wall had two gates. Each one opened to either end of a wooden dockside where boats were lined up two and even three ships deep. Rufus pointed and said, "Look guys, the dockside is filled with soldiers. They're getting on the ships. Looks like we missed the war."

"There will be plenty of war to go around before this is over," Faustus said. "Now, you see the dockyard, don't you?"

"Yes sir," came back a flood of answers.

"Okay, go inland three blocks. Do you see the large building that takes up a whole city block, the one that is mostly courtyard?"

"Yes, sir."

"Okay, that's where we will live, train, and house our horses. We will live above our horse."

"That will stink for sure," someone belted out.

Faustus continued. "You will be thankful for the heat coming off the horses in the winter. Now, do you see the big building next to it on this side?"

"Yes, sir."

"That is the headquarters. That is where Germanicus and his family live. In other words, we will be living in the best neighbourhood, so watch yourselves."

"Sir, what is that huge round building in the corner next to the river?"

"That, Rufus my boy, is the Amphitheatre. It's for the games." He looked back and got mostly blank stares. It was then that he realized just how uncivilized these men were. He remembered having to teach them how to bathe. A few of them had never even used a toilet before joining the army. That did not matter to Faustus. Most of them had the stuff to make the best soldiers in the Roman army. He even felt a measure of pride as they entered the city through the gate.

They were quickly settled into their new permanent quarters. There was no time to waste. Their training began immediately. The next day, more legions arrived. The small city of Xanten was crawling with soldiers. Later that day, they were given time off. Before they were let go, Centurion Faustus formed them up to address them. He stood in the last afternoon sun and observed them. He could not help noticing how much Rufus did not match the picture. His uniform was a mess and his armour was dull. He made a mental note to address his deficiencies before letting the others free for the remainder of the day. He was worried about the effects the recent rebellion would have on his impressionable troops. He wanted to head off any trouble before it began.

"As you may or may not know…if you don't, you will. Shortly after the death of Augustus the soldiers here rebelled for various reasons. Germanicus was appointed and put it down. That is why your training was not shortened like we had expected it would be…rather it was lengthened, waiting for Germanicus to get control of the situation. He has control now. What I want you to get clear in your heads is that these issues are not your issues. If I find any one of you causing trouble about the rebellion, you will be dealt with in the harshest terms. Is that understood?"

"Yes, sir."

"Okay, you may be off." He pointed his cane to Rufus. "Not you, you horrible fat little man."

The rest of them headed to one of the town markets where all manner of Roman uniforms could be observed. The traditional Roman legionnaire with their red tunic was outnumbered by the plethora of auxiliary troops wearing green tunics under their chain mail. Syrian archers with their round shields and pointed helmets had just arrived and were staying outside the city walls in fortified camps. Greek and African troops were everywhere, along with German irregulars still garbed in their traditional costume of wool pants similar to the Celts. With them came constant rumours about when they were going to move into Germania Major.

Getarix, Cullen, and Jodoc were enjoying the colourful sights of Xanten when Ortwin the infanteer found them.

"Getarix, Cullen, you are summoned to Centurion Faustus along with a Jodoc and Rufus."

"I am Jodoc. Rufus, the lazy little sod, did not pass his inspection. He looked like a bag of dirt wearing a helmet. He's back at the barracks. What is it you want?"

Ortwin sheepishly looked down and said, "I…I…don't know, but a messenger came to Centurion Faustus from Portius Itius. I recognized him. Maybe it's about the other night." At the thought of Aquilla and Cassius laid out on the stone of the patio, Ortwin could not help but smile.

As the four of them stood in front of Faustus, they could see he was furious. "Okay, you block heads, we spend untold amounts of money to train you, feed you, pay you, and just when we can actually employ you…you pull this stunt."

"Sir—" Jodoc started.

"Shut up, you!"

Jodoc froze. He had never seen Faustus so angry. He pointed his mace toward the three good soldiers. "You three are the best cavalry soldiers I have ever seen and you jeopardize all my hard work for this!" He looked at Rufus, who had a bit of a hurt look in his eyes. He was not in the mood for it. "Wipe that look off your face, you, or I will…you must know that you are a waste of barley." He calmed down and thought a bit. "Okay, you four are equal to the infantry rank of Miles, so it was equals to equals. Not like those two did not deserve it. I consider the matter about Aquilla and Cassius closed. That's all."

All four saluted and did a precision drill movement turning around to leave. Faustus called back. "Getarix and Jodoc, stay." They turned back around. Faustus waited until the other two were gone. "Listen, you idiots. I can blow off the clobbering of those two morons. You actually did the Roman army a favour. But I cannot blow off this other matter."

"Other matter, sir?" Jodoc asked.

"You know, Jodoc, you must think I am stupid. Everyone in Portius Itius knows that no one trusts the stables in the village." Faustus paused to let this revelation sink in. "He's calling for your blood. He has demanded you go before the magistrate to stand trial. And it gets worse. He's a Roman citizen. You're not. Get the picture? That little bout of self-made justice might well cost you your freedom, possibly your lives."

Centurion Faustus' optie knocked on his door and announced that the messenger from Portius Itius had returned, needing an answer.

"Keep him in that room."

"Yes sir." Faustus turned and followed his aid out of the room, leaving the door open. "Miles Gius, I just finished a search but unfortunately the four soldiers you seek were sent north by boat to join Germanicus in North Germany. By now they should be at sea off the coast of Germany. As far as I concerned the matter with Aquilla and Cassius at the inn is a dead issue. Soldiers of equal rank often settle their disputes in like manner. As for the matter with the stable master, when they return from that campaign I will personally put the chains on them.

Until then there is nothing we can do, sorry. Please give my regrets to Centurion Domitus."

"Yes sir." Miles Gius saluted and left to prepare to return.

Faustus returned to the room, where Getarix and Jodoc were waiting at attention. "Okay, you two, I just bought you about six months. If you're lucky you will get killed gloriously in battle and this whole problem will simply go away."

"Thank you, sir...I think," Getarix said.

"Now, the four of you will be pulling special duty. This way we can keep you out of sight for a bit. Mess this up and I'll hunt you down and personally kill you myself."

XVIII

A GARDEN RETREAT

The gardens of Senator Damianus were amongst the most splendid in all of
Rome. They were situated facing the southeast, where they received the full
effect of the morning sun. By afternoon the gardens were in the shade when it
was most required. Antonio loved the gardens in the fall. The morning heat during the summer made them almost unbearable. Watering the plants during the
summer was a test of endurance. The heat made Antonio feel like he was wax
on a hot stove. The intense sun burned his skin until it blistered, but he had no
choice but to comply or face the whip. After the sultry heat, the autumn breezes
brought relief to all, slave and master alike. By late fall, the winds blew colder,
and the mornings in the garden were warm and comfortable. A welcome reprieve
from the cold autumn nights. It was Antonio's job to water the plants before his
daily tasks were assigned. The senator believed that slaves should never be idle.
If their work was completed he would find something else to occupy their time.
Long after sunset, his army of slaves would still be toiling at whatever tasks they
were assigned. The warm morning breeze swept across Antonio's face, bringing
what almost amounted to a shot of joy through his body. It seemed to all that
it was forbidden for the slaves of the senator to feel pleasure of any kind. It hit
Antonio that if the senator knew he enjoyed his morning chores during the fall
season he would be reassigned to something unpleasant.

As beautiful as the gardens were, they still constituted Antonio's prison. It would not be so bad if his master would leave him behind when he went on his frequent trips to the countryside. There was that one time when he was left behind, the day when the senator went charging out to the emperor's villa. The same day Centurion Cornelius made his escape. Once the senator cleared Esquiline Hill, Antonio noticed that a great cloud lifted from the estate. Within an hour he even heard laughter. Late that night the master returned. Antonio had never seen the senator in such a state. He had five slaves tied up and he whipped them until he almost passed out. Two of the slaves, one a woman, died from his ministration. Antonio had never been so close to killing the senator with his bare hands before or since. He had fantasized that night of slowly pushing the life out of him. Slaves of a household became even closer than many natural families. To see strangers murdered and tortured to death before your own eyes was bad enough, but to have it done to family members intensified the horror.

Rumours ran rampant of how Centurion Cornelius escaped the iron grip of Senator Damianus. Every slave celebrated his escape. It became a vicarious victory for all the captives. Even the three who survived their whippings felt it was worth seeing the small victory. The two who died made their own escape. That fateful day, like the garden, Antonio loved and hated all at once. Oh how he longed for the freedom to love someone or something wholeheartedly and without complication. He dare not dream of the family he left behind. The pain was far too great. The best he could hope for was another day when the senator might again leave him behind. That day never came. For some reason the senator took Antonio wherever he went. The only other hope the family of slaves clung to was to die before their master. Antonio shook these thoughts from his mind. He looked around him and laid his eyes upon a marble statue of the goddess Floras. The goddess of plants, flowers mostly. Antonio thought of the festival in her honour each spring. A festival that at times past was a celebration of the beauty of flowers which morphed into late-night licentiousness acts of depravity. All dedicated to the goddess. Antonio loved looking at the marble statues. *How could a culture so cruel produce such beauty in art and architecture? Or how could a culture so rich in beauty be so cruel?* Antonio lifted the water can to the top of a beautifully carved marble urn that sported a palm from some far-off corner of the empire. He poured the water slowly, allowing the sun to warm his body. He poured it slower than he needed to. The official reason was to prevent the water from overflowing. The real reason was Antonio wanted to slow the day down. He did not want this hour to end. As the water poured, feeding the thirsty soil, he scanned the garden, taking in the beauty of all the plants and statues. His eyes fell on the beautiful red blossoms of an unknown fall flowering bush. He was taken aback by its beauty. It was at moments like these that he realized how much his soul longed for beauty and love. Anything to replace the fear and hate the senator seemed to draw out of him.

As he was musing about this is he heard the voice of his master. That voice which dug deep into the pit of his stomach, destroying the peace known just a moment before. Unconsciously he crouched down, trying to be invisible. The senator was walking from the house, following the meandering path paved in interconnected mosaic that imitated a flowing stream. The artist had imbedded fish and reeds and pebbles that the small tiles gently flowed around. Antonio remembered when the senator had it built. He sent throughout the empire the message that he was in the market for a slave with a gift for this art. When the slave markets could not produce his required artist, he found a freeman who was so gifted. Through deception and treachery he bribed a wine merchant to testify that the artisan had stolen wine from his cellar. Senator Damianus, being the law-conscious man he was, took it upon himself to ensure justice was done, pursuing that issue until the freeman was not longer free. If it happened that Damianus ended up owning the man as his slave, that was just the luck of the draw. He should not have stolen the wine in the first place. Antonio avoided thinking of what the senator had done to the family of his victim. After losing his freedom and then his family, all on trumped up charges, he was sent to the garden to build the mosaic path. He was under threat of a whipping if it were not done in time for the festival. Singlehanded, he accomplished this difficult task. For his labours and sacrifice he was sent to one of Damianus' farms, where they found him one day hanging from the rafters of the stable. The gossip was that Damianus arranged it. He was heard to have said that no one would benefit from the talents of his hapless possession.

"Alexander, I have called you here because I am interested in buying a young girl," Senator Damianus greeted his favourite slave trader.

"That should not be any trouble. What would you be looking for, a dark one or maybe something a little lighter?"

"I have one in mind."

"Okay, no problem. Do I own her or is she—"

"You don't understand. Now shut up and listen. This girl is not yet a slave, but I think she will soon be."

Alexander looked at the artwork of the path and smiled. "Ah, I understand."

"No you don't, now keep your peace. This girl I have had, when I was in Germania. Our troops are there now, exacting some revenge on those pigs for Teutoburg Forest. Now get yourself up there and find her. If she is not killed in the fighting, I want her, do you understand? And I do not care what you have to do to get her. Now, her name is Isolee, or something like that. It does not matter. Her father owns the Boar's Head Inn. I have it shown on this map right here. Is that clear?"

"Germania...up there? But sir—"

The Senator shot him a look that said the discussion was done."

"Sir." Alexander bowed his head.

"Do not fail me, or you might just become one of your own products."

"Yes, sir." Alexander hustled to clear the garden, fearing he'd been sent on an impossible task. Before he could get away, the senator called him back.

"Ho, and one more thing. She has a brother, a feisty one with fire in his eyes. Get him, too, if you can. I will enjoy slowly killing him in front of her. And don't worry about your expenses. Get her and I will make you a rich man. Fail me and..." He left Alexander to finish the threat.

Antonio's mind went back to Germania and the Boar's Head Inn. He remembered Centurion Cornelius' narrative once they had returned to Rome. *Do the gods not care at all about justice?* Antonio just then remembered the many stories of the gods acting no different than the senator himself. *If you ask the gods to curse the innocent just because you are filled with hate it would be done, if enough money was presented. The gods are always fighting and killing just for the pleasure of it.* Antonio felt sick, so much so he dropped the copper watering bucket.

When it hit the ground it made a loud bang, bouncing off the marble base of the large urn.

"What...who is there? Show yourself now!"

"Sir." Antonio approached his master with his head down.

"What were you doing there?"

"Watering the pla—"

"You were spying, were you not?"

"No s—"

"It will be the whip for you."

And so it was.

XIX

A STRANGE PLACE TO HIDE

Getarix stood guard to the right of the passageway that led into the atrium of the house, Cullen to the left. He had never seen the likes before in his life. The atrium of a Roman house formed its centre, around which all the rooms of the home were found. At one time in the past, it had been the bedroom of the mother of the family next to the hearth where the fire was kept. These days it was a beautifully decorated roofless room centred by a pool used to collect the rain. The roofline slopped inward, directing rainwater into the centre. This was a perfect style in the warmth of southern Europe. In the north where it got cold, the Romans had developed an ingenious heating system. They built the walls of their buildings hollow. Under the house, slaves kept fires burning. The walls acted like chimneys, circulating warm air under the floors and through the walls, which radiated the heat. In spite of the cool day, all in the home felt the heat from within the walls and floor. The atrium did not open into the street. Instead there was a long hallway leading from the main door of the house into the atrium. No matter how noisy the streets became, it was always peaceful in the atrium.

Getarix and Cullen did not understand were the warmth came from. They were simply thankful for it. As they stood there they were also thankful for their centurion protecting them, for without his intervention they would have by now lost their lives to the gallows. Getarix and Cullen discussed at length the strange stroke of fate that landed them in the home of the next emperor when justice demanded their death. Instead they stood guard, protecting the family of Germanicus himself. The atrium alone of Germanicus' Xanten home was larger than the house Getarix grew up in. As he stood on guard, he was awestruck by the beauty before him. Flowers, still in bloom, blended perfectly with the beautiful walls. On the walls, artist-painted scenes of peacocks, fish, and all sorts of wild animals, all framed in red. The morning sun danced off the pool in the central part of the atrium. The bright red tiles of the inward sloping roofline still shone from the early morning rains. Under the pillar-supported roof, an open passageway ran around the pool, connecting the entire house. Directly across from them was the bedroom of Germanicus and Agrippina.

Agrippina was the daughter of Julia the Elder, making her the granddaughter of Augustus himself. As the symbol of homeliness, the atrium was the centre of all domestic life. Everyone passed through it, and Agrippina spent much of her day there. It also acted as the location where guests were entertained. This meant that the guards were close to the family most of the day. They saw and heard more than their station in life merited. After the mutiny of the more seasoned troops, the guard duty was handed to newly trained soldiers who, they hoped, had no sympathies one way or the other with the recent rebellion. Centurion Faustus had taken this opportunity to hide his errant soldiers.

Germanicus was not in Xanten. He had quickly departed with his newly pacified legions, six in all, on a campaign to exact revenge upon the Chatti, one of the tribes responsible for Teutoburg Forest, where the Roman army's humiliation still burned. Word filtered back about the brutal battles where whole villages were massacred. By doing this, Germanicus gave vent to any anger left in his rebellious troops on the hapless Germans and not on Roman leadership. Any booty collected was distributed amongst the soldiers, alleviating the financial stress due to their low wages, a major sour point felt by Rome's disgruntled army.

Their shift had just begun on the first day of the third week of guard duty. Getarix was looking straight ahead, just above the water of the pool. As the early morning sun was rising into a new day, its light bounced off the water right into his eyes. At first he was not even sure if he was hearing right.

"Soldier, salute me."

It sounded like a pixy was talking to him. But then it came again in a toddler's Latin.

"I am not telling you again, soldier. You will salute me!"

Getarix could see nothing. The next thing he heard was Cullen snickering. As he looked over to his partner, he felt something lightly kick the armour covering his shins.

"I am not telling you again to salute me!"

Getarix looked down at the most amazing sight he had ever seen. There before his eyes was a little three-year-old child. What was amazing about him was his outfit. He wore a complete Roman centurion's uniform, resplendent with bronze armour and red cape. On his feet were well-crafted miniature army boots. He held his little child-size helmet under his arm like all centurions did. At such a sight, Getarix could not help himself but to laugh.

"I said salute me!"

Getarix stood tall and gave him the grandest salute he could muster. After that, he bent down on one knee next to Rome's youngest centurion. Getarix had seen him before but only briefly. He knew him to be the son of Germanicus and Agrippina.

"What is your name?" he asked in simple Latin.

"I am Gaius Julius Caesar Augustus Germanicus, and I am a centurion. Emperor Augustus is my grandfather. That means you must do as I say."

"That's quite a name for such a little guy. I think I will call you Caligula. Do you know what that means?" Gaius just looked at him.

"It means little boots. Literally, little army boots." As he said this he pointed to the child's feet. The child's face lighted up at this revelation.

Their little conference was broken by the voice of Agrippina, his mother.

"Gaius, there you are. Don't just run off like that."

Getarix and Cullen returned to their proper stance, ridged as statues.

"I am Caligula. Centurion Caligula."

Agrippina could not help herself but broke into a smile. "Indeed, Centurion Caligula. Now come with me and stop running off like that."

Before she could leave, two soldiers entered the atrium, appearing between Getarix and Cullen. They saluted Agrippina. She bowed her head in recognition of their salute. "Forgive us, lady, we have been sent here to relieve your guards." With that she departed with her little centurion.

They addressed Getarix and Cullen. "You two are to report to Legion Headquarters." The two dismissed guards looked worried, fearing that they had been discovered and were now being sent back to face their punishment. The replacement guards, knowing their worries, reassured them. "Don't worry, you two. You are saved by the waves. We lost a number of ships in the North Sea last week and apparently you were on one of them. You're going to Germania today, in fact. As far as Portius Itius is concerned, you are dead. Therefore you shall live. In all my life I have never seen luck like yours."

The weather had turned cold and the two of them remembered their guard duty and its warm wall with fondness. Nonetheless, they would never have traded this for anything. 40,000 Roman soldiers were in German territory. The Fifth Legion held the right flank. Once again they faced Arminius and his coalition of German tribes. Germanicus was not going to make the same mistake Verus had by leaving his flanks exposed. Germanicus divided his legions. He kept back two and sent them after the Chatti. The other four Legions under Caecina were sent to attack the Cherusci and Marsi.

By the time they arrived at the frontier, much of the Chatti had been wiped out. Stories abounded about the Germans abandoning their women and children to their fate at the ends of Roman swords. Stories of the men swimming the river to save themselves meant that their villages ceased to exist. It also meant that much of their fighting forces remained intact.

As they approached the river Adrana, they were informed that their duty was to assist the engineering officer in building a bridge for the legions to pursue the swimming Chatti, now camped safely on the other bank.

"Okay you lot, grab your shovels and get your backs into it. I need a hole here and one here."

As the soldiers were shedding their gear, securing their picks and grabbing shovels, Cullen was kicking the ground where the engineering officer indicated. It was a small depression about ten paces from shore. It had been carved out by the river earlier in the season when the water was higher and the current stronger.

"By the gods, you guys, this is going to be a hard go. Look at the size of these boulders. Forget your shovel. Get down here and help me with this stone. We will have to lift it out with our hands."

Jodoc got on his knees immediately and began to get hold of the stone. Rufus just watched, being careful not to use up his limited storehouse of energy.

Bending to join them, Getarix began to grumble about the prospective workload set before them. Cullen, more accustomed to hard labour, welcomed the challenge and chided Getarix. "Don't you start!" Cullen began. "This is what you want, right? To be in the Roman army…living the dream."

"No, this is what you wanted. Remember the day we joined? If you would have kept your porridge hole shut, we would be—"

"Slaves! Probably digging big stones out of some farmer's field. A farmer who would own our hides. Besides, you're the dreamer. Welcome to your dream."

"More like a blinking nightmare."

"Would you two shut up!" Jodoc silenced them. Rufus just stood there looking at them, leaning on his shield, which faced the river.

The shadow of the engineering officer loomed over them from the height of the embankment created by the earlier current. He was reaching high with his cane, ready to strike the closest to him, bellowing, "All of you just shut up or I'll—"

"Cullen, did you see that?"

"What?" Cullen asked, looking up. He was knocked down by the full weight of the engineering officer, who fell in their midst with a spear that had gone clear though him.

Rufus still just stood there, more out of shock than anything else.

"Over there. Jodoc, look!" Getarix yelled, looking over the protective embankment their officer had fallen from. He was pointing across the river. "Rufus, get down!"

Another spear came screaming for Rufus, hitting his shield, going right through it and between his legs, stopping only when the shaft was halfway through the shield. The sudden hit woke him from his fear-induced trance. As he tried to take a step for cover he tripped over the spear wedged in his shield. His full weight landed on his now-dead officer. He rolled down the embankment, joining his three friends in the shallow depression, landing on Getarix.

Getarix fought his way out from under him. He looked over the edge to assess the situation and noticed the trajectory of the enemy spears and arrows. He yelled to all his comrades on the beach to get their shields and provide top cover. All over the beach soldiers did what they were told, not caring who gave the commands. They followed them because they made sense. Once again Getarix looked to assess the situation. He noticed a number of soldiers dead and dying on either side of him. One look at the shield of Rufus told him they had to get out of there right away. All it took was for a spear to hit at full thrust at a weak spot on the shield. He looked again over the crest wondering why his leadership was so silent. One look told him. Most of them had been standing in clear view at the water's edge when the attack commenced, and now all lay either dead or dying just like the engineering officer. Getarix muttered to himself, "I did not come here just to die like a human sacrifice."

"What was that?" Jodoc asked.

Getarix ignored him. "How many spears do we have?"

They counted up seven. Getarix ordered them all brought to him. He then stuck his head up and yelled across the beach for each group to gather all their spears and appoint their best spearmen to get ready to return the German spears along with a few Roman ones as interest. He counted about nine identifiable groups.

"Okay, when I say go, spearmen give them hell, the rest of you head back to safety. It's about fifty paces until you'll be safely out of their range."

Getarix took a deep breath and gave Rufus a smack. "Did you hear me? You will need to move that fat carcass of yours."

"I understand."

"Okay, go!" With his command he threw the first spear, which fell short. He cursed in frustration. He was gratified that by the time he gripped his second spear all the soldiers around him, including Rufus, were gone. He also noticed a number of spears were being launched. Two Germans fell into the river and their bodies were floating away as Getarix launched his second spear that went high into the tree line. Again he cursed himself for not paying attention to his aim. As he threw his third spear, it hit him that he had not planned an exit strategy for himself and his spear-throwers. In an instant it came to him.

"Okay spear-throwers, get ready to run on my command!"

He gathered his four remaining spears in his hands, three in his left and one in his throwing hand. He jumped up on to the embankment and yelled, "Go!" and launched his remaining spears. The second one hit its mark. At that he quickly spent his last two and ran like never before, spears bouncing all around. Just as he was about out of range, one of the German spears found its target, landing in his back right through his old leather bag that never left his side. He felt a pain in his back and fell to the ground splashing sand like it was water. Cullen ran forward without hesitation and grabbed him, screaming his name. His muscular arms dragged his lifelong friend a few paces to safety.

"Cullen, blast you, you are tearing my arm out."

"Getarix, you're not dead." Cullen almost cried.

"Not yet. Now let go of me before you finish the job."

"But Getarix, I saw the spear hit you hard. Your chain mail must have saved you."

"Not just the chain mail." Getarix righted himself, pulling his leather bag off his back, the spear firmly attached. When he opened it he found that the spear had cut cleanly through, firmly lodged in the gold buckle of the belt that once adorned the King of the Gauls. As he pulled the spear free, Cullen laughed at the irony of it all. The arm torque had slowed the spear but not stopped it. It still cut through the chain mail and into Getarix's back. Not far enough to kill him, but far enough.

XX

PROMOTION

As a precaution, Cullen was tasked to take Getarix to the unit physician. When they arrived at the hospital tent, the orderly told Getarix to strip to the waist and wait for the doctor. He warned them that the doctor had just arrived and was still unpacking. They waited for about a half an hour and were talking quietly when they had a feeling someone was watching them. Turning, they saw the frozen figure of the physician just inside the tent flap. The light of day surrounded him, blacking out his facial features. He just stood there, silent. Getarix and Cullen began to feel extremely self-conscious. They faced the doctor in silence, almost at parade attention.

"It appears...I am looking at the dead," the doctor said quietly.

Fear streaked though the two of them. Did he recognize them? Would they be turned in? Would they be sent to the gallows after all? Not wanting to give themselves away, Getarix played dumb.

"Dead, sir? I do not know what you—"

"Don't play dumb with me, Getarix."

At that moment, they both recognized the voice of Gullis.

"Duplicarius Gullis, is it—"

"No, it's Physician Gullis now. I just completed my training as a doctor." He ended this statement of revelation with a skip in his voice. "I heard that you were killed when your ships went down. So you survived the shipwreck?"

"No, we were never on the ship—" Cullen added until shut up by Getarix's elbow planted firmly in his ribs.

"Ah, so you finally found a protector to keep your sorry backsides out of the fires you're so skilled at setting."

"You might say that." Getarix explained.

"Well let me look at that back of yours. From what I have heard, you distinguished yourself today. They didn't give me any names, just the story of a young hero. They said that a new soldier just arrived from Portius Itius was the hero of the day. If you were a centurion, you would have received a medal of honour for your effort."

"What effort, saving my hide?"

"Well, you did not just save your own hide, you know. And it did not go without notice. Why am I not surprised you two would be my first cases even when you're supposed to be dead?" They all laughed and caught up on the news.

Gullis cleaned the wound that was not very deep but was only a hand's distance from his spine. He sent them on their way relieved that they were alive. He could find a bit of peace knowing that he was not responsible for their death by talking them into joining the army.

Once Cullen and Getarix arrived back at their tent area, Centurion Faustus impatiently inquired about his injury.

"I am fine, just a bit sore. Do you know who our new doc is?"

"Don't care. Get your horses both of you, and full battle armour."

"But...?"

"No buts. We have been given a mission. It turns out that some Germans in a village about ten miles back have taken this opportunity to rebel. I have no idea what they were thinking with over 40,000 soldiers massed here. Suicide, if you ask me." He paused and looked at Getarix. "As you know, Decion Caecilius was killed in that little action you distinguished yourself in. Getarix, you have been promoted. You are now Decion, a section commander. A commander of fifteen to thirty soldiers. Oh and before you ask, it does not come with better pay, just more responsibility and a greater chance to get killed."

He began to walk away, but stopped and turned around with an afterthought. "Oh yeah, I have assigned Rufus to you, since you seem to like him so much."

"But sir..." Faustus beat a hasty retreat before Getarix could protest any more.

Faustus quickly gathered his cavalry troop of about forty mounted soldiers. The thirty he had trained and brought to the frontier, plus ten augmentees that included Duplicarius Romanus, who acted as the troop commander. Once mounted with their missing kit replaced by the quartermaster, they thundered out of the camp as fast as their mounts would carry them.

By the time they arrived at the edge of the village, their horses were winded and needed a break. Getarix's back was killing him. Faustus hid the troop in the low ground under the cover of a copse of trees. From that vantage point, they assessed the situation. They could see the bodies of five Roman infantry soldiers who had been assigned to occupy the village and keep the peace. The rebels had failed to kill all the Romans and one escaped, shedding all his kit, including his sword belt. He arrived at Germanicus' field headquarters with nothing more than his sweat-soaked tunic, a lightweight woollen shirt that reached his knees. The sweat made the customarily light green tunic look much darker. He could hardly talk, but before long he gave his report. It appeared that the attack had corresponded with the timing of the attack at the river.

"The village was likely a diversion designed to draw the Romans from the river. The main force is across the river. This much I know. If we all went chasing after that village, it would allow the Germans to cross at ease and fall upon us from the rear," Germanicus said as if he was talking to himself. "That is why I am sending such a small contingent back to assess the situation and subdue the rebels if possible."

They were told that all male captives belonged to the legion's tribune. He would take them and sell them to one of the slave traders who plied their trade in the wake of the army. All female and child captives were to be divided amongst the surviving soldiers. All gold found in the village belonged to the tribune. Any gold found outside the village belonged again to the surviving soldiers according to rank.

Germanicus gave Faustus his orders. "Centurion Faustus, you are tasked to do a recce and clear the village if possible. If not, call back for reinforcements. I am expecting the main thrust to cross the river at any time now."

As they hid behind a small embankment observing the village, Faustus concentrated on the now quiet village. As they waited, Rufus asked, "Why did the tribune want only the male slaves? Are they more valuable than the female?"

"Technically everything belongs to the tribune. He is being very generous. I figure he told us to hand over all adult males to him to save your fat carcass, Rufus."

"How's that?"

"Think about it, boy. When you come up to a big brawny barbarian. You think you could get a bag of money for him so you try to save his life. I can assure you that he would not try to save yours. As you are dreaming about how you are going to retire on all the cash, he will usher you to your final retirement. As you hold back, he strikes. Now go and gather some firewood."

The village seemed quiet and it appeared that the rebels didn't have any sentries posted. The town amounted to no more than a small town square that looked more like an off-shaped triangle. They were stationed on one of the long arms that came to a point to their right where it met the other side of the square. Their side of the triangle sported only two buildings. Both of them were to their left, close together and near the corner of the next arm of the three-sided square. There was a dirt trail running between their hiding place and the side of the square. The trail ran behind the two white buildings to their left before it rejoined the Roman road that ran behind the buildings opposite them. Other than the two buildings, their side was clear. It opened up to the rest of the town square that housed nine other buildings. All were white single-story buildings with thatched roofs. The square was paved with cobblestones, and in the centre sat the village well. They could see five two-story buildings facing them across the square. They appeared to have a dual purpose of having the shop on the lower floor and the home of the village shopkeepers above. Just then a man stumbled out of the last building on the right, across the square where it narrowed to a point. He appeared to be drunk and was rooting around in a small pile of firewood. He was unarmed.

Faustus knew he had to grab him to get some intelligence. He pointed to two soldiers closest to him and told them to run and grab him. Glancing over, he noticed one was Rufus and quickly changed his mind. "Not you. I need someone who can run. Jodoc, Cullen, get over there now and grab him. And keep him silent."

In a flash they were across the opening. On their return they were dragging their panicking captive with them. Cullen had his hands in his mouth, almost choking him. He could not get a sound out at all. They took him deep into the trees to squeeze some information out of him. Before long he was gushing information faster than they could understand. Faustus, not knowing the German language well, soon became lost. "Jodoc, what the hell is he saying?"

"He is saying that the leader comes from an inn down the road where the two roads converge. This fellow is called Fritz and he forced the village to rebel. He finished with a weak Hail Caesar."

"I heard that. Where's this leader now?"

"He says he is back at the inn with the bulk of the rebels."

"Okay, that's all I need. Kill him."

Jodoc looked up at him with a question in his eyes.

"Look at his clothes. Do you not see the blood? Roman blood! According to the only surviving soldier, these villagers did not need any encouragement." Faustus gave Jodoc a little nod. That was all the encouragement he needed. As they looked down, they noticed the German's blood began to mingle with the drying Roman blood.

"Rufus, light a fire over there." He pointed to a place deeper in the woods that was in a depression, so no one from the village could see the flames. "You lot, cut some of these fir branches and place them by the fire, not too close."

After that was completed, he ordered his troop to enter the village quietly, dismounted. They split up into groups of three. Three men per building, as instructed. They waited for the signal to fall upon the whole village at once, catching everyone by surprise. Faustus stood in the centre of the square beside the well with his mace held high. As soon as everyone was in position, he dropped his mace. Everyone moved at once. The first man kicked the doors in, the second and third moved in rapidly, swords in hand, screaming at the top of their lungs. The village did not know what hit them. They attacked just before the evening meal hour, where the people would have been least on their guard. It was over before it began. As instructed, the soldiers killed only the men who offered resistance. The rest were taken captive. There were few men in the village, and those few were drunk from celebrating their temporary victory.

Getarix, Cullen, and Jodoc were sent to the closest building just to the right of their hideout. In spite of his protests, Rufus was tasked to attend the fire. Faustus did not have very much confidence in his fighting ability, as he explained it to a few of the other troops before they launched. "I'm afraid he might encounter some irate child and die in his first encounter." Cullen thought it was an unfair assessment but laughed despite himself.

Faustus had chosen Cullen to kick the door in. A quick scan of the little home showed it had no other rooms. The fire pit was in the centre of the one-room hut. There were two bed spaces lengthwise against the wall to the left of the fire pit. To the right were provisions gathered during the summer to hold over the winter. The light of the fire blinded them from seeing the back wall. At the fire pit they made out the figure of someone caught stoking the fire. Jodoc was second in order of march. He went straight for the only person they saw. Getarix went stiffly to the left of the fire pit. His back was beginning to give him serious grief. Nonetheless, he hid the pain from the others. Cullen went to the right to clear the back of the room. All he found was firewood stacked up against the wall. Jodoc, however, discovered a worthy adversary. As he came upon the occupant he was greeted with a red hot poker across the right side of his face. The poker hit his cheek-plate hard, bending it wildly. Where it made contact with his flesh it cut deeply. First he saw the yellow of stars followed by blackness and finished off in the red of rage. He pulled his sword back fully, about to take his second life of the day. As he thrust it toward the offending occupant, his sword was knocked down with a powerful blow. It was almost knocked out of his hand. Jodoc thought they had come upon a den of rebels. He began to swing wildly until he was tackled. When he looked around from the ground he noticed all was quiet with Cullen's full weight on top of him. Getarix still stood on the stone edge of the fire pit with his sword propped into the side of the rebel soldier. He looked like he was in pain. Cullen was getting off Jodoc when he realized it was Getarix who had knocked his sword down and Cullen who had tackled him.

"What the blazes are you doing? Did we come here to kill the enemy or to save them?"

"We were told to kill any men who showed resistance."

"Well what the hell is this?" Jodoc pointed to his cheek where the poker bruised, cut, and burnt him all in one hit.

"It's a woman, Jodoc," Getarix said.

"A what?"

"A woman. You know, like men, but different."

"I know a woman—" Jodoc said as he gave her a good look, only then recognizing her long dark-blond hair. She was a handsome woman about ten years older than Getarix but as tall with broad shoulders and well built. Her eyes told them she was not to be trifled with.

"Okay, so she's a woman, so what! Look what she did to me."

"We are under orders, only the men!"

"Okay, let's say I kill her and we report her as a man."

"Her dead body will testify otherwise."

"I'm not so sure about that." Jodoc was ready to thrust her.

Getarix countered. "After what happened on our last stay at Portius Itius, we are still in deep water. I don't want to push it."

Jodoc knew he had lost the argument. "Okay, but let's keep this a secret, understood?"

"Sure, I'll keep my part secret if you can hide that," a grinning Getarix said, pointing to the now-blistering wound. It glowed red and the swelling caused it to protrude out from his cheek. It did not bleed because the red-hot poker had cauterized the blood vessels as it cut. The cheek plate of his helmet stuck out at a right angle.

"Oh by the gods, I'll never live this down, will I?"

"Not if I have anything to do with it," Cullen said with a smile.

Jodoc submitted himself to his fate. "Well, I don't want her as my war booty, even if they force her onto me." ·

"I would never accept you as a master," she spoke for the first time. All three men just stopped and stared. Not only was she speaking perfect Celtic, she spoke it with an accent that placed her from somewhere in western Britannia.

"What is your name?" Getarix asked. She hesitated until Getarix turned his sword that was planted at her side.

"Gainer," she said defiantly. She looked straight ahead, saying no more.

After they gathered all the captives in the village square, about seven soldiers were tasked to grab fir bows, dip them into the fire and set the village alight. Many of the children were crying but when the homes began to burn the women began to protest and cry out loud and the few men shouted out in anger. They were easily silenced at the tip of a sword. The children on the other hand could not be consoled.

Faustus had the captives moved into the trees and left a small detail to guard them. He gathered the remainder of his troops to move on to the village inn down the road. This time Rufus was mounted with the assault troops.

As they were about to leave to go after the main group of fighters, Faustus got a good look at Jodoc and asked him what had happened. His cheek shone brightly and his helmet was crudely repaired.

Getarix piped up with a sly grin. "He tripped on the door post."

Faustus glanced over to Gainer and simply said. "Yeah, sure he did." He could not hide the trace of laughter. He looked at Jodoc. "Make sure that when you are drinking yourself handsome at some inn, you tell the girl that you faced off Arminius himself or you will just waste your wine." Those in hearing range joined in laughter at Jodoc's expense.

XXI

DON'T HURT HER

They rode at full tilt along the Roman road built by the very hands of the soldiers lost five years before in the Battle of the Teutoburg Forest. It was a short distance to the inn and it appeared they were approaching it from the rear. As the trees cleared, they could tell that the road they were on converged with another and the inn sat on the inside of the fork. They dismounted, using the trees for cover and observed their target.

To the left side of the inn stood a small barn. It appeared that the main entrance to the inn was situated in the centre of the long side across from the barn. A garden shed formed the far side of what amounted to a small courtyard of sorts. Faustus quickly assessed that this would not be as easily taken. He could see holes punched through the wall on the second-floor level at the end of the building.

"Split up! Get near the building, fast!" Just as he said that what he feared happened. Through the holes in the wall, arrows began to rain down on them. Off to his left and back he saw one of his soldiers get hit and fall to the ground. Another arrow hit the shields of other soldiers but did not penetrate. Once they split up and became more difficult targets to hit, the enemy's arrows became ineffective. As soon as they were against the back wall of the inn, they were safe. The barn and shed were quiet. Faustus sent a recce into the barn and around the building.

They returned with news that the barn was clear. It only held a few horses, mostly farm types. They also reported that the rebels had punched holes in the lower walls about eye level. Faustus split his troop into two. Duplicarius Romanus led one group of nine soldiers. He was tasked to clear the back of the inn, circling around the inn, ending at the front door where Faustus would meet them with his group. Faustus led his troops in front, keeping low and silent to hide their movement. As they passed the improvised holes in the walls, Faustus thrust his sword in each opening. The first two holes produced blood on his sword. By the time they reached the third of the four holes along the wall, the Germans inside had learned that it was not a healthy idea to be standing there peering through the holes.

Getarix was just behind Faustus, followed by Cullen and Jodoc. Once they stopped, Getarix took a couple deep breaths and tried to calm the pain from the damaged muscle in his back. When he regained his composure, he looked up. Above the inn door he noticed a sign in the shape of a Boar's Head. Someone, possibly a child, had painted eyes and tusks on it. There was no writing, just the picture.

They had to wait at the door for Duplicarius Romanus to arrive. He had twice the distance to go.

"Sir." Getarix interrupted the thoughts of Faustus.

"What is it?"

"What is the name of this place?"

"I don't know."

Getarix pointed to the sign Faustus missed seeing, having concentrated so much on the holes in the walls.

Getarix guessed. "The Boar's Inn, or the Painted Boar?"

Faustus gave one look and knew instantly. "The Boar's Head Inn."

"Wait a minute, the Boar's Head Inn. Isn't it the place?"

"Yes, it is, or was very popular with men…who felt the urge. Maybe that's why we were selected to do this. They know that none of us have developed sympathy for the master of this house. I just wish I was given a full century of eighty men and not just the thirty or so I trained plus a few extra."

When the duplicarius arrived, Faustus wasted no time. The order of march was Duplicarius Romanus, Centurion Faustus, Getarix, Jodoc, and Cullen, followed by the remainder of the section not otherwise tasked. Rufus was to the rear. As they waited, Faustus had made a quick calculation of his number. He had started with forty men. He had three injured in the village. Left seven to guard the villagers and care for the injured. *That makes ten,* he thought. He lost four on their approach to the inn. *Down fourteen.* He had left seven more to guard the horses and three were guarding the windows on the backside of the building. *That makes twenty-four.* In addition, he had three more stationed at the back door leading from the kitchen. That left him with only thirteen soldiers, including himself. *Getarix's section of five—well four, I cannot count Rufus—plus myself, my duplicarius, and six others. This might be suicide, trying to take an entire building full of rebels with only eleven untried men.*

Unlike the village, this door was assumed to be heavier and barricaded. They had taken one of the support poles from the barn and used it as a battering ram. After the third solid hit from the oaken pole, the hinges gave way. As the door fell it pushed away the tables and benches that had been propped against it. Duplicarius Romanus charged, yelling as he entered. He drove his sword deep into the first belly he came to. Someone charged him from the left. He pushed his shield up into the face of a young blond warrior. The warrior fell backward. Romanus was on top of him in a second, pulling his sword out of the belly of his first victim right into the belly of his second. The youth screamed in pain as his life fled from him. As Romanus pull his sword clear, he bent over the dying blond. A third rebel appeared out of the blackness and drove a dagger up under his amour, deep into his vitals. Romanus turned on his heels. His face showed the shock of death with his eyes opening fully. Mustering the last bit of life left in him, he pulled his sword out of the body at his feet and landed it expertly between two ribs and right into the heart of his third kill within thirty seconds. Having accomplished this task, he collapsed, joining them in death.

Faustus stepped over his now-dead duplicarius. With his second-in-command dead, his plans had to change on the spot. He noticed a single door that let into two rooms at the end of the building to his left.

"Decion Getarix, go left, clear those rooms. Cullen and you two go with him. The rest of you follow me!"

The inn looked like it had been well-kept at one time. Across from the large central door stood a big stone fire pit. The main floor consisted of only three rooms. The kitchen shared the north end with the storage room, which Faustus directed Getarix to clear. The largest room on the ground floor was the great room. The tables were now pushed up against the walls and the door. On the south wall to his right, Faustus saw a staircase. It led to two rooms on the second floor. A narrow balcony walkway ran across the wall in front of him to two more rooms at the north end. These rooms were above the kitchen and storerooms.

Arrows began to shower down from the upper floor. Faustus noticed two of his soldiers fall. Without hesitation he headed for the stairs before the arrows could do any more damage.

Getarix, just as eager to escape the same arrows, darted for the door to his left. The door was positioned in the centre of the interior wall that separated the two smaller rooms from the great room. You had to turn left into the kitchen or right into the storeroom to avoid running into the end of the wall separating the two rooms. He went left into the kitchen but found it empty other than a mature lady who looked like she had been victimized by life itself. She screamed and ducked below the large heavy oak table that dominated the centre of the room. Cullen checked behind the table and found nothing there other than the whimpering old woman.

Once the kitchen was cleared, they entered the storeroom. Getarix noticed the light of the day was fading. Before entering the windowless room, he grabbed two torches leaning by the small door that led outside. They produced a weak orange light but it was enough to do their job. Getarix had Jodoc hold one in each hand as high as he could without setting the inn alight. With torches in hand, he ran behind Getarix and Cullen across the open door into the other room. All three stopped short at a horrific sight that made their blood run cold. There, in the middle of the room sat a man who appeared to be in his early fifties, dead. Getarix froze with visions of a ritualistic killing much like the one he had barely escaped himself. The same kind of killing he had witnessed as a child. Sights and smells he had hoped never to experience again came flooding back. The man was tied to a support post. The victim appeared to have been afflicted by more than twenty stab wounds. Getarix knew he was looking upon a murder scene, a sadistic murder where the culprit or culprits took their time and slowly tortured their victim to death.

Out from between the storeroom shelves a rebel darted for Getarix. Getarix stood there transfixed, fighting a war of memories. Jodoc caught sight of the young rebel and brought the torch in his right hand firmly across his head, knocking him out cold. As he fell back unconscious, the inn went strangely silent. The silence was broken by whispering that came from above them.

That was broken by words of instruction in German. "Stay behind the door. When they come in and engage me, you ambush them from the rear." It took a while for the words to register in Getarix as he regained his presence of mind and translated the German in his head. Before they knew it, they heard shuffling of feet above them as one of the Roman soldiers entered the room. Within seconds his body fell heavily on the floorboards. Getarix looked up and saw the armour and then blood began to drip between the boards. Then a second soldier fell. His blood joined the first and splashed down on them from above.

Without saying a word, Getarix darted out of the storeroom across the great room toward the stairs. He cleared the great room within seconds and was up the stairs running along the adjoining balcony. Halfway across the balcony he was met by other members of their troop yelling at him not to go in there. "Getarix, we have already lost three in that room, including the centurion." Getarix did not even hear their voices as he thundered on past them. As he burst through the door he ignored the man in front of him and swung around to his left, pivoting to the man behind the door. He deflected the first thrust that came from behind the door with his shield. In one fluid motion, still advancing, he used his body's momentum to drive his sword all the way to the hilt into the soft belly of the young assassin. Before he could withdraw his deadly instrument, he felt a sharp pain in his exposed right side. He felt the point digging into his ribs. When he glanced over to his right he saw a young man desperately trying to pull his narrow sword free from the torn chain mail that gripped it. The loops of his chain mail had grabbed tightly onto his sword blade and would not let it go.

The German was a well-built strong youth with long white flowing hair. As he jerked his sword back and forth shallowly cutting and stabbing Getarix, the pain almost caused Getarix to pass out. Getarix dropped his sword, unable to grip the hilt anymore. He had run so fast he outran the others and he knew he was alone. It was clear to Getarix that if he gave up the fight at this point it would be over for him. He mustered his last bit of strength, ignoring the ripping pain of his side and the stiff pain of his back. He dropped to his knees, forcing the sword from the hands of his white-haired opponent. When he landed, his right hand fell onto the hilt of his fallen sword. He tightened his grip and lifted himself to his feet, ramming his sword upwards under the ribcage of the young warrior. Getarix was now face to face with him. He noticed a scar across his left cheek. The dying German suddenly opened his eyes. Getarix was taken aback by the depth of blue in his dying eyes. He stared at him as his life took its leave.

The white-haired youth muttered through the blood now pouring from his mouth. "Don't hurt her." He became heavy on Getarix's sword. Getarix could not look away from his fading eyes. In his mind, Getarix heard his last words again. *Don't hurt her.* It had sounded like he was pleading, even begging. As his life slipped from him, his weight became too much for the injured Getarix to hold. He let go of the blood-soaked sword. The young German fell to the floor

153

with a thud, his white hair scattered across his face. Getarix stood there and just stared at his open eyes. *Don't hurt her.* Who was he talking about? Just then the room seemed filled with Roman soldiers. It occurred to Getarix that from the time he entered the room to now had been less than ten seconds. When Cullen and Jodoc arrived, they almost knocked him over. Once the room was declared cleared and safe, most of the soldiers left, leaving the three friends. They just stood there and stared at the dead youth. Jodoc said that according to the description of the villagers he must have been Fritz, the leader of the rebellion. They were interrupted by a voice from the floor.

"Decion Getarix, I will make sure you are recognized for your valour here. If it's the last thing I do, which it might be." His little speech was broken by a bout of coughing that sent him wincing in pain.

When Faustus recovered, Getarix asked, "Sir, did you hear what he said? Don't hurt her?"

"Yes...yes, I did. Whoever she is, she is yours." By this time, Faustus was on his feet being escorted from the room by two other soldiers.

XXII

SPOILS OF WAR

etarix just stood there. He felt weak all over. So weak, in fact, he had to sit down on the little bed mounted to the wall in the corner of the room. The type made from heavy oaken beams with rope fed through holes creating a weave that held the sleeper up. On top of that was a straw-filled mattress. He landed heavily with all his weight, causing the ropes to stretch some more. As he settled, he felt something under the bed. He did not have enough energy to investigate until he heard some crying. The kind a small child does when they can no longer hold back the tears.

Weak and hurt, Getarix threw his weight to his left, using his momentum to turn himself around. He slid off the bed and gently landed on his knees. He lowered himself until he sat on his feet, steadying himself on the bed with his good arm. Lowering his head slowly, he caught a glimpse of something. He could not make it out because the light was too low. It looked like an animal or a small child. He could hear the muffled sounds of a child's failed attempt to suppress his cries. Getarix took a deep breath and painfully drove his right arm under the bed, grabbing what felt like the arm of a child. As he began to pull with painful effort, he felt the child fighting him. His right side burned badly with pain as he felt his wounds tear open again. It put Getarix in a sour mood. His muscles would not respond, so he rolled backward, using his weight to pull the belligerent child out from under the bed. As he rolled on his back, the child landed squarely on top of him. She screamed for all she was worth. The commotion drew the attention of the soldiers from the next room, where they were searching for anything of value. As Cullen and Jodoc entered the room, they broke in laughter. There on the floor was an irate girl-child, kicking and fighting with all fours. Getarix was so hurt that at this point the fight was about equal. Cullen finally pulled the child off his friend and others helped him to his bed.

"Well Getarix, it looks like we discovered who 'She' is and according to the centurion 'She's yours...congratulations." He finished with a chuckle.

As they were dragging her out, Getarix yelled at them. "Do not hurt her!"

Jodoc cut in. "That makes two, because you also get the one in the village. No one else dare take her on and you kept me from killing her, so again she, too, is yours."

Later, as Getarix was gaining his strength downstairs, he noticed the child was being held by the old gal from the kitchen. Some of the soldiers showed an unhealthy interest in the girl. Koran, a dirty little man from western Gaul, tried to pull the child from the protective arms of the old lady. She struggled desperately. In response, Koran gave her a terrific belt across the face, knocking her off the bench. She held out one of her arms to break her fall and Koran successfully dislodged the child from the old lady's hold. He held her up and tried to kiss her. She screamed, fighting a losing battle. Koran pulled her by her golden hair. She began to cry out of fear more than pain. Suddenly, Koran dropped her, reeling in pain.

As he slipped to the floor holding his head, Isolde saw Getarix standing there with a club in his hand. He gestured to the old lady, now recovered, in simple German. "Take care of her." She nodded, happy to fulfill his wish.

By the time they joined the other villagers, it was almost midnight. The fire was burning brightly. On their approach the villagers craned their necks, trying to spot their loved ones amongst the survivors of the battle. Many of the mothers began to wail when they failed to see their sons as their worst fears were confirmed.

The bleeding had stopped again, and Getarix was feeling better fortified with some crude mead seized from the storeroom of the Inn. They'd had a celebration of sorts before putting the inn to the torch.

Getarix got up and took Isolde by the hand. She did not fight him as he walked her to Gainer and said almost apologetically, "I want you to take care of her for me. Apparently she is mine."

"Apparently...so am I", " she spat out with bitterness.

"Yeah, so I understand." He gestured over to some of the half-drunken soldiers gathered around Koran. "Keep those buggers away from her."

"I'll kill anyone who touches her."

"I wouldn't recommend that."

"Even you!" she muttered. Getarix felt she was serious, and chose not to fight over the issue. He could rest assured the child would be as safe as she ever could be.

They could not move very fast with their newly captured slaves. It was nearly daylight when they arrived back at the winter camp where Germanicus was poised to repel the main German onslaught. As they traveled back, Koran rode up by Getarix on his right, next to the edge of the stone-surfaced Roman road, and said sheepishly, "Hey, Decion Getarix…hum, no hard feelings eh…you know I did not know she was yours. I inquired with the centurion if I could have her but he told me you already had her." Getarix just ignored him. "I don't blame you. I would want to keep her to myself. She is awfully pretty. I bet you could get a really good price for her from the slaver. Girls like that go for a premium. Personally I would just keep her and enjoy her myself."

Getarix looked at him, not knowing what he was talking about. "Girls like what?"

"You know, like her…?"

"No, I don't know what the hell you're talking about. Like what?"

"You know, a man-pleaser."

"A what?"

"A man-pleaser…a prostitute. Hey, I tell you what, I'll buy her from you. Did you hear there was a chest found in the inn containing a large amount of money? Because it was not found in the village, legally it belonged to the surviving soldiers. I'll give you my share in exchange for her."

Jodoc, riding in formation just to the left of Getarix, cut in. "I hear it amounts to three years' pay. A sizable sum, Getarix, about twice what you would get from the slave-trader."

"Whose side are you on, Jodoc?" Getarix began to get irritated.

"What's your issue? She is only a slave. You know, a thing?" Koran said.

Getarix was now getting angry. "Yeah, and twelve hours ago she was a free person, a child, a daughter."

"Technically, yes, however, from what I hear, even though she was the daughter of the innkeeper she was sold to patrons for their pleasure. Therefore, in reality, even then a slave," Jodoc added.

Getarix shot a glare at Jodoc. The sudden movement caused him no slight pain. "Jodoc, what the hell is wrong with you? How old is she? A dozen years at best. Do you want me to turn her over to the likes of him?" Getarix pointed to Koran.

"Well, no, but let's be real here. When you do sell her, Getarix, she will inevitably end up where she was a few days ago, probably, in a brothel somewhere in Rome."

"At least with me you know where she is," Koran said, beginning to sound desperate.

Cullen was riding behind the three of them, listening to their conversation. He sensed his lifelong friend becoming more than a little angry. He noticed that when Getarix took his helmet off for a bit the skin on the back of his neck was getting red. When Koran spoke, Cullen saw the veins popping up on the neck of his friend and he knew that Getarix was about to launch. He kicked Epona forward, forcing himself between Getarix and Koran, sending Koran and his mount off the road.

Getarix yelled at Koran to get into formation, ridding himself of one of his irritants for the moment.

Cullen remained to the right side of Getarix.

"What will you do, Getarix? You can't keep her. If she was older you could grant her freedom and she could take care of herself, but she's just a kid."

"I'm aware of what my problem is, Cullen."

Cullen knew that the kid was not his only problem. He leaned over, catching a glimpse of Getarix's face. His face was ashen white and the look of pain could not be missed. Cullen noticed he was leaning to one side and he was holding his side.

"You're hurt?"

"Not bad."

"Not bad, you're about to fall off your saddle."

"I'll see the doc when I sort out this kid."

"If you don't die first."

"I'll be okay."

"Well, you might not get much for Gainer, but you could at least offload her."

"She is just as likely to kill the slave-trader as to let him sell her. But that still leaves the problem of the kid."

Getarix looked behind him, where Gainer was walking with the child in her arms.

What am I to do? Getarix prayed to the empty air, not knowing if anyone was listening. *What to do?*

It was not until noon that all the paperwork was complete, making legal the ownership of all their recently found booty. The newly created slaves were held in the dirt square of the legion's temporary encampment.

By noon, everyone was tired and badly needing a bath. The weather had turned cold. No snow fell, but it was bone chilling. Getarix, however, did not feel cold. In actual fact he felt hot and flush. With papers in hand he sought out his booty. As he entered the square, he ran into Cullen. Cullen noticed that his colour had returned, but now he looked red and sunburnt. As they searched for Gainer and the child Getarix asked, "So how did you fare, Cullen?"

"Oh, some old lady. Barely got anything for her. However, I think I got better off than you."

Getarix found the child peacefully asleep in the tired arms of Gainer. He did not want to disturb them. He had no reason to. Getarix had not solved his dilemma about the child's future.

Getarix and Cullen became distracted by a small commotion not far off.

Koran was in a bad mood, having been given the old hag he belted in the inn. Centurion Faustus informed him that since he had hit her for no reason, she was considered damaged goods. "Ergo she is yours to do as you please." He only owned her a few minutes before he convinced the slave-trader to take her off his hands.

"What am I to do with her?" Alexander the Greek slave-trader asked.

"Sell her."

"As what? There are few calls for decrepit old grandmothers. She's at the end of her useful life," Alexander said, dismissing Koran.

"Okay, take her off my hands. I'm a soldier. What am I to do with her?"

"Do what many other soldiers do. Set up an apartment in town and keep your new lover there. She might just please you in ways you never knew possible," Alexander said with a chuckle, clearly enjoying Koran's predicament.

"Very funny. Now what will you give me for her?"

"Okay, all I will give for her is two *As*."

"That would only buy a loaf of bread!"

"Then enjoy your meal."

"What?"

"A loaf of bread or nothing."

Once Alexander completed that deal, he dropped his eyes on the child. He looked around frantically. "Who owns that child?"

"I do," Getarix said, narrowing his eyes.

"Where did she come from?"

"The same battle we fought yesterday, you twit."

"No, did she come from the village or did she belong to the Boar's Head Inn?"

"The inn. Why?"

Alexander took his cane and woke the child by pushing it hard into her shoulder. She awoke with a start. In one swift motion, Gainer instinctively swung her hand, knocking the cane to the ground. Alexander recovered it, raising the cane high in the air, ready to beat her for all her life.

Getarix stood between them and simply stared him down.

"My apologies, good sir," Alexander said without conviction. "But my advice to you is to beat such behaviour out of your slaves early or you will wake up one night with a knife pinning you to your bed."

Koran took this opportunity to explain their short history with Gainer, making her un-sellable. Getarix felt like he could break him in two.

"I am not at all interested in the woman. It's the child that interests me." He began to address the child in a gentle voice, speaking in perfect German. "What is your name, child?"

She looked at him through her dried up tears. She was tired and her eyes were bloodshot. In spite of redness, the blue of her eyes still shone through. Getarix noticed Alexander getting down on one knee to look at her in the eyes. "It's okay dear, I won't hurt you. What is your name?"

"Isolde," she said weakly.

"Did you live at the inn?"

She nodded.

"Your daddy was the keeper of the inn?"

At the mention of her father, she shrunk back a bit, but nodded.

"I will take her," he said with too much excitement.

"Hang on here." Getarix felt things were moving too fast. "It sounds like you were looking for her."

"I have a client in Rome who might be interested in a child like her."

"A child like her, or this child?"

Alexander knew he had been found out and dropped the ruse. "Hum, he seems to be acquainted with her. He could make your efforts worth their while."

"What does he wish to do with her?" Getarix did not like where this was going.

Koran took this opportunity to muddy the water. "It's obvious he was a past customer of hers and now he sees his opportunity to have her for—"

"Alaris Koran, do you not have something else to do at this time!" Getarix used his newly acquired rank to rid himself of Koran.

"Good sir, my client can make you not only a rich man, but he has the power of promotions."

"I don't think I am interested just the same. Besides, I was just promoted, thank you very much."

"Let me warn you that my client also has the power to break careers."

"I am a common soldier. I have no career. Good day. She is not for sale. Now leave me alone. Gainer, bring the child!" Getarix began to walk toward his tent line.

Cullen quickly got in step at his side. "Okay, now what?"

"Like I said, I don't…wait a minute. How much did they say we were getting?"

"Nothing, remember, you're not selling."

"No, idiot. The money found in the inn."

"Oh, that. About three year's pay, I hear."

"How much would it cost to set up an apartment in Xanten?"

"Less than three year's pay, I would say."

"I think I have the solution."

"What about Gainer?"

"She is my solution."

"What?"

"Who do you think will take care of the child?"

"You mean you would spend all you just earned on that child?"

"What's wrong with that? From what I hear she earned it in the first place, against her will at that."

Cullen could not help wondering how this was to work as they left the square.

XXIII

LEFT TO DIE

"Getarix, you're done! Look at this mess. What the hell is wrong with you? You should have gone to the doc, or at least taken a bath before sleeping fifteen hours." Cullen tried to pull Getarix's tunic free from his injured side. The green wool was stained with dry blood and white puss that had begun to build up. As he tugged to remove the stiff fabric, it began to tear the wound open again. This time it was not only blood that poured from the tear. Cullen stopped before he caused more damage. The smell was putrid and seized his lungs. When he saw that the skin around the cut was swollen and red, he gently placed his hand near it. It felt like there was a fire burning just below the surface. Infection killed more soldiers than the enemy, and it appeared Getarix was growing a good one. Cullen jumped up. "I'm getting the Doctor."

"Don't be silly, I can walk there."

Just as Getarix stood up, messenger from Centurion Faustus poked his head into the leather tent. "Decion Getarix." Getarix nodded. "Centurion Faustus has ordered you to Germanicus' tent, now. They are there waiting for you now, Decion."

"Well, there you go. Get my chain mail, would you, Cullen." He cinched his sword belt on and slowly and carefully walked to his appointment.

The soldier's tents were all made of leather. The common ten-man tents were of natural brown leather, while the tent complex of Germanicus was a wonder.

The leather of his quarters was painted to make the large complex resemble a solid stone and wood building.

On the inside walls were painted scenes of waterfowl and wild animals that decorated the reception room. On the wall facing the entrance there was a door to the next room. Getarix saw the figures of Apollo and Mars. Presumably they were painted there to guard the door. He sneered at the idea of the gods protecting Germanicus. *If anything,* he thought, *Germanicus would need protection from the gods.*

His musing about the gods was disturbed by voices coming from the room just in front of him. "What did you find, Centurion Caius?"

"Well sir, we probed deep into the Chatti territory and it appears they have retreated to their winter camps for the season."

"Do you have any confirmation of this?"

"We captured a number of Germans and under interrogation they all confirmed the same."

"All of them? You mean to tell me that they were all so willing to divulge the whereabouts of their army with a smile on their face?"

"Well sir, we did have to use persuasion on a few and the ones who survived were too happy to talk," Caius countered.

"Well, I'm not sure if I want to trust my rear flank to a few tortured Germans."

"Sir, we also saw evidence of their movement, and their camps are abandoned. Even most of the civilians have left and they have burned all their farms and villages."

"They could be trying to make us believe that they have left. When we return to Xanten, they attack."

Once Germanicus had finished, another voice spoke for the first time.

"Sir, our supplies are almost exhausted and getting more has become a dire problem. We have more than 50,000 legionnaires, auxiliaries, and non-combatants who need grain, beans, meat, and leather, not to mention metal to repair our armour and many other things. None of which we can take off the land here. Sir, we must return the legions back to the Rhine or the army will begin to starve. We have very few roads established here unlike in Gaul. Moving supplies in the dead of winter will be almost impossible. The few farms here about have been burnt and their grain hauled off."

Germanicus gave it some thought. "Supply-wise, how much time do we have?"

"Four weeks at most…and that is with rationing, sir."

Germanicus cut him off, directing his next question to Faustus. "Tell me what you think about that little adventure you were on, was it a diversion?"

Getarix heard the tired voice of his commander for the first time. "From what we can tell, sir, it was a local incident unrelated to anything else. It was disorganized and by the time we arrived all of them were half-drunk celebrating their little victory. We interrogated all the men and half the women without a single word being said about any bigger scheme. It appears it was all about revenge centred around a youth from the inn. He seems to have begun his little rebellion by the ritualistic murder of his own father."

"Bloody barbarians. So you can say with confidence that it was not meant to be a diversion."

"Everything we saw and heard points to a local event."

"Okay, in what state did you leave the village?"

"What village, sir?" Faustus said with a smile.

Germanicus chuckled at that and made his decision. "Alright gentlemen, prepare the army to move back to Xanten. I want to be clear of this place by the end of the week. Is that understood?"

Getarix heard a number of men declare their concurrence, accompanied by the loud chest-slapping salutes. They began to pile out of the inner room, their minds occupied with the many tasks to be accomplished. As a postscript, Germanicus yelled to Centurion Caius to double his scouts deep into enemy territory as a precaution.

"Now, Faustus, where is this hero of yours?"

"He should be outside waiting, sir."

In a few seconds the door opened again and the tired face of Faustus appeared to summon Getarix.

Germanicus was a tall man. Erect and the very vision of a soldier. The bridge of his nose was straight as a ruler and a bit too long, but this did not take away from the handsome figure he cut.

Getarix by now was light-headed and his fever was beginning to make him feel like he was in the midst of the summer heat and not the cold of early winter. He stood as steady as he could, but he felt like a top turning on its base. He had to concentrate on not moving.

"Decion Getarix, I have been given to understand you have distinguished yourself in battle on two occasions since your arrival here less then thirty-six hours ago. Is this so?"

"I was just doing my duty, sir."

"Mmm, Faustus, I understand you trained this man and many of the others that put down the rebellion?"

"Yes, sir. Decion Getarix is one of the best."

"It would appear so." Germanicus was silent for a while. He turned his back to them and toward his beautiful wooden desk that stood on carved sweeping legs ending in lion claws grasping glass balls. The highly polished top was covered with all kinds of documents and scrolls. Without facing his two guests, he asked. "I understand Duplicarius Romanus was killed in the inn?"

"Yes, sir."

"Too bad. He was an outstanding soldier." Germanicus turned and faced Faustus fully. "So you are short a Duplicarius, are you not?"

"Yes, sir," Faustus said, clearly knowing where this was going. Getarix was still just trying to remain on his feet. Germanicus turned to Getarix and proclaimed, "Congratulations, Duplicarius Getarix. What do you say to that?"

Getarix, not sure what was going on, noticed that Germanicus was smiling. He simply replied, "Thank you, sir."

As they walked back to their tent line, Faustus did not even notice how unsteady Getarix was getting. "Well, two promotions in less than a day. This one comes with a pay raise, you know? That's what Duplicarius means: two times the base pay. Tell Cullen and Jodoc they have both been promoted to Decion. Not bad for a couple of lost Britannians. At this rate you will be Emperor by the end of the month." Faustus laughed. As they approached their tent line, Cullen and Jodoc met them looking concerned.

"Congratulations, Decion Cullen and Jodoc." He paused to let it soak in. "But before you get too excited, you're still outranked by Duplicarius Getarix here. What's wrong, you look like I'm bringing you bad news?"

Jodoc and Cullen were looking at Getarix. Faustus glanced over just in time to watch him collapse.

"Okay, why in the hell did you people wait so blasted long to bring him here?" Gullis was angry.

"Doctor, will he live?" Faustus asked in a matter of fact way. He had learned years ago you may have friends, even brothers of the sword, but you never invested your emotion in them or your mind would not survive. Occasionally he succeeded in doing this.

"He had a chance if I was able to clean his wounds as soon as he arrived. Now look at this, even his earlier wound on his back has festered up. He will not be able to be moved if you want him to survive at all. He must stay behind and if he is strong enough he just might recover."

"What are his chances?"

"None, almost none if he is lucky."

"If we take him with us?"

"Absolutely none."

With 50,000 soldiers and others, there will always be a small group who cannot be moved. A small detail of eight soldiers were left to care for the infirm, unfortunately none with medical training—none could be spared. They were instructed that when the sick and injured were well enough or had died, they were to follow behind, that is if the weather made it at all possible. No one in the detail felt any sense of honour at being left with the sick, injured, and dying. As they assessed their situation, not one among them had made a very good impression upon their respective leaders. The Duplicarius who was left behind had charges laid against him. Charges he refused to divulge.

Ortwin had earned his place amongst the detail. He knew that his infantry centurion saw him as weak and expendable. It was no secret that their chance of survival was slight to none. Their duplicarius knew this very well.

"Alright, this is how it's going to work. There is only a small amount of rations left behind for all of us. The sick will receive nothing. Is that understood? Let them starve. All the rations…we will eat and we will come out alive and maybe this winter might even be comfortable. Is that agreed?"

All agreed with the duplicarius. Ortwin felt it was wrong but lacked any courage to speak up. Besides, he was out-ranked and such arguments lasted no longer than five seconds. And if he felt inclined to fight it out in a sword battle with anyone in their little detail, it would last half that time. This did not stop him from going into the large tent of the wounded and lighting the fire so they would not freeze to death. As he lit the fire it gave some light throughout the tent. He wandered from bed to bed, seeing if any had died. Some had. One patient he noticed had difficulty breathing. When he got closer, he recognized him from their days in basic training.

"Getarix. Getarix, wake up."

Getarix awoke enough to mutter, "Get Cullen!"

"Cullen is gone. He went to Xanten with the rest of the army for the winter."

"Get me some food. How long have I been out for…why is it so quiet?"

"The army is gone."

"Gone…why, where? Did Cullen go with them?"

At this Ortwin knew Getarix was not taking anything in. When he went to the duplicarius about the request for food, he was strongly rebuffed and threatened.

He wandered through the burnt-out ruins of the camp, scrounging for anything to help. All that remained of the once-large encampment were their two tents. One held the dying and the other was for the detachment of eight soldiers left to care for them. Ortwin felt he owed Getarix for saving him back in basic training. His mind rehearsed the incident where he was overheard mocking their instructor, Cassius. He would never forget the look on his instructor's face as he went after Getarix, yelling, "Who wants to die?" Ortwin felt the same fear as he had so many months prior. Getarix took a beating for him when all he needed to do was reveal who made the comment. He even heard Getarix telling others that they were not to report Ortwin. *That's it. I will do whatever I can, even if it means giving my own rations to keep him alive.*

"Where do you think you're going?" the duplicarius yelled at Ortwin as he was leaving their tent with his ration of porridge. Before Ortwin could get a word out, his commander answered for him. "You are taking that food over to one of the dying rats. Get back here and I want to watch you eat that right here, right now." He looked up and finished as Ortwin sat on his bunk and began to eat the bowl of porridge. "This man is never to leave this tent with food and at every meal he will be observed eating. Is that understood? Otherwise he, too, will be left to starve." The other six soldiers all agreed in chorus.

Once Ortwin had finished his fill, he went to Getarix wanting to explain why he was unable to bring him some food. When he arrived, he saw that Getarix was much worse off than before. He felt like he was giving off more heat than the fire. Then Ortwin saw the wound on his side. When he opened the dressing, he almost lost the newly placed porridge. The puss was oozing out, giving off a terrific stench.

"I need to clean this." It hit him then that all the medical supplies the doctor had left were gone. A quick inspection found them in the other tent in a trunk under the fat backside of the duplicarius as he played dice, losing his pay to the great joy of the rest of the other soldiers. Ortwin withdrew before his presence was noticed. The light was fading and late afternoon brought some clouds that threatened snow. He was lost and did not know what to do. He had always hated himself for being weak and inadequate, but never so much as now. To his great shame, he felt like he was going to cry. He wandered over to where the kitchen tents once stood. When he was off duty, he would go and help the cooks. It was the only place where his work was appreciated. He just stood there looking at the scars on the ground where the tables had stood. He stood at the spot with worn grass, where he had made the bread for Germanicus and his staff.

"Bread!" He said aloud. Before they had left, they threw out a large amount of bread. Most of it was spoilt but some was still edible. He remembered that they had tossed it over the small embankment.

He gathered up a couple of armfuls and took them to the tent where the sick were held. He was unsuccessful in rousing Getarix. It was then he got the idea to use the worst of the bread and treat it like bandages. He went back to the embankment and gathered the green-covered bread and stowed it under Getarix's cot. He carefully removed the old dressing that wrapped around Getarix. Ortwin heated some water on the fire and found a rag. He washed the wounds, making sure to clear the puss out as best as he could. He placed the mouldy bread over the wounds. He took the old dressing, wrapping it tightly around him, holding the bread in place. As he was stowing the extra bread under the cot, he discovered a leather bag. When he examined it he discovered that the cover had been repaired. Inside he found woollen leggings of the Celtic kind worn in Britannia. Instantly he knew that the bag belonged to Getarix. He threw it on the ground, feeling guilty for invading his personal things. As it landed, he heard the distinctive sound of a heavy kind of metal. Curiosity got the better of him. He examined the contents and discovered the arm torques and dagger at the bottom of the bag. It hit Ortwin that the rest of the crew left behind overlooked the idea of looting the personal belongings of the sick. He knew that it would not take long for the idea to rise to the surface. He panicked at the idea of these things being looted. He jumped up and darted out of the tent with the idea of hiding the bag in a small pit where it could be recovered later. He ran blindly away from the two tents, looking over his shoulder to be sure no one saw him. As soon as he looked again in the direction he was running, he landed right in the chest of the duplicarius returning from relieving himself.

"What the hell? Ortwin, where are…what have we here?" He rudely ripped the bag from his hands. He did not bother to unbuckle the straps. With a mighty tug, he tore open the bag and dumped the contents on the ground. The gold glittered in the moonlight as they tumbled, landing hard on the frozen ground. "Now look here?" He picked up the arm torques and dagger. "Looting the sick, are we?"

"No, sir." The Duplicarius grabbed Ortwin by the neck, almost breaking it.

"Don't you lie to me, you maggot. It would bring me great pleasure to execute you for this crime today. I haven't killed anyone lately and you seem to give the urge." He let go of Ortwin, who fell to the ground gasping for air. "But tonight I feel generous and I will spare you." He gave the gold a closer examination. "I will, however, need to confiscate these items. You can keep the leggings. I was wondering about you. To think I thought you were trying to save the lives of those dying rats. But all along you were farming them for their belongings. You and I might just get along. We'll have to be sure that whoever owned this gets his reward coming to him on the other side of the river, eh?"

"Sir," Ortwin muttered weakly.

"Show me the bed space of the owner of this."

Ortwin's mind was reeling. After all of his efforts to save the life of his friend, he now was forced to lead his murderer to his bedside. He felt weak, weaker than ever before in his life. His self-hate burned deep in his soul. As he approached the tent he had visions of turning around and killing the duplicarius before he realized what hit him. But he knew he lacked the courage to do anything. With that thought, a wave of shame swept across him. As he entered the tent and walked toward the bed space, he seriously contemplated ending his own life later that day. But alas, he even lacked the courage to do that.

"He is still alive, but barely. Let's speed it up a bit, eh?" The Duplicarius pulled out the golden dagger looked at the blade and drove it deep into the body of its victim.

"You know, it's actually funny." He rudely pulled the dagger from the now-dead body. Ortwin just gave him a mystified look.

"To be killed by your own blade." The Duplicarius laughed at his sick joke as he left the tent, wiping the murder-soiled blade on his red cape.

Ortwin fell on the stool, completely defeated and only wanting death for himself. He felt the body to see if he was still alive. His chest was silent and no air came from his mouth or nose.

He got up and slowly walked to the other end of the tent and sat on the stool next to Getarix. He thought at least he had saved the life of his friend, if not the life of an unknown comrade.

XXIV

UNLIKELY HERO

As Ortwin sat there trying to make sense out of what had just happened, he heard the rest of the guards come toward the tent. *The bread! If they find the bread, they will kill Getarix for sure.* He got to his knees and quickly pushed the bread under the leather tent flap. When the guards thundered into the tent, his head was clear under the cot of Getarix.

"What the hell do you think you're doing?" the first one through the door yelled, drawing his sword and moving toward Ortwin.

"Leave him alone, you," the duplicarius yelled back. "He is just getting ahead of us. It appears our little Ortwin has been farming the sick all along." The duplicarius laughed. "What did you find there?"

"Um, nothing, the bed space is completely empty."

"Okay boys, each one of you get one. It's like a lottery. Ortwin, you already have your prize." They all laughed at the perceived misfortune of Ortwin. As they dug into the belongings of the dead and dying, some won a great prize, others—like Ortwin—collected nothing.

The guards quickly retreated with their treasures to their own tent. Ortwin was so thankful that they had forgotten to kill their victims. He quickly replaced the bread lest someone noticed it outside. Over the next few days he spent most of his time with the dying, keeping their tent warm. Getarix did not change much. He felt like he was burning up. Most of the time Ortwin would uncover him and at times pack a little snow around his head. It made sense to him that if something was too hot, cool it down. Twice a day, he removed the old bread and replaced it with new pieces of the flat bread he had helped the cook make. Soon it was impossible to find any without it being covered with green mould. His mates thought he had lost his mind. As the sick died off, he would tell the duplicarius, who simply responded, "Let them rot where they die." Ortwin began to fear for his own life. He lacked courage but not intelligence. He knew the duplicarius would not risk leaving him alive. It seemed obvious that they planned to desert and strike out in the opposite direction of the Roman winter camps. Ortwin would certainly be killed on their way out.

As the days built into weeks, Ortwin noticed that Getarix was beginning to cool off. One night when he went to stoke the fire in the dead of the night, he heard a noise behind him.

He had let the fire die down to a few coals, so they only gave little light. Ortwin feared that he was about to be ambushed. He turned around unarmed, willing to accept whatever fate stood before him.

To his utter delight, it was Getarix himself sitting uneasily on his cot. Ortwin squeaked out his name, holding back sobs of joy. This was the first time he could remember accomplishing anything praiseworthy.

"Water," Getarix said weakly. Within a second Ortwin held the ladle full of cold, fresh water to his dry, cracked lips. When he took a large gulp it hit his empty stomach with a bang.

"How long have I been out?"

"Almost two weeks."

"By the gods I'm hungry. Where is Cullen? Where is everyone?"

Ortwin outlined the situation quickly as he rooted under the cot and found some old bread with as little green on it as possible and apologetically handed it to his friend. Getarix quickly ate the bread, ignoring its condition as Ortwin filled him in on all the details, including the dubious leadership of the duplicarius. As Getarix heard the narrative he began to get angry. When it boiled over, he stood with the intent of running into the other tent. As he quickly stood up his head went blank and he almost fell back on Ortwin, who was sitting next to him. Ortwin steadied him and as he settled back down his head cleared enough to regain control.

"I think you need to gain your strength before you try anything. The duplicarius may not be an ethical soldier, but he is a good one. I will bring whatever food you can eat. Unfortunately, it might only be that green bread."

"It may not please my mouth, but I am sure it will strengthen my body."

Over the next few days, Getarix regained his strength on mouldy bread and water. At night he worked out the kinks in his body, first with short walks, then short runs through the forest. After a week he felt almost as good as new. He knew he had to confront the wayward duplicarius before the dead of winter trapped them. The last of the other sick soldiers all had died, leaving no reason to remain. In the mind of Getarix the time was now.

The fire was almost out and Getarix and Ortwin could feel the cold enter the tent. There was no reason to stoke the fire. Now was the time to confront the others in the next tent. Once Ortwin had explained what had happened to the gold from his leather bag, Getarix had begun nursing a grudge that had grown to full maturity over the weeks.

"I'm sorry, Duplicarius Getarix, but they have all the weapons locked up in one of the chests. I dare not ask for them. I was able to slip mine out without notice."

Getarix took hold of Ortwin's infantry sword. It was shorter than the longer cavalry sabre Getarix trained on. The infantry swords, or *gladius,* were made shorter to reach just past the shields. This enabled the foot soldiers to thrust their swords into the enemy as they piled up against their shields without elbowing the row of soldiers behind them.

Getarix made a mental adjustment as he held the sword, feeling its balance.

"Okay, Ortwin, I want you to hang back and get ready to grab a sword if someone drops his. Otherwise, stay back. It would be a waste for you to jump in unarmed. Is that understood?"

"Yes, sir." Ortwin could not believe his ears. He had never in his life ever felt a part of a team. For that matter, he did not remember ever being valued at all. At that moment, he felt a wave of courage come over him. He felt like he could even die for his newfound leader.

Getarix was dressed only in his green tunic that was badly in need of a wash. It was stained with dry blood where both the spear and sword had torn into his flesh. Around the tears there was a build-up of dried puss. On his legs he wore his old Celtic leggings to fend off the cold. He chose not to wear the cloak his mother had made him. Instead he wore Ortwin's red cape, that of a Roman soldier. When he entered the tent he did not want to be mistaken for a German and have the whole group pounce on him at once.

Ortwin was in his green tunic covered with chainmail. Getarix thought of wearing Ortwin's chainmail, but quickly concluded that Ortwin's small stature ensured it would never fit, and armour was not known to stretch.

Earlier that evening, Getarix had sent Ortwin over to the other tent to inform them that he had died, leaving no more sick to tend to. As the two had hoped, the crew broke open the small ration of wine left behind for them.

"Duplicarius Getarix, why didn't we tell them you were dead this morning? By now they would be blind drunk and could offer no resistance."

"By now they would be ten miles away. If I were them I would not hesitate to clear the area while the weather holds, killing you before departing. They would not want to travel at night, so they will wait until morning. It would only be logical that they would lighten their load of a few wineskins with a celebration."

As they peered through the tent flap, they saw the scene of the duplicarius at the far end, half-drunk, dancing like an idiot, creating a spectacle for the others to cheer and egg on. Getarix noticed they wore only their green tunics. Their leader had tied his off at the waist with the belt stolen from Getarix. The golden dagger hung off it on his right hip and the arm torques adorned his upper arms. Seeing his family heritage on the body of such a good-for-nothing, Getarix had to remind himself of his plan and not to act on impulse. The duplicarius stood at the far end of the tent on the low crate he had been using as a seat. He grabbed the dagger of Vercingetorix the Great with his right hand and began to swing it wildly, recounting his great victory in killing the weapon's owner. His audience faced him, sitting on cots that lined either side of the tent. This left an aisle open leading straight to the main attraction.

Getarix pulled out an old iron knife he had brought with him from Britannia and handed it to Ortwin. It was too worthless to steal.

"Here, take this. Hang back by the door. If you need to defend yourself, use it. Otherwise, lay low. If I am killed, you had better head to Gaul at full speed."

Once he had given Ortwin his final instructions, Getarix threw back the tent flaps and thundered in, pointing Ortwin's sword directly at the duplicarius, proclaiming in Latin, "I am Duplicarius Getarix of the Fifth Legion and I arrest you in the name of Emperor Tiberius for murder and treason." Getarix was hoping for resistance. His anger burned so deeply in his soul that killing the lot would do him good.

By the time he had finished his declaration he had advanced to the middle of the tent. To his left sat three stunned, half-drunk soldiers and three to his right.

The soldier seated directly to his right spoke up as he drew his sword. "Hey, you are supposed to be dead!" He began to rise to his feet, sword fully drawn.

Without taking his eyes off the duplicarius, Getarix quickly drove Ortwin's infantry sword deep into the soldier's heart.

Still looking at the duplicarius, Getarix said, "Now, you are dead!"

He let his first kill fall, freeing his sword for the next one who would make a bad choice. The remaining five junior soldiers just sat there, stunned.

"Now get down from there and put my dagger away."

"Your dagger? I killed the one—" He went silent, knowing he had confessed too much.

"You thought you killed me?"

"Ortwin, I'll personally—" the errant NCO hissed.

"You will do no such—"

The duplicarius lunged for him. As he jumped, Getarix drove his sword at the belly of his adversary. Without seeing his hand move, the duplicarius used the gold dagger and practically knocked the sword from Getarix's grasp. Getarix knew he had to get his bearings quickly or he would die even quicker. He had regained much of his strength, but not all. He drove his shoulder into his adversary's chest, throwing him back. The duplicarius fell to the floor among the cooking utensils. His arm hit the handle of a pot of porridge, knocking it on him. The hot wheat paste spread across his chest, scalding him. He was not on the floor very long, but enough time to give Getarix a chance to regain his balance. When the duplicarius had fallen next to the hot stove, Getarix was facing the third soldier on his left. The soldier had his short infantry sword out, ready to thrust into the temporarily disorientated Getarix. Getarix did not hesitate. He thrust his gladius deep into the man's chest. One of the other soldiers near the tent's door stood to attack Getarix. He began to lunge forward. Seeing this, Ortwin came from behind, covering the mouth of his victim with his left hand, pulling him back and sliding the knife across his voice box with his right, silencing him forever. He fell to the floor, grasping his throat as his life flowed from him. Ortwin just stood there realizing he had responded just as they were trained to do. To his great relief no one noticed. Their attention was on Getarix.

Getarix quickly freed his sword from the chest of his last opponent. The duplicarius was using both hands to recover from the floor, giving Getarix the opportunity he needed. Without any ceremony, he thrust the sword into the belly of his treasonous counterpart. He did not wait for him to fall before he pivoted around, sword in the un-guard position, before he could be attacked from behind.

He saw Ortwin standing before their fourth kill of the day.

"I am Duplicarius Getarix, and I am now in charge of what is left of this detachment. We will leave before light tomorrow. You three will spend the night preparing a funeral pile for the poor victims you let die like rats." Hearing this and realizing they were down to three, they knew they were defeated. Getarix had Ortwin confiscate their weapons, locking them in one of the trunks.

After he had placed the key around his neck, he said, "Now, you three gather together all the bodies of your comrades murdered and build a proper funeral pile for them. Now." He looked down at the dead guards. "These four the wild animals can have. Ortwin, where are the horses kept?"

"No horses, sir."

"No horses?"

"No, sir."

"Well, we have little time to lose. Weather pending, we leave before first light tomorrow. We'll burn the tents and bury what won't burn or we can't carry. Now make me some of that good army porridge." With that he sat down heavily, having exhausted what strength he had gathered. It was apparent he had not fully recovered, but the greatest challenge was out of the way.

The weather was good and their three offending soldiers did not cause any grief for fear of their lives.

XXV

ABANDONED

When first light came, Getarix felt as tired as he ever had been in his life. A Roman soldier was expected to be able to march up to twenty miles a day with full kit. He figured that they would have to do better than thirty if they had any chance of making it to Xanten before the dead of winter froze them in place. Getarix calculated that they could make the distance in five days at thirty miles a day. His two fears were his own condition and how co-operative his three captives would be. The first day was a success. They were dressed in all the heavy woollen clothes that could be scrounged. They had discarded their heavy armour. During the day they shed a few layers as the constant movement warmed their bodies better than any amount of wool could. Ortwin rejoiced with every meal cooked because it meant he had to carry less weight with every bite. The first day they covered thirty-five miles before Getarix felt the need to bunk down for the night. He ordered the three captives to gather a large pile of wood to keep a strong fire burning in order to fight off the cold of the night. Ortwin prepared a healthy dinner of wheat porridge and everyone ate heartily. They divided the night watch amongst the five of them, Ortwin taking the first and Getarix taking the last watch.

After four bowls of the warm porridge, Getarix could not stay awake even if he tried to. In his sleep he had vivid dreams of being lost in the cold. First he felt like he was burning up. Later the heat gave way to bitter cold. He felt like he was shivering in his dreams. He forced himself awake. Getarix opened his eyes to the darkness of the night. As he awoke, it hit him he had not been dreaming about the cold.

The fire was out.

Only a few embers remained in the fire pit. He desperately peered through the darkness as he stumbled toward the pile of wood only to discover that it, too, was gone. He grabbed some dry grass, placing it amongst the hot coals. When the grass ignited, it gave an intense light for a few seconds. That was all he needed to survey the situation. The wood pile was truly gone. The footprint of the fire explained why he had dreamed about burning up. Someone had taken all the wood and placed it on the fire. It was totally consumed, leaving nothing to burn. He heard Ortwin in a fitful sleep but the bed spaces of their three captives were empty. It all became clear to Getarix. They had built up the fire so it would burn for a long time, thus giving them a head start. Then Getarix discovered that all their weapons were gone, including the bow and arrow needed to hunt game to supplement their wheat porridge. *Wheat porridge…* "Ortwin, wake up!"

"Why is it so cold…?"

"The wheat?"

"It's gone, and so is my sword."

Getarix felt for his leather bag only to discover his arm torques and the dagger were missing.

He was so mad he swore and cursed the ground the three of them walked on. "Okay Ortwin, let's get moving. We have no reason to remain here. Besides, sleep will not come back to me." Without hesitation they grabbed their cloaks that passed as a bed and continued down the path as fast as they could. Their pace began to slow as the morning sun began to warm them. After a short rest when they ate some snow for water, they were back on their way again. By nightfall, Getarix figured they had travelled about forty miles. They were absolutely dead tired. All they wanted to do was to sleep. Unfortunately, their tinderbox had gone along with their weapons and the food.

"Ortwin, do you know how to make fire from rubbing sticks together?"

"Can that be done?"

"Well, that answers that. Get up, let's go," Getarix said with determination he did not feel. "We can't just sit here waiting for the shore of death's river to arrive."

"I thought you didn't believe in that. Crossing the river of eternal life?"

"I don't…I don't think I do. I feel we will know soon enough, though?"

They stiffly got off the ground and slowly began to move toward their goal or death. They were not sure which. The temperature dropped dramatically. As their muscles loosened up, the wind increased, throwing snow in little swirls. Then it began to really snow. Ortwin took hold of the cape Getarix was wearing because at times he could not see his friend who was no more than an arm's length away. The snow hit their faces and melted from their breath. When the newly melted water landed on their short beards that had grown in the last few weeks, it froze in place. By midnight they both were sporting long icicles from their faces. Many times they would lose the path, only to discover their error when their shins would run into fallen trees. They would stop, look around, get back on the path and slowly carry on. Just before dawn, the temperature took another dive, and their clothes could no longer keep them warm. Getarix was really feeling his weakness. He began to wonder if it had been a bad idea to leave their camp so early. It might have been wiser to have gained his strength before heading out. He felt his head spin and he feared he was going to pass out. He could no longer feel his legs. When it came to his feet, he was astounded how something so numb could hurt so badly. His knees gave way and he hit the trail. Ortwin, walking directly behind, fell on top of him.

"I mu…I mus…I must stop jus…just for a moment…just a little rest…"

Ortwin was so tired he did not protest, in spite of the grave danger stopping would pose. Within seconds, he heard Getarix snoring, then he was scared. He grabbed Getarix and shook him violently. "Getarix…Getarix, wake up. Wake up, will you."

"No…leave me alone. I want to sleep just a little sleep…" He snored again.

"Get up, you, or you will freeze to death."

"What are you talking about? I'm not cold at all. I feel warm and sleep…"

Ortwin knew he would surely die if he let him sleep much longer. Having grown up in a colder climate, he remembered losing a friend in the freezing weather. He looked around and found a broken branch about the size of a man's arm. He stood up and began pounding Getarix mercilessly. After the third hit on the back, Getarix awoke completely. He stood up to defend himself from the offending branch. "Ortwin, what the hell is wrong with you?"

"You're awake now, are you?"

"Yeah, you jerk." Getarix could barely get that out, he was shaking so violently. "I was comfortable, you idiot. Now I feel colder than ever before in my life because of you."

Ortwin began screaming, "You British pigs are just weak! You can't handle anything!" As he said this he was poking him with a stick.

Getarix was getting visibility irate. "Ortwin, what the hell is wrong with you? I'll snap you—" He lunged for him. Ortwin jumped out of the way and ran down the path, Getarix hot on his heels. About a hundred paces down the path the angry Getarix caught his prey. He threw him to the ground mad enough to kill him. Ortwin fell on his back and instantly Getarix was sitting on him, his fist deployed, ready to strike. He paused because Ortwin was laughing in hysterics. "What the…have you gone mad?"

"You're warm now, aren't you?"

Getarix paused and realized that he had stopped shivering and indeed felt warm. Even in his legs he felt the warmth from his blood running through them when he had been running. Getarix realized that Ortwin had once again saved his life. He stood up, helping his benefactor up. He, too, was laughing. "Looks like I owe you my life again, eh?" They began to walk, not wanting to stop moving again.

"We're not home yet."

"No, but if we make it, I owe you. Mind you, if you tell a soul about this, I'll kill you." Ortwin just laughed. "How did you know?"

"I grew up in the forest of Germania. Every year someone would get lost in the forest and die. That teaches you a few things."

"Obviously the right things. I thank you."

"Not necessary. Hell, if you died I would not stand a chance."

The storm of the night gave way to morning sun that warmed their bodies. In the light of the sun they saw a mile marker. They were dismayed that they had only traveled five miles all night. They found a small hillock that faced directly toward the sun and out of the wind. In spite of the cold, the direct sun had melted some snow into a little pool of water. They drank their fill. As the cold water hit their empty bellies they felt the pain of hunger that reminded them just how famished they were.

"Getarix, I recommend we sleep here, safe from the cold during the day and carry on later today and into the night, when constant movement is needed to stay alive."

"But we will lose the best travelling conditions."

"Yes, and avoid the best dying conditions."

"You win, forest man."

As they were getting comfortable, Ortwin said, "I don't understand something."

"What?"

"That girl you got. Why don't you sell her?"

"Would you like to be sold?"

"No, but, she's just a—"

"Just a slave? What made her so? Born to the wrong person? Did she commit a crime deserving to lose her freedom?"

"No, I guess not. But nonetheless she is still a slave."

"One I own and as such I can do as I choose, right?"

"I guess."

"What I don't understand is, if I choose to rape her and then sell her to a brothel, no one would say a thing. But when I choose to treat her like a human…"

"I guess most people would just…" Ortwin was slipping into sleep.

"I am not most people." Getarix joined him in slumber.

Getarix was woken by something scratching his leg that slipped outside his cloak. He looked down and saw a small woodland animal crawling over him to reach the pool of water. The second the animal reached the water, Getarix in lighting reaction had his neck in his firm grip. As furious as the animal was, Getarix was more so. Ortwin woke up by the commotion.

"Lunch, anyone?" Getarix asked with a smile. It was a few hours after midday. Fortified with more water and a meal of raw badger meat, they moved fast, covering ten miles by sunset. That night they covered another ten, however the next day the weather had disintegrated to such a degree that sleeping during the day would have resulted in the same fate as their second night out. They bashed on, hunger and exhaustion slowing their progress as much as the weather did. The fifteen miles they managed during the day were the longest in their lives.

This time Getarix kept Ortwin going. "Only a day's march to go, I figure. We can do it. We must do it." As he said these words, he did not believe them himself. He noticed he had lost his peripheral vision. It was like he was looking through a pipe. Soon they were no longer walking. They were simply stumbling toward their goal. By morning they were just stumbling. The mile marker told them they had gained only six miles all night, and a clear night at that. They could hardly notice it, but the sky was gathering her troops for a mighty onslaught on the land. The clouds were dark and the wind gave warning of the impending battle. It was a good thing they did not notice these things. They would have simply given up, choosing the warmth of a frozen death.

Neither of them knew where the warm hand came from. *Maybe this is what it feels like crossing the river to the other side,* Getarix reasoned. When they awoke, they found themselves in the warmth of the all too familiar leather army tent. Ortwin thought he'd had a crazy dream and they were still back at the frontier.

"You were almost gone. Thank the gods we found you."

"Who are you...where am I?"

"I am Marcus Sabilius. Of the Fifth Alaudae, Duplicarius of the patrol who discovered your half-frozen corpse."

"That's good. My friend?"

"He's okay, almost fully recovered. If you are ready today, we will head back. We were expected back two days ago."

Some weeks later, Getarix was in the bath. People had noticed that he favoured the warm bath. Matter of a fact, the warmer the better. He spent much of his free time there. On that day, he was called to the entrance, where two dishevelled soldiers stood with a bag in their hands.

"What is it?"

"Duplicarius, are these the three who escaped your custody?" They emptied the bag, and three heads fell to the ground. In an instant Getarix knew they were the three.

"Well, sir, I'm told these must be yours as well." The senior soldier handed him his lost leather bag. "We found this on the three frozen soldiers last night." Getarix felt the bag for the gold when senior soldier said, "Don't worry, friend, it's all there. Anyone who clubs those two morons, Aquilla and Cassius, is a friend of mine."

Getarix thought back to the night of their course party when they had dropped their course instructors, never realizing that such an act would offer them so much good will. He could not believe his fate. Once again, his family gold miraculously returned.

"Did they give you a fight?"

"Not a bit. The gods froze them to a tree. They just sat there quietly waiting for us, and they were extremely co-operative."

The army used the rest of the winter to train, preparing for the spring campaign. Getarix had Cullen to thank for saving his two new charges from the clutches of Alexander the slave trader, who had become obsessed with the little girl. Even the astronomical sum he offered for her was rejected. The other soldiers thought Getarix had gone mad turning down such a profit. Instead, he was forced to spend all his money on an apartment he did not even live in just to keep a slave girl safe.

In his report about their escape from the winter, Getarix highlighted the role Ortwin played throughout the adventure. He recommended he be assigned to Gullis the physician as an intern. As his report stated, Ortwin had a natural instinct for all things medical. He very quickly became qualified and in a few short years he was assigned to the III Augusta Legion stationed in Ammaedra, Africa, as a physician. Like Getarix, he could never absorb too much heat. For him Africa was perfect.

XXVI

SNATCHED

Spring could never come soon enough for Getarix. It seemed he spent most of his free hours at the bath. He favoured the heat of the caldarium. After the warm baths of the tepidarium, he would spend most of his time in the much warmer caldarium. These baths had their floors heated from a crawl space below, where some hapless slave would expend his short life keeping the fires going, keeping it so hot that the bathers were issued wooden clogs to prevent them from burning their feet. Getarix would just sit there for hours, soaking in the warmth. He found he could never get enough of it, the hotter the better. He would sit there and talk with his friends. He would sit there and watch the entertainment put on by the bath. He would sit there and listen to one of the lecturers the bath would engage. He would eat at the bath. It became his second home. However, he never set foot in the cold bath, the fridgidarium.

When he was not in the bath, he was busy training, rebuilding his strength and keeping fit, counting the minutes until he could return to the heat of the bath. He hardly set foot in the apartment rented for his two slaves. As it turned out, Gainer was a trained midwife and had built a sizable practice among the young wives and girlfriends of the soldiers. The money she made paid for their food. Getarix let her live as if she was a free woman—it was easier that way. It solved his immediate problem: what to do with the child. The rare times when Getarix stopped by, he would just sit there and watch. He was afraid to do anything more for fear of Gainer. During his visits he could hardly keep his eyes off Isolde. The light would shine off her light golden hair with the brilliance of a bronze mirror. He seldom saw her deep blue eyes. She would look down at her feet whenever Getarix spoke to her. He was always sure to keep his voice low and gentle. She never once looked at his face. Getarix wrestled with the memory that he was the one who had killed her brother. He knew at the time he'd had to, but wished he hadn't. His dreams were haunted with the vision of those blue eyes and the last word of a dying brother. *Don't hurt her.* He wondered why he was not like the others, and some days questioned if he should sell the two of them and be done with it. He had no quarrel with her brother and admitted he would probably do the same if the Romans were in Britannia. He knew Isolde had seen him do it. Maybe in that room he had made a covenant with the young rebel and felt bound to keep his dying wish by protecting that only thing the young man valued, his sister. Maybe Getarix identified with the sister, having spent the greater part of his life in a place where he, too, was powerless and used for the benefit of others. These did play a role in his desire to protect Isolde, he knew, but he had to admit that when he looked upon her he saw what amounted to a perfect work of art. Such art deserved to be treated with respect and the only way he knew how to do that was to keep her no matter what.

Whenever he was around, Gainer never left the one-room flat. She would even position herself between them, ready to pounce on him if he tried anything. If she had to leave the child alone, she would kick him out before she left. Getarix did not mind this. He felt that the child could not have been better protected than by her overbearing matron. This gave a great measure of peace to Getarix, especially with Alexander the slave-trader hanging about the place. His friends were of a different opinion. They chided him continually about what they called his pets, expensive pets at that. "If you don't lay with them, at least sell them for all they're worth," was the ever-present remark from his fellow soldiers. Cullen was the only one who never mentioned them.

As the spring winds thawed the cold earth, activity intensified. No verbal orders were necessary to let the soldiers know that they would soon be on the march again. The soldiers trained harder and harder. The farriers re-shoed all the horses; large stockpiles of supplies began to appear. All of this testified to a long campaign to come.

One spring day, early in the morning, the leadership of Getarix's cohort were called together in an open courtyard. "Okay, you lot," Centurion Faustus said as he began his brief. "We leave for the frontier first light tomorrow. Get your kit sorted out. By now you should be ready, but if you need anything, get it now."

No one was in need of anything. Faustus' cavalry cohort by now was a very tightly knit unit. It made him proud to lead them.

With that bit of administration out of the way, he continued. "Now, this is the plan for our first mission. We will march into Germania Superior against the Chatti. Our goal is to destroy this settlement…here." He pointed to a spot on a leather map. "After that we will proceed to the Upper Weser. That's all I have for now. Okay, any questions? As we get closer we will get more details. We have been tasked to cover the right flank. Germanicus will not make the same mistake that Varus made in Teutoburg." He straightened up. "Now go and get your troops ready. We have a lot of new troops who are green and I am depending on you to keep a good grip of them. Duplicarius Getarix, your troop will take the lead when we step off. Duplicarius Drusus, your troop will take the lead after the noon rest. Any questions?" No one had any. "Okay, now get your troops ready and oh take note: our mission's objective is not to be shared with anyone. This brief was for you, not your troops. I imagine the Germans have their spies everywhere, even in our ranks. Let's not forget that Arminius once fought hard as a Roman. Okay, off with you."

The leadership of the cohort departed to get their troops ready for the long march ahead of them. Getarix had mixed feelings about heading back to the frontier. The idea of heading to where he well-nigh froze to death hit the pit of his stomach like the fists of Aquilla or Cassius. On the other hand, he was on the move again and for him that always brought relief. In the middle of the day it hit him that the rent for the apartment was only paid for until the end of spring. He just then noticed Koren standing about with nothing to do. Faustus did not particularly like him and had tried to have him transferred out of is unit but could not. So he put him in the rear party. They were left to man and guard the unit lines.

"Koren."

"Yes, Duplicarius."

"I need you to go to Martius Gaius the Greek and tell him he has to come here to receive the rent for the summer." Getarix thought it very arrogant to name yourself after the god Mars as his landlord did. *Maybe some people just need a little help*, he mused.

"Yes sir," Koren said sharply and was off. Getarix wondered if he had misjudged him last fall. He had avoided him throughout the winter, holding a grudge for his meddling with Alexander the slave-trader and the girl the previous fall. Getarix had no time to deliver this message himself and he could not bring himself to trust Koren with the money.

Martius Gaius arrived at lunch a little put out. Getarix paid him not only the summer rent but the fall as well. After the previous year's experience, he was taking no chances. The extra pay also seemed to turn Martius' bad mood around. Getarix even invited him to lunch, but Martius declined, thinking that if he wanted poorly cooked porridge he could eat where the city's poor were fed.

The preparations went well, but the mountain of tasks to be accomplished busied the troops right through the night. A few hours before dawn, the troops were sent to ground to catch some sleep. Getarix, Cullen, and Jodoc met just inside the gate intent on sacrificing a wine skin in celebration and to help them unwind and maybe aid their own quest for sleep. They settled themselves on a few woven baskets filled with wheat. The baskets were set there ready to be placed on the pack horses at first light. As Cullen cracked open the wineskin, Jodoc ran his finger along the now-healed scar on his face. It ran down the right side of his face clear from his ear to the end of his chin. He started to tease Getarix.

"Well Getarix, do you think you can go to war this time without making it more difficult than it has to be?"

Getarix noticed his fingers tracing the scar. "We'll be okay if you don't meet any more Amazons," Getarix shot back, referring to the scar Gainer had placed on his cheek.

"You're one for talking. She has you whipped, and you're the master. A point you seemed to have missed."

"She serves her purpose. She whipped you in battle, don't forget."

"Oh yeah, I would have won that one if the two of you didn't jump me."

"We just didn't want to see you get hurt anymore." Getarix smirked.

"At least I know how to leave a war with grace and not freeze in the wilderness." Jodoc sported a smile on his face.

"And to think how much you hate being uncomfortable," Cullen added with a chuckle. By now he had the wine open and began to pass it around.

"Things will run as smooth as a bronze mirror, I assure you."

"How would you know? You have never seen one." Cullen and Jodoc laughed.

"Shut up, the two—"Screams and the panicked voice of a woman interrupted him.

"Getarix! Getarix! They took her!" The voice was screaming British Celtic. Instantly Getarix knew he was hearing the voice of Gainer. All three ran to the gate. Getarix ordered it to be opened. The guards complied and she ran right into his arms. Getarix barely recognized her. She was no longer the strong pillar of power he knew. Her face was stained red and her brown hair was dry with blood.

"They took her...they took her..."

"Who took her? You mean Isolde?"

"Yes...that slave-trader, the Greek one. When he entered the apartment I fought his slave but I was hit over the head, hard."

"How long ago?" Getarix guessed at least an hour by the dry blood on her head.

"I don't know. They hit me...I was out...they took her."

"Which way did they go?"

"I don't...they hit me...I didn't see...they took her." Getarix spotted Koren at the doorway to one of their barracks. What was noticeable was the smirk on his face. Getarix pushed her away into Jodoc's arms, who in spite of himself was enjoying her weakness but felt some discomfort in holding her and was in no frame of mind to comfort her. She put her head into his chest with a sob. As soon as she felt the cool of his chain mail on her forehead she looked up at his face. Her face was no more than two fingers away from his. The second she recognized him she became strong again. She roughly pushed him away and stood apart, watching Getarix approach Koren. Jodoc could not help himself as he smiled at her. She shot back a look of hate at him before returning her attention to Getarix.

Koren saw Getarix approach, his eyes flashing anger, his hand on the hilt of his sword. Cullen and Jodoc close on his heels. He turned to make his escape. Getarix grabbed him by the back of the soldier's green tunic. It was all he had on. Koren fell awkwardly backward off the threshold onto the ground. He landed at their feet on his back. Getarix had his sword out, pushing it to his neck.

"What do you know about this, maggot?"

"Nothing. You can't hurt me...the army will—"

Cullen broke in. "What are you talking about? I saw you attack the duplicarius."

Jodoc threw his army issue utility knife on the dirt next to Koran and added. "Hell, I saw you go at him with your utility knife."

"You wouldn't..."

"At that, Getarix pushed the sword deep enough to begin to choke him but not enough to cut the skin. Koran looked into the eyes of his duplicarius and saw the anger burn like a volcano. He began to panic as the conviction of his imminent death was near.

"He is taking her to Rome, to some senator. He's heading there right away. He would be on the Via Roma by now, moving as fast as his donkeys can—"

"What does this senator want with her?"

Koren look at him and gave a little smile of arrogance. "His sex toy…"

That's all Getarix could handle. He put his full weight on the sword hilt, ending Koran's confession with his life.

Within minutes the three of them were mounted, charging through the abandoned streets of Xanten heading for the west side and the road that led to Rome.

Once they cleared the city walls, they pushed their horses full out. All three were intent for different reasons. Jodoc saw the girl as nothing more than a possession of Getarix. His indignation only went as far as seeing Alexander as a thief. Getarix on the other hand realized he was seeing the girl in a totally different light. He did not see this as a theft; he saw this as a kidnapping. As he rode for all his might, he realized he simply feared for Isolde. Cullen was indignant that anyone hurt his closest friend. He realized then that he would go to the wall for his friend. Added to all that, the three friends saw Koren's sin as a betrayal of a fellow soldier. Getarix knew he had to deal with this here and now. If the slave-trader got her to Rome it would be too late. No matter how illegal the acts of Alexander were. He would get away with it. Gainer had told him of some senator who had visited the Boar's Head Inn a few years back and turned the girl's world upside-down. If it was him, Getarix knew that the same senator had ways of turning justice upside-down.

The predawn light was beginning to brighten the sky. Up ahead they saw a small caravan of about five people. Two were mounted. They looked like large strong men. Behind them was a donkey with what looked like a bundle over its back. Tied to it were three men in chains, walking. Getarix thought that with Alexander moving so slowly he must have been supremely confident that he would not be pursued. He probably figured that the army would be marching in the opposite direction by now. He never calculated in, nor expected to meet the determination found in Gainer.

Alexander felt like he had accomplished the feat of his life. He imagined the look on the face of the senator upon his arrival. Not to mention the great reward.

He was smiling broadly at this thought. He looked over to his slave, Cana. His big Egyptian had taken the brunt of the woman's wrath. The first thing he'd felt was her knee in his groin. When he had hit the floor, the next thing he'd felt was her foot directly in his left eye. Within minutes it had swollen to where he could not see out of it at all. The saddle was none too comfortable either. Cana had to stand in the stirrups to stave off the pain. If Alexander had not come in and clubbed the woman from behind, Cana was not too sure he would have survived the encounter. Cana had wanted to kill her but the child began screaming and his master told him to grab her and keep her quiet. The child fought hard but brute strength subdued her. Aside from his physical pain, Cana was not feeling good about what he had done. He remembered as a child himself being ripped from his family just as he ripped this child from hers. He also knew that her fate would be significantly worse than his own. He knew of the senator and did not feel all that noble about his acts of the night before.

"That little girl can really fight, eh?" Alexander broke through his thoughts.

"Yeah, she can really use those claws of hers."

"We will have to de-claw her, eh?" Alexander chuckled. "Maybe I'll just pull them out."

Cana could no longer join in such revelry.   "The senator will surely tame this one. You can count on that," Alexander continued with a laugh. "Did you see—" He stopped and listened. "What is that?"

Cana, standing in his stirrups, turned quickly in the saddle. "Master, three men on horse, moving fast. Soldiers, I think."

"Grab the girl, leave the others. Get moving."

Cana quickly turned his horse around and grabbed the bundle on the donkey. The child had made such a fuss they wrapped her like an Egyptian mummy in gunny sack material.

She began to kick and squirm wildly. Cana could hear her scream through the gag that was tightly bound around her head. As Cana grabbed her and slid her onto his horse in front of him, she drew her bound legs up and her knees landed right where Gainer had once been. The pain was blinding. He had to concentrate not to throw up. They began to ride full tilt with the hope that their fresh horses could ride longer and faster than the soldiers' mounts which already had five miles under their girth. What he did not count on was that the soldiers' horses also trained with the soldiers, making them much fitter than the mounts of the slave-traders. Cana felt like he was going to die with every step. He could no longer suspend himself off the saddle with the extra weight of the child. His body landed hard on the saddle with every stride of the gallop. Before long he could hardly see straight. He glanced back and noticed that the soldiers were closing in fast, swords in hand. It became clear in his mind that he could not escape and would likely be killed once they caught up with them. He concluded that there was no fight left in him. He pulled on the reins, turning his horse to face his pursuers and simply waited. Isolde began to squirm again. He heard her muted screams. He tried to soothe her but she could not hear anything in her state.

As the soldiers arrived, the lead solder, the biggest of the three, nailed him in the right eye with the hilt of his sword. Cana felt like he deserved this punishment. In a perverse way it was like punishing the one who had stolen him from his home. Cana fell from his now-winded horse. As he slid from the saddle, someone grabbed the child.

Getarix held Isolde in his arms as he dismounted. He noticed that the rider he clobbered just laid there not moving. He thought he went down a little too easy. As he unwrapped the child, he kept an eye on the fallen figure.

Jodoc and Cullen went after the other rider. Before long they returned with the dead body of Alexander lying across the saddle of his own horse.

Jodoc said, "Do you think they will let us keep our war booty?"

"It's not war booty. I expect that the government would take it all. I don't care to get anything from that dead snake." Getarix spat.

Cullen looked over to Getarix, who was now holding the child tightly. Isolde, unbound, had her arms and legs around him in a death grip. Getarix held her, rocking her back and forth, soothing her gently.

XXVII

THE SIEGE

"Can you explain to me why you insist on leaving a trail of destruction in every town we leave?" Faustus was spitting as he spoke. "It wasn't good enough to beat up a Roman citizen and a few soldiers like the last time. This time you had to kill the buggers."

Faustus violently pointed his index finger directly in Getarix's face. "You killed a Roman soldier!"

Jodoc interrupted. "In self defence, sir, it was—" Faustus froze in place, his face going crimson red. He looked like he was about to explode as he pivoted on his heels, landing his pointed finger and glare directly on Jodoc. He spoke in an unnaturally quiet voice, struggling to maintain control. "Jodoc, why is it that every time you open your mouth I get this uncontrollable urge to kill something?" He looked back at Getarix, pointing over his shoulder with his thumb toward Jodoc and Cullen. "These two clowns tell me that Koren went after you with his utility knife. Is that so?"

"Yes sir, he did."

"Tell me why he would do that?"

"I seldom understood how his mind worked, sir."

"Mmm…do you have your utility knife on you?"

"Yes, sir." Getarix produced his instantly.

Faustus turned on the other two. "Show me yours."

Cullen produced his just as quickly as Getarix, but Jodoc did not have his. Faustus zeroed in on him, speaking quietly, only a few fingers from his face. "Jodoc, could you be so kind as to explain to me, why you do not have yours?"

"Sir…um, I must have lost it in pursuit of the felon."

"Felon. It's pretty presumptuous for you to call anyone a felon." He turned to his desk and picked up a utility knife. "Maybe you can explain why I found Koren's utility knife with his kit."

"It's my story, sir, and I am staying with it," Jodoc said.

"How about the two of you?" Faustus asked Getarix and Cullen.

"It's our story too, sir."

Faustus threw the utility knife into Jodoc's hand. "You better stick to it. Now, that other matter of the slave-trader. His big Egyptian slave has confessed to stealing your slave. He also mentioned Koren meeting with his master about you three deploying, making the way clear. So you had better stick to your stories. How many times must I cover for you three? Now get out there and mount up. You've delayed us enough." Faustus muttered to himself as they left, "Let's see you three top this one."

Faustus knew they were as guilty as the devil, but like last year he did not want to lose soldiers who appeared to have such a natural ability in battle. He also reasoned that Koren was a deviant who he would not trust to care for his dog. He reasoned that he had just lost one poor soldier, why lose three of his best in the deal? As far as the slave-trader, it was an open-and-closed case. *Next time*, he mused. *I'll lock them up in cells the night before we head anywhere.*

Before the week was over they had forgotten their little adventure. As they marched through the forest, they laid waste to everything they saw. Their armour would rattle in time and in step with their marching. The cavalry would make the distinctive sound of iron horse shoes striking the stone of the Roman roads. Roads laid by some of these very soldiers back in the day when this part of Germania was solidly in Roman control. When they did encounter the Germans, most of the fighting had to be done by the mounted troops. The Germans fled upon either sight or sound of the Romans, only to set up ambushes. They were slowly wearing away the fighting effectiveness of Germanicus' troops. Only the cavalry saw any battles to speak of, when they would be sent in pursuit. Rome's army was best in pitched battles in open fields. Skirmishes in the trees were dwindling her numbers and morale alike.

After a few days' march through the forest, they came upon the settlement of the pro-Roman Germanic leader Segestes, where he was held captive by forces loyal to Arminius.

"I assure you, sir, he is there, not of his free will," Adulfus, their German spy, informed Germanicus.

"How is he guarded?"

"He is in the lower level locked in a room. It's guarded by only two guards."

"That'll be easy, eh?"

"But sir…" Adulfus said.

"But what?"

"He is held in the basement of the armouries…in the centre of their stronghold."

"So he is not guarded by two soldiers? He is guarded by everyone, right?"

"Mmm…yes, sir."

"That changes things. We will lay siege. That will be all, Adulfus." Germanicus turned to his adjutant, Caecina. "Pay the man." As Caecina went to a strong box to get a small leather bag of coins, Adulfus interrupted the proceedings.

"Sir, there's one more thing." Germanicus simply looked at him, waiting for him to finish. "Segestes is not the only important person there. His daughter and son are there."

"Thusnelda, you mean?"

"Yes sir, it's her for sure."

"You saw her?"

"With my own eye I did."

"The wife of Arminius?"

"And her brother Segimundus, sir…and, and she is pregnant."

"This just gets better. Imagine the capture of the wife of Arminius, and pregnant no less. Caecina, give Adulfus a bonus for his services, would you?"

Once the spy had left, Germanicus said to Caecina, "The capture of Thusnelda and her brother would only fan the flames of war in the heart of Arminius. Now, if I know Arminius, he just might be drawn into open battle. This fighting amongst the trees in small groups is killing us. I know that our better-trained and disciplined troops would dominate on the traditional field of battle over his undisciplined German fighters."

"That would be better than going hither and yon accomplishing nothing," Caecina added.

"Caecina, I need you to take the army of Germania inferior and attack the Marsi again. If my plan works, this will prevent them from supporting the Chatti. And if we are lucky, you will keep the other tribes busy as well. Maybe even the Cherusci. After that, I want you to proceed and attack the Bructeri along the Upper Ems again. What do you think?"

Caecina looked a bit distressed. "Sounds good, other than that fact I'm being sent off on a diversion…you know, missing the good parts."

"There will be plenty of good parts, Caecina my friend." Germanicus chuckled.

"Getarix, look at this." Cullen was pointing to the legs and chest of Epona, his mount. Cullen took his utility knife and lanced a festering sore. Getarix inspected the numerous cuts and bruises on his old horse.

"This fighting through the forest is hard on the old girl, eh?"

"I don't know how much more of this they can take. And look at our legs."

"Do you realise that we, you and me, have never once been in a battle we trained for? The big ones? Mighty armies lined up on a large field and all that."

"Come here, you two, don't just stand there lollygagging. Mount up!"

Without another word they were both mounted in line of battle facing the walls of the well-defended town. It was built upon a small hill, allowing a good line of sight in all directions.

For over a week they laid siege, cutting off all aid. They attacked the surrounding area, herding the survivors toward the town, where they choked the streets of the stronghold and were consuming all of their provisions. By the hour of battle, they had been without water for five days and the weak had already begun to die. With nowhere to bury their dead, the Germans were forced to dispose of the bodies over the walls.

Getarix was mounted in front of his troop of ten soldiers, who were lined up behind him in single file.

"Well here we go, our first real battle, boys." Getarix turned around in his saddle, talking to his small troop. He saw the tense face of Cullen directly behind him and the overeager face of Jodoc at the end of the line.

The infantry had conducted raids on the strongholds almost continually. The only weapons the Germans had for defence were their arrows and what spears they had. After a week and a half of continual attacks, the German supply was exhausted. By the day of the battle, they were ripping their homes apart, fashioning crude spears that did not fly straight. The last of the arrows the Romans had to contend with were their own recovered from dead defenders off the ramparts. Now the fort stood defenceless and exhausted.

As Getarix sat waiting, he watched the infantry approach unmolested. Once they got within spear range, the infantry blackened the sky with deadly effect. As the projectiles found their targets, the thin-tipped spears bent all out of shape.

This ensured the defenders could never throw them back, rendering them useless to the enemy.

They could hear the cries from the streets of the fortified town as the Roman spears fell among the people. As soon as the infantry had unloaded their deadly missiles, the large catapults let loose. These huge engines of war could hurl the weight of a large man for over a mile. The projectiles chosen were terra cotta jars filled with flammable tar. The small opening of the jars was stuffed with cloth they lit before launching. As the jars smashed on the ground, the cloth would ignite the spilling tar, covering everything in its path with fire not easily extinguished. The smell of burning tar filled the air. Wherever the wind blew from behind the troops, black smoke obscured their vision. When the command was given, the sky was blackened again, this time from the many trails of burning tar. Getarix and his friends had never seen these in action and were overwhelmed by their murderous power. A few of the projectiles fell short of their mark. As they landed, the bursting missiles exploded into a field of fire three times the size of the hut Getarix grew up in. One jar fell so short it landed right in front of the formed-up infantry. Some of the tar splashed back and onto a few soldiers in the first rank. They instantly fell to the ground, their mates covering them with their capes, smothering the flames. The real damage took place in the streets of the fort, where the women and children were. The men were under cover, protecting themselves so they could live to fight. In a very short time these wooden buildings were engulfed in flames, forcing the fighters to exit onto the ramparts of the walls. Once they were in position, Germanicus adjusted fire and let loose with another barrage of burning tar. This time their targets were the walls. With amazing accuracy, most of the flaming jars reached their target. Some cleared the wall and few fell short, one landing right in the midst of the cohort of infantry. As Getarix watched, he could not help but imagine what it must be like for the women and children in the burning fort. He was already able to smell the distinct odour produced from burning flesh.

As the fires did their work, the wooden walls began to give. The moment a breach in the wall came open, the soldiers of Germanicus began to pour in with orders to fight their way toward the main gate from the inside. Watching the infantry pour into the fortress, Getarix's heart began to pound wildly. His breathing became laboured. When he was a child, an old man had worked for his brother. One day when Getarix was about ten, they were running the dogs. Suddenly the old man stopped. He held his chest, barely able to breath, and then died. This scene ran through his mind, now. As the pain increased, Getarix truly believed he was about to die like the old man. He tried unsuccessfully to breathe deeply. He began to have difficulty focusing on anything, as the pain in his chest made him feel like it was about to explode like sour wine in a wineskin. He noticed the world begin to blacken. The thought hit him that it might be good to have some sort of a god to pray to at times like this. Instantly he countered that thought. *No god is worthy of my homage or my prayers.* Fear gripped him as he thought he would soon be at the mercy of those wolves.

The gate opened and Faustus ordered, "Move, now!" He took off, leading his cohort forward through the new opening.

Cullen kicked Epona, bumping Getarix hard. Getarix instantly kicked Cabello. As they charged the 200 paces up the hill toward the open gate, the feeling lifted from Getarix and his vision came back.

Once inside, the choking smoke with its pungent odour almost unhorsed the riders. All around lay dead Germans with a few Roman infantry mixed in. Cullen was sickened by the sight of the children strewn about. His anger boiled as he realized that the defenders had not put them under protection. Rather they left them to feel the full thrust of Rome's war machine.

Their orders were to take the central building, where the Roman-friendly Segestes was held. It only took a few seconds to reach the building. Most of the defenders had been ushered to their death on the walls by burning tar. The few left offered little resistance. Where possible they ran, but they had nowhere to go. Most found their death at the end of a Roman sword. Getarix had drawn the lot and been selected to lead his troop into the building in search of Segestes, father-in-law of Arminius. When he was selected for the task he felt the honour. Now that the moment had arrived he was not so sure. The burning tar had done its work on the building. When they arrived, one troop went left around the building, the other went right. Their job was to ensure their prize could not be spirited away out some back door. When Getarix got to the door, he signalled Cullen to kick the oaken door. It gave way without much of a struggle, having been weakened by fire. Without thought, they charged into the building, Getarix leading, Cullen directly behind him. Getarix felt the hand of Cullen tightly gripping his cape, as the man behind Cullen gripped his, all down the line ending with Jodoc. They had trained this way so that no one would get lost in the smoke and confusion.

Getarix began to wonder if he should just turn back. *What fool runs into a building fully engulfed in flames?* He could not see a thing. Matter of a fact, they could not even open their eyes nor even breathe, the smoke was so thick. He had been instructed to enter the building and go only five paces, turn left, and at mid-wall there would be a staircase leading deep into the cells where Segestes was reported to be held. Getarix muttered to himself, "That rat had better have told the truth or I'll kill the little—"

A deafening thunder filled his ears and shook his bones. Cullen pulled violently on his cape. Getarix lost his balance, landing his full weight on the already fallen Cullen. He screamed at him. "Cullen, what the hell…?"

Cullen could not hear what he'd said with the roar of the fire. There was another great crash. Their eyes were closed so tight they did not even notice that the central part of the roof had fallen in, letting the morning sun shine through the choking smoke from above. Cullen felt the weight of his friend on him when he pushed him violently off. He knew that if they did not clear the area soon they both would die. He was so disorientated that he forced his eyes open for a second only to discover that the missing roof was at their feet. It gave him just enough light to see the stairs along a stone wall, leading down. He jumped up, grabbing Getarix, who opened his eye, peering through the pain behind him and searching for the rest of his troop. What he saw horrified him. The rest of the troop was buried under the timbers of the roof. Cullen dragged his friend to his feet and bolted for the stairs just as the remainder of the roof gave way. Getarix was so blinded by the smoke that when he reached the stairs he simply fell onto Cullen, knocking both of them down the stairs. They tumbled down, skinning their bodies as they went. The debris from the roof filled the stairwell behind them. They had to roll sideways into the room to avoid being killed by the broken timbers. The deafening crash was replaced with an ominous silence. For minutes they laid there, wondering if they were dead. It hit Getarix that he could breathe without choking. He dared open his eyes, saying, "Cullen, is this what death is like?"

"No, I think this is what the basement is like."

Getarix saw that the room was lit by torchlight. It was a small stone room with three doors off each wall. The other wall was where the stairs had come down.

"This might not be what death is like, but I have the feeling it might be the last of earth for us."

"Come now, Getarix. This is nothing for you."

"Your faith in my ability to survive gives me great comfort!"

"Your ability to survive? I was talking about my ability to survive and my ability to save your hide. I'm here for you. Where are the others? Did you see them?"

"I did…unfortunately."

"Unfortunately?" Cullen said weakly. Getarix did not need to explain any further.

Getarix felt like he wanted to return his rank and the extra pay that came with it. "You know, Cullen, when I was promoted all I thought about was the increase in pay. Not the burden of something like this. They were my men… Jodoc, a friend."

"They were all my friends."

Getarix felt ashamed that he was talking to Cullen like he hadn't lost anything. "I'm sorry, brother."

"Don't be. Now, how about getting out of here?"

"First the doors. I guess the guards probably fled when the building was set alight."

The doors were locked and no keys were at hand. Using the hilts of their swords, they began to pound on the three doors. Two doors produced an answer, both in German. Getarix asked their names but the doors were too thick to understand anything.

"The keys, Cullen. Check for the keys."

They took one of the two torches still burning, bringing it low to the flagstone floor. The search only produced a few dead rats.

"Keep those. We might need to eat later," Cullen said.

"It's more likely that we'll join them before we get hungry." Getarix held the dying torch up to the roof. Cullen looked up from the floor and noticed the smoke billowing through the cracks into the room.

"That explains why it is getting so hot in here. Soon we will be without light," Cullen said.

Getarix began to examine the stones next to the doors. "Cullen, quickly get up here and bring your sword. Here, before the light goes between the stones." The mortar began to give way. The years of water seeping through and the stress of the collapsed building had done their work and compromised the mortar. The hinges were bolted to the thick oaken doors but they were only attached to the wall by one spike imbedded into the now-cracked mortar between the stones. To secure them into the wall, the mason had used a number of smaller stones surrounding the spikes. This was their weakness. As Cullen worked on the bottom hinge, Getarix worked feverishly on the top. Getarix experienced more success, and just as their last torch was giving way the door began to fall. Getarix grabbed Cullen, pulling him out of the way of the falling door. It broke the silence as it thundered on the floor.

"Who is in here?" Getarix yelled in Latin, knowing that the one they were after was fluent in the Roman language. The answer came back in German. Getarix asked again in Celtic. The man answered. It was not Segestes.

After some violent curses, Getarix yelled at Cullen to follow him to the next door. He felt his way along the wall. Once he felt the wood of the door, it was not long before he discovered the hinges. As he began to work at the mortar, he called into the room through the door. It also produced a voice. As they worked on the stones with their now badly scarred swords, the smoke burned their eyes and irritated their lungs. They chipped away at the stone just shy of full panic. Cullen, having cleaner air closer to the floor, worked faster and was done before Getarix. As with the first door the second crashed open loudly. They repeated the question but this time got the answer they sought. They had found Segestes.

"Well, we found him, Getarix. What now? Just the satisfaction of knowing that we accomplished our mission before we die?"

"Now you're being dark, Cullen—" The ceiling of the outer chamber began to crack and give way. Instinctively, Getarix looked up at the ceiling of the cell they stood in. It appeared to be holding. He noticed something. "Light, a pinprick of light." He went to it and placed his hand to discover that it was coming from outside through a gap that had opened in the stone of the outer wall. Suddenly they all were able to see. A dull orange light illuminated the oppressively hot room. Cullen gave an expletive of delight at being able to see again.

"I would not be so happy about the light, brother, when you think it comes from the ceiling."

Cullen looked up and noticed that the ceiling began to glow orange. He also noticed that smoke was violently billowing into the room. At that sight, he gave a different expletive.

"Cullen, unless you wish to see where death comes from, I suggest you get your sword out and help me here." Getarix was straining to reach the top of the wall where the light shone through. Getarix yelled in Celtic to the German prisoner from the first cell who had followed them into the cell holding Segestes. "You! Get down so I can get on you to reach..." He did not wait for a response. He simply grabbed the German by his long hair, pulling him down. As he stepped on him, he heard Segestes explaining to the other German what was happening. Getarix cut in. "Sir, with all due respect, I suggest you join your countryman and allow my mate to join me up here or we'll all die."

Before long they were both chipping away in a cloud of smoke perched on the backs of the two prisoners. Eventually they were forced to lie down on the floor to catch some air before returning to their task, no different than if they were working under water.

"Getarix, this one!" Cullen grabbed his friend's hand, guiding it around a large stone about the size of man's belly.

"Got it." Getarix began to work on the mortar holding the stone in place as Cullen went down for a breath. After a few minutes that felt like an hour, they had most of the mortar cleared away.

Where the mortar once was they were able to see outside, but could not detect any movement. Getarix quickly concluded that they had neither the time nor the luxury to call for help. They had to do it themselves.

"Okay Cullen, let's pry it out!" Getarix dug his sword deep and they pried with all their might. The stone began to move slowly, giving them encouragement.

Cullen put his whole weight into it. The stone moved some more, then the sword gave way with a loud snap. Cullen fell into the broken end still lodged in the mortar, cutting his lip badly and losing his balance. He fell onto the strained back of Segestes. Getarix dropped down to the floor to get a breath of air.

"You okay, brother?"

"I'll live."

"Not for long if you don't get up."

Cullen felt weak all over and was shaking. He was at the verge of giving up when he heard the roof begin to crack. That was all he needed to find the energy to move again. He jumped up, joining his friend using his broken sword and with new vigour began to move the stone out little by little.

Suddenly the stone tipped and fell, landing silently on the ground.

Cullen looked for Getarix but could not see him. *The sound was off. The stone sounded more like it landed on a pillow or...* "Getarix!"

"Quit yelling!" As the dust settled, the light streaming in through the smoke revealed the previously dark room. When the stone had begun to fall, it pushed Getarix onto his back and out of the way. The light revealed the dying body of the hapless prisoner bearing the crushing weight of the fallen stone. Segestes just stood there. Getarix jumped to his feet, grabbed him, and almost threw him through the opening. As soon as his head poked through the hole, Getarix put his shoulder against the backside of Segestes and launched him outside. The beams began to crack loudly. Without looking or hesitating, Getarix grabbed Cullen and fired him through the hole under protest. The second Cullen landed outside, he pivoted and stuck his head back into the hole where Getarix was just mounting the stone. He grabbed the arms of his friend and heaved with all his might, wrenching Getarix through the opening.

Before he knew it, Getarix was outside. Burning timbers soon covered the opening. They just lay on the ground looking at the sun, unable to process what had just happened.

XXVIII

ROUGH PASSAGE

The three blackened figures lay exhausted and motionless. If one did not know any better, they could easily have been mistaken for the dead.

"Well, Cullen," Getarix laboured, "did I not promise you adventure?"

"You can keep your adventure."

"I'm not sure if I want it anymore myself." This was his first taste of losing men he was responsible for. He did not like the feeling at all.

"Duplicarius Getarix!" a voice bellowed from a distance.

"Sir?" Getarix moved his head toward the voice without getting up.

It was the voice of Faustus.

Faustus stood there looking at the three bodies. "Well, did you find him?"

"Sir, may I present to you Lord Segestes."

Getarix pointed to the blackened body of Segestes, who was barely moving.

"Sir, are you okay?" Faustus asked. Segestes nodded. "General Germanicus is anxious to see you, sir."

"He won't be able to see me through this soot," Segestes said as he sat up and slowly stood on his unsteady legs. "How about one of your famous Roman baths?"

"We will see what we can do, sir." Turning his attention to Getarix, Faustus said, "Get your troop. Apparently we are marching out first thing tomorrow." He looked around. "So...where is your troop?"

"This is my troop, sir." Getarix held back his emotions.

"What? Where are the rest?"

Getarix simply pointed toward the remains of the building they had barely escaped.

"What do you mean? I just saw Jodoc with the horses!" He pointed to the area where they had left their mounts. Once they managed to get to their feet, they saw him standing there. They forced themselves up on painful limbs and stumbled toward their friend.

"Decion Jodoc, what's the meaning of this? What are you doing here? You should be with your troop." Getarix could not help but smile as he reproved his friend. It was such a relief to see him alive that they embraced in a powerful bear hug.

Jodoc looked like he was in shock. "How did you...I thought you were... when the building?"

"That story we reserve for a skin of wine. You're buying."

"With joy." Jodoc laughed.

"How did you get out?" Now it was Getarix's turn to ask.

"Out, I never got in. I was holding on to Scipio and just as I crossed the threshold he was gone, with the building. One of the roof timbers fell and knocked me flat but out of harm's way. You two look like hell."

"That's where we just spent the last hour," Cullen said with a smile.

Faustus stood there wondering, *How do these three continue to survive the scrapes they insist on encountering?* "Okay, that's enough. Break up your little love fest. You two get cleaned up and be ready in an hour. Jodoc, take the other mounts to the stables and turn them over to the army, then get ready to move. The rest of the cavalry is getting ready."

"What's up, sir?" Jodoc asked.

"You'll see. The summer has just begun. There is a whole season of fighting waiting for you. If you don't want to miss it, I suggest you get moving."

For the balance of the summer, they were continually in battle, seldom seeing any rest. The battles went both ways and by summer's end things looked like a draw. By late season, they found themselves on the river Amisia.

"We're going back."

"Back?"

"Yes, back."

"How?"

"By boat. There must be at least a thousand ships on the river."

The new soldiers assigned to Duplicarius Getarix were passing the usual gossip soldiers seem to discuss throughout the ages. They had proven to be good soldiers, giving a good account of their training. Getarix had lost only one during the summer. And he had died when he fell from his mount, landing his head on a rock.

"Okay, shut up you lot. For once you happen to be right. We are going by sea."

"Oh great, Quintus here gets seasick just looking at dew on the grass." The troop broke out in laughter.

"You better not barf on me, Quintus," Getarix said, breaking up their banter. "Okay, we are going back home. And we are the lucky ones who get to ride it out on the boats and not on the saddle. Now if your mount is lame in any way, it has priority. If your horse is healthy, it might have to hump it back. So when you get back you'll be without."

"No way, I don't want to be separated," Quintus said.

"Fair enough, Quintus has just volunteered to go with the road party."

"Well, maybe I can see myself through our separation." Quintus smiled.

"I thought you would."

The next day when they were loading they noticed that, to their dismay, the hold of their assigned boat was being filled with the lame horses from the road-bound legions. After their own lame mounts were loaded, they were allowed to load their healthy rides.

"Sorry, the hold is full," the loadmaster yelled from below. Faustus, assigned to the same vessel, began to protest, stating that there were very few of their horses on board.

"Sorry sir, but we are already over our limit. You better pray to whatever you pray to that the seas stay calm as it is."

Faustus, frustrated, had to accept the loadmaster's recommendation. He looked from the deck and noticed that the only troop not yet loaded was Getarix's. "Duplicarius Getarix."

"Sir!"

"Your horses will be walking back. Assign one reliable soldier to take them."

"Sir. Jodoc, you're it."

Jodoc was standing a few feet away and looking forward to just sitting around for the week the trip would take. Maybe kill a few wine skins.

"Getarix, you're killing me here."

"Get over it, brother. You could always pray for bad weather."

"I might just do that."

The declining summer weather was dry and calm and it promised to be a restful trip. The plan was to load up on the shores of the River Amisia and proceed to the North Sea, heading south toward their winter quarter in Xanten. Germanicus sailed on the flagship, leading his floating army close along the European shore. Many of the boats were not ocean-going vessels. The day they departed, the weather was so calm they despaired that with no wind to move them along the trip would take much longer than originally planned.

The accommodations Getarix and Cullen shared with the soldiers and horses left a lot to be desired. They were all crowded down in the hold. They strung hammocks between the horses. The tired men awoke often when the ship rolled and they were crushed with the full weight of their horse. They would curse and swear whenever that happened. When they could take it no more or their hammock was needed for the next shift of sleepers, they would jump down with bare feet right into the loose manure freshly minted by the nervous horses. With the smell of the fifty animals and the noise of sixty soldiers decompressing, many with the help of wine, this trip could not compare with their first trip by boat from Britannia. There was no paneled stateroom, nor servants taking care of all their needs. That notwithstanding, they would never trade this trip for anything. On this passage they were men, not lost children scared with no apparent future. Getarix and Cullen spent most of their time topside ensuring they kept clear of the sailors. There was no love between sailors and soldiers, but it could get even uglier when the soldiers got in the way of the working sailors.

As they stood there leaning on the railing talking out their experiences of the summer, Cullen noticed Getarix just staring west into the sea.

"Getarix, do you ever miss home?"

"What's to miss?"

"Oh I don't know…family, friends?"

"Ha, family, please. My uncle, yes." Getarix dared not mention his mother. The idea that she knew about the plan to sacrifice him and did nothing about it was too painful to think of, let alone mention. "And as far as friends go, I brought him with me. For that matter, I brought my family with me in him."

They fell into silence and just looked at the expanse of the sea. In the distance, they could faintly make out the outline of Britannia.

"Do you think we will ever see her again?"

"Not me."

"Getarix, look." Cullen pointed to the horizon. In the distance they noticed gray clouds growing, rapidly turning black. The clouds did not escape the notice of the sailors either. They had worried looks on their faces as they hurriedly tied down everything in sight.

"They really seemed worried," Cullen said as Getarix turned, looked the other way and gazed across the ship's deck to the horizon on the other side.

"Cullen…I think we might be in for a rough ride."

"I guess we will see just how well Quintus does, eh?"

"I tell you, if I find out that Jodoc actually prayed for this I'll—"

"I thought you didn't—"

"Didn't believe? To bring suffering to man I do believe they are more than capable."

"You two get down below and stay out of our way!" This time it was the captain of the ship yelling at them. They complied without protest.

Below things seemed to be quiet and no one was aware of any danger. Getarix gathered his troop off to the port side hull near the stairs. He figured he should keep them together.

"What's up, sir?" one of his soldiers asked with concern.

"Nothing, really, just a bit of rough weather. I thought we could be together to help clean up after Quintus." The little joke helped alleviate the sudden tension. It was not long before the boat began to rock. They noticed that they had turned east toward the coast of Germania.

"They are turning in to find a port to ride out the storm. See, nothing to worry about."

"Yeah, but the winds seem to be blowing west," Quintus said. The wind soon picked up in earnest and the ride became very bumpy.

A loud voice bellowed below, ordering the men to extinguish all lights or fire of any kind. They were also instructed to tether the animals as tightly as possible. Just as they were about to engage in their tasks, Quintus gave loose right on Cullen. Getarix just laughed and went to work. Once the animals were secure, they returned to their position to wait out the storm. By this time, Quintus was on the floor with dry heaves. No one was joking now. They had to hold onto whatever they could grab. At one moment they were almost floating in the air like a bird, only to be thrown on the deck, smashing hard on whatever was in the way. Getarix held tight to his leather bag, just grateful that he had remembered to grab it the last time he was with his kit. Water began to pour into the hold through any opening it could find. Fear began to really grip the soldiers.

Then Getarix noticed that some soldiers were leaving the hold for topside.

"Where are you going?" he asked a fellow duplicarius.

"I'm not dying down here. These sailors obviously need some help keeping this bucket afloat—we're going up to help."

Getarix began to think that maybe he was right. *Who the hell wants to die like rats in a ship, anyway?* He was about to get his troop ready to do the same when he saw a pair of legs coming down the ladder. They were sporting centurion shin guards. Since Faustus was the only centurion on board, Getarix hesitated.

"Maybe he is coming down to take us up to help, Cullen."

"I hope so. I can't take much more of this."

Getarix looked at him and said, "You mean to tell me that Cullen has found his limit?"

"I'm not ashamed to say so. An hour of this would finish off the gods themselves."

"Of course it would. They don't like to suffer, you know. That's what we are here for, to suffer on their behalf."

Faustus had managed to make it down the ladder. The moment he stepped on the lower deck, he went down hard in the manure and the many meals brought up by almost everyone below. The ship rolled sharply to starboard, causing Faustus to slide rapidly across the centre of the deck. He slid right underfoot of one of the frightened horses. His weight knocked the legs out from under the horse. The startled horse was held up by ropes tightly binding him to the ship's under-structure. With his body suspended, the animal began to thrash wildly, kicking Faustus. Unlike the soldier below, Faustus was wearing his full amour. It saved his life. The horse got in a few good hits before Getarix pulled Faustus out of range. The roll of the ship aided them, throwing them right into the stairs. They both grabbed onto the wooden stairs with all their might.

"Sir, you okay?"

"Good enough." He glanced down at his bruised arm. "This is like a living hell down here." Faustus tried his best not to bring up his lunch. As a centurion, his accommodations were topside in a cabin shared with the ship's commanders.

"What's happening up there, sir? Do you want us to go and help with the ship?" Getarix asked, glancing up the stairs.

"Absolutely not. I came down here to tell you to stay here because those idiots who have already gone up are just getting in the way and a few have already been washed overboard."

"What about this storm…why haven't we found a cove by the coast?"

"The winds are now from the south and we are nowhere near the German coast. We are closer to Britannia, I am told." The thought of that was horrific to

Getarix. He looked over to his superior and noticed that the horse had kicked his armour apart.

"Sir. What are our chances?"

"If we are lucky, we will be blown ashore somewhere in Britannia. If not..." He left the statement unfinished.

"Can you swim?"

"Not well."

"Well, I recommend you lose your armour."

Faustus looked down at the expensive armour he had taken a year to pay for but concluded a year was not worth his life.

Water continued to pour down the stairs as they talked. Suddenly a sailor almost fell down the stairs yelling at the soldiers to start pumping. He grabbed a few quickly, instructing them how to pump the water out of the hold. Once he accomplished this task, he found Faustus holding onto the stairs.

"Sir...I'm sorry, but we are going to have to lighten the load." Faustus, not sure what he was getting at, just looked at him.

"Sir, we are going to have to throw some of the horses overboard." It took a moment for this to sink in. The last thing a cavalryman could conceive would be to sacrifice his mount. Faustus was broken out of his shock when the ship almost capsized and an immense amount of water flowed down the stairs on him.

"Okay." Addressing Getarix, he began his orders. "Select the lame horses—"

"Sir, no...sorry, they all go...or we all go!"

"Very well. Duplicarius, make it so."

In the midst of the storm, they had to drop the ramp, secure it in place and try to lead horses frightened out of their minds topside. It would have been bad enough to lead healthy animals, but lame horses proved a special challenge. The ramp was no wider than the width of a horse. It led from the upper deck down to the hold below. As the frightened and already injured mounts were being led up, they would rear up and thrash about, occasionally crushing the equally frightened soldiers. A few soldiers even lost their lives in the endeavour. It took a better part of the night to accomplish this hellish task. The only good that came out of it was that the men were too busy to be sitting around slowly sliding into a panic. As difficult as the task was, it accomplished the goal. As dawn began to filter through the storm clouds, the boat was still afloat. The day, however, did not relieve them of Poseidon's fury. The loadmaster found Faustus now dressed in only a tunic like the rest of his soldiers, soaked to the bone.

"Well…are they all off?"

"No, there are three left."

"Get them off. No one, even you, can keep his—"

"They are not mine, they're dead."

"Well, go down there and get them off."

Sea spray whipped his face, but Faustus hardly noticed. "Why don't you go down there and pick them up and toss them over. I'm sure the ten soldiers I lost last night will make up for the three horses still on board." Faustus was spitting mad. Not only had he lost ten soldiers overboard, he had to say goodbye to his own mount who had been with him for the last ten years.

The loadmaster knew enough not to push the issue. He was aware that lifting such large animals in this weather would be deadly work if not impossible. "Sir, cut them up and get rid of them. This boat was not built for these seas and the storm does not appear to be weakening any." He then went about the business of throwing all the provisions overboard. Before the day was done, they had thrown everything not nailed down and a few things nailed down that the storm had not already broken free, including all their arms.

The storm raged on, and the soldiers were sent back below. Getarix was tasked to secure the ramp back up with the hope that closing the ramp would slow down the water intake. The pumps could not keep up with the amount of water slowly sinking the vessel. Cullen was on one rope and Quintus on the other. They heaved with all their strength on the coarse ropes that burned their hands raw. As he directed the work, Getarix held onto the main mast that protruded down from the upper deck secured to the keel. The mast seemed to be getting larger.

Then he felt the mast pull apart.

He looked up through the hole still open from the ramp and all he saw was water. It looked to him like they were in a temple of the sea. Even above his head he saw only water. The ship began to list to port. Suddenly all was silent. And he realized he was under water. Held tightly to the mast, not sure what to do, he simply held tight. Just as suddenly the noise returned and he was able to breathe. This time he was no longer on board, yet he still had a death grip on the main mast. He frantically looked around trying to orientate himself. As he looked down the mast, he noticed Cullen holding on for all he was worth. At one moment they were deep in a valley of sea water. The next second they were on top of a crest looking down into a different valley. As they crested the wave they anxiously sought their ship. At one time they thought they heard a loud cracking sound but saw nothing. The worst part was the cold. Their limbs became weak and at one point Getarix felt he was losing his grip. He let go just a second to throw his arms around the mast again. The second he let go it seemed Poseidon himself pulled the mast away from his grip. The wave pulled him away and when it descended he began to sink under the water. He figured if he was going to die, why spend the last moments in a panic. He calmed his mind and accepted his fate. He continued to hold his breath because that's what we do. He did not wish death, he just accepted it. When he could hardly hold his breath anymore, and he was preparing himself for what came next, his feet hit bottom. The sea bottom woke him from his semi-spiritual state and he realized that if the water was that shallow he must be near land. He recoiled his legs and shot up with all his might. When he broke the surface he searched the horizon once again. This time he was able to see the dark shadow of land. He forced his numb limbs to move and began to swim toward the darkness. With the help of the waves, he soon felt land under his feet. Only then did he realize how tired he had become. With the last of his energy, he crawled up away from the water onto the beach, his leather bag dragging on the sand. Finding a large stone he sat, leaning against it, facing the sea, hoping and almost praying for any sight of other survivors, particularly Cullen. He could hardly keep his eyes open.

XXIX

BACK HOME

In spite of himself, Getarix could no longer keep his watch. Forty-eight hours without sleep and the continual strain of nonstop toil and strain had taken its toll. He could not help himself. Sleep invaded his mind and without even knowing it, he was in a dreamless slumber. He had reached the shore shortly after sunset. By the time he was found, the morning sun was in full bloom and he was being harassed by the sharp end of an unfriendly spear poking at his side.

"Get up, you. I said get up!"

So deep was his sleep that Getarix dreamed he was back home, for he seemed to be dreaming in Celtic again. Three fierce-looking tribesmen stood by him. They were dressed for war with spears and swords each. One of the three took the handle of his spear and began to beat Getarix. He woke up in short order. He was greeted with the sight of the sun behind the three figures, creating dark silhouettes. Being awoken to such a vision struck fear deep into his soul. He thought he had died and now was at the mercy of three hateful gods. His fear intensified when he clued in to the fact he understood every word they said. Words spoken in his own language. Words spoken with an accent he recognized. As he came around, he comprehended that these were not the voices of the gods—they were the voices of his own people. He scrambled around on all fours, placing the sun behind himself. Once done he confirmed to his horror his greatest fear. He was not only in Britannia again, he was in the hands of his tribe's greatest enemy, the Trinovantes. Fear gripped him as he recounted in his childhood the many stories of horror about the Trinovantes. Stories of how they ate their own children and killed anyone who wandered into their territory.

It was this very tribe that his own sacrifice had been intended to protect his family from, his death through which his adopted tribe, the Icenian, sought divine protection from these Trinovantes. They became agitated as they poked him with their spear, telling him to get to his feet. He felt he better comply, but just before he stood one of the three gave the same command in broken Latin. Getarix, by then, found his footing and stood instantly.

"These Romans are so stupid they do not even know the language of the gods." That's when it hit Getarix that he would be safer as long as he kept silent.

After a short walk, they entered a small village that sat with its back to the sea. It was a farming village surrounded by farms and in the village itself livestock were free to roam. Getarix recognized the people as mainly farmer types, little different from his own family. As Getarix rounded one of the twenty huts that surrounded the village common area, he spotted what looked like about ten Romans dressed only in their tunics. They all looked, as he did, tired, dirty, and distressed. Getarix noticed there were as many well-armed guards surrounding the prisoners. His eyes scanned the small crowd searching in vain for Cullen. One of the guards gruffly pointed his spear to a spot on the ground and said in rough, mispronounced Latin, "Here, sit!"

As he sat, he whispered to no one in particular, "Has anyone seen Decion Cullen or Alaris Quintus?" He received a negative answer followed by questions about their own friends. He finally had to tell them that once the ship broke up he was on his own and saw no one.

"Silence there, you!" one of the guards screamed in Celtic, putting an end to their meeting. As the morning sun burned their exposed skin, Getarix chastised himself for not somehow saving Cullen. He was so lost in thought that he did not notice a large delegation of Celts enter the village common from the north. The entire village tensed up and their guards became more alert, holding their spears in the defensive stance. Getarix was broken out of his self-assessment by a voice dreadfully familiar to him.

"We demand you turn these Roman pigs over to us."

"Ha, you do, do you? We found them in our land and they are ours. Look at them—they are strong and will command a good price."

Getarix looked up shyly just as Cunorix turned and looked in his direction. As soon as his brother's eyes landed near him, Getarix shot his head down, covering his face.

"A little timid to command any price." His laughter was joined by his mates.

"They will fetch a good enough price," returned Broiiox, Chief of the Trinovantes.

"Well in that case, it would only be fair to share the profits," Cunorix said.

Broiiox considered Cunorix's suggestion. It angered him that Cunorix, the new chief of the Icenian, dare interfere with Trinovantes affairs, let alone demand a share of their prize. *Such arrogance to come here and claim anything from us...*

Cunorix broke his chain of thought. "I expect you would only return these invaders of our sacred land back to your masters."

"The Romans are not our masters! We are a free people...free to call whomever we wish our friends."

"Romans have no friends—" Cunorix stopped himself because of a commotion in the centre of the square. Some Trinovantes fighters were escorting another group of Roman soldiers into the village. They doubled the number of Romans gathered from the coast.

As the new group of soldiers arrived, Getarix held his arms across his face and peered between his arms in hopes of sighting any men from of his own section. He finally saw his friend toward the back of the crowd. He had tucked his leather bag under his legs, trying to keep eyes off it. He especially tried to keep Cullen from recognizing him. If Cullen blurted out his name, that would be it.

"Wait a minute!" Cunorix yelled. He jumped from his pony and ran toward the Romans with his sword drawn. The Trinovante guards jumped in front of him, preventing Cunorix from reaching them. He never took his eyes off Cullen. "Cullen...Cullen, is that you?"

Cullen looked directly into his eyes. "Cunorix?"

Cunorix could not believe his eyes. Not only had Getarix evaded his sacred duty to the gods, but now they had joined his avowed enemy. *To wear their hated uniform...to dare to wear them here on sacred land, especially after denying the gods their rightful sacrifice.*

"Where is Getarix, Cullen? He can't be far, that little coward. Getarix, show yourself. Getarix, the gods have returned you here to fulfill your duty."

This was one of the few things his brother had ever said that Getarix truly believed in.

"What's the meaning of this?" Broiiox demanded, forcing himself between Cunorix and the guards. Cunorix did not even notice him at first until Broiiox was yelling right into his face. "Do not forget you are standing in Trinovante territory and I, Broiiox, I am the chief here and not you!"

Cunorix looked him in the eyes and hissed, "Oh yeah? Why do you harbour and protect those who have offended the gods? Those," Cunorix looked over Broiiox's shoulder and addressed the Romans behind him, many of whom looked at him in wonder, "who the gods have called for in sacrifice, but are too cowardly to answer to their sacred duty. Too selfish, thinking only of themselves, not of our people. All our people."

That was all Getarix could take. He stood and called out to his brother. "Cunorix!" Cunorix stopped in midsentence and just looked at his younger brother, hair cut short, shaven and wearing the green tunic of a Roman soldier with their hated eagle painted on the front.

"You freaking coward…you are a curse to the land." By this time Cullen was standing next to his friend. "And your useless friend—"

"That's enough of that," Broiiox cut him off. His endurance had been pushed to the limit. "Clear yourself—"

"No! We take what is ours. These two belong to the gods. We will take them, you may sell or kill or give back the rest. I really don't care."

"How dare you come here and order me and my people around like you're the king of all of Briton. You're not even a Briton yourself, Gaul. Matter of a fact, I don't believe a word you said, Gaul," Broiiox said, stressing Cunorix' Gaulish origin to combat the attempt to usurp his authority beyond his adopted tribe.

"Fine. That leather bag, look in it. Go ahead and open it."

"What's so special about that?"

"I made it. He stole it and you will find the gold of Vercingetorix, my great grandfather, inside." He stood to his full height, looking around, and continued trying to win the favour of the whole crowd. "Vercingetorix, the great Celtic King who defeated the mighty Roman General Caesar. Until he was betrayed by cowards like these two." He pointed at his brother. "You will find in that bag a dagger, maybe arm torques, if they have not already sold them to the first Roman they came across."

Broiiox indicated to one of the guards to open the bag, where they found exactly what Cunorix claimed would be there.

"You come forward," Broiiox commanded Getarix. He advanced, steeling himself to face his brother. This time he was determined not to cower. He was a

Roman soldier who had killed more men than his brother. He reminded himself that he was better trained in sword fighting. No matter what, he felt he was not going to show weakness. He walked with his back straight and looked Cunorix straight in his eyes.

"I see that my little baby brother appears to have found his spine. At least he walks like a man for once."

"How is our mother?"

"She rejoices in your death. Yeah, she thinks you're dead. That's what I told her when our uncle could not find you in Gaul. After the shame of your cowardly acts, she rejoiced in your death."

"You lie!" Getarix almost betrayed himself. He choked down all emotions.

"Now she rejoices in her new daughter-in-law, Boudica." Getarix did not show the hurt in hearing the girl he had admired for so many years would take to the bed of Cunorix. "And our mother is kept busy with her granddaughter, named after her mother. And yes, Cullen," Cunorix said, looking beyond Getarix to where Cullen still stood, "your father could not bear your betrayal and took his own life a week after your treason." Cullen just stood there in shock.

Cunorix addressed Broiiox. "We will now go with what is ours and finish that which the gods demand."

"Not so easy," Broiiox interrupted. He addressed Getarix. "Tell me, is what he's telling me true?"

Getarix spoke for the first time. "Can a snake ever tell the truth?"

"So you do know him." Broiiox smiled, Cunorix shot Getarix a look of hate.

"Tell him, coward. You were called upon by the gods to be sacrificed for the protection of our tribe. Tell him, coward!"

Getarix confirmed that he had been selected for the dubious honour. Broiiox asked, "And what border were you to have been sacrificed on?"

Cunorix did not answer, knowing that the right answer would offend. Getarix saw his opportunity to destroy any hope of Cunorix making off with his prize. "On our south border."

"Oh, I see, so you were to be sacrificed to protect against us. In other words, you were to be sacrificed in order to place a curse on me and my people. Is that not so, Getarix?"

"He offended the gods!" Cunorix screamed, not giving Getarix a chance to answer.

"Gods you were attempting to bribe to destroy us. The gods spoke when he escaped."

"The gods are speaking by bringing him back. We will take him to finish what the gods so clearly demand. Demand, you hear—they demand it."

"You demand it."

"Yes I do demand it!"

"Would it offend you if we turned him back over to the Romans?"

"More than you could imagine," Cunorix snarled, sword in hand. He realized he was losing ground with the Travertine Chief. He also knew that he had not brought enough men with him for a fight. A battle at this time would not likely go his way, as the Travertine were stronger and better armed.

"It would offend you?"

"And the gods."

"Not from where I stand," Broiiox declared, and turned facing his guards. "Release the prisoners. Feed them and bind their wounds." Broiiox smiled. He turned and looked straight into the face of Cunorix, broadening his smile. "Oh, and feed them meat. They will be loaded on our boats and returned at this evening sail. You," he said to Cunorix, "can leave now. Our business is done."

Cunorix glared at Getarix before departing. "I pray for the day we meet in battle where I can send you to your death."

"You would not last two minutes in battle with me, brother. But for our mother's sake I would never kill you." Getarix had never stood up to his brother. Cunorix felt completely defeated. He mounted his pony and departed the village as quickly as he arrived.

Getarix just stood there, filled with a thousand emotions. Relief and joy on having survived, hate and anger over the news about Boudica and his brother's insistence that he be killed. But the main emotion was fear that Cunorix spoke the truth about his mother being pleased about his death.

XXX

QUICK RECOVERY

The news of the disaster at sea reached the Germans, encouraging them to prepare for a late-summer war. They felt the storm was an omen from their gods. An omen interpreted as the gods intervening on their behalf.

Germanicus was so distraught from the great losses due to the storm, he was inconsolable. Until he got word of the German preparations.

"It looks like the Germans have renewed hopes of driving us back again, repeating their victories of seven years ago. I will not let that happen. They misinterpret the meaning of the gods. They do not know that the gods rescued our army. This is unquestionable proof that the gods favour us. This surprise can and will work in our favour."

"Yes, sir, it is truly a miracle, however we did lose a lot of men and horses, not to mention arms."

"I know, Silius. But Arminius thinks we are wiped out. Destitute, even. Far from it…and that works to our advantage. How many men could you muster?"

"Given replacement arms and horses, I could field 30,000 infantry."

"Not destitute at all. The storm at sea was not a disaster at all—it is an opportunity handed to us by fate. An opportunity we dare not ignore. I want you to take your 30,000 troops and I'll top you off with three thousand cavalry. How long will it take you to sort yourself out?"

"Where are the horses and armour we sent by land?"

"They are due back today or tomorrow."

"Then I will be ready in two days."

Germanicus pointed to the map. "Good, then. Silius, I want you to head here and hit the Cattians hard. I will take the bulk of our force over to here and invade the Marsians. Word is they have buried at least one of the eagle standards in a small grove of trees. And if what we have heard is true, it is not well-guarded. When you engage, with your force right here, I expect they will all rush to the aid of the Cattians, leaving a clear path for my army along here to the supposed location of the standard. Which I believe should be right in this area. After the disaster of the sea, they will at first think we are finished but when we hit them hard they will be convinced we are actually invincible, able to ride any wave of misfortune, coming out even stronger than before. They will say, 'Even with their fleet in ruins, their arms lost, their horses and men rotting all along the shores, they attack and win the same.' They will think we are gods ourselves."

The forest, even in the bright sunlight, was filled with ghosts. The three of them, Getarix, Cullen, and Jodoc, were used as scouts employed as a small recce troop. Their assignment had changed. With the loss of so many men, Getarix, the less experienced leader, lost his troop. Most of his men perished in the fire and were not replaced. With so many lost at sea, command decided to employ their three best riders as scouts.

They had been rescued and reunited with their horses, and attached to Caecina's army. They were assigned to one of Germanicus' colonels, Lucius Stertinius. Their assignment was to be the eyes and ears of the army. This was not far from where Varus had lost his legions and his life.

"I don't like this place," Getarix said quietly to no one in particular, wondering when this summer would end. Cullen, riding by his side, simply nodded. Jodoc grunted in agreement. They were riding a path through the dark forest. When the sun did manage to find its way past the branches of the stately pines, the heat was intense. It was two hours before noon and they felt the rapidly rising temperature causing them to sweat under their newly issued armour.

"Do you smell that?"

"They must be burning the fields," Jodoc said.

"That's not the fields burning, that smells like a village going down," Cullen said.

"We had better be careful. If they flee this way, I can guarantee you they will not be in a friendly mood—" Before Getarix got it out, they heard the sound of horses' hooves behind them.

"Up here, quick," Getarix whispered, not wanting to be heard. *No matter how well-trained they are, three Roman soldiers cannot handle an entire angry village.*

To their right the bank ascended sharply to a small plateau the height of a three-story Roman apartment house. They found a rarely used path that led directly to a small clearing that seemed to lead to an opening of a cave situated just over the crest of the grass-covered plateau.

Getarix dismounted just short of the vine-covered cave opening. "Jodoc, secure that cave. Cullen, hide our mounts. We will hide in there if need be."

Jodoc moved the vines aside. Ensuring the cave did not hold any disgruntled Germans, he moved in for a closer look. Getarix fell on his belly to peer over the crest as Cullen led their horses into the tree line, out of sight of the clearing. Just as Getarix peered over the edge, he was shocked to find the hooves no more than fifteen paces away, moving rapidly up the embankment toward him.

"In the cave!" he yelled, not caring who heard him.

Jodoc, from the mouth of the cave, turned to see what was going on. The moment he turned, he was knocked flat on his back by the muscular bulk of Getarix. Cullen followed, sword drawn. From inside Jodoc heard the sound of swords meeting. Battle had erupted.

From his vantage point, Jodoc saw his two friends fighting for all their worth. Their bulk filled the mouth of the cave opening. The first German who reached them was on the ground within seconds, holding his belly. He was quickly replaced. Jodoc assessed that there were eight to ten villagers queued to replace any dead or injured. With the opening too small for the three of them, he could not join the fight. Jodoc searched around and noticed that the cave was a storehouse for weapons. Most of them were Roman and rusting badly. He found a long spear with a strong shaft and went to work with great effect, poking it between his friends into unsuspecting Germans. He quickly took down three unwary villagers.

The battle continued until they were all exhausted. Getarix had seldom seen men so determined to win. Jodoc wondered why they were so willing to risk their lives for a few rusted weapons. They were fighting with all their might. Jodoc noticed that Getarix was slowing down due to fatigue. He knew that this was when men got killed, even the best of them. His sword was becoming heavy. A large villager who obviously skilled in sword work was quickly getting the better of Getarix. Jodoc unsuccessfully attempted to drive his spear into the muscular German. With a sixth sense, the villager moved out of the way each time. On the third attempt, he even grabbed the spear but had to loose his grip to defend himself. Sweat poured down Getarix's face. He could hardly see. This did not escape the giant's notice. He pulled his sword back, ready to thrust it deep into the now-stumbling Getarix. Jodoc grabbed Getarix by his cape, pulled hard and threw him backward into the cave, thrusting the spear deep into the unprotected belly of the well-trained German. He gave a look of shock, dropping his sword as he stumbled backward to the middle of the clearing. When he fell on his back, the spear stood proudly in the sky like a broken standard. He lay there dying about five paces away from the four other dead who lay at the mouth of the cave. By now, the warriors had to reach over the dead to engage each other. The three unengaged villagers just stood there staring at their best warrior as he died.

Getarix got hold of his breath and began to search for a new spear like the one Jodoc had. All he could find were the typical Roman spears with their weak, thin shank, most of which were bent beyond use. The light was not very good in the cave. He began to frantically search for a stout spear, knocking aside a large stack of neatly arranged Roman spears. They stood against the cave wall creating a curtain. When they fell, Getarix noticed a bulge on the cave floor. It looked like a large tablet set on the floor and covered with a mound of dirt. When he touched it, he noticed whatever it was had been recently buried and wrapped in an old Roman centurion's cape. The red had faded and the dirt made it look more orange than red. He picked it up. Again whatever it was it was heavy—very heavy for its size. Getarix hastily unwrapped it.

The sight of a wonder greeted him.

The solid brass wings were exposed first. Then the heavy eagle that stood proudly on a platform. On the face of the platform blazoned into the brass were the Roman numbers XIX. Under this was a small brass rod that extended beyond the length of the wing tips, a thin rod that a small red banner had once hung from. Then Getarix knew what he held in his hands. It also explained why the Germans were fighting so tenaciously. Getarix sat for a moment, staring at the Eagle Standard of the nineteenth legion. One of the legions Arminius destroyed, one of the standards that Varus lost. Getarix looked to the cave opening and noticed that Cullen was slowing down. Jodoc was holding his own. Matter of a fact, he looked like he was enjoying himself, almost too much. Getarix grabbed one of the least-bent spears and ran to the cave opening, landing the spear right into the chest of Cullen's opponent. The fighter Jodoc was against stopped short at the death of his mate just long enough for Jodoc to finish him off with one blow of the sword across the neck. Once he fell, there was a deathly silence. The remainder of the Germans had fled at the sight of their best warrior's death in the clearing. They stood, soaking in the heavy air and the silence.

XXXI

EVIL PLANS

Antonio was beside himself. He had always thought that as a man grows older his life should know more peace until his retirement, when he could rest and those he loved could take care of him. For Antonio, life went the other direction. His master's abuse had grown as the years passed. He tried not to think of his retirement to the mines. Lately things had grown worse. Ever since the trip to Germania, the senator seemed to have lost the final shred of humanity that resided in him. First there was Centurion Cornelius who made his narrow escape. Then there was the death of the old Augustus. Tiberius was not like his stepfather. He could not be manipulated in the same way. Augustus never forgot that he was not born into an empire. He never forgot that his position was dependent upon the grace of the Senate, or at least he believed so. That was all Senator Damianus had needed to maintain a measure of control over the last emperor. Tiberius would not even give him the courtesy to look at him when they talked. He just sat there looking like he was sulking. As of late, it had become difficult to even get an audience with him. The new emperor spent very little time in Rome, favouring the quiet of one of his country villas, cutting himself off from those who wish to influence him. But the final blow came when he failed to gain ownership of the little German girl. He became obsessed with it, making the lives of his slaves a special breed of hell.

"I want that girl! Every reasonable man has a price," declared the senator.

"True, sir...however, we have not yet found his price."

"Then find it!" the senator bellowed at his hapless slave. "Explain to me what he sees in this worthless child?"

"I don'—"

"Don't talk to me unless I address you."

Antonio looked around the beautifully decorated room to see if the senator was addressing someone else who might have entered the room, but they were the only ones there.

"Tell me, what would he want with that thing?"

This time Antonio kept his peace.

"Answer me, you bag of dung!" Punctuated with a whack across the head from the small cane the senator carried.

Keeping his head down, Antonio answered, "Who can understand the minds of such people, sir?" Antonio frantically searched for an answer he feared did not exist. The best he could hope for was to at least pacify the senator enough to keep him from striking again.

"How is it that he lives after killing Alexander? I sent him to get that girl and this, this...thing...has the gall to kill him. This foreigner not even a Roman!" The senator was red in the face. Antonio feared that if he did not calm down, he would die on the spot, sending him and the other slaves to the mines.

"Lucius, get in here!" the senator said, calling for his new military aid.

Lucius Caius Asinius was the unlucky centurion who had replaced Cornelius.

"Yes, sir." Lucius entered the room, still buckling his breastplate on.

I want you to look into why that maggot still lives after he killed Alexander the slave-trader."

"Sir, we have already—" Lucius was still learning to keep his mouth shut. "Sir, Germanicus personally looked into it."

"Shut up! I don't want to hear that ever again."

Their stormy conversation was broken up by a messenger who looked like he had just ridden from the end of the Empire. Lucius didn't care if he had come from the land of the dead, he was just glad someone broke the senator's tirade. The messenger went straight to the senator and spoke quietly. Neither Antonio nor Centurion Lucius could hear a word. They, however, could see the effect upon their master. He gave a look of surprise and almost shock, followed by anger. His face was getting redder as he clenched his fist hard. Suddenly he exploded in an angry rampage seldom seen even from the senator.

"You mean to tell me that little pond scum actually found the Eagle Standard... my eagle standard, the one I found and that waste of rations Cornelius lost?" He began to pace in a circle. Once again, Antonio feared for his life. Lucius was not sure if the interruption was so good.

As he came by the messenger again, Senator Damianus raised his cane and began to beat the messenger in the face without mercy. "Do you have the gall to tell me that the murderer of Alexander actually found an eagle standard?"

"I'm sorry, sir," the messenger said through his tears as he held his hands over his face for protection. He fell to the ground, utterly confused as to what was happening.

"Stop protecting yourself!" The senator grabbed his hands and threw them down, and continued to hit the messenger, screaming, "When I want to strike your face, you do not have the right to deny me. Do you understand me?"

"Sir."

Antonio thought frantically. If this continued someone might die, possibly his master. He was not ready for the mines. "Sir!" he blurted out before he knew it.

The senator stopped his beating. Antonio looked at him. He was red in the face and quivering with rage.

Catching his breath and thinking anxiously, Antonio said, "Sir...um...this may not be all that bad."

His master slowly approached him, still shaking with rage. He was now whipping the palm of his left hand with his small cane like he was about to launch upon his head slave. He gave the impression that it took all he had to control his voice. "How in the name of all the gods is this not all that bad?"

Now it was time for Antonio's voice to quiver. Lucius just looked at him as if he was looking upon a man who just asked for a painful execution. Antonio was just thinking about his adopted family of slaves. "Well, sir, if he is already noticed by Germanicus...as a hero and all...well, maybe it would be better to add your voice to the chorus of praise."

"What!"

Antonio began to panic a bit, as the senator was still crossing the red marble floor toward him. "If you...were to add your voice of praise...to the tune of demanding the young soldier even be promoted to centurion, with citizenship granted by a grateful Rome for his recovery of the—your—standard, you can have him transferred to the Praetorian Guards...here in Rome."

"What!" The senator was almost within striking range.

"Sir, if this little arrogant soldier was moved here to Rome, he would also bring the—"

"The girl." The senator stopped his advance dead. Slowly he regained the old evil look in his eyes. He paused and then his face lit up as if a new idea had just struck. "And if I was responsible for such a huge leap in his career, he would owe me. That rotten little maggot will melt once in my hands. I think the proper payment would be…what? Merely an untrained, useless little slave girl?"

Senator Damianus was back in control. Antonio was relieved for that, but felt sick at his part in the assured demise of that little girl he faintly remembered from their trip to Germania. The fate of the young soldier did not matter to him, as he was unknown, but the girl. Antonio had no illusions about his boss. Once he had the young soldier in his grasp, he would never stop squeezing until he crushed him, promoted or not.

"Where is Germanicus now?" Senator Damianus now addressed his messenger as if nothing had happened.

Trying to recover, the messenger said, "Well, sir…once the Eagle Standard of the Nineteenth Legion was found—"

"Nineteenth, eh?"

"Yes, sir…hum, Germanicus himself went to the country of the Marsians, where the standard was found—"

"Lucius, get my horse ready. I will see that emperor whether he wants to see me or not. I have to do Rome a great service by having one of her adopted sons properly rewarded for his indispensible service to the empire. This I know Tiberius will listen to."

XXXII

HEROISM RECOGNIZED

The late summer sun burned mercilessly wherever it found a way through the thick carpet of trees. The summer heat caused the pitch of the Teutoburg Forest to release its sweet pine perfume.

Getarix did not know whether to enjoy the smell or be horrified by the sight. Before his eyes lay the carnage of the three lost legions. The entire army of Varus lay where they had died. The bleached out bones shone where the sun hit them. They looked like stars on the ground. Getarix sat mounted on Cabello, near Germanicus. Ever since the discovery of the Eagle Standard, Germanicus had assigned the three of them to be his personal guards. Germanicus dismounted and just stood there. Getarix glanced over and saw a tear roll from his eye. Germanicus bent down and freed a rusting sword from the grasp of a bony hand. "It's okay, brother, you may rest…we are here to relieve you." Only those close to Germanicus could hear his words. They were not meant for anyone else. He looked up and took in the remains of the 20,000 lost that day six years prior.

"Caecina, bring him here." Caecina signalled to a young soldier, who marched sharply to Germanicus and gave him a proper salute. He stood waiting to be addressed.

"Relax, son…so tell me. You were here before, right?"

"Yes sir, I was here with the delegation two years ago."

"You mean, with the honourable Damianus Aurelia Marius Gius, Senator of Rome."

At such a noble title, the young soldier paused. "Yes, sir…I…I mean, we found the standards."

"According to reports, the senator claims to have found them himself."

"Yes, sir…I must be mistaken, um, wrong."

"No, you're not. Now tell me the truth, the real truth as you saw and experienced it."

"Umm…yes, sir…this way, sir." They walked for a time up a trail used by the deer of the forest. "Up here, sir, is a great stone, an outcrop of sorts…and they were leaning there. In those days the forest was full of the enemy." The young soldier peered around him as if he were back two years ago. The fear was noticeable on his face.

"They are gone now. I can assure you of that," Germanicus said.

They reached the place where some of the sub-unit standards were still standing. Many of the poles had fallen and the weather had warped them beyond use. On the stone floor at the base of the standard poles were some torn, faded pennants. Where the outside folds were exposed to the elements, they were bleached light orange. Their gold lettering was barely visible. On the trees that surrounded the stone outcrop, the Germans had mounted a number of human skulls. The sight of this angered Germanicus, but not as badly as the altars they found, complete with the remains of their human sacrifices.

The young soldier stopped and seemed as if he could go no further.

Germanicus stopped beside him, just short of the ledge where the standards stood. "Then what happened, son?"

The young soldier began to labour in his story. "We came up to this spot, myself and Miles Crassus…" He could not move his eyes off the remains of a soldier that appeared more recent than the rest.

"What happened then?"

The young soldier simply pointed to the ground where the crumpled remains of a Roman soldier lay.

"He has not been here as long. Who is he?"

"That is Miles Crassus. He was my brother."

"Ah, yes, the report…the soldier Centurion Cornelius got killed." Germanicus left the statement open, allowing the young soldier to make any correction, which he did not. This did not matter to Germanicus, as he knew very well where the guilt of that day rested.

After the soldier reported the events of the day, they gathered up all the standards they could find. The eagle standards of the XVII and XIIX Legion were not found.

"Just what I figured, like the XIXth they are hidden somewhere near here… Caecina."

"Sir."

"I want you to send out search parties for the lost standards. Make sure they check every cave they come across."

"Yes sir."

"And once they are gone, start gathering the remains for a proper burial. I'll do the rites myself."

"Are you sure that's wise, sir?"

"Maybe not, but it's the least I could do for the fallen."

"What about the animals…horses, mules and such? It will be difficult separating them from the soldiers."

"Then don't. They died together…bury them together."

The few soldiers who had somehow escaped the battle six years before also guided Germanicus to where the key events happened, including the suicide of their general, Varus. They also pointed out where Arminius stood and heaped insults onto the standards. Germanicus finally stopped one soldier and said, "Enough. I've heard enough." He walked away to be alone with his thoughts.

Once the funeral rites were completed, Germanicus ordered a great monument built to honour the dead. The evening of the funeral, a messenger arrived from Rome, seeking Germanicus. The message bore the seal of the emperor Tiberius.

"You are beyond belief." Faustus was in shock. He just stared at Getarix in utter astonishment. Getarix just sat there, unable to take in the meaning of the news Faustus had brought from Germanicus.

"Centurion…what does this mean?" Getarix almost gasped.

"More money," Cullen answered for him with a smile. He was just happy for his friend.

"And women. Women go for centurions, you know. And a better quality of them," Jodoc added.

"Really? Would someone tell the girls I meet?" Faustus quipped. "Promoted by the emperor himself. Who do you know? I know finding the standard has stirred Rome up, but this…" Faustus continued in wonder, still unable to grasp the new development.

"What?"

"Whoever he is you know…"

"I don't know anyone."

"Well he knows you, and whoever he is, and he knows Tiberius, and has a measure of pull with him. Well, it's time we get to the tent of Germanicus. By the way, you two have also been promoted to duplicarius. With Centurion Getarix' new promotion, I am down three duplicarius and I need the two of you for this next battle. I hear it's going to be the biggest yet. Come on, brother centurion, let's go. And remember, next month when you are made Emperor, don't forget this centurion in the forests of Germany."

As they left the tent, Jodoc called out, "Hey, how is it that every time Getarix gets made up it's in front of Germanicus, and all we get is 'oh by the way, you're promoted?'"

"I can take it back if you want."

"It's okay, I kind of like the simple approach," Jodoc acquiesced with a smile accompanied by the laughter of the others—except Getarix, who was still in shock.

In spite of the banter, both Jodoc and Cullen sat there stunned as their good news sank in. It also hit them that their paths were about to part, possibly never to meet again.

"Centurion Getarix, you are a remarkable man," Germanicus began. "I have never seen such a rise in my life. It even makes me worry about my own job," Germanicus said. "I was going to reward you with a bronze phalera. This medal of honour is for your work at the Boar's Head Inn. That will still happen before you leave today. But, apparently the emperor will be honouring you with a gold phalera for finding the Eagle Standard. That will happen once you arrive in Rome."

"Today?"

"No, when you get to Rome."

"No, sir, am I leaving Germany today?"

"Oh yes, today, it's all here," Germanicus said as he picked up the document the messenger brought. "Never before have I seen such direction. As of today, you are no longer a member of the V Alaudae Legion.

"Sir?"

"Its right here. I'm going to miss you in the final push of the summer, but you're transferred to the Praetorian Guard." At hearing this Faustus felt pangs of jealousy. For years he had tried to join this elite unit. Tasked with guarding the life of the emperor, they lived life in the centre of Rome.

"Yes, sir." Getarix did not comprehend the significance of such a transfer. It angered Faustus a bit that he did not. Germanicus was silent. He stood there reading the order that had arrived that morning. His eyes narrowed and he asked, "Centurion, did you campaign for this transfer?"

"Sir?"

"Who do you know who could do this for you?"

"No one, sir. I know no one in Rome…no one at all, never even been there."

"Then what looks like a blessing just might be a curse."

Faustus jumped in. "Sir, are we sure we have the right person?"

"Yes, it's very clear. Getarix, are you from Britannia?"

"Yes sir."

"Well, you're a Roman citizen now."

Getarix just looked in wonder.

"Are you one of the heroes of the battle of that inn last year?"

"I'm no hero, sir."

"According to this you are."

"Did you receive a little slave girl from that battle?"

"Sir?"

"Did you?"

"Yes. But what does that have to do—?"

"Well, that's pretty narrow. We have our man. All that is left is to congratulate you. Now it says you're allowed to pick up your slaves in Xanten and proceed to Rome soonest. Rome is paying for their transport as well."

"My slaves, how do they know?"

"The emperor is divine, they say. Maybe he simply flew here on his wings," Germanicus said a bit irreverently.

Getarix began to wonder about his good fortune. He had that same feeling he had when he first landed in Gaul. He had a strong sense of abandonment and lonely vulnerability.

"Sir."

"Yes."

"A request. I know it's a lot, but could I take with me Duplicarius Cullen and Jodoc? The roads are dangerous and—"

"Well, how can I refuse the emperor's favourite soldier? You have my permission. Faustus, make it so."

"Sir," Faustus said stiffly.

235

With that command given, the meeting was over. The two centurions stepped out into the sun. Faustus was ready to burst.

"What the hell was that?"

"What?"

"You are not even thirty…you are barely off your mother's teats. Only ninety men are promoted a year and one of them has to be you. The Praetorian Guard? And 'Can I take Jodoc and Cullen with me!' I just had them made up because I needed them for the campaign, you boar's ass. They are the best I have."

"I'm sorry, sir. They are all I have." Faustus stared at Getarix. Like Germanicus, he has a bad feeling about this good fortune. As he turned to comply with his orders, he said flatly, "I'm sorry Getarix…you're right. And stop calling me sir. We're the same rank now."

"Yes, sir."

XXXIII

AWAKENING

"You know you'll be making money like never before. Just imagine how many women you'll have all over you now?" Jodoc spoke over the rhythmic clopping of the hooves on the stone road that led directly to the bridge and then into Xanten, their winter quarters.

"Jodoc, what's wrong with you?" Cullen looked at him in mock disgust.

Jodoc defended himself. "Listen, haven't we risked our lives? He—" pointing to the so-far silent Getarix, "damn near died more than nine times. You, Cullen, almost died with him and I almost died five of those times. So what does that tell you?"

"That we should avoid him?" Cullen said with a smile.

"No, dopey…it begs the question, why should we not enjoy a bit of, how shall I say it, comfort?"

"There's more to life than sex, Jodoc."

"Yeah, I know, there's wine…" All three laughed at the little joke. "Maybe we can go back to Portius Itius and you can find Beaudin the bar wench for a little—"

Getarix shot Jodoc a hostile look. Cullen broke in. "Yeah, but this time you can do it right." The two of them almost fell off their mounts with laughter.

"Hey!" Jodoc added. "We could find Cassius and Aquilla, just to order them around."

"We will do no such thing. Portius Itius will be avoided completely. That's a direct order from your new centurion, boys. Gents, did it not strike you as odd that my promotion and posting message mentioned Isolde?"

"Yeah, it made me feel very uneasy," Cullen said.

"This posting may not be the party you think it," Getarix said.

"So much for sex and fun," Jodoc concluded.

They rode in silence for a few miles, then Cullen continued the theme. "Besides, Jodoc, Getarix will have to buy all his armour now. He will not get it issued like we do, and he'll need to buy a good set that shines in the presence of the emperor."

"Well, I still think we should spend what's left on—"

"Would you two stop arguing over how to spend my money? Besides, there's not much left. It's going to be tight just buying the armour. Keeping Gainer and the child has not been cheap."

"Sell them. Then we could—"

"Jodoc, I'm not telling you again."

"Okay, okay." Jodoc said nothing more as they entered the open gates of the military city of Xanten. Once in the city, they quickly went to their unit lines and cleared out, receiving any pay due and paying any dues owed.

"Now that we are cleared out of the quarters, where will we stay?" Cullen asked.

"I'm staying at my apartment," Getarix announced.

"Yeah, that's if your slave allows you," Jodoc said.

"Shut your cake hole, Jodoc."

"Getarix, we will be at the Legionaries Rest Inn," Cullen said before Jodoc could dig himself a deeper hole. Cullen noticed that as they got nearer to Xanten, Getarix had become quiet and sullen.

"I'll see you there in the morning."

"We'll reserve a room for you," Jodoc joked. Getarix chose to ignore the comment as Cullen was pulling Jodoc in the direction of the inn. Once they were on their way, Getarix slowly rode on to where he had rented his apartment.

Finally alone, he had time to think. Time to feel. He was trying to sort out why he felt so ill-tempered and irritable. In the pit of his stomach, he felt a tightness he did not understand. The memory of the spring rescue of Isolde ran vividly through his mind in amazing detail. He longed to see her. He feared for her. *What if they were gone? What if others came by to take her away? What if Gainer just packed up and left?* He was so busy over the summer—so much happened—that he seldom gave any thought to Xanten and his two slaves housed in the city. That term caught him wrong. *Not slave...family maybe...no, not family, but certainly not slaves.* He tried to comfort himself with the thought that Gainer would protect the child with her life. He tried to think other things, any other thing, but his mind immediately returned to the spring when he had almost lost Isolde. The argument continued with the thought that Gainer would have learned from that event and she would be more diligent than before. On went his internal debate until he arrived at the apartment. His heart was pounding and perspiration covered his body. He ran up the stairs to the third floor. He stopped at the second door to the right. He listened carefully to see if he could hear anything. He heard nothing. He began to worry, wondering if they had run away. The thought almost put him into a panic. *What the hell is wrong with me? I fight hand-to-hand with killers, survive fires, shipwrecks, almost being turned over to Cunorix to be sacrificed and here I am, in a panic about a small girl-child a slave child.*

He took out his key. Following the events of last spring, he had paid for a lock to be put on the door with only two keys made. One for Gainer and the other sent to him. He turned the lock and it engaged. As he opened the door, the first thing he noticed about the two-room apartment was that it was occupied and kept in good order. Immaculate, actually.

"Gainer, how did it go?" The small sweet voice of Isolde came from the other room. Getarix's heart almost stopped on hearing it. For a second he lost his peripheral vision. His breath went short and he sat down on a small trunk by the door. It was the first time he ever heard her speak with such confidence. He barely recognised her voice. From it, he could tell she had grown. She also spoke perfect Celtic.

"Gainer?" she repeated. This time there was a slight air of concern. He heard her footsteps as she got up. "Gainer, did it go okay?" The moment she entered the room she froze in her tracks. At first, she gave out a quiet shriek of fear until she recognized him. He just sat there taking in the most beautiful sight he had ever seen. Her golden hair was tied back to keep it out of the way. This exposed her long, delicate neck that led to the most exquisite face he had ever seen. Her ocean deep blue eyes were alert and noble. Her straight nose was dainty and fitted her stunning face perfectly. His eyes lowered to take in the entire vision. When he looked below her chin, he noticed she was no longer a child. Womanhood had taken residence in her petite frame, and the sight caused him to lose his breath to the point he become light-headed.

She didn't move at first. She noticed the round medal of honour. She did not understand any of it, other than the fact it meant he did something great and was recognized for his acts.

"Sir," she finally got out. "I thought you were—"

"I'm sorry, I must have scared you."

"No, not at all, master...welcome home. Do you want a drink? We only have water...master."

"Water...would be good. And don't call me master, okay?"

"What should I call you?"

"I—I...don't know. Getarix."

"No sir, Gainer would never allow—"

"Well, we can sort that out later."

She went to a small clay amphora leaning in the corner and drew out a cup of water. It was amazingly cold and Getarix drank deeply, enjoying even the taste of the ground that the clay gave the water. He was strangely elated just to drink water offered from the hand of Isolde. They spent the next few hours talking about all that happened over the summer. As they talked and laughed, he noticed that not only did she have the beauty of a goddess, she was also articulate and quick-minded. The only interruption was when Isolde had to get up and light the lamps as the sun was setting. Getarix had never enjoyed himself more than these three hours, the fastest three hours of his life. The intoxication he felt was greater than the finest wine could produce.

The Legionaries Rest Inn was a very clean-kept inn, not much different than the barracks. The white-washed wall sported a large variety of old swords, spears, and shields, representing the various legions that had been posted to the city. After securing their lodgings, Jodoc and Cullen met in the great hall against the north wall across from the main oaken door. It just so happened that they sat below the section littered with armour from the Fifth Legion, the Larks. Above it all hung a crude red banner about a man's armspan square. It had a walking elephant and the words V LEG embroidered in gold on it.

"Well, Cullen, here's to our old legion, the Larks."

"The Larks." Cullen held his terracotta cup high.

They both drank deeply from their cups. Just as Cullen was about to mention that Getarix must have made it into his apartment, the door opened and in walked their new centurion, down-crested. Jodoc was the first to speak.

"We reserved you a room, boss." Jodoc laughed heartily, but Cullen noticed that something was different. Getarix walked over to them as if he'd heard nothing.

"Is everything okay, brother?" Cullen asked with concern. Getarix did not answer right away. Cullen got a little worried. "They're all right…Getarix?" He held his breath a bit until Getarix spoke up.

"Ah, what? Hum, yes, they're fine, doing well as a matter of a fact."

"Then what's the problem?" Cullen said.

"There is no problem!" Getarix said.

"The problem is that his master, the slave, has kicked him out of his own home."

Jodoc laughed. Getarix tried to ignore him. "There is a solution, you know. And I will be proud to administer it personally."

By now Getarix noticed that he somehow found his patience and a bit of his sense of humour. "She would clean your clock, Jodoc."

"She already did," Cullen said.

Getarix looked serious and broke into their revelry. "Gents, I think we need to get going, and fast. Gainer told me that a man from Britannia visited. She said he wants to see me."

"Someone sent from your brother?" Jodoc asked.

"Don't know, don't care. I don't plan on running into him. We leave tomorrow. Gainer is presently giving away or selling many of the household things, and I have arranged for a pack mule—"

"How did she take the news?" Cullen asked.

"Isolde, great. Gainer, not so…we should be on the road by noon tomorrow. You two be ready."

They worked into the night, then went to ground for a few hours before getting up at sunrise. They were on the road right after the noon meal. The mysterious visitor had told Gainer he would return the next evening. Getarix was determined not to be there when he returned. The thought of putting miles between himself and his brother gave him solace. The more miles the better.

XXXIV

ROME

Rome, a wonder to the eyes, ecstasy to the senses. Art for the viewing, wine for the tasting, music for the ears and every sensual pleasure for body and mind. Rome, a living organism; breathing, living, and groaning with the weight of the world on her shoulders. There they stood, overlooking the greatest city constructed by man.

"If Cunorix could see this," Cullen said to Getarix.

"It would shut him up for good."

Before their eyes stood a city of over one million inhabitants. It seemed to them that the whole world wanted to live in this one spot. Below them, the thin roads were crowded with travellers. From a distance they looked like ants that moved slowly, thousands of them streaming to and fro. They stood there for ten minutes, trying in vain to absorb the sight before them.

"You know, Getarix, when we were growing up I thought our village was the centre of the world. I thought that no place in the world could be bigger. Imagine, three hundred people all living in one place. Was it not the place where all the farmers went every week? Was it not the place where all the fishermen sold their fish? To me, as a child it was the centre—"

"As a child? Two years ago you still believed it was the centre of the world." Getarix chuckled. "But as a child even our village can seem a city if you only have a few points of reference. Now this is one hell of a point of reference. Look Cullen, did I not tell you that we would be seeing great cities?"

"Yeah..." Cullen almost whispered.

"Well, they don't get greater than this."

"They say that it never sleeps," Jodoc said.

"You will be able to find all the wine and women you can handle here, Jodoc," Cullen said as he put his arm on the shoulders of his friend.

"He can handle women?" Getarix could not resist. Gainer could be heard laughing from behind. Jodoc gave Getarix a look of hostility. Getarix simply smiled and gave the command. "Okay everyone, enough standing around. Let us join the millions who call Rome their home."

Once in the city, they spent the better part of the day lost, searching for the Praetorian Guard's lines. By noon, they found what they sought. Once the three of them were cleared in, Getarix was sent a few blocks off where he could rent an apartment. Within a few days they had begun to settle in when their commander called all three into his office.

"Well, well, here we have our political appointees." Centurion Gius Velius Marsallas looked at the three of them with distain. Centurion Marsallas commanded the city cohort of the Praetorian Guard. "Do you know much about the Praetorian Guard?"

"No, sir."

"No. I see...you mean to tell me that you had strings pulled, putting you here, and you know nothing about your...unit of choice. That tells me that this unit means nothing to you. We mean nothing more to you than just a step up the ladder on your political career."

The three of them stood at attention before their new centurion, Getarix in the middle and slightly in front of Jodoc and Cullen. The two subordinate soldiers became a bit confused and looked at each other. Getarix kept his eyes on his new commander.

"Well, let me enlighten you, boys. The Praetorian Guard is an elite unit... made of only the best soldiers in the Empire. Her ranks are filled soldiers who have proven themselves...proven themselves in and out of battle." Getarix began to feel uneasy as the hostility grew. "Soldiers who have proved themselves time and again, year after year, on a continuous basis. Understand what I am getting at? Not some piss-ant little foreign boys who just happened to stumble across a standard. Where were you three two years ago?"

Getarix glanced quickly right to left at his two friends before building up the courage to speak. "Basic, sir."

"Basic. Yeah, basic. Two years ago while you were being taught how to hold a wooden sword, there were hundreds of worthy soldiers waiting to get into this unit when an opening came…who still wait. Soldiers a hundred times your better who had earned their spot…and now you three, using whatever influence you seem to have, just jumped over them."

"Sir, we know no one—"

"Shut your porridge hole!" Marsallas got up and approached Getarix with his pace stick in his hand. "Don't you lie to me, son, or I'll ram this stick down your throat until you have a third leg to walk on. Do you think I am stupid? I haven't walked these streets of Rome for all these years without knowing how things work around here. Nobody just gets a posting here without either earning it or buying it. The three of you sure as hell did not earn it—you obviously had to buy it. It must have cost you a bundle, eh, bringing your own body guards." Their new centurion pointed contemptuously to Cullen and Jodoc. "I don't know what your thing is, but I don't like you and I don't trust the three of you. Maybe you're hired to get close to the emperor and repeat the treachery done unto Caesar. Maybe you bought the position to get close to the emperor, eh? Is that your game?" He paused for effect and then continued. "I did a little digging. I found these in your kit." Marsallas opened the contents of a cloth on his desk. As he opened the cloth, it revealed the dagger and arm torques. "Now these are not the possession of some barbarian peasant. Maybe the contents of a barbarian prince or the booty of a thief. Who are you, boy?" Marsallas looked directly into the eyes of Getarix.

"They're my great-grandfather's," Getarix said flatly.

"Great-grandfather, eh?"

"Yes sir, my great-grandfather, Vercingetorix the Great."

"The Great, eh?"

"Yes, sir."

"I know that name. Not so great, beaten by Rome's first citizen. Was he not that Celtic king Caesar had killed in the Forum? Strangled, I believe, slowly if I heard right." Centurion Marsallas was looking right into Getarix's face. He returned to his chair behind his simple oaken desk and just leaned back and looked for a reaction. None came.

Getarix had come to terms with his family history years ago. He had never bought into his brother's life mission, to keep the hate alive. The same hate that deprived him of his father, killed at a young age, and turned his brother into a hateful bitter person who reeked as if he were dead. Besides, he saw no benefit in getting worked up over ancient history. And when all was taken into account, the Romans brought far more to his people than they took from them.

Marsallas finally gave up on the reaction he sought. "Okay, you three. There will be a public ceremony where Tiberius will present you," pointing contemptuously directly at Getarix, "with your gold phalera. Apparently the divine Emperor has decided you two will be receiving silver medals of honour on top of his gold one. I will be there every step of the way. If I see you step out of line just once…if I had my way…" Marsallas placed his hand firmly on the hilt of his sword. "We are tasked to protect the emperor's life, and I will not fail in it. After that ceremony, you will never be near the emperor again. Is that understood?"

"Yes sir," all three answered in unison.

"I don't know when this little ceremony will be. Sometime after Germanicus has finished with those Germans and he has had his Triumphant Parade, at least a year from now." Marsallas looked at some papers on his desk and continued in a businesslike manner.

"I am assigning you three to the Subura district. It's a job below your rank but still above your abilities. There you can deal with the drunkards and prostitutes to your heart's content until the ceremony. But you will never get near Tiberius after that ceremony, that I can guarantee you. That is if I cannot find out what you're truly about before the year's out. Centurion Getarix, I leave you in charge of the night watch for that district, and your two 'body guards' will each lead a patrol."

"Yes sir."

"You will not wear armour in the city unless you are on formal function. You are to wear your red guard's tunic with your sword belt only. It's a long tradition that Roman soldiers do not wear their armour within the city walls unless it's for formal events. Oh yes, on that subject, centurion, you will need to purchase a proper set of armour for such events. Talk to the quartermaster about where you can have them made."

"Sir, I do not have enough—"

"Not my problem. You wanted to be a centurion. Now show some leadership, initiative, and solve your own problems for once. I will see you in a month's time fully kitted out…understood? Maybe your political masters will pay for it."

"Yes, sir."

He pointed to the arm torques and dagger. "I want to see you wearing these when you are presented with your phalera. The irony will be too good to miss."

Marsallas grinned. "I'll let you know when you will be presented your medals of honour you so deserve." Marsallas dismissed them.

Their duty began that very night. The Subura was a dirty, un-kept community in the Vertus Creek valley that was defined by the Viminal and Esquiline Hills right in the heart of Rome. As the three entered the Subura, Getarix commentated on his disappointment and disgust. Jodoc saw it differently. "This is great," he said loudly.

"Great?" Cullen said. "All I see is nastiness, filth, and unpleasantness all crowded into this little valley. It's not great, it's scary."

Getarix kept silent, watching each step, making sure he would not end up spending his evening cleaning some un-nameable filth off his sandals.

"You see, that's the problem with you two. You cannot see the opportunities right in front of you."

Getarix paused his search. "You mean cheap wine and easy girls."

"So you do see it too, eh? Just look around." He turned around, waving his arms all round him. Suddenly he went silent with a resounding crash as he hit the ground, out cold. Pottery shards flew from where they hit his head.

"What the...?" Cullen said as both became alert, looking all around seeking their attacker. Finding nothing, they both studied the now-silent Jodoc lying in the narrow filthy street with broken red pottery surrounding him.

"Hey, Getarix, is that a broken chamber pot?"

"I would say so, and it appears to have been full." In perfect harmony, they looked up to the upper apartments.

"You know, Getarix, if this has not killed him, it's just funny." At that moment, they saw Jodoc come to and they both laughed with abandonment.

Cullen patrolled one side of the Vertus Creek and Jodoc, nursing a sore head, led the patrol on the other. By sunrise, they were exhausted, having battled drunks, thieves, prostitutes, and—for one of their number—a head-pounding throb all through the night. All this had to be handled amongst the thousands of carts restocking the many shops, most of which sold wine and trinkets.

This went on throughout the winter months unabated, including the odd missile from the upper floors. Many nights they had to do battle through the freezing rain and the half-frozen mud of the streets of the Subura. As spring arrived, they had mastered their duties to such a degree that Marsallas could not find any fault, to his frustration.

XXXV

CHANCE ENCOUNTER

Antonio took his usual shortcut from the estate of Senator Damianus on Esquiline Hill down the slope, using the winding Clivus Pullius road that led to the Subura. Antonio hated the stench of the Subura, where everything from dead cats to table scraps sat rotting in the Vertus Creek, mixed with the ever-present smell of vomit and human waste. As he looked upwards toward Viminalis Hill, he noticed the sun just showing itself. Soon the bitter cold of the early spring night would be chased away by the day's warmth. Antonio became lost in his thoughts, recreating the beating of the night before. The senator was becoming increasingly impatient about the little German girl. He blamed Antonio for the present situation. *'Where is she? It's been over a year,'* he would bellow at his hapless slave. Last night, Antonio's master drank the last of their good wine and in his drunken state went after Antonio.

"If I don't get my prize and soon, I'll have you killed, you worthless worm," the senator screamed as he commenced to beat Antonio. Antonio's greatest mistake was putting his arm up to shield his face from the blows. The moment he did that, the beating grew savage. It would have continued further if the senator had not grown exhausted.

Antonio had noticed that his ability to 'take it' was not growing with age. Rather, as he grew older, he longed for his freedom even more. His desire for dignity and a measure of respect matured with each painful year. He also noticed that he began to have an increasingly difficult time controlling the anger within him.

It was still early and the senator would sleep off his drunken stupor well into the morning. As much as Antonio hated the Subura, he was glad to be off Esquiline Hill and away from his master. He also knew that if his owner woke up to discover the wine cellar empty of his favourite wine, Antonio would once again pay for it. Antonio, so distracted in his thoughts, did not notice the soldier wearing his red tunic and sword belt.

"Hey, you. Drunkard." Jodoc stopped directly in his path. Antonio continued on, as if walking a deserted street. Jodoc placed his hand securely on the hilt of his sword and stood firmly in place. Antonio walked directly into him.

"Watch where you're going, pig!" Antonio said before he even noticed that it was a member of the patrol. Jodoc had his sword out and struck him across the face with the broad side of his weapon. This did not cut him, but left a terrific addition to his bruises collected the night before. Antonio fell backward, right into the mud and filth of the streets. The night rains had been heavier than normal, making the narrow roads of the Subura a quagmire. As he landed hard in the mud, Antonio let loose a tapestry of profanities at Jodoc. By the time he was finished, his face was as red as the tunic worn by Jodoc.

Further down the street, Getarix saw the commotion and began to run toward Jodoc. He loved Jodoc and if he ever had to choose a person to be by his side in battle it would be Jodoc. However, he was not blind to the faults of his friend. It would not take much to encourage Jodoc to lance a sword right through some offending drunk. Getarix had visions of explaining why they had killed some nobleman's favourite slave, or worse yet some kinsman of Tiberius. In the muddy streets of the Subura, the high and the low rubbed shoulders together alike. It was the one place you could get what you wanted without questions asked, and the streets were filled with young nobles seeking the thrills of the flesh. As he approached, he saw what looked to him like the figure of a man broken of all his dignity. He was spitting incoherent words as he talked. When Getarix got closer, it appeared to him that the man was crying through his words. Mucus flowed from his nose and tears from his eyes. Once Antonio was composed, Getarix spoke.

"Jodoc, what's up?

"This drunk assaulted me."

"I did not...I was lost in my mind and did not see you." Antonio attempted to regain some sense of dignity.

"Centurion Getarix, I have a mind to run him through," Jodoc said as he drew his sword back to point it directly at Antonio's chest.

"Duplicarius, stand down."

"What! He assaulted me!"

"That's an order, duplicarius!" Jodoc lowered his sword, but kept it at the ready.

Getarix directed his attention to the simply dressed man sitting in the mud in front of him. "Who are you?"

"I am Antonio, the chief slave of the noble Damianus Aurelia Marius Gius, Senator of Rome."

Getarix gave him a look. "Can you explain the bruises on your face? You must not be a very good slave," Getarix said. Antonio sat there, wanting them to believe he was a valued slave of the senator. He placed his muddy hand on the growing welt just granted to him by the sword of Jodoc. "This, your partner here can explain."

"Get up!" Getarix said. He had learned that to maintain control of a situation with the drunks of the Subura, he had to be a bit gruff, always letting the offending citizen believe that if they did not comply they could lose their life.

Antonio shot him a look of hate as he got back to his feet. He was a head shorter than Getarix. Getarix grabbed him by the back of his thinning brown hair, forcing his head back a bit so he could smell his breath. There was only the smell of an early breakfast.

Why are you wandering the mud streets of the Subura and not the marble halls of the senator's home?"

"I come to buy wine for my master." Antonio shook his head from the grip of Getarix.

Getarix become irritated by this mark of defiance, but continued on with his questioning.

"Why buy wine at sunrise, as the shops are closed?"

"The wine arrives at night, as do all things in Rome. If you want the best, you have to be there first...and my master always wants only the best. And he can be cruel to anyone who deprives him of what he wants." Getarix noticed he was getting more and more defiant, to the point that his last statement could be seen as a threat. In spite of that, he thought better of escalating the situation any more.

"Ergo the marks?" Getarix asked.

"Ergo the marks."

"Be on your way. And mark my words, watch where you're going or I'll let this one have his way with you, old man."

Antonio was seething inside. He glared at Getarix with a burning hate as he complied and went on his way.

There was silence between Getarix and Jodoc until Antonio was out of earshot. Jodoc was first to pierce the air. "What the hell was that!"

"That, my friend...was saving your life."

"Saving my life, are you mad, he's just a useless slave...I could have—"

"Yes, you could have, but do not forget he is the possession of Damianus Aurelia Marius Gius, Senator of Rome."

"So what!" Jodoc was now red in the face, unable to comprehend the situation.

By this time, Cullen had joined them. "Let's walk, gents." They walked for a bit, allowing Jodoc to cool off the greater part of his frustration. "Do you remember Alexander the slave-trader?"

"Oh yeah, that was great," Jodoc said, remembering with joy the night they had killed him. It even brought the biggest smile he could muster. The memory of killing the thieving slave-trader broke the last of the spell for Jodoc.

"Do you remember what the slave-trader said the day I got Isolde?"

They both looked puzzled, then Jodoc said, "I remember he told you that you should beat Gainer."

"Not that, you fool."

"It's still good advice."

"No. Now listen, he said it was the child he was interested in, not Gainer."

"So what? Everyone seemed to be interested in that child. And as it turns out, no one seems interested in Gainer."

"Yes, but he said he had a client who wanted Isolde herself. Not just any child, but that child. Remember what he said: 'My client can make you not only a rich man, but he has the power of promotions.'"

"Yeah, so what?"

"He also said, 'Let me warn you that my client also has the power to break careers.'"

"Okay, Getarix, you're not making sense," Jodoc said.

"He was so determined to get the girl that he even sent Alexander to kidnap her, and the slave-trader lost his life in the process."

"Yeah, that was great...but I still don't get it."

"You dolt—"

"I get it," Cullen said. "He was backed by a client and that client is—"

"Here in Rome," Getarix finished.

"So what?" Jodoc still did not see the connection.

"My client can make you not only a rich man, but he has the power of promotions," Getarix repeated.

"Promotions..." Cullen gasped.

"Let me warn you that my client also has the power to break careers," Getarix continued.

"Okay, you are killing me here," Jodoc said. "What does that have to do with that slave?"

"Damianus Aurelia Marius Gius, Senator of Rome. Remember when we arrived, Centurion Marsallas asked who our sponsor here in Rome is, who has the power and influence with the emperor."

"Yeah, so? Are you suggesting that he was Alexander's client...our sponsor?"

"Is the client."

"Are you sure?"

"No, but I have heard a lot about him and he seems to fit the description."

"I still don't get how you saved my life."

"I hear that this senator will kill if need be to gain revenge or settle a score, or even to avoid paying a bill. There is a story about a walkway in his garden and not wanting to pay the artisan. He eventually had him killed. If you killed his valued possession, or even delayed his wine shipment...I would not think it wise to give him a legitimate excuse to have me killed."

"I still don't get it," Jodoc said.

Cullen and Getarix both smiled at their friend's confusion.

"Jodoc, you may be able to survive the prostitutes and thieves of the taverns of wine that would kill most of us, but you know nothing of the taverns of power. I recommend you stay clear of them."

In the middle of their banter, a young slave they recognized as belonging to Marsallas approached them in full sprint. They were instructed to report in all haste to their commander. When they reported in that morning, they were told to go home and clean up and get to the Servian Walls in the Campus Martius on the other side of the river, mounted and in full armour. They were given only two hours to be ready. Upon enquiring, they were told it was the beginning of the Triumphant Parade for Germanicus. The general would be awaiting their arrival. Later in the afternoon, they would be presented their awards in the forum. Marsallas did not tell them anything more. He seemed tense and very upset, like he was giving them some very bad news.

XXXVI

TRIUMPH

"Isolde, grab that bag there, would you?" She grabbed the large cloth bag Gainer used to hold the tools of her trade, handing it to Gainer.

"No, take it," Gainer barked as she hurriedly prepared herself to leave.

"What?"

"You're coming with me, now. Get ready."

"What…?"

"I have decided it is time for you to attend your first delivery. Your apprenticeship has now begun. I am determined to give you a trade so you can earn your way on your feet and not your back. Besides, I want to keep a close eye on you. Rome has become a madhouse since the latest victories in Germania, and is out of control since the troop's arrival in the city."

"I'll be safe here."

"No, you won't, The Triumph is today and every soldier will be drunk… first with the flush of victory and then with wine. Actually, you have never been safe and the danger has increased. Besides, it is high time you start your training, giving you more value than just a thing to bring pleasure to men."

Isolde had mixed feelings. She wanted to start her training, but she lived for the times when Getarix would visit and that only happened when Gainer was away. If Gainer were home, Getarix would do his business with Gainer and then depart. When she was away, he would bring her small gifts. Trinkets mostly, but for the first time in her life Isolde felt special. She felt wanted, just for her, not what someone could get out of her—she wanted to believe someone cared. Gainer cared, but more in a matronly, restrictive way. With Getarix, Isolde had feelings she had never experienced before. He never tried anything. Matter of a fact, he never came close to her. They would sit for hours and talk. At times they just sat and look at each other, their moments broken only by Gainer's return home or the hour Getarix had to leave to take up his duties in the Subura.

"Hey, wake up girl. I said get me those towels. The messenger indicated that Lady Livia was very advanced and we have no time to waste."

Isolde shook herself out of her dream world and grabbed the towels, following Gainer out the door to their next appointment.

The streets were alive like few could ever remember. On the lips of everyone was only one name, Germanicus. Germanicus was finally being granted his Triumphant.

Some believed that he could, if so inclined, walk up to his uncle and depose him on the spot and the city would have gone wild in support. The weather on this spring day was perfect, warm with only a trace of a gentle wind.

"So, what do you two know about one of these parades?" Getarix asked.

"I know nothing," Cullen answered.

"Well, I have this friend and she—"

"She, you mean an employee, Jodoc?" Getarix cut in with a smirk. Cullen laughed.

"Well yes, I might pay her but she is connected and has lived in Rome all her life, so she has the ability to know a little. She has a brain, you know."

"Now how would you know?"

"Cullen." Jodoc could not hide the frustration in his voice.

"Okay, so what did this friend have to say, brother?" Getarix said.

"Like I was saying, she said the ceremony begins outside the Servian Walls in the Campus Martius, on the western bank of the Tiber, where we are heading now. Germanicus, the *vir triumphalis*, will enter the city in his chariot through the Porta Triumphalis, which is only opened when a triumphant parade is granted."

"Yeah, I know that."

"Do you want to know the rest?"

"Go on."

"Okay, as he enters the city he will be met by the senate and magistrates, and he will legally surrender his command to them. The parade will then follow the

Via Triumphalis to the Circus Flaminius and then on to the Circus Maximus. Any captured enemy rulers or generals that are paraded might be taken to the Tullianum for execution."

"I imagine my great grandfather was strangled there. I wonder if Thusnelda will be displayed," Getarix added.

"I am told both she along with her newborn will be in the parade as prized trophies. And her brother, Segimundus," Jodoc said.

"Do you think Germanicus will execute them?" Cullen asked.

"It's not like Germanicus, but you never know."

"No, my friend said they intend on allowing the boy to grow up and enter the ring as a gladiator. Anyway, the procession will continue along the Via Sacra to the Forum and ascend the Capitoline Hill to the Temple of Jupiter, their final destination."

"It looks like the route will be lined with cheering crowds," Cullen said as he surveyed the growing crowd.

"At the Capitoline Hill, Germanicus will sacrifice two white bulls to Jupiter. He will then enter the temple to offer his wreath to Jupiter as a sign that he did not intend to become the king of Rome. Once this part of the ceremony is over, temples will be kept open and incense burned all night on the altars. The soldiers will disperse to the city to celebrate. This will be a great day, eh boys? Getting drunk with the Larks, it'll be like old times."

"Tell you the truth, Getarix," Cullen said, "I sure could use some friends like we had back in the Larks. I'm tired of being the legion's unwanted."

They fell silent for a moment, all lost in contemplation of how lonely they truly felt.

"Okay Jodoc, that's what you know, now tell me what you don't know. Why do you think we are here?"

"Extra security, obviously, I'm sure no one has this day off," Getarix said. "I hear you about having friends, brother, and I know you want to cut loose, but no rest for us tonight, boys. Be ready for the worst night in the streets yet, especially since the drunks will be those we fought alongside."

As they approached the Porta Triumphalis, they noticed a large group of men all wearing togas as white as doves. As they got closer they saw that the men were predominantly older, with just a few younger men in their midst. Then they noticed the distinctive purple stripes lining every toga. The only thing distinguishing one man from the other in dress was the thickness of the purple stripes. The wider the stripe, the higher on the social ladder they could be found.

"Looks like the Senate is ready," Cullen said quietly. They rode as far as they could to the left of the road, trying their best to go unnoticed. Nonetheless, they heard a call from the crowd of noblemen.

"Centurion Getarix...Centurion." The three soldiers search the crowds mystified who would call after them. Who from this esteemed assembly would even know one of their names, or care to know?

"It came from in there—one of the senators," Cullen said as all three halted their mounts.

Soon the small sea of white opened and one of the largest men any of them had ever seen stood in the centre surrounded on three sides by his peers.

"Centurion Getarix, I am Damianus Aurelia Marius Gius, Senator of Rome, and I assume these gentlemen with you are Duplicarius Cullen and Jodoc." As he said their names, he turned to each in their turn, indicating he knew them and knew them well.

"Yes, sir...what merits us such an honour to be noticed by such a great man of Rome?"

Damianus turned to his crowd and declared in a loud stage voice, "Ha ha, just listen to him, gentlemen: what merits, have you seen such humility?"

"We have done nothing, sir," Getarix said, utterly confused and not a little nervous.

"Ah, but you are wrong, my boy. You are a great man of Rome...you and our great General Germanicus." At that, the Senate gave a cheer. "It is not enough you recover the lost standard...the same standard I...myself discovered but a few years ago, only to be denied possession by the bumbling of an incompetent." He stopped himself for fear of breaking the moment. "But never mind. As I was saying, it was not enough to recover Rome's honour. I have been informed by Segestes himself of your heroic rescue from the fires of hell. And on top of all that, I just learned from our great general that on your very first day of battle you saved the day and later you bravely saved the life of your centurion in the Boar's Head Inn, and wear the bronze phalera in honour of that action. Am I not right?"

"Yes si—"

"Yes indeed. You know, I too had to deal with the same proprietor of that inn. A terrible man indeed."

"Yes, sir."

"Now, I also heard from our great general of your remarkable ability to negotiate with the enemy."

"Sir...I do not know—"

"The shipwrecks, son, the shipwrecks. You forget your heroic deeds so quickly." The senator laughed and turned his attention to his peers, who joined him in their praise of the trio.

"But sir—" Getarix attempted to correct the perception of the senator.

"But nothing. It's reported that due to your skilled negotiation, not only did our enemy release all of our captured soldiers without a demand for ransom, but—and no one knows how you did it—you turned two of their tribes onto each other and they fought a war between them."

Getarix tried not to show surprise. To be honest, he had hardly given much thought to the incident once they left Britannia. He knew nothing of a battle between the Cantiaci and the Trinovantes.

"Duplicarius Cullen!"

"Sir?"

"I understand you were there?"

"Yes sir, I was."

"And you speak the language of the negotiations, do you not?"

"Yes sir, I do."

"And what do you have to report, my good man?"

Getarix said, "Yes Cullen, please report the events as you saw them?"

Cullen looked to his superior and friend and said, "Yes sir, I would be pleased to do just that." He turned to the senator. "It is exactly as the noble senator has said, sir."

Damianus turned to his peers and declared in triumph. "Am I not always right about the character of men, eh?" To which the peers gave a great cheer of approval. "You better hurry if you are to make your timings. I'm sure Germanicus is even now wondering where his heroes are." Before they could answer, the senator turned his back and soon once again vanished in a sea of white, leaving three very confused soldiers to continue on their way.

As they moved out of earshot, Getarix could not hold it in any more. "Okay, now what the hell was that?" Getarix fought his anger.

"Getarix, one thing I have learned since coming to Rome."

"What's that?"

"Never contradict a superior, especially if he is wrong."

"But that is not even close to what happened over there."

"Maybe, but his version does us no harm."

"It will if they ever—"

"No one but the two of us understood a word that was spoken."

"Where did they get that version?"

"Not from me," Cullen said as Getarix gave him an expression of exasperation.

As they progressed to the middle of the parade where Germanicus would be, they passed carts with the spoils of war followed by the two white bulls destined for sacrifice, then the captured weapons and standards of the Germans. It was just after these they saw Thusnelda and her baby in a cage for display. They stopped to examine her. She was naked and un-kept. She wrapped herself around her baby boy in maternal protection. She looked up at them with hateful contempt. A look that made them a bit uncomfortable.

"Hey, Getarix, there is Germanicus and the Larks beyond," Jodoc said.

When Getarix looked up, he could see Marsallas in deep conversation with the general. He did not look pleased.

"Centurion Getarix, there you are," Germanicus declared as he walked to the three of them. Getarix noticed that Marsallas went the other way but glared back at him in warning not to step out of line.

"There you are. We have been waiting for you."

"Great to see you again, sir, I have…we have all missed being with you more than we can express. Rome can have my promotion back if it means returning to the brotherhood of the army."

"Yes, I feared that you have not been fully accepted here. Well it is to be expected, jumping the ranks as you did, and before you ask, no to your demotion. Anyway, it's great to see three of my best fighters again. Now, as you have been briefed, you three will be right behind me leading the legions, starting with your own Larks."

"We leading…sir, what are you…?"

"The Triumph, man. You will be leading the legions, bearing the standard of the Nineteenth Legion. Tomorrow we will honour your great deeds. You weren't briefed?"

"We—no, sir, but that's okay." In spite of the difficult relationship with Marsallas, Getarix felt it wrong to say anything that would do his superior harm.

The crowds were oppressive. Gainer became worried and when she worried, she became very cross and short-tempered. It didn't help that they had almost lost the baby. The father even threatened that he would see to a whipping if anything happened. It was a very tense operation, but all went well and the baby boy delighted the father, who gave her a large tip. Her hatred for Rome grew even more. One moment a whipping and the next being showered with gifts over something none of them had any control over. Now she was becoming fearful that she might lose Isolde in the pushing and shoving of the infernal crowd. She was not in the mood to celebrate a war that took everything she valued. The parade had arrived on the street they were walking. It filled with the procession of the Triumph, and the crowds were reacting to whomever or whatever passed by. Gainer tried to stay next to the buildings in an effort to be more secure. That way she would only have to worry about people on one side of her. Maybe the child was right and she should have been left in the apartment. The crowd was becoming more excited to the point that Gainer could not even hear her own voice.

"Isolde, now keep close…take my hand…Isolde…Isolde!" she yelled in a panic. She scanned the now-hysterical crowd. She began to work her way back, calling Isolde, fearing the worst. When she finally spotted her, Isolde was seated on the base of a large statue mounted on the top step of a noble-looking public building, engrossed in something in the Triumph. Gainer burned with rage at the thought that she had just stopped to watch some mindless Roman parade. When she finally reached Isolde, she roared, "Isolde, what the hell is wrong with you? Do you have any idea what you just put me through?" Isolde just stood transfixed, without any indication she had heard any of Gainer's harsh words.

"Gainer, look." She pointed to the road below where they stood. "It's master. He is in the parade," she said in wonderment. Gainer looked and there mounted proudly on Caballo was indeed her master, Getarix. He sat holding a stout pole with a gleaming eagle mounted atop it. On either side sat Cullen and Jodoc riding their horses, both wearing skins with the wolf head atop their own. They both held a standard of minor units recovered from the forest.

Getarix could not believe what was happening. The crowds were cheering him as a great hero. After a year of being hated amongst his fellow soldiers, it was difficult to comprehend. Ahead of him, he could see Germanicus riding his grand chariot pulled by four perfect horses. Behind Germanicus stood a humbly dressed man whispering something into his ear. Riding with him were all his children, Caligula wearing his full Centurion uniform right down to his little boots, truly a crowd-pleaser. As they passed one of Rome's many public buildings, the road widened and the crowd ascended up the stairs in a similar fashion as found in the theatre. It was there he spotted her, sitting on the base of a large statue looking directly at him. He could see Gainer saying something to her but she did not seem to notice. Her hair gleamed in the warm sun, framing a face of the purist beauty he had ever seen. Her slender body showed itself through her dress as the wind gently caressed her skin. He wished he were with her and not in any Triumph. He turned to her and bowed slightly, giving her honour. The crowd sought who he was paying tribute to. They looked around until their eyes fell upon her and they gave out a loud cheer. Far too soon, the parade moved on and he could no longer see her.

"Ho, Gainer, did you see that he stopped and recognized us?"

"It was not us he was noticing."

"Yes he was, I saw him look directly at me."

"You're right...directly at you. Now that he has passed, let us get out of here." Gainer did not know what to think of this. Did he truly admire and value her, or was he like the rest of them with only one thing on his mind? *Time will tell.* Her hopes were not set very high.

"Getarix, look at you! If Cunorix could see you now."

"Quit saying that, Cullen."

Getarix stood in full ceremonial armour on the morning after the parade. He was wrong, they had not been on duty the night before. They spent the evening with the closest brothers a man could find. Brothers welded in the furnace of battle. Cullen and Getarix were careful to celebrate but not at the expense of clear minds the next morning. Jodoc was not so careful. Getarix's armour was not the gold-plated armour like that used by the emperor, but the highly polished bronze shone with a brilliance Cullen had never seen before. The breastplate surrounded the front of Getarix, buckled to the back plate at the sides. The artist had shaped the two plates to resemble the chest and back of a naked man in the peak of health and fitness. There were two laurel reliefs pounded across the chest on the front.

"Cullen, hand me my helmet, would you please?"

Cullen went to the crate that was delivered months before and pulled out an equally polished helmet boasting a large red feather plume that resembled a lady's fan. It was mounted on top by a centre post and it stretched from one ear to the next.

The wool kilt was covered by leather straps that ended in points, each crowned with a bronze tip. He'd even had to buy new sandal-like boots that laced up to the knees.

"Ho, Getarix don't forget your new cape. My god, Look how bright it is, and heavy. Wow, we don't get issued such good quality."

"You can have it."

"Really?"

"Yeah, once you pay for it."

"Yeah, very funny. How did you pay for it anyway?"

"I paid half the day I ordered, using all my pay, and next pay period I will pay the rest."

"Plus interest?"

"Plus interest, of course."

"How do you live?"

"I eat at the mess."

"Porridge, your favourite."

"Yeah, great."

"So Gainer won't let you near your apartment today, eh? I wonder what she thought of your little stunt yesterday."

"I don't care what she thinks of it and it was not a stunt...now drop it."

"Okay, so what about your other expenses?"

"I am at the mercy of Gainer. She has a thriving midwife business. Within a week of our arrival, she found some pregnant women...she has taken Isolde on as an apprentice, so she will have the same trade."

"So, you will be able to sell her trade and recoup some of your money. This way you do not have to worry about how she will be used—your concern dealt with, and a hefty profit to boot."

"Cullen...even you don't get it, do you? Get me my dagger and arm torques, would you?"

As Getarix was putting them on, Cullen said, "I was just thinking of how many times you almost lost those things." Cullen held the belt in his hands and examined the repair done by the smith to the gold buckle. He could still see the scar left by the spear that almost ended Getarix's life at the river's edge in their first engagement.

"Yeah, who would have thought it, eh? Remember basic? Cassius and Aquilla almost killed us." They both chuckled in nostalgia, then fell silent.

Cullen broke the quiet. "Getarix, what do you plan on doing with Isolde? Marry her?" Cullen laughed. Getarix didn't. Cullen noticed in his eyes that his friend did not want to talk about it anymore. Getarix began to fidget with his arm torques, pulling them high on his biceps above his tunic where they could not be seen.

"Put them at your forearms, like you did for the triumph. You were ordered to wear them...be bold, brother. Show them, all of them, especially the emperor, that a lowly Celt saved the day. Show them you're not a peasant but a prince in your own right."

Getarix thought for a moment and slid them down with a sudden jerk. "Be bold you say. Okay, bold it is." The arm torques, belt, and dagger were in full view.

At that point, Getarix was ready to buckle his leather straps that held his medals of valour. They covered his breastplate and already held two bronze phalera. The top strap was empty, ready for his gold phalera.

"Well, what do you think?"

"Very noble."

"Well, let's get Jodoc and be on our way."

The senator still felt the wrath of Bacchius, who visited those who indulged in too much of his elixir. The ill effects from the evening before had only subsided marginally throughout the day. Due to his immense size, his litter needed four extra slaves to carry it. Even with eight men carrying him, the ride was no smoother. If anything it was rougher. At one point on the journey, he almost turned the litter over when he leaned to the side and dropped his lunch on one of his slaves as the poor man strained under the extra weight on his side.

He closed the curtain to clean the vomit from his face over the next few blocks until the smell became too much and was about to make him sick again. "Open the curtains at once!" Antonio, who walked beside the litter, immediately opened the curtain as ordered. The senator leaned out a bit, trying with all his energy to balance his stomach and head. It seemed to be working. As his head cleared, he looked around at the people in the streets. He noticed a very proud-looking woman walking as if she had an appointment of some importance. He was about to look away when he noticed that in her wake a young girl followed. *That face. No, it could not be, she was too old—no, she would be older...that face, I know that face, it is her, yes it is...*Suddenly the senator did not feel the sickness at all. He saw her, the object of his latest desire. *So, Antonio's plan did work. She is now in Rome, close to my grasp. And tonight after the ceremony I will strong-arm my young protégé into giving her up for good, if he knows what is good for him.*

They worked their way through the Forum crowded with people streaming in for a chance to get a glimpse of the emperor. The day before he was nowhere to be seen, as the day had belonged to Germanicus. Unlike Augustus, Tiberius was seldom in the public eye. If he had his way, he would never step foot in Rome again.

The senator's boredom was very noticeable. The award ceremony as usual took too long for his liking. He took special interest in the young centurion he had promoted and brought to Rome. He was struck again by just how young Getarix and his companions were. He thought that it must have caused a sensation in the ranks of the Praetorian Guard when they arrived. He figured that once he got the girl, he would toss them and their careers onto the trash heap. But until then they would be his favourite.

The sun beat down on the recipients of the awards without mercy. At times during the long ceremony, they fought to stay awake in the heat of the early spring day, barely recovering from the night before.

Tiberius buckled a silver phalera onto the chest of Getarix without saying a word. Getarix was taken aback by this, as he understood that he was to be awarded the gold phalera. He chalked it up to political fickleness or simple miscommunication. Once the phalera was secure and the emperor turned, Getarix began to move to descend the podium, only to be told by Marsallas to stand firm. Without hesitation, he steadied up just in time for the emperor to buckle an additional phalera next to the silver one. This one was made of gold.

"Centurion Getarix...truly remarkable career for such a young man. Should I be worried about my job, son?"

"Absolutely not, sire," Getarix answered Emperor Tiberius with a smile, as the emperor pinned his gold phalera on the strap that strung across his chest.

"Some days I would be willing to let you have it, my son." Tiberius broke into a smile, a very rare occurrence for such as sour-looking man. Centurion Marsallas stood just to the side, a bit too close for the emperor's liking. Tiberius became irritated by his overbearing presence. After a few moments, he stopped addressing Getarix and looked straight at his personal bodyguard. "Centurion, is everything alright?"

"Yes, sire. Everything, sire..."

"Then move off the stage." Tiberius dismissed him with the wave of his hand. As Marsallas departed, he glared at Getarix. It hit him that he had ordered the new centurion to wear his Celtic dagger, a weapon, and now he could not protect the emperor from it.

"Now, centurion, I understand you distinguished yourself from the first day you arrived on the battlefield to the last. Even when you were captured you outdid yourself."

"Just doing my duty, sire."

"Just your duty, eh? Just think, if everyone just did their duty." With the second phalera now firmly mounted, Tiberius was on to the next soldier in line. Cullen and Jodoc had received theirs earlier in the ceremony. A large group of soldiers had distinguished themselves in battle throughout the empire. Most, however, gained renown in Germania.

Once they were dismissed, Getarix looked into the crowd with the faint hope that Gainer had brought Isolde as Getarix had asked. He could not see them, but he did recognize the face of the slave they had scuffled with in the early morning two days prior. He was standing by the very large senator they spoke with the morning before in miles of toga all fringed in thick rich purple.

Not only had the slave cleaned up and recovered his dignity, he seemed to be glaring at Getarix with a burning hatred. Getarix felt guilty of some crime he was unaware of committing until he put it out of his mind with irritation.

XXXVII

GARDEN PARTY

The sun had set as they arrived at the emperor's palace for the reception. Once again, they were amazed by what lay before them. The entire building appeared to gleam. The invited guests entered by a gate in the wall that led directly into the palace garden. They quickly assessed that the reception would be held outside. They walked into an eerie daylight created by thousands of torches lit throughout the grounds. The light danced off the polished marble of the massive palace walls like a joyful dance of the spirits. They gazed with wonderment at the many statues and fountains found in the gardens. Even in the darkness of the night, they were a wonder. All of the guests lined up along the path, waiting to be greeted officially. As the line moved forward, the three looked about and wondered how these gardens appeared during the daylight when the flowers could boast their full palette of colours.

When the three young guests arrived at the front of the line, they were met by the most stately lady they had ever laid eyes on. She stood as straight as a soldier's spear. Her raven-black hair was held back, exposing a beautiful but stern face.

"Greetings gentlemen, I am Lady Julia Augusta."

"Greetings, m 'Lady," all three answered her.

"By your accent, you're the Gauls I hear so much about," she said with an air of superiority.

"Yes, Madame, we two are from Britannia, and Duplicarius Jodoc is from—"

"Interesting. We are making noblemen of them before we conquer them and make them our slaves...how backward." Lady Augusta spoke as if she was irritated by their lowly presence. After saying her piece, she turned her back on them and greeted the next guest in line.

In a shocked silence, they moved on.

Cullen whispered, "Well that takes the shine off the building, eh?"

Jodoc broke in not so silently. "Give me a bowl of wheat porridge and a group of farting soldiers just out of battle any day. Even in basic I never felt so worthless."

"Don't let it worry you. You will be retired and enjoying your family around you long after her funeral pile is cold and forgotten," Getarix said.

"Family? You can't raise a family in a brothel, can you?" Jodoc said.

Getarix smiled. "You're hopeless."

Once in the centre of the garden, they were served wine and were free to mingle. The first person to congratulate them was an older man in noble robes who spoke Latin well, but with a German accent.

"Centurion...my, my you have done well for yourself, my son."

Getarix just looked at him, not recognizing him at all. "Sir, you must forgive me," Getarix said with a slight bow.

The older man seemed to enjoy this as he laughed and looked directly at Cullen. "And you, you do not remember either, Duplicarius?"

"I am sorry, sir."

"Well, I do not blame you at all. The last time we were together we were all black from head to toe...from the fire and smoke."

"That village in Germania, Getarix. Remember the burning Armouries," Cullen said with triumph.

"Yes, Segestes, sir. I see you made out well."

"Very well indeed. They gave me a villa on the coast not far from here. I see you have met the noble lady Augusta."

"Yes. Who is she?" Getarix asked, not quite recovered from their encounter.

"She is the mother of Tiberius. She was known as Livia.

"Livia? Is she not the widow of Augustus?"

"Yes."

"But Tiberius is not the son—"

"No, he is from her first marriage. She was such a devoted wife of the divine Augustus. A perfect example of what a wife should be."

"That sounds wonderful, sir. What of Thusnelda, your daughter, and her brother Segimundus?" Getarix said.

Segestes seemed uncomfortable and Getarix got the sense that he did not want to talk about it. "Well...they're here in Rome. Thusnelda had a baby...a boy you know, he...he's the son of Arminius."

"Yes, we saw them yesterday," Jodoc said.

"Well I must be going. Well...have a good evening...men." Segestes could not bring himself to call them gentlemen. He was already beating a retreat as he finished the last of his statement.

"Well that's two for two," Cullen said flatly. Jodoc laughed.

"What are 'you' laughing at, idiot?" Getarix asked.

"Men like that do not merit honour, even from the lowest scum in the mud of the Subura. Did you see her brother Segimundus in the parade?" Jodoc asked.

"No, didn't see him."

"He was naked and in chains, walking, not in a cage. Meanwhile, your Segestes that you risked your life to save stood beside the emperor and watched it all, unmoved. Like he had never seen them before. You think your brother is bad, imagine a father like him."

Getarix brought him out of his musing. "My brother's worse."

"Oh, really. He did not parade you through the streets, did he?"

"No, he was going to sacrifice me to some blood-thirsty gods."

"Yeah, but he did not humiliate you, did he?"

"He was going to cut my nipples off in public."

"Yeah, but you would have been dead."

"No, you idiot, they do that while you're still alive, and if you're so inclined you can watch them do it to ya."

"Your people are savages."

Cullen broke in, knowing that Jodoc was pushing too far. "Jodoc, what about you? We know nothing about your past."

"Nothing to tell," Jodoc said evasively. They were interrupted by the overwhelming presence of their admiring senator.

"My boys...you are truly heroes of Rome and in my humble opinion you have not yet been fully recognized. If you remember, I'm Damianus Aurelia Marius Gius, Senator of Rome. You may call me Damianus." He put his arm around Getarix and looked him directly in his face. "So, you are the discoverer of one of the eagle standards, eh?"

"Yes sir, we all discover—"

"Yes, yes indeed. As mentioned before, we have something in common." He took Getarix by the arm and led him away from his companions. Getarix could not help but notice the overextended middle. He was so large that Getarix had to bend sideways around his middle to bring his head closer to the senator when he lowered his voice.

"We do, sir, in common?"

"Yes we do. I also discovered that standard, and all the others, including the other two eagle standards. From what I saw, there were all the subunits standards present. Most of the cloth banners were even present but not in good repair."

Getarix could not believe his ears, considering the senator's size and obvious lack of mobility.

"Yes, a few years ago the Divine Augustus sent me to Arminius himself, to negotiate peace, but he would not have it—he was so bent upon war, you know... well, on the way we came across the battleground where Varus was betrayed. He was my brother-in-law, you know. You know the site. "

"Yes sir, I do. A terrible sight."

"Yes indeed, that's the one. Well, there we were in front of all the standards. They were all together, all of them. The standards, that is, on a ledge you see... all of them."

"I remember the ledge you're talking about. We found all the subunit standards there, but no eagle standards of the legions."

"You were there, at the ledge itself?"

"Yes, sir, with Germanicus and a young soldier who was with you."

"What did he say? I'm afraid that we did not have good quality soldiers with us on that mission."

"He said nothing other than that some of the standards were missing from before." Getarix felt it better not to reveal much more. He had a feeling that he could get himself into danger.

"The Eagle standards?"

"Yes, sir."

"Yes, I heard they moved them after my valiant attempt. We almost had them, if not for my incompetent and stupid centurion."

"It would have been a great service to Rome, sir."

"Yes, but now you are the hero of Rome. And not your only heroic act, eh?"

"Well, sir, we were only doing our job. And as far as finding the standard, well, we fell upon it, literally."

"Baa, you're too modest. You run yourself down too much. You have a great future here in Rome. Rome has made many a great man in her time, men who inspire these very marble statues. Men, great men whom others study and learn about for generations, immortality even. I'll let you in on a little secret."

"Secret, sir?"

"Yes." The senator lowered his voice even more, so that Getarix had to bow down even further in order to hear him.

"When I heard about all your heroic deeds, crowned by the discovery of the nineteenth standard, I was moved to tears. I thought 'here, a son of another country dedicating himself to the glory of Rome, a selfless servant who obviously believes in all things Roman. One who left his own home and the fortune it could offer him.'" The senator went quiet for a moment, catching his breath, showing tears before he went on. "To give up all…just for a chance to serve Rome, to serve Rome as a simple soldier, to give his life for such glory." The senator stopped once again, as if getting control of his emotions. "It still moves me to think that there are still such men alive…men like you. I must confess that when I heard about your selfless service, I went directly to the emperor myself and personally spoke to him about you. That is why you have been discovered…promoted."

"You, sir?" After their encounter at the day of the Triumph, Getarix had felt sure this was his sponsor. Now he truly began to worry. What did he want? What was this going to cost?

"Yes, my son. You know, Rome is in trouble. Were you greeted at the gate by a lady?"

"Yes, Lady Augusta."

"Lady Julia Augusta indeed. Her name is Livia. It is said—" the senator dropped his voice to a whisper. "—she poisoned a path to the throne for her son. Fair warning…stay clear of her. Be careful with her. She is known to take a shine to young centurions."

"That should be no problem. No shine there, I can guarantee you."

"I'm not so sure. You have a brilliant future before you, my son. She dropped her first husband the moment she saw the star of Augustus rise. They say she is quite the expert in poisons. The divine Augustus would not eat from her hands. So she poisoned the figs while they hung on the tree."

"Well this is one centurion that will double-check anything served by her. Besides, I don't think anyone will take notice of me."

"I have."

Getarix went silent and just nodded. He did not want to either encourage the conversation or offend his unwelcome conversationalist.

The senator went quiet for a moment and continued in a more serious tone. It seemed to Getarix that he was guarding his words, even a bit nervous. "You know it was my privilege—nay, honour—to have you promoted. I did it at great personal and political risk, you know. I cashed in many favours owed me." He paused to let the last statement sink in.

Getarix thought, *ha here comes the toll.*

"I even created a few debts to make it happen."

"Sir, I am sorry that I caused you so much trouble, but I never as—"

"No, no, think nothing of it. Nothing…well, there is one thing you might be able to do for me, and if I hear right it would also lift a great burden off your shoulders."

"Sir?"

"Well, I find myself in a bit of a bind. The slave markets are empty of what I need. You see…my wife, who lives in a villa on the coast, insists on one type of slave, a little girl, about fourteen or fifteen years old. She needs her as a personal attendant. She wants her to have that Germanic look—you know, the yellow hair and all that. My wife can be such a demon when she does not get her way. So, you see you would be doing me such a deep personal favour. I will be very much in your debt. I do pay generously for what I want."

"Well sir, I don't—"

"Know what to say? Think nothing of it I hear you cannot afford her anyway. Your armour here almost broke you. Am I not right?"

"Well sir—"

Damianus, sure of his success, chuckled. "At your age and position in life, you should be swimming in money and loose girls. I can even arrange that for you."

Getarix had to speak up before he sold Isolde without knowing it. "No, sir, you don't understand. The girl is not for sale."

"What? You are mad. You cannot afford her, she is nothing but a burden…a burden you can ill afford. My son, listen here—"

"Centurion Getarix…excuse us, Senator." The smiling voice of Germanicus broke their meeting.

"Sir, it's so great to see you—"

Germanicus took Getarix by the arm and led him away, to the sheer delight of the young centurion. The senator turned and stormed out of the garden.

"Did you enjoy the parade, Centurion?"

"Yes sir, an experience of a lifetime." As they talked about old times, Germanicus led Getarix toward a small group centred by Tiberius. Once out of earshot, Germanicus leaned over to Getarix and whispered quietly in his ear. "Be careful, Rome is full of jackals, much more fierce then those Germans you spent the last few years fighting."

"Yes, sir, I think I know what you mean." By then they were in the company of Tiberius and Getarix dropped any further comment.

XXXVIII

CHOICES

"You stupid...useless...maggot!" Damianus bellowed as he landed three blows in quick succession, corresponding to each insult, upon the hapless head of Antonio. "You should go off and die you worthless pig!"

Antonio did not know what had hit him. Throughout the many years of abuse, he usually knew when something was coming. Build-up of tension, or some political intrigue would indicate to the household slaves that an explosion was imminent. This night, however, there was no such indication of trouble. The senator had been positively buoyant on their way to the reception.

"The prize, Antonio, is within my grasp...I can feel it now. And to think it was your idea," Damianus was almost giddy as they travelled to the reception. Antonio walked by the litter with the litter-bearers, struggling under their burden. As he walked, he was unsure if he wanted the credit for a plan to destroy a child's life, but survival is what it is—just that, survival. So as the blows came the moment the senator appeared through the garden gate, Antonio was caught off his guard.

"Get out of my sight before I kill you!" Antonio did not hesitate another second. He darted into the darkness of an alley that led away from the garden down into the valley. He ran with all of his might but none of his dignity. The only solace was that their plan had not worked and the child was still safe, for now.

"So tell me, Centurion," Tiberius said. "They tell me that you were in the fight the moment you arrived on the battlefield and managed to stay in it for the duration. Are such tales true, or is my adopted son here exaggerating the accounts?" Tiberius had a wry expression on his face as he gestured toward Germanicus standing by his side.

"It wasn't boring, sir, I can tell you that."

'Not boring indeed. Your senator, Damianus, seems to be quite smitten by you. To hear him tell it, you won the war alone."

"I was never alone sir, ever."

"But what about your winter adventure? Left to die, I'm told. Were you not alone then?"

"No sir, there was one other loyal soldier. He saved my life."

"Well, in saving your life he helped save the dignity of Rome."

Getarix noticed Centurion Marsallas closing in on their group. He was glaring hatefully at Getarix.

"Sir," Marsallas interrupted, maintaining his glare at Getarix.

"What is it?" Tiberius growled. "What is it now? Leave me alone, man!"

"I'm sorry, sir, your mother wishes to speak to you."

"What does she want?" He addressed the small crowd again. "That was the best part of war, being away from her. One of these days, I'm going to set her up on an island somewhere. Maybe I should send her to war. We would win that one for sure, eh?" The small crowd chuckled, including Getarix until he caught the glare of Marsallas. The message was clear. *You are not part of this group and have no right to laugh.*

Once Tiberius left to find out what his mother wanted, the group dissipated, leaving only Germanicus and Getarix.

"So, Centurion, where did you meet your benefactor the noble Senator Damianus?"

"Tonight, sir."

"Tonight?"

"Actually, just before the Triumph, sir."

"Do you have any idea how you got to Rome?"

"That was only revealed tonight."

"By the senator?"

"Yes, sir."

"He must have some persuasive ability to convince the emperor to bring all three of you here to Rome, with promotions on top of that. I take it Centurion Marsallas and the officers of the Praetorian Guard are not too happy about it?"

"Marsallas, mostly. The rest of the officers are too overworked to care about much. They are just happy someone else is taking the Subura patrol."

"Subura, is that where Marsallas put you?"

"Yes sir, it too isn't boring."

"I should say not. Watch out for Damianus. He must really want something you have. To convince the emperor to promote you three and add you to the roles of the Praetorian Guard and all that comes with it is no small feat, considering Tiberius's opinion of the revered body of senators. Men fit to be slaves, he calls them."

"Well, he revealed that tonight as well." Germanicus gave him a look that said carry on. "Apparently I have a slave he wants."

"Let me guess. A girl slave, a young one?"

"Yes sir."

"How young?"

"Now I would say thirteen, fourteen—marriageable age, I guess."

"He's not interested in marriage, and she seems a little old for what has become known as his tastes."

"Oh, he wants her for his wife, sir. That is, to give to his wife, who lives in a villa by—"

"By the sea. She is a prisoner there, you know. He has not seen her for years. He couldn't care if she lived or died. Actually, dying would be his preference."

"Well he wants the slave for her, or so he says."

"No he doesn't, he wants her for himself."

"Well, it seems he sent his agent Alexander, the slave-trader, to Germania two years ago to kidnap her."

"Who?"

"Alexander the slave—"

"No, who did he kidnap?"

"Oh, Isolde, my slave—she was about eleven at the time."

"Now that makes sense. Alexander...wait a minute, was he not killed by...?" Getarix simply raised his left hand. "It was you who killed him. You do attract attention. So what did he offer you for her?"

"The senator, tonight?" Germanicus nodded. "We did not get that far. He only said the price would be a great one."

"And why not, I'm sure you could have made out very well. When he wants something, he usually gets it and is usually willing to pay for it. My advice is to just give her to him as a gift for the promotion."

"She is not for sale, sir."

"What are you, mad? You could make a sizable sum, not to mention the promotion. But if you refuse him…"

"I already did."

"You fool. I would watch your back, especially since Marsallas already has his sword pointed at it. You are inviting trouble."

"I know, but she's just a child and not—"

"Well if you insist on being a fool, I will warn you to keep a very low profile. Even disappear into the paving stones if you can. There is one thing that is to your advantage." Germanicus paused.

"Sir?"

"Well, I'm sure it took a lot of persuasion to convince Tiberius to move you here. Damianus the senator could not very well go back to the emperor demanding you be broken back down. He might just have to leave you as you are. He has made a legend out of you and cannot now tell the world it was false. But he could still hurt you."

"Mmm, something to look forward to."

"Don't take it so lightly. What doesn't make sense here is why would you want to keep her? Is she that good in bed?"

"I don't know."

"You don't know? Then what is…? Don't tell me that you have feelings for her?"

"Yes, sir, I guess I do."

"You little ass. Must you insist on committing suicide?"

"Sir?"

"You have a good career. If you survive this storm, you could reach knighthood. Were you or your parents ever slaves?"

"No sir, no one, ever."

"You could make knighthood. All you need is 400,000 *sesterces*. Tiberius just changed the laws. But to marry this slave you will close these doors of opportunity forever."

"Something to think about, sir."

"Think about it…it's not worth it, Centurion. You owe that girl nothing and she can only give more expenses. Rome does owe you and can pay handsomely.

Think about what you are doing. If you go one way, you will have wealth, honour, and a career—a future. Go the other way…think about it."

"I will, sir."

XXXIX

SECOND ENCOUNTER

By the time they finished the talk, Getarix noticed the party had died down significantly. He also noticed his two friends were nowhere to be found. Someone told him Cullen and Jodoc had retired with some of the other medal recipients to the Guards Inn drinking hole to carry the party on throughout the night. Getarix was glad for that because he needed to be alone to mull over his options.

He took the longest way home possible, giving himself time to think. Sleep would not be his companion that night at any rate. Working in the Subura every night had turned his day around. Besides, he had far too much on his mind—it wandered everywhere. For a moment he was in the heat of a battle, then at sea in the storm followed by rescuing Isolde from Alexander. It then slipped into his childhood. He remembered the disgrace he had lived under. Walking down the streets of their village, wrapped shamefully in the rages of poverty. He, the descendant of the great warrior king, reduced to nothing but a pathetic waif. As he walked and wandered through the streets of the greatest city to ever exist, he became more conscious of his present station in life. His armour shone brilliantly when any torch light bounced off it. Even though it was the middle of the night, the streets were full of merchants receiving their produce from the farms. Wood for burning and building, trinkets of all kinds, wine of every quality and grain of every type were all delivered once the majority of the citizens were safely in bed. It hit Getarix that as he went about, people moved aside for him. Wealthy merchants greeted him with respect. Cart drivers bowed their heads for him, and if he found himself at a crossing, they would give deference to him, allowing him to cross first. *You owe that girl nothing and she can only give expenses. Rome does owe you and can pay handsomely.*

I could get used to this. He began to walk straighter, holding his chin up and chest out. At one point, he even threw his thick red cape over his shoulders, revealing all of his armour and medals of honour. Even his dagger and arm torques were clearly exposed. He noticed that as he began to strut like a peacock, people gave him even greater respect. He began to really enjoy this new special status. He reasoned to himself, *I have earned this, through battle and hardship. Why should I be without? After all, am I not of royal blood? Do I not merit this as an inheritance? An inheritance that skipped a few generations but now is mine.* He thought about his great grandfather. *Was it like this? Did he wear the dagger and arm torques in this manner?* Getarix congratulated himself on bringing them back to the life of honour and respect they deserve and were made for.

The moment his mind was convinced of his own self-importance, he saw the eyes of Isolde as she was pulled from her kidnapper. The eyes of her dying brother—*Don't hurt her.* Visions flooded his mind of their quiet times together, of her on the base of the statue with the light illuminating her hair. He stooped a little as he mulled over thoughts about her pure heart and clear, intelligent mind. These thoughts challenged any desire for wealth or status. He thought that they would be happy farming a small plot away from the politics and the wars of the world. But then the conviction returned that she was already lost to the senator. *He has the power to grab her, and not only she but also I would be destroyed.* Getarix had made a commitment to the Roman army. It was his life, now, and he knew he could be called away to serve another posting at any time, possibly somewhere he wouldn't be able to offer Isolde any protection. The thought of her falling into the senator's hands tore him up inside, but even with his status as a centurion in the Praetorian Guard, he was powerless against such a devious and well-connected man. But he was a centurion, and that was a remarkable achievement in such a short time. He felt proud of his station, and his fellow soldiers were his family, now. The only true family he had left. He could envision a long, successful military career ahead.

But Isolde…

On he went throughout the night, his mind leaning one way then the other. Whichever way he went, whatever path he chose, it would cost him dearly. This was a strange feeling; for the first time in his life, he had something to lose. He did not like being put into this place.

When Getarix left the emperor's palace, he headed north through the forum. From there he continued north and east, keeping clear of the Subura. As the night wore on, he noticed the carts disappearing. By that hour, he had looped back and was in the valley below the palace by the great Circus Maximus, where the gladiatorial games were held in want of a proper amphitheatre to hold those festivals of blood he hated so much. *Human sacrifices by another name, sacrificed to the gods of public opinion.* Getarix was tired and frustrated, so he decided to head north through the valley that ran north and south to the east of the emperor's palace. Just before reaching the Subura, he passed a vast swampy area to his right, a great eyesore. Not only was it an eyesore, it was a great place to go to do things you do not want the public to see. Once he hit the Subura, his mind was so conflicted all he wanted was wine. He knew it would only cloud his situation more, but at least it would be a happy cloud. He stopped at a few wine stalls but found the drink scarcely palatable. The merchants knew not to waste their good stuff at this hour. By the wee hours, a man either was already drunk or only wanted to be. Either case, the cheap wine would do. He knew that further down, near the winding Clivus Pullius road that led out of the valley up to Esquiline Hill, there was a tavern where good wine could be found.

The front of the wine shop was completely open to the street. Before Getarix, a thick oaken counter went into the tavern and wrapped around the merchant. When he entered the place he noticed only one other figure left. He was slumped over the counter between two tall wine amphorae that jutted out of the counter. The merchant was bent under the counter, carefully placing the last of his wine shipment away. He heard Getarix arrive, placing some coins on the counter.

"We're closed." When he turned and looked, he recognized Getarix. "Sir… forgive, I did not notice you. You're not patrolling tonight, are you?"

"No, not tonight."

"You are surely dressed the part, but not any part for the Subura."

"No, I attended a little party tonight."

"I heard. Congratulations, sir."

"Little party indeed!" yelled the reviving figure.

Getarix chose to ignore him. "Julius, your finest, please."

"For you, Centurion, anything."

"Yes...for you the finest...only the finest, eh? Not like the life led by us slaves, eh?"

Julius said, "Antonio, mind your tongue. Do you not know who you address?"

"I know who I address...just another Roman pig."

Getarix was getting irritated. He stood from his stool. "Hey, you drunk, shut your porridge hole. You're lucky I'm off duty or else I'd—"

"Or else you'd what?" The drunk got up, working himself around the counter into the light. "Or else you'd beat me again."

Once he staggered into the light of the oil lamps near the open end of the tavern, Getarix recognized him from the other morning with Jodoc. "You...go home, slave...to your master with you before you end up dead."

Getarix sat back down, determined to ignore Antonio.

"You would love to do that, eh...what is wrong with you?"

"What the hell are you talking about?"

Antonio lost all discretion. "Why don't you give the senator what he wants?" His words slurred.

"What do you know of your master's business or mine?" Getarix was getting angry. He stood to his full height with his back to the open street. To complete his authoritative stance, he threw back his cape revealing his medals of honour and the brilliant armour of an imperial centurion. The glow from the numerous lamps caused his armour to shine like many lights. Antonio stopped and just stared as if he were in a trance. Antonio began to shake. His face became red with fury. Before he knew what hit him, Getarix was on his back in the muck of the Subura with the animal-like slave on top of him. Antonio had grabbed a knife that stood erect on a cheese board. The cheese long exhausted, the knife had been left to be cleaned and put away after closing.

"Where did you get that from, you murdering imp, you...I'll kill you... you bastard you...." As Antonio gasped these words, he drew the knife high with both hands around the handle and his chest behind the hilt. He threw his weight down upon the weapon, but the greater strength of the younger Getarix prevailed and threw him off onto his own back in the mud. Julius was yelling at his old friend to stand down, but by this time Antonio could hear nothing, see nothing, and for that matter feel nothing other than uncontrollable rage.

Antonio thrown clear, Getarix was on his feet within seconds, dripping with puke-inspired mud, his sword in hand, ready to kill the offending slave. Antonio saw the determination in his eyes and decided that tonight was a good night to die. He ran toward the armed centurion, determined to leave this world for the next. Just before reaching his goal, he was knocked out from behind, landing unconscious in the mud. Getarix looked up to see Duplicarius Arius standing before the slave lying between them. The night's patrol had witnessed the entire event from down the street. It took everything in Getarix not to bend over the slave and pin his heart to the muck of the ground. Instead, he stood there as they hauled the slave away to certain death. After they took Antonio away, he returned to the wine shop and depleted Julius of some of his cheap wine with the goal of making the night go away. Julius never said another word, sick to his soul by the altercation.

There they sat together and watched the sunrise from within an amphora.

XL

DECISION MADE

"What the hell happened to you?" Cullen said with a laugh. "Did you get drunk with the emperor?"

"Did you get some girls?" Jodoc added. "I bet he only gets the best."

"Jodoc, shut up or else—"

"Cullen, as we were drinking ourselves handsome…alone, he was rolling around with some young prostitutes. From the looks of things, you did it in the streets of the Subura."

"If you must know, and it appears you must, I was attacked last night by some crazy slave. You know the one. The one I did not let you kill last week and yes, it was in the streets of the Subura. And yes, maybe I should have let you kill him." Getarix filled in the blanks as he undressed. He moved painfully slow, still in a drunken haze.

"Tell us about the girls."

"Just ignore him, Getarix. He is just sore that he could not interest any young ladies last night."

"Hey, that's not true."

"Granted, once he started to pay for it, he found all kinds of interest."

Getarix realized that if he were not drunk and hung over simultaneously, he just might have found that comment funny. However, he was not in any mood to entertain or be entertained. Deep down, he knew he had made a decision sometime after Antonio was gone. It made him sick to think of it, but his mind was uncomfortably made up. He was going to sell his slaves and be done with it. "Okay, guys, not this morning. Bugger off and give me some peace to recover, will you?"

"No."

"What?"

"We came here to deliver a message."

"What message? Make it and go away and leave me in my hellish peace!" he said a little too loudly, which made him wish he hadn't because his head felt like it was about to explode.

"We can't, we're under orders."

"Whose orders? Because I countermand them."

"You can't, we're under the orders of Damianus Aurelia Marius Gius, Senator of Rome."

"What the hell does he want?" Getarix said, even though he did want to talk to him—he did, but just not right then.

"He has ordered us to bring you to him."

"Now?"

"Yes, now or a few minutes ago," Cullen added, to give the situation a bit of urgency.

"What time is it?"

"Just after the noon meal."

"Tell him I'll see him later," Getarix said weakly as he laid back down.

"Nothing doing." Cullen and Jodoc grabbed him to rouse him back to life. When they touched him, they discovered he was still slimy.

"Getarix, what did you do last night?"

"I was rolling in the mud in front of the taverns of the Subura...now leave me alone."

Jodoc said, "Getarix, are you aware that half of the mud in front of those taverns is pure vomit?" The stench was almost too much for them to stomach, but they soldiered on and got their friend cleaned up and dressed to a somewhat presentable standard.

The sun was almost more than his spinning head could handle, but Getarix slowly made his way to the home of Damianus, owner of Antonio. Many times, he stopped in order to slow the spinning in his head and settle his stomach. In the semi-drunken state, everything works at half capacity at best. When he arrived, a slave met him at the door and showed him in. Once inside he had to stop again for a moment to allow his eyes to adjust and his stomach to calm down. It was not as bad as before. The slave was a dark-haired young man who coldly introduced himself as Marcus. As Getarix walked through the many halls of the senator's grand home, all the slaves gave him cold, hateful stares. This made Getarix very uncomfortable, causing him to wonder what he had done to these people. When they crossed an open atrium, he noticed a young female slave digging out a dead plant from the small flowerbed that framed the pool that collected rainwater. Something about her caught his eye. He stopped and stared at her, desperately telling his own eyes to focus. Marcus stopped impatiently. The girl looked at Getarix with a hateful scowl.

"Marcus…what has happened to this girl?" Getarix was shocked at the bruising on her face.

"The senator does not tolerate insubordination or laziness," Marcus said in a monotone voice that told Getarix he did not believe his own words.

"He raped m—" the girl tried to say, but Marcus was there in a second, crouching down and covering her mouth with his hand.

"Quiet, Helen…you do not need to be heard."

Don't hurt her. Getarix could see the deep blue eyes of Fritz looking down on him. A wave of guilt hammered at him.

Marcus looked up at Getarix, who was simply dressed in his red tunic and sword belt. "The senator runs his house as efficiently as you run the army." Marcus wanted to get the message across without being disloyal to his owner.

"Yeah…but I don't rape my soldiers." He was pointing to her face. "Is this common, slave?" Getarix asked, looking down at the two slaves on their knees.

At hearing the question, Marcus quickly got up, walking past Getarix toward the direction they were heading before they saw the girl. "The noble senator will meet you in here, Centurion," Marcus said as they entered a very large room.

Getarix knew he was treading in unfriendly territory, so he pushed the issue of the girl no further. The walls of the grand room were plastered in a warm cream colour framed in red borders. Instead of the usual painted scenes of flowers, birds, or fish, the centre of each red-framed panel held armour and weapons. As Getarix waited for the senator, he became aware that he had almost recovered from his self-inflicted amphora sickness. The weapons interested him greatly. Many of them he recognized. He noticed one wall was totally German, another Roman, while others looked exotic and strange and he could not place. On the far wall, he noticed weapons that were clearly Celtic. He walked toward the end wall, studying them. His eyes then caught sight of weapons that looked very much like those from Britannia. In the centre was mounted a distinctive Gaulish sword. He could not quite make it out. The distance was too far, and his eyes were still in the remnants of a haze. He stood transfixed until the senator filled the room with his bulk.

"Centurion." The senator stopped and looked at him. It was evident that the smell Getarix emanated was not lost on the senator. "Welcome to my home. It would appear the table has shifted a bit on our affairs. I still want the girl...for my wife that is...but it seems I also owe you for that disgraceful attack last night by my slave Antonio."

"Well, sir, it was truly unexpected."

"Indeed...especially for me."

"I assure you, sir, I never once thought—"

"To be sure...understood, but the fact still remains that Antonio attacked you. I have prepared remuneration—you know, compensation for your troubles." The senator pronounced the words very carefully as he tried to hand Getarix a small leather bag of coins. This was outside the normal way Damianus dealt with his lessers, but considering his own advocacy of Getarix in front of the emperor and the fact it appeared that Germanicus had taken a liking to this young man, the senator felt it wise to use honey rather than vinegar.

"Thank you, sir, but I cannot accept this."

"Don't be so silly...take it."

"No, sir. You see, even though I was not on duty, per say, I was in uniform and this is simply part of my job, my duty, sir." Getarix did not want to be in any way indebted to the senator.

"Very good. As you want. This is why I was able to spot you so easily. You have qualities seldom seen these days." Getarix knew that the senator could care less about the happenings of the previous night—he just did not want to be in a disadvantage in the negotiations for the girl. Getarix had been well prepared to sell the girl when he arrived at the home of his unrequested patron. This had changed somewhat after talking to the slave girl in the atrium. The eyes of Fritz intruded on his mind and his words were becoming difficult to silence.

The senator knew he had lost some ground that could not be made up by a bribe. The only card he had left was his plans for Antonio. "As for that worthless slave, I have plans for him."

"What plans would that be, sir?"

"Well, I no longer own him, you see."

"I thought you never sold slaves, sir."

"Normally not, but this is special. I sold him over to the gladiatorial school. He is held there, and will fight in the upcoming games. When his day comes, he will die the most painful death imaginable. This should please you?"

"I am not the greatest fan of the games, sir."

"Well on that day, yet to be determined, you will be my special guest in my box and together we will watch as your revenge is meted out, not to mention Roman justice." The senator knew he was not gaining much ground, so he thought he would change the subject once more before moving on to the slave girl.

"I noticed you were rather transfixed by some of my collection."

"Yes, sir, I recognize many of the weapons. Some I have used and many have been used against myself."

"Do you recognize these?" The senator pointed to the wall with strangely shaped weapons.

"No, sir, I have not had the pleasure of meeting any of those."

"They are from the eastern Roman Empire. You are only familiar with the west. Is that not so?"

"Yes sir, but I noticed that Gaulish sword there." Getarix pointed to the wall of British weapons.

"That one I found in battle. I was a Tribune some years back, and fought in Gaul. You were not aware of that, eh?"

"No sir, not at all."

"We are soldiers both, are we not?" The senator hoped he had found his point of contact.

"It would seem so, sir," Getarix said, his mind now spinning with more questions than answers. "Now the girl...." Getarix just wanted to get out of there.

"But before her. Marcus!" the senator bellowed.

"Master?"

"Get that sword down, at once." He pointed to the Gaulish sword. "Wrap it up for our guest. I believe this gift will be appreciated. And as it turns out, I have no reason to hold on to it anymore."

Marcus dutifully took a ladder, detached the sword from the wall, wrapped it tightly in a linen cloth, and handed it to Getarix. The last thing Getarix wanted was a gift from the senator, but he could think of no graceful way to refuse without provoking this dangerous man. He fought to keep the look of disgust from his face as he held the cloth bundle.

"Sir, I thank you for the gift, but I must tell you that my mind is made up about the girl."

"Do not trouble yourself about that. I'm sure you will make the right decision in due course."

At that, Getarix knew that the meeting was over. He paid his respects, wondering why the senator did not apply greater pressure on him. He knew that the sword was a bribe to soften him up. He returned home with his new gift, which he simply threw in the corner without opening. Getarix did not want to see it, as it was a sickening reminder of his willingness to turn Isolde over to the likes of Damianus. He made his decision to keep Isolde and maybe someday marry her if she would consent. He did not want to lay eyes on his new bribe. He felt a release within his soul that he had made the right decision in the end.

XLI

COMING CLEAN

"What are you up to!?" Centurion Marsallas belted out with a hostile voice. "You tell me that you know no one. 'I have no sponsor,' you tell me. Then I see you and the senator hugging like lovers at the reception the other night. And where did you go, this very day? Nowhere, but his house. I have watched you three and did some digging. It would appear that Damianus, Senator of Rome, *is* your sponsor. You knew that…you are a lying little—" Marsallas checked himself before he crossed the line. He was not sure just how far the senator would go to protect his young protégé. "What I can't understand is why? What could you possibly have that that old man could ever want? What…is it sexual?" Marsallas knew that was not the answer by the instant look of disgust on the face of Getarix.

Getarix had learnt over the last year to keep his business to himself. He knew he could not trust his superior officer. Too many times, Centurion Marsallas tried to trip him up. He even had him followed during his patrols. On more than one occasion, Getarix had heard from the merchants that Marsallas had questioned them to see if Getarix and crew had taken any bribes or if they let anything slip. The three of them were an enigma to Marsallas. He could not understand why the senator would have these three promoted and moved to Rome if they could not provide a valuable service. Damianus would never do a good deed simply out of the goodness of his heart. It was a well-known fact that no goodness could be found there. Marsallas could not figure it out and not knowing was killing him.

"So, your senator gets you promoted and brings you here to Rome. For whatever reason? The gods seem to be keeping the reason to themselves, as are you. So he brings you here, and then once here he sends his slave to attack you."

"No sir, the slave was acting on his own accord. He was drunk and filled with rage. I was nothing more than a convenient target. The senator had him sent to the gladiatorial schools to be publicly executed. He would not send his slave to do his bidding and then put him to death for doing as he was commanded."

"You do not know your senator. This also tells me that you and your senator are talking regularly. You seem to know his business. I had you followed yesterday right to his door. But you do not know your sponsor very well. He would send a slave to try to kill you and then he would send him to his death just as easy."

"Like you said, I don't know him, sir."

"Don't lie to me, Centurion. And can you explain to me why there is this man who claims to be from your village back in Britannia…a relative no less, desperately seeking you? He indicated that you are avoiding him." The look of worry that crossed Getarix's face told Marsallas that there were many layers to this mystery.

"I cannot imagine who that might be, sir."

"You don't lie very well, Centurion Getarix."

Getarix decided that he had spoken enough and kept his peace. After a few more fruitless questions, Marsallas gave up and sent him on his way.

As Getarix left, Marsallas vowed to get to the bottom of this and when he did, all the help of the gods would be of no aid to his young centurion. He was a bit conflicted. On one hand, he hated Getarix with every fibre of his being. On the other, he and his team worked extremely well. The Subura has never been kept in such order. The nights they patrolled, the worst rabble-rousers stayed indoors rather than face them. Their sense of duty was an inspiration and their attention to detail was faultless. That being what it was, Marsallas still hated political appointees and his determination to destroy this one was heightened by his efficiency. *What the hell is he up to?* Marsallas could not wrap his head around it. Marsallas was also resisting pressure from his superiors to assign the new centurion a job in line with his rank. The last thing Marsallas wanted was for these three to shine in a more public arena.

Getarix and team were back on patrol that night. When he stopped by to talk to Julius, his tavern was full. His usual customers were mostly young single men from wealthy families drinking the finest Julius had to offer. After they had drank themselves handsome, they would proceed to the brothel to honour the prostitutes with their patronage.

"Centurion Getarix, welcome. Have some of my best. It's Greek, just in last night."

"No thank you, Julius. I am still recovering from the other night and I vaguely remember making some vows never to drink again."

Julius chuckled as he withdrew the cup. "Centurion, I'm glad you're here. I want to talk to you about Antonio."

"What about him?"

"What is to happen to him?"

"He is already in the hands of the gladiatorial school."

"Public execution," Julius concluded sadly.

"Why are you so worried? He's a drunk, is he not?"

"No not a drunk. Antonio, never."

"Well that's the side of him I saw, and an angry one too."

Julius kept his counsel to himself and quietly mourned the fate of his friend. Getarix continued his patrol, trying to forget the night before.

When the night's patrol was finished, they dragged themselves home, exhausted, with the ever-present mud caked on their feet.

"You know it's going to take hours putting my sandals back in order," Jodoc said.

"The cost of business," Getarix said without much sympathy.

When they arrived at the barracks, the armourer was waiting for them. "Centurion Getarix, sir…um, I am sorry to inconvenience you like this…but, hum…things have changed."

"What things?"

"Your payment scheme, sir."

"What's wrong with it? Did I not pay you for half already?"

"Yes, sir," he answered a bit nervously.

"As per our agreement…?" Getarix was getting irritated, to the great discomfort of the armourer.

"Yes, sir, but as I mentioned, things have changed. I need the second payment now. If you do not have the cash, I would be willing to take some property in exchange."

"Property indeed." Getarix was quick to see the hand of the senator in all of this. "When do you need your money?" Getarix said in menacing tone as he walked up to him, doing his best to intimidate the craftsman, to great effect.

"By the end of the week, sir…in two days, sir," the fear-filled armourer said. He lowered his voice even more. "I'm sorry, sir, but I—"

"You'll get it. Now go, thief," Getarix said as he grabbed his sword in the most threatening stance possible. He was livid.

"What was that about?" Cullen asked.

"That, my friend, was the work of the senator. What am I to do? Without that armour…"

"Let him have it back. You've finished your ceremony. You might even get your down-payment back," Jodoc said.

"First, Jodoc, if you open your eyes you'll notice that I need that ceremonial armour at least once a month. Second, he made that armour to fit my body, no one else's, and I can guarantee you he will not give me back one single *As*. And as far as the property is concerned, he was referring to Isolde, not armour."

"What would he want with Isolde? And how would he even know? Hey, why not give him Gainer?"

"Jodoc…it's a wonder we let you live. The senator put him up to it, so I would be forced to give up Isolde and he could get his hand on her…literally."

Cullen looked worried. "Getarix, if I were you I would check on them."

Getarix did not need much encouragement. It took only a few minutes to arrive at the apartment. He found Gainer gone on a call and Isolde he roused out of bed. She had her nightclothes on. It was a one-piece linen frock. It clung to her petite womanly body, almost causing Getarix to faint. When she saw him, she smiled broadly. Her smile was the most beautiful thing he had ever seen. Her skin looked like it radiated light and the deep blue of her eyes almost drowned him. He just sat there looking at her, almost forgetting the purpose of his visit. He was just glad he did. It hit him that they were both so busy that over the last year they had not seen each other as much as he wanted to.

"I hear you are doing well in your training."

"Yes, I will deliver my first baby soon, Gainer said."

"Good for you. That is wonderful." He could not have been more proud. He marvelled at the sight of her. She was a woman full of beauty and shy confidence.

"I heard that the emperor awarded you a gold phalera for finding the Eagle Standard, and a silver one besides."

"A small thing, really."

"Nothing about you is a small thing." She regretted letting it go as she burned red, blushing. She'd had strong feelings for him from the day he pulled her from the kidnapper's arms. She feared men, especially strong men, but there was a gentleness to her owner she had never seen in another. She ran over the scene of the Triumph in her mind. But that was just it: he was her owner and she a slave, a thing. And that was all he would be and all she would be—he just an owner and her nothing but a possession. She would occasionally allow herself to believe that he saw her in a different light, but those thoughts were soon dashed and put aside. How could he ever be attracted to her, a lowly slave that had been with more men than she ever wanted to think about? She saw herself as nothing more than broken goods. She would often ask herself, *Why would he keep me? Is he trying to find some use for me?* That is why she figured he had Gainer teach her the trade of midwifery. She figured that once she had enough skill, he would sell her for a handsome profit. She wished he wouldn't. Life now was good, better than she could have hoped. She felt it would be even better if only he noticed her. Whenever she dared to believe that such was possible, Gainer was there to remind her of its impossibility.

Her blushing did not escape his notice. It gave him reason to hope. He could never believe that the man who killed her brother, right in front of her eyes, could ever be anything but an object of hate. He marvelled that she would even seem to enjoy being in his company, which she seemed to. He chalked it up to that fact she was scared of her owner and did not want to offend, lest something unpleasant might happen. The blush after the compliment was something different. He knew he could order her to his bed or even order her to marry him, but unless she desired the same, he wanted nothing of it.

They went quiet for a while, both afraid to speak. It hit Getarix that he had been consumed with her fate and protecting her, yet had never once talked to her about what she wanted. He built up the courage.

"Do you like midwifery?"

"Yes, sir. Are you going to sell me...?" Isolde could not believe she had just said such a thing.

"Sell you, what ever made you think...?"

"Well, is that not why you had Gainer train me?"

"By the gods, no...that was Gainer, it was her idea. Actually she did not even run it by me." They both chuckled at that. They went silent again.

"Then why...why do you keep me?"

"Because—" It was time for Getarix to go red as he thought about the question. He realized that he loved her, or at least had feeling that resembled love. He wanted to say it but was afraid.

He decided he had nothing to lose.

"It's because...I love you, Isolde." He looked down, fearful that her look would say otherwise. As he said it, it felt like a wave went through his head, giving him the same sensation as strong wine.

She sat there, silent. When he did have the courage to look up, she was smiling broadly and he could see a tear working its way down her cheek. He almost exploded inside with happiness, for in that tear he found his joy.

XLII

THE VISITOR

Getarix and Isolde sat there filled with unspeakable happiness. Their heavenly silence was broken by angry steps and the deafening slam of the door.

"Ooh he's insufferable. Isolde, I need water."

"Gainer, what is it…?" Getarix said.

Gainer had walked into the room and spotted him.

"You…you worthless piece of—"

"Enough! I will not have you speak to me in that way." Getarix stood. Gainer stopped in her tracks. He had never spoken to her in that manner. She had noticed a change in him over the last year. He had become more confident, less willing to simply take it.

Once all was quiet, he calmly asked, "Now what is the problem?"

"The problem," Gainer started with a strained voice that gave away the fact she had to use every bit of her inner strength not to yell. "The problem is that you…you not only lied to us—" she pointed to the still-sitting Isolde, "—you cheated us along the way."

Getarix could not get his mind around her statement. "Cheated you? I put you up in this apartment, let you have total freedom to practice your profession, and ask nothing from you. On top of that, since you have moved to Rome I have even paid all the rent for this apartment, which—"

"You have not!" Gainer's rage was back. "You have not only left the rent unpaid, but the landlord has tripled our rate…because of you. And on top of that he has demanded back rent for the past year. He said he has been too kind, allowing us to stay here with only your promises but never a single *sestorii*.

Isolde said, "We will have to move…"

"We can't. Ever since Germanicus has returned with his entourage, there's no place in Rome to be had." Getarix said gently. He then addressed the still-angry Gainer. "Gainer, you must believe me. I paid him personally, every *As* I owed… every month. I don't know how I am going to pay for this. I assure you we will figure something out. And I know who's behind this." He explained about his armour payment, but nothing about the senator.

"You can make all the excuses you want, but as far as I'm concerned you are not welcome here and you may never talk to this child again."

"I'm not—" Isolde was silenced with one look from her matron. She sheepishly looked down to the floor.

"Let me remind you of our little legal arrangement we have here," Getarix said.

"No, let me remind you that whatever you did we now have to pay triple the rent."

Getarix knew that this was not the time to have a showdown with his strong-willed slave. He had to own up to the fact that he had let the situation get to where it was by not establishing his authority from the beginning. He simply said, "I'll get it somehow."

"No, you don't need to."

"But how will we…?"

"No *we* here. I will pay the rent."

"How can you?"

"Midwifery pays, y'know. I, *we*," she said, again pointing to Isolde, "we're saving to buy our freedom…our freedom from you. Until today, we almost had enough to buy both our freedoms. As far as the back rent is concerned, I have already paid it with our freedom money. That leaves me—us—with nothing… absolutely nothing." There was a choke in her voice.

Getarix had never felt right about owning another, but he could not bear seeing Isolde leave his life. It hurt him that she was part of the scheme to buy her freedom to get away from him. "Where will you go when you are free?"

"Nowhere, because the way you seem to orchestrate things, we will never be free." Gainer once again fought to control her voice, but the defiance remained.

"We're going as far away from you as possible. Britannia, where you cannot go, where there is no memory of Rome or anything Roman, especially…you. Isolde could forget her past where no one could know how you Romans used her. I could forget my capture and return to my people, bringing her with me. Now go, this is no longer your apartment. We pay for it, we own it. I can assure you that we will not run. We will double our work and give you your precious money for our freedom."

He looked down at Isolde who looked back with disappointment and hurt. He withdrew, defeated. Of all the things ever done to him, this was one of the worst. The moment he won the heart of his loved one, it was ripped away.

Getarix left the apartment and went straight to the favourite watering hole of the Praetorian Guards, to swim in some cheap wine. Ever since the Triumph, the three of them had earned a place in the unit. Going to the Guards Inn had become a place of acceptance. He had completely forgotten about his plan to avoid the place because it was known that his mysterious Brit was hanging about the place asking questions about him and Cullen. If he had remembered, it probably wouldn't have made a difference. He felt utterly crushed. He thought maybe he should grant them their freedom, turn himself over to his brother's agent, and leave this world for the next. It couldn't be worse. As he sat by himself in the greatest bout of self-pity he had every experienced, he decided to simply grant both ladies their freedom that very day. Maybe that was best. If Isolde went to Britannia, she would be well beyond the grasp of Damianus. Getarix accepted the loss of Isolde, for the love of Isolde.

This plan was short-lived. In discussion with some fellow centurions, he learned that by owning the two ladies he was protecting them. As free single females without any family or agent such as an owner, they were totally exposed to whatever depravation the worst of Roman society could throw at them. He had no doubt about Roman depravity. He was also informed in confidence that the senator had approached a few of his brother centurions to keep a watch on him. There was an offer to pay handsomely. The senator left them with the impression that the slaves had been acquired in an illicit way, that the senator was the rightful owner. It became apparent that the moment they were free and out of his protection, the senator would scoop them up without hesitation and with impunity.

"Centurion Getarix, sir, there you are." Cullen approached the small huddle of officers, giving a smart salute, making sure he used the proper title that his lifelong friend had been granted.

"Duplicarius Cullen, what is it?"

Cullen hesitated for a moment, making the two other centurions believe he was bringing some official business to his superior officer. They knew the drill and retreated out of earshot.

"Cullen, what is it? I am in no mood, nor any shape to deal with the dregs of the Subura. If Marsallas wants to take a strip off me he can just wait in line."

"None of the above. You know that relative who has been looking for you?"

Getarix woke fully from his stupor. "What about him?"

"He is here."

"I know, I was informed."

"No, I mean he is here, right here."

Getarix stood, drawing his sword. "Let him try to assassinate me here of all places."

"You idiot!" Cullen said, motioning for him to sit down. Getarix just looked at him with hostility. "It's Cunhail, your uncle." Getarix exchanged his look of fear for a look of astonishment. "He has been following us across the western Empire. He tracked you down here…and he is standing right there." Cullen pointed to a dark figure just inside the door of the inn. He looked out of place, being the only man not in uniform.

Getarix had to focus in on the man by the door. The light from the open door blinded onlookers from within the dark, smoky room. Getarix just stood there, and Cullen had to signal Cunhail forward.

Cunhail had explained to Cullen that he was not sure if he was allowed in the inn. Nor was he convinced that his nephew would want to talk to him, the way he fought to avoid him. When Cullen had assured him, Cunhail countered with, "That may be so, but am I welcome into the life of my nephew? Whenever I seem to get close, he runs."

Now Getarix and Cullen watched Cunhail warily approach. "He was not sure you would want to see him," Cullen said. "I assured your Uncle that you still hold him in the highest esteem and see him as the means of our survival. I hope that is okay?"

"Yes, thank you, brother."

When Cunhail reached Getarix, they embraced for what seemed a long time, enough to attract some attention. Cunhail had had the foresight to ensure he was dressed as a wealthy Roman merchant. The attention was short-lived and as soon as all three sat to a hearty meal, Getarix playing host, everyone went back to their business.

"Getarix my boy, look at you. You're a centurion now, I'm told, and in the elite Praetorian Guard."

"Just think of what Cunorix would say," Cullen added.

"I don't have to think, I was there." All three laughed. Within minutes, Jodoc had found their table and was introduced. Over the next few hours, all three filled Cunhail in of their adventures, starting with basic training. The stories included Beaudin the barmaid, to the mortification of Getarix. The more mortified Getarix got, the deeper his friends embellished. Getarix got back at Jodoc, explaining how he was branded with a fire poker on the right side of the face. Cullen and Jodoc also filled Cunhail in all the heroic exploits of their new centurion. They began with the thumping of their old instructors and their first battle by the river, where Getarix won his first phalera, and on to the battle of the inn where he won his second, and gave details of what they referred to as the battle of the standard that caught the attention of the citizens of Rome. They did not mention the shipwreck and the understanding in Rome that Getarix caused a war between Cunhail's tribe and the next.

When the food was exhausted, the conversation turned serious. Jodoc assessed the situation as deteriorating, and quietly slipped away to a livelier table where revelry was still the order of the day.

The three remaining were once again silent. Cunhail studied the quiet figure of his nephew. Cullen cleared his voice and with difficulty asked the question foremost on his mind. "Cunhail, is it true about my father? Did he take his life?"

"I'm afraid so, my boy."

Cullen went quiet, and Cunhail appraised his nephew with pride and concern.

"You look tired, my son."

"Oh, we were up all night patrolling, and due to some situations I did not get any rest today. I'm afraid I will not be great company. It doesn't help that wine makes me sleepy."

"You know, my son…you have not asked after your mother." Getarix shifted uncomfortably in his chair. "Do you not want to know?"

"I'm sure she is fine. Otherwise you would have volunteered—"

"You're right, but that not the point."

"Well there we go, eh?"

"You know she had no part in it."

"The village is small, and there is no way—"

"But it's true."

"It seemed that Cullen and I were the only ones without any knowledge."

"You were not the only ones."

"You knew."

"I did."

"And yet you did not come out and tell it to me plainly."

"Getarix, I know, and I chastise myself daily, but you know that to try to dissuade an awaiting sacrifice would gain only the wrath of the gods, not to mention standing before the elders."

"Wrath of the gods indeed...I ran from their bloody sacrifice and look at me now. If those gods exist, then I choose to spend eternity somewhere else. They're powerless, worthless things and only destruction is found in their wake."

"That, I now know. I'm sorry, my son, for not making it clearer, but I'm afraid in your state of mind you would not have believed me anyway."

"That may be true, but you could have tried. What am I talking about...in the end it was clear enough, and you gave us a means of escape."

"Unfortunately not enough for two...and here you are stuck in the Roman army."

"If you haven't noticed, it seems to be working out for us."

Cunhail went quiet again and then said, "But your mother truly knew nothing and now lives with the guilt that she played a part—the feast and all. Now she lives with Cunorix and Boudica with their two little ones."

"They have two, now...she must enjoy her grandchildren."

"Not that much. Boudica never lets her hold them, nor ever leaves them alone with her. And ever since the night you had to flee, your mother has not spoken to your brother, other than for things of business. She cut herself off from him completely. That makes the home very tense. I'm not allowed to stop by. If I can find a place to stay, I might try to see her, but Boudica has made her a virtual prisoner in her own home."

"I had no idea."

"It will bring her great joy to know you still live and are such a success."

"I'm not any success."

"What are you talking about, son?"

"Remember that girl we told you about, the little slave? Well, she's not too little anymore." Getarix filled in almost the entire picture about the present frustrations he had on his hands. He talked about the senator's demands and his armour payment, but nothing of his love for Isolde or his recent experience with Gainer and the apartment.

After an hour of conversation, Cunhail got up. "My boys, I must excuse myself. I am carrying an entire amphora of wine that is past due to explode."

"Oh, down the street on your left. I'll come, too," Cullen said. He was about to get up when Getarix grabbed his arm. Cunhail did not notice, because his urgency drove him to the door as he was getting directions.

"Getarix, I'm dying here. I need to—"

"You can die later…I want to talk to you about today." Cullen kept quiet and let Getarix finish his monologue about the apartment rent and his words with Gainer. He was visibly shaken.

"You know Getarix, this, in a way, is an answer to your prayers."

"I didn't pray for anything."

"Okay, whatever, but it does solve your problem. They are self-supporting and yet remain under your protection."

"They are not under my protection if I never see them. They could easily be kidnapped and I would never know. Besides, I want—"

"To see them?"

"No, not *them*."

"By the gods, Getarix, you do have feelings for her."

"And she for me, or at least until Gainer…" At this point he completed the narrative about his many stolen moments with Isolde and his profoundly strong feelings for her.

"She is something to look at, that's for sure. What do you want to do? Bring her to your bed? Gainer would kill you."

"I want to marry her, Cullen." The second he got it out, a wave of emotions swept over him that affected every fibre of his being.

"Um, brother, have you thought about the implications of this? Getarix, your career."

"Not you too, of all people."

"No, Getarix, are you willing to pay the cost?"

"Yes, but right now I can't even pay the rent." They both chuckled at that. "Besides, Gainer will never allow me near her again, and the look in Isolde's eyes told me that she felt the same. They know nothing of the senator and what I've done for—" Getarix stopped short with the return of his uncle from the bathroom.

Cullen got up and excused himself for his turn at the privy.

Uncle and nephew talked for the next hour as the sun set on yet another difficult day for Getarix. Then they noticed Cullen was still gone, and were about to seek his whereabouts when he walked in with a big smile on his face. Getarix had caught his second wind, and the party went on until his uncle had to excuse himself, being too tired to carry on.

XLIII

PAYMENT

The next day, Getarix slept hard, recovering from his forty-eight-hour stretch without rest garnished with plenty of wine. Marsallas, true to his word, made the life of Getarix and company a living hell. Their weekly day off was cut to a monthly day off, and their shifts were extended by two hours either side. During the day there was no need to patrol the streets, especially in the early morning when the streets were abandoned and everyone was sleeping off the night before. For the last two hours of their shifts, they would patrol completely deserted streets. They did not even have anywhere to sit and wait. They simply walked their patrol and talked. They spent the rest of their time taking care of only essential personal needs and sleep. The early summer rains meant that somehow they had to make time for cleaning their uniforms and digging their sandals out of the nightly cakes of putrid mud. They scarcely had time to see the visiting uncle. This did not bother Cunhail much, as he kept himself busy with his Roman business contacts, arranging deals for goods from Britannia.

"You know, Getarix, this is getting old. I mean, I can't remember the last time I visited my favourite brothel."

"Just think of all the money you're saving, Jodoc."

"I'd rather spend it. Besides, I'm sure they have bought some new girls and they're only good if you get them fresh."

"Jodoc, you do know you're talking about people, right?"

"Yeah…I wouldn't consider anything else, although if you want, I have connections…"

"No, stop."

"Just thought I'd ask. You never know." Jodoc was laughing.

Cullen walked in silence and chuckled at their banter. Then he broke into their conversation, changing the subject. "Getarix, have you heard from the armourer?"

"Not a word. Tomorrow I intend on paying him a visit. I expected to have been hauled up before Marsallas about non-payment of a bill by now, maybe tomorrow."

"Tomorrow, today you'll find me with all the new girls—"

Cullen just ignored Jodoc and cut him off. "Getarix, do you intend on visiting Isolde today?"

"No." Getarix left it at that. He wanted to say more, but did not know how to verbalize it. Jodoc was now lost in his own world and probably couldn't have heard them if he wanted to.

"Getarix, I think you should visit. You never know if the senator arranged things with Marsallas to keep us out of the way." He left the rest unsaid.

"No need, I asked my uncle to check in with them daily. If there was a problem he was to come here to the streets of mud and inform me."

"I still think you should take the time—"

"Cullen you don't understand…the look in her eyes…"

"Just do it," Cullen said like it was a ruling.

Later that day, Getarix submitted his weekly report to Marsallas. He expected to receive the full blast from his superior, but received nothing. If anything, he received a disinterested cool reception. Once that was done, he quickly changed his uniform and headed out to see the armourer.

"Welcome, Centurion Getarix." He greeted Getarix as he would greet his favourite patron, not a delinquent customer.

"Good day to you…hum, about the second payment for my—"

"Yes, I thank you for it and I apologize. I know we had an arrangement, but you see I was about to lose my—"

"Payment?"

"Yes, your agent…three weeks ago. Now, what can I get for you? We have some new helmet plumes in." He turned his back to Getarix, facing a shelf where he was lifting a brightly dyed red feather plume. "You can never have too many,

310

you know, if one gets broken. They are so easy to—" When he turned around, Getarix was gone. "Soldiers, they're so fickle."

Back in the barracks, Getarix caught up to Cullen, who was sitting on his cot washing the caked-on mud from his sandals. "Cullen, do you know someone paid for my armour?"

"Maybe it was the optie. You know that you had it arranged to have your pay diverted."

"That's impossible. We do not get paid until next week, nor will I be paid enough. Besides, I have too many other debts with the unit."

"How were you going to pay for your armour?" Cullen asked without looking up from his task.

"I hadn't figured that out."

"It looks like you don't need to, now."

"What do you mean? Who do I owe, now? And what will the interest be on this one?"

"Never mind that. Now go visit your slaves and make sure they are safe."

"If I return with a scar on my face matching Jodoc's, I will ensure you get one, too. Now where is he?"

"Where else?"

"Donating his pay to needy ladies of the night, eh?"

"Yup, now get going before your ladies are gone on their rounds for the day."

Getarix just stood there for a moment.

"You're stalling."

"I'm the centurion, Duplicarius, and I will stall if I want to."

Cullen looked up from his almost-completed work and gave him a hard stare.

"Okay, I'm gone."

When Getarix got to the top floor of the apartment, he could hear laughing inside. He hesitated, thinking he had found out what he came to know. *They are safe and by all accounts happy...happy that I am no longer part—*

Then he heard the loud sound of laughter that can only come from the throat of a man. *What the...what man would they...?*

He took out his key, but the lock had been changed. That was the final straw. Livid, he began to pound on the door, yelling, demanding to be let in. In quick order, the door was opened by the hand of Isolde. At the sight of her, he lost all the anger in him. He became light-headed and weak in the knees. His heart pounded like it was about to take its leave. The thought that the male voice was here for her was too much to bear.

"Centurion Getarix, please come in."

As he entered the apartment past the short hall that led into the main room, all his fears and anger subsided into shame for acting in an irrational manner. "Uncle...?"

"Getarix my boy, come sit...did I not say I would make sure they were safe?" Cunhail looked at the ladies. "He was so worried about you and your safety that he made me promise to check in on you daily."

Getarix looked at Isolde, who was blushing and looking to the floor. Gainer looked out the window, noting the position of the sun in reference to the hills in the east. "Isolde, get the bag. It's time to start our rounds. The butcher's wife is due anytime and she will be your client." In short order they were out the door and gone, leaving the two alone. As Isolde closed the door, she stole one last glance and caught his eyes. He wanted to reach out and hold her forever.

The moment the door closed, he connected the payment to the armourer with his uncle. "Uncle, did you make a payment...?"

"To the armourer? A small amount, really."

"I want to pay you back."

"No need. You're family."

"Still, I want to."

"As you wish, but with what?"

"How about...I own nothing."

"How about two slaves? I can own them and upon my return to Britannia, let them free. They can stay with me or they can go wherever they wish. Whatever works for them."

"Two, eh...? I guess that would be best. Um, by the way, what happened here? You are not aware, but Gainer—"

"Gainer told me all about it."

"About what?"

"About how you have struggled to keep that child out of the hands of that decrepit senator."

"Wait, how did she know?"

"Cullen told her. You don't think that it took an hour for him to use the toilet that night I arrived? She respects him, you know."

"The only man she respects."

"Not the only one. She respects you, but will never tell you."

"She seems to like you."

"We understand each other."

"So, you would take them to Britannia for me? And they will be safe?"

"I would with joy, my boy, and yes they will be safe. But, I recommend you sell them to me legally, let's say at the end of a working day and I leave with them immediately. I'm sure your senator has eyes and ears in all government offices. If we are quick, we can make a break before he could react."

XLIV

THE ESCAPE

"There, that's now legal. Sir, you are now the proud owner of two healthy slaves," the consul Caracalla said to Cunhail. He looked at the young centurion next to the older merchant and a question crossed his eyes. "Why would you sell two young, healthy slaves for a *sestorii* each?"

"I owed the merchant a debt and this makes us equal."

"Whatever. It must have been a very large debt indeed. That young one could easily fetch over 6,000 *denarii*…24,000 *sestorii*. Do you know how much land you could buy, or houses, or if you want a new promotion?"

"I have enough of each, thank you very much. How about you mind your business and not mine." Getarix just wanted the business done and for them to be on their way. The only happy one of the four was Gainer. A dream she had scarcely dared to dream was actually coming true. Isolde just looked to the floor, keeping her sorrow to herself. Getarix felt that this was best for all. He embraced his uncle, who was sad to be leaving his young nephew. Getarix made him promise to return as soon as possible with news of his family. Once Getarix disengaged from his uncle, he stood back and formally said his goodbyes to the ladies. Isolde never took her eyes off the floor. With that done, he left the building and joined Cullen, who was waiting outside on the street. Getarix walked right by him and headed home at a quick clip. All he wanted was to be done with it and away from this place. He was torn inside. He had just said goodbye to the only one he truly loved, never to see her again. His only comfort was knowing that in a few weeks, Isolde would be forever beyond the reach of the likes of the senator.

"Getarix…brother, why did you sell her with Gainer?"

"It's for the better, Cullen. Soon she will be safe and secure. Besides, I'm convinced she would never be happy with me."

"What are you talking about?"

"After that fight with Gainer in the apartment last month, I'm sure she changed her view of me permanently."

"What makes you say that?"

"I saw it in her eyes, and she was never the same to me after that."

"No, you were never the same after that. And tell me, when in the last month have just the two of you been together?"

This thought brought a great measure of discomfort to the mind of Cullen's lifelong friend. "Just shut up, Cullen. What's done is done. I forbid you to bring it up again. Understood, Duplicarius?"

"Yes sir," Cullen said, knowing that this ended the subject. Cullen feared this was the beginning of a dark mood in his friend, which had almost disappeared. They walked for some time in an uncomfortable silence. Cullen racked his brain to come up with a subject that might help change things. "What are you going to do about the apartment?"

"Well, Gainer paid the rent to the end of the month, so I guess I'll stay there. I need the break from the barracks anyway. Besides, if I cancel the rental agreement too soon, the senator would definitely know something is up."

Cullen was about to say, 'he's going to find out anyway,' but kept his words. Their disappearance would be noticed when the consul reported it, when the clients who were depending on the midwife services noticed them gone. Cullen feared there was no way to keep this one quiet.

When they appeared back at the barracks, Jodoc was about to head out for the evening.

"Hey! Where were you two all day? I'm heading to a new place they say has only fresh girls—wanna come?"

Cullen was about to tell him no for the both of them when Getarix said, "Yeah, let's do it." Cullen, who never indulged, went along to keep an eye on his friend.

When they arrived ten minutes later, the party was just about to start. There was no shortage of girls. Some were clearly experienced and did not show any shyness. Three of the girls were all over the new customers upon their arrival. Wine was liberally provided and they were ushered to a cushion-covered couch.

"You'll like this place, boys. Classy. We even lounge on couches like the rich aristocracy of the city do."

"We will probably have to pay like the rich do," Cullen said.

"Where do you think I invest all my money, boys?" Jodoc said, clearly in his element.

Once they were settled in, scantily clad women began to bring them their food. "You don't order food here, it's a set menu. The good thing is that whatever you wanted to eat will eventually arrive."

"And my money will eventually depart," Cullen said to himself.

Getarix felt numb and mindlessly followed without much thought of his surroundings. He happily accepted his second cup of wine and it went down as fast as the first. When one of the girls chose him as her mark for the night, he did not protest. The girl next to Cullen was not so warmly embraced. By that time, Jodoc had two girls and seemed to be in his own form of heaven. As the evening wore on, more men disappeared with the young female slaves to rooms on the upper floors. As the crowd thinned, Getarix noticed some girls against the far wall. All of them were extremely young, children really. But what was striking about them was that they were all extremely fair—white or yellow hair with blue eyes. He sat up to focus on them better. The keeper of the brothel noticed this and went over to him, shooing away the woman by his side.

"I see you have very refined tastes, sir. You have noticed the beautiful girls. All are from Germania—all are very young and tender. Only our best customers indulge. The price is higher, but not too high for a noble Centurion of the Guard, especially one who brought home the Eagle Standard. I know all about you, my son. My good friend the noble Senator Damianus has told me all about your heroism. I was with him when the emperor awarded you your gold and silver phalera." He looked back at the far wall and continued. "I have two more besides these three. They are now with customers. Let me know which one you desire and I'll have her taken to a room for you, Centurion. And tonight, consider it a gift from me."

"Too young, my friend. They should be in bed after a hearty day of playing with their dolls."

"Ah, yes indeed. I personally do not indulge in such, but some do like it. I have a line on another, a bit older by about four years, with heavenly yellow hair and ocean deep blue eyes. My friend the senator tells me that he intends on giving her to me as a gift in gratitude. He tells me he has even had her and she is like heaven. And she comes with experience. She should be here I am told within a few days, as she is about to come available."

"Thank you, if I want, I'll come back," Getarix said just to rid himself of the snake. The keeper took the hint and departed to more-profitable endeavours. The chosen prostitute returned to Getarix's side.

Getarix lounged back, sipping his wine, accepting the caresses of the girl. *Four years older.* The thought struck him like lightning. He bolted up, throwing the girl on the floor. *Four years older!* the thought screamed in his head. He got up and approached the three remaining girls who sat sadly by the wall. "How old are you girls?" he asked in Latin. He got no response. He repeated the question in his broken German and got the return of ten and eleven. The keeper of the brothel saw him talking to the girls and went over to enquire.

"Noble Centurion, I see you have changed your mind. Their beauty does radiate…"

"When did the senator inform you of this new girl?"

"This very evening. I was a guest at his home. I just returned from there…"

"How did he say he was getting this girl?"

"He said she was wrongfully taken from him and he was about to win the case."

"A legal case at night! Seems odd?"

"Yes, but who am I to question?"

"Who else was there?"

"No one."

"Are you sure?" Getarix said with ever-growing agitation that began to scare the keeper. The three girls looked upon them with wonder, enjoying their master's discomfort.

"Wait, one more arrived later."

"Who?"

"Caracalla."

"The consul Caracalla?"

"Yes, that was him." At this point, the keeper was cooperating fully, being a natural coward who confined his bullying to the powerless and weak.

"When were you told about the new girl?"

"I told you, this evening at the dinner."

"No idiot, before or after the arrival of the consul?"

The keeper gave it a bit of thought. "After. When he first arrived, they went in conference alone in another room. The announcement was made when they returned."

"How long were they away in this meeting?"

"About an hour…they missed a whole course."

That's all Getarix wanted to hear. He could care less that they missed a course of the dinner while they planned the destruction of the only thing that held any meaning to him. He ran out of the brothel, grabbing the bored Cullen, but had to go to the upper floors and dislodge Jodoc out of the arms of now three girls.

"This better be good, Centurion, or you owe me mon—"

"You might be able to kill someone tonight, Jodoc."

"That's good enough."

"Getarix, what is going on here?" Cullen asked. Getarix explained what he had just learned.

"So we go back to the barracks, get our instruments of death and go play a tune, with enough time to finish the night off in the arms of my beauties. You seem to have arranged the perfect evening, Centurion." Getarix let Jodoc babble on until he was finished.

"No, we do not do this on our own. The senator has far too many strings that he can pull around our necks. It has to be official and we need allies."

"Where will we find allies? The last I looked, we run alone."

"Marsallas."

"Marsallas?" they both said in astonishment as they stopped and tried to take it in.

"Keep up with me, I'm not stopping." The two heeded his warning, running to join him.

"Marsallas will eat you alive," Jodoc said as he walked quickly by Getarix.

"Getarix, I'm not sure about this," Cullen said.

"We have no choice. It must be legal."

XLV

FULL DISCLOSURE

"This better be good, Centurion Getarix," Marsallas said through irritated, sleepy eyes. Marsallas had never married. The army was his bride. He seldom socialized and never took an apartment or house in the city. He had purchased a farm outside the city with plans of retirement but otherwise lived in the unit lines. It was easy to find him for he was seldom away.

"I need you to help me, sir," Getarix said shyly.

"Help? What kind of trouble have you found now?"

"Sir, you once asked, why would the senator have me promoted and brought to Rome?"

"I believe I asked that a number of times…go on."

"Well it was not to do me any favours, I can assure you. I did have something he wanted."

"Had?"

"Yes, sir…do you remember I had two slaves I put up in an apartment not far from here?"

"Yes, the landlord mentioned you were negligent in your payment. You must have sorted that out because he did not come back."

"Ah, yes sir. Do you remember when Augustus sent a delegation to Arminius?"

"Headed up by the senator. Some say that he damn near started the war. Yeah, so, what has this to do with you?"

"Yes sir, nothing sir, other than that they stopped at an inn in Germania to and from the meetings. There was a girl, a mere child, with—"

"Yellow hair and eyes of deep blue," Marsallas finished.

"Sir…how do you know?"

"Never mind, carry on. I know what he did to that child."

Getarix looked with inquiring eyes. "Well sir, she later became mine. That is what…whom the senator wants."

"How did you get her?"

Getarix quickly explained the history behind his getting and almost losing Isolde.

"How is it you no longer own her?"

Getarix explained about his arrangement with Cunhail.

Marsallas sat quietly, soaking in the new information.

"Okay, now your uncle has her. What do you want me to do? Go get her back?"

"Sir, I believe he no longer has her."

"You believe? You got me up for this?"

"No sir, let me explain." Getarix described what he learned at the brothel.

"You know I hate political appointees."

"Yes sir, you mentioned that as well."

"Many times."

"Yes, sir."

"I really do not care about a slave girl, but I do care about what that fat pervert gets away with. I have been looking for an opportunity to clip his wings. This just might be it. Are sure you have your information right?"

"Absolutely, sir."

"I thought you were a favourite of the senator, sent here to spy on us or do his bidding, maybe to get you promoted to some position of power and authority. To have one of his minions in a position to influence the army would only enhance his power. You see, the senator is held in absolute contempt in the army. I have deeper personal reasons I'll not get into. I knew, before you three arrived, who had you promoted and moved here. I truly thought you were his agents. Let's not waste any more time. Do you know where your uncle was to camp for the night?"

"Yes, sir, they took the Via Flaminia north along the river. There is a small grove of trees about six miles from the city wall next to an old abandoned mill."

"I know the spot, very secluded."

"Yes sir, we thought it better not to be noticed."

"That may have been your intent. All you did was give the enemy the tactical advantage of cover and seclusion. They should have camped by the road where hundreds of people camp every night. Safety in numbers."

"I see that, now."

"Manius," Marsallas called for his adjutant from the barrack room next to his.

"Yes, sir," came the sleepy response as he stumbled into his commanding officer's room.

"Rouse one troop and tell them to mount up with full armour. This is not an exercise. Centurion Getarix and his two duplicarius will be joining us."

"Us, sir?"

"Yes, I will be going with them."

"As you wish, sir."

"Who is on duty?"

"Aulus, sir."

"Send him immediately to Centurion Spurius to inform him we are pursuing some criminals outside the city and to meet us on the Via Flaminia at the public camp site six miles north of the city."

Centurion Spurius was the commanding Officer of the Praetorian Guard, tasked with the safety of travelers to and from Rome. In no time, twenty soldiers were thundering north on the Via Flaminia, where they met up with Spurius. It was important to keep everything legal, and having Spurius along gave them authority to operate outside their jurisdiction. They rode at full gallop until they arrived at the secluded campsite by the abandoned mill. They could see the embers of a dying fire. Marsallas jumped from his mount to feel the rocks by the fire. "Warm…this fire did not go out that long ago and it was let go, no water was put on it…it was just left."

Further investigation revealed evidence of a hasty retreat and some kind of struggle. One of the soldiers looking further afield yelled back, "Someone's over here….he's alive."

They made a beeline to the site. Recognizing his travelling clothes, Getarix was by the side of his uncle within seconds. "Uncle…Uncle, can you hear me?"

Cunhail was rousing and responded in Celtic. "They got them…both of them."

"Who got them, uncle?"

"Thugs…they looked like criminals…."

"We got another over here…this one's dead, though." Getarix stayed with his uncle helping him sit up.

Cullen and Jodoc helped turn the body over, revealing a sharp gash across the dead man's face and a fire poker embedded deep into his chest, right through the heart. They looked at each other and said in unison, "Gainer."

"What was that?" Marsallas asked.

Cullen answered. "Just a theory, sir."

Jodoc added, "A pretty good one, though. We believe we know who killed him: the woman slave, Gainer."

"It does not matter who killed him, what matters is who is he." One of the soldiers had resurrected the fire, giving off light. "Bring him by the fire. I want to get a look at him. Cullen and Jodoc mentioned that they recognized him from the Subura taverns. They did not know his name, but knew that he was a nasty drunk and only bought the cheapest wine available.

"From the smell of him, he was pulled from one of the taverns tonight," Cullen said.

Marsallas said, "Maybe being drunk allowed this woman get the jump on him."

"You don't need to be drunk for her to get the jump on you," Jodoc said, unconsciously running his fingers across the matching scar on his face.

Marsallas looked at him and quickly pieced it together, chuckling, to Jodoc's discomfort. "Well, your friend over there is right. They were thugs. This one is—was—known as Publius, not his real name but a real thug. And I know who he works for. It seems, Centurion Getarix, your story is holding water. The gang this one plies his trade with is known to do the dirty work for your friend."

"No friend of mine, sir."

"It would seem. I have a very good idea where we might find your slaves. This gang is headed up by a disreputable merchant know only as Babudius, in a small warehouse on the river right by the new mausoleum they are building for Emperor Augustus in the Martius district. I'll bet my next year's wages they have them there. It would not be prudent to have them taken near the senator's house tonight. Your brothel owner said she would be delivered over the next few days, right? Okay, we ride hard to the construction site for the mausoleum and go quietly on foot from there. Centurion Spurius, you coming?"

"I'm up now."

"Okay, let's do it." Marsallas pointed to two soldiers and told them to stay with and escort the still-recovering Cunhail to the apartment.

Within the hour they were dismounted and approaching the warehouse on foot. All was quiet and dark. This did not escape the notice of Getarix. "Sir, why would they not be receiving goods at night like the rest of Rome?"

"Because they haven't used this building as a legitimate place of business for years."

"How does he get away with it?"

"Do you see that construction site?"

"Yes."

"Well, who do you think donated the land?"

"So this Babudius is respectable?"

"No one would ever be caught in public with him. He's a freeman, an ex-slave. Only money gives him a veneer of respectability. Okay, Duplicarius Gaius, you take these ten soldiers and cover the right side and the right hand of the dockside facing the river. Centurion Spurius, you take the remainder to the left. When you meet in the middle, send me a signal. Centurion Getarix, you take Cullen and Jodoc and cover that door in front of us. Your uncle said there were only ten of them. One's now dead, making nine, and I am sure their ringleader went off to report to Babudius. If my plan works they will try to escape out this way." He stopped and pointed to Spurius and Gaius. "When you enter the building, make it loud. Break those doors down. They're half rotted as it is, so it should be easy. But make it noisy—yell, scream. I want them to drop their hearts and run like rats. We will get them as they come out this door in front of us. Got it?"

Everyone answered in the affirmative.

Marsallas looked at Getarix. "I want to see if the three of you are as good with the sword as reported."

The warehouse sat on a patch of land too big for the building. The brambles and weeds had grown wildly around the un-kept single-story structure. In the early dawn light, they could see that the white paint had yellowed considerably and the customary red lines had faded to a light orange. Many patches of plaster had come loose, exposing the building's inner construction of loose mortar reinforced with small willow branches. There were two small windows and one large central door on the landside of the building, facing the construction site. Nothing on either side of the building, but the front could open up to the riverside. It took more time than they wanted to work their way around the building because they had to fight the undergrowth. The entire riverside of the building consisted of lightly constructed wooden doors that were mostly rotten. All four of the wooden doors were secured. When all were in position, Centurion Spurius gave the signal.

The quiet of the early morning was shattered as the big cargo doors went crashing in. It was not long before their first victim crossed the threshold of the back door. Jodoc ran forward, driving his sword deep into the unsuspecting man's stomach. Once the sword was all the way to the hilt, Jodoc used the man's momentum to lift him by the blade and throw him over his head and aside in one swooping motion, making the way clear for the next two that kept Cullen and Getarix busy. Marsallas did not even get a chance to get one for himself. His three political appointees moved too quickly, depriving him of even one score during the entire fight. The next person through the door was Jodoc's. He raised his sword parallel to the ground at eye level and was about to drive it home when he recognized Gainer. She gave him a hostile look that said, "Just try it." He grabbed the front of her dress and threw her into the arms of Marsallas. There came a yell from within, warning the others not to use this door. Jodoc charged into the building, bringing the warning cry to a quick end. Cullen and Getarix quickly followed, and discovered that the other soldiers had killed all but one other. This one they had captured.

"Where is the girl?" Getarix said.

"The pretty one?" He smiled through a filthy mouth. "You just missed her. I imagine she would be on her back by now." He laughed.

It was too much for Getarix to take. He began to beat the man mercilessly until he went limp.

"Marsallas, I know where they are taking her," Getarix said as he ran for the door and mounted Cabello. Within a minute he was out of the building, heading south on the Via Flaminia that led into the heart of the city. Cullen and Jodoc were right on his heels, Marsallas and company not far behind them. They rode at full gallop through the streets to the brothel where Getarix had learned about the plot. Caballo almost lost his footing on several occasions. People had to jump out of the way, and when they came up against carts, they simply jumped up onto the sidewalks, throwing drunks into the street. As they approached the back of the brothel, Getarix caught sight of a dark figure leading a smaller slight figure by a rope or light chain. The two had just reached a small wooden door that led into the herbal garden of the brothel. Getarix spurred Caballo on as fast as he had ever run. The ground was soft, muffling much of the sound of the pounding hooves. He aimed right for the larger of the two figures standing to the left of the door. When Getarix was no more than a few paces from his target, he swung his right leg over the head of his mount, riding side-saddle. Just as Caballo was about to crash headlong into the wall, he turned sharply to the right, just missing the smaller figure, now in the doorway. Getarix leaped toward the wall with the full velocity of Caballo's charge. He held his sword with both hands and had it pointed directly for the man's chest. The noise caused the man to turn just as Getarix was flying through the air. Getarix slammed into him, breaking all of his ribs and his right shoulder. The sword drove through his sternum and spine, pinning him to the plaster wall. Dying as he was, the sword held him in place, giving the impression that he was just standing there quietly. Getarix bounced off the man and landed backward on the street. He was up in seconds, hissing in the dying man's ear, "I hope you live out your eternity in the same hellish existence you were about to deliver this girl to." His message delivered, he took hold of Isolde, who was crying out of fear, out of the sheer emotion of it all, but most of all out of joy.

Jodoc and Cullen were there within seconds, having witnessed the whole event. Marsallas was next, closely followed by the others. Getarix looked up at his commanding officer. "I found him dead sir, when I arrived. Someone beat us to him."

Marsallas answered, "Well then, you had better take your sword out of him." The men laughed. Getarix let go of Isolde, grabbed the sword, and wiggled it to dislodge the man. As he fell to the ground, the keeper of the brothel opened the gate, roused from his bed by the din. Marsallas addressed him. "My good citizen, I believe you were to have a delivery of a slave today?"

"Yes, sir…?"

"Well, there he is. His name is Babudius. He's slightly used." The men all laughed as they turn away to head back to their unit lines.

XLVI

NEW DAY

The apartment was directly on the route to the unit lines. They arrived there just as the morning sun was cresting the hills to the east. Isolde rode on Caballo, attached to Getarix tighter than a soldier to his sword in the midst of battle. When they arrived at the apartment, Cunhail and Gainer were already there and anxiously waiting.

The moment Getarix got the door closed, Isolde let him have it. Through her tears, she screamed, flailing her arms at him, "How could you? How could you sell me and send me away?"

"Isolde, I thought it was for the best. My uncle would take you to freedom—"

"Don't you get it? I don't want freedom—I want you. I am free when I'm with you." As she said this, she went quiet and fell into his waiting arms.

Cunhail and Gainer just sat there, stunned. Gainer, who had fought the idea of their love, and Cunhail, who had no idea about it.

"You said you loved me!" Isolde's muffled voice challenged him.

Getarix melted with these words. "I do love you; I thought you wanted to go."

"No, never...where did you get that idea? Did you ever think of actually asking me what I wanted?"

He held her tight, almost crushing her into his breastplate. "I'm so sorry, my love."

From the street below, Jodoc yelled, "Centurion Getarix, Marsallas awaits you, sir. Official business."

"I must go," he said and kissed Isolde for the very first time, a long passionate kiss that was disrupted by—

"Come on, Getarix, the wine shops are about to close."

Isolde laughed and gave Getarix's armoured chest a slap and told him to go. "But you better come back and never again send me away."

The wine shops were indeed closed, but the baths were just opening. There they could warm up, get clean and, as it turned out, get drunk, which Jodoc did.

They sat on highly polished marble benches and talked. Getarix much preferred the bathhouses to the taverns. The walls were beautifully decorated with mosaics of birds and panoramas of the gods. They were clean and always warm. Jodoc and Cullen were celebrating their latest adventure with the other ranks, leaving their centurions alone.

"Well, I guess I was wrong about you three," Marsallas said. "I have seldom seen fighting like that. I would never want to see the business end of any one of your swords. That move you did at the brothel…did you practice that?"

"No…just lucky, I'd probably kill myself if I ever tried it again," Getarix said with a smile.

"And that Jodoc is an animal. I really thought the three of you were useless with a sword…you know, just agents of the senator sent here to bring me down."

"Why would he want to bring you down?"

"Battle can bond men as brothers. My own brother is a waste of skin, but I found a friend in another centurion who became that brother. Cornelius Pricus… we fought in those forests of Germania first, you know? You know that standard you found?"

"Yes."

"Well that was my unit. The only other unit I served in besides this one. We served in Germania together, Cornelius and I. It was tough going in those days. We built the very roads you marched on. I fought side by side with him. He is one of the bravest men I have ever known…we started in the army together. He made centurion before me, having far more natural ability. When I got my centurionent, we were both selected for a transfer to the Praetorian Guard here in

Rome. That was just before Varus lost the legions and that standard you found. Did you know that Varus was the brother-in-law to the senator?"

"Yes, I heard."

"Varus changed the assignment for Cornelius. He must have known what the senator was like. We managed to keep him in the Guard for a time, but that did not last. Varus hated Cornelius."

"Why would he—"

"Cornelius criticised his treatment of the Germans...he confronted him. I got posted here to the Praetorian Guard and he was to be posted to that bag of maggots. Once Varus died, though, we had his orders changed and he served in the guard until the senator got his hands on him and almost fulfilled the wishes of his brother-in-law. So you see, I have a personal reason to hate the senator. No centurion wants to be posted to him; it's like a death sentence. For some it became so, usually by their own hand."

"What happened to Cornelius?"

"The senator was about to crush him, but through his own cunning and a few strings I pulled, he made his escape. Not much of an escape, though. He went to hell on earth."

"Where did he go?"

"The one place you do not want to go. The most easterly province, out in the desert, a desolate barren tract of land everyone seems to fight over, amongst an unhappy, quarrelling people...Judea."

They were silent for a while, then Getarix asked, "And how did you know about Isolde and the senator?"

"He was there, Cornelius was, he told me all about the trip, how the senator got a good soldier killed."

"The one by the ledge where the standards stood."

"Yes, him, and almost had the rest of them slaughtered. Then when he got back, the senator blamed Cornelius to cover his own failure...he blackened the name of my brother."

"He made mention, not by name, of some centurion he blamed for the failure of an earlier rescue of the standards."

"A fine leader we have in that senator."

"Do you expect to hear from the senator about tonight?"

"Not a word. Damianus is not on the best of terms with the emperor right now, still trying to figure him out, I guess. Tiberius is a hard one to understand. I'm sure he'll figure him out, but for now he'll keep this quiet and disassociate himself with anything that causes disruption in the streets of Rome. Rome is a volatile place, over a million people. One third are slaves and many of the citizens are lowbrow uneducated and unemployed. Our job is not to corral the drunks of the night. That's just to keep us busy until we are really needed. What do you think the games are all about? Free bread to keep their bellies full and the games to distract them. No, he'll keep it quiet, but mark my word, he never forgets and I'm sure something will come of it. The gods forbid if he ever gets in good with the emperor. My advice to you is to keep low. The only colour you should show now is gray.

"Do you think he will try this again soon?"

"No. For one thing, we just killed all his thugs, including their leader. And even though the senator will not be mentioned in my official report, I will tell Germanicus verbally about the connection. This way, Tiberius will be informed. If I know Germanicus, he will also drop a hint to the senator, letting him know we are aware of the connection."

"That won't go over well."

"It will at least shut him down for a bit, eh. Now, the fridgidarium. You joining me?"

"Not on your life. Too many winters in Germania."

"Too many? You were only there—"

"One was enough," Getarix said with a smile

That day was the first time Getarix slept in his own apartment. When he arrived later in the morning, all were asleep. He slept like never before. Marsallas returned their hours back to normal, and soon Getarix found himself doing many more tasks in line with his rank. He put Cullen and Jodoc in charge of their own patrols, giving them soldiers to lead for the first time since entering Rome. They also noticed that they were now fully accepted into the ranks of their new unit.

"My boy, you need to marry that girl."

"I know, I want to, but...I can't."

"What is wrong with you? Waiting for a better? I doubt you'll find one."

"It's not that, Uncle. She is a slave and as such she is a possession, a thing, according to Roman law."

"So?"

"So...a person cannot enter into a legal contract with a thing, and that's what a slave is. According to Roman law, it would be like selling land to your horse."

"This Roman law of yours—"

"It's not mine, and yes it can be inflexible, but it does keep the peace."

"Then free her. You own her...simply grant her freedom."

"I already tried that. I can't."

"Let me guess." Getarix joined him with, "Roman law!"

Getarix said, "She cannot be free until she turns thirty."

Their meals arrived. Most of Rome was in the many restaurants in the city by that hour.

"To hell with Roman law," Cunhail said.

Getarix waved his hands, indicating for him to speak softly. "Uncle, talk like that might go over well back home, but here I'm charged with suppressing 'said' expressions."

"No, no my boy, marry her anyway."

"I can't."

"What Roman law states you cannot go through the ceremony and publicly declare you're married?"

"None, but it won't be legal."

"Legal? Most marriages in Rome are common-law anyway. She'll still be your slave, but—"

"The old Roman Patrician marriages were like that. The woman became the slave of her husband. So I guess we will just have to settle for an ancient aristocratic marriage. Besides, Roman marriage requires no license or state officials. Essentially the consent of the couple as an act of personal union is all that is needed; it has to be done in person. That's the law."

"Then you should show up."

They chuckled as they ate their meal.

Getarix continued, "So tell me how it goes, the ceremony that is? It cannot be entered into by letter, messenger, or proxy. This public act could consist of the joining of hands in the presence of five witnesses, or the bride letting herself be escorted to her husband's house, which I don't think will work, here."

"You have given this some thought and a measure of study. You do want this, eh?"

"I want this to be recognized and legal...but I guess this is all we have... Yeah, I want this."

"There you go, m' boy."

"You're right, who's to say...okay then, but I want to do this before you leave."

"It must be done within the week, then. I'm already late and must get back."

"That's just as well, because within a week the spring festivals begin and nobody will be getting married for six weeks after that."

"Sounds good. But you had better talk this out with your bride. I'll talk to Gainer. She will represent Isolde's family, and must announce your betrothal."

"Will she allow it?"

"Absolutely. We've talked; it's okay. I will represent you."

"So, Uncle, you and Gainer...?"

"Mind your own business, boy."

They needed a few days to get everything together. Getarix was unable to find a wedding gown. Normally, Isolde's dress would have been ordered months before the wedding and it would have been woven to fit the bride perfectly. It would have been seamless and white, woven the old-fashioned way on an upright loom from a single thread. It would have been long enough to fall to her feet. He did however buy her a new dress of white she could also use for any formal occasions.

On the morning of her wedding day, Isolde was dressed by Gainer, who played the role of her mother. Her new dress was fastened around the waist with a band of wool tied in the knot of Hercules, which only Getarix was privileged to untie. Over her head she wore a flame-coloured veil. Gainer divided her hair into six locks using the point of a spear Cullen supplied. These locks were coiled and held in position by ribbons.

"There. Your hair is done up just like the Vestal Virgins wear theirs."

"I am hardly a virgin..."

"You are purer than all the Vestal put together, my dear." Gainer smiled at Isolde. "Now, where is that wreath of flowers and sacred plants you gathered this morning? Getarix will wear the other wreath on his head."

For the ceremony, the required five witnesses were there. Marsallas completed the requirement. "The part of the ceremony where I place a coin on the scales representing a purchase, we will skip." Everyone laughed at the joke, knowing Getarix already legally owned her. He turned to Isolde and said in a soft tone, "But I will present you with this gift." He took a small gold ring from Cullen and placed it on the third finger of her left hand. It was believed that the nerve of this finger ran directly to the heart. The ring was of pure gold and where a stone would have been was the gold-embossed figure of two hands joining.

Isolde looked into his eyes and asked, "Where did you get the money?"

"Well, you will notice one of my arm torques is lighter."

She could not help the tears that clouded her vision. With immense pride, she provided him with a small dowry. It consisted of enough coins she had earned to pay one month's rent. What Getarix did not know is it included all the money Gainer had earned as well.

Normally, the house of the father's bride was the place of the ceremony. In this case, they held ceremony at the apartment. It was decorated in the traditional manner with flowers, boughs of trees, bands of wool, and tapestries. The omens had already been taken before sunrise and pronounced favourable. The bride and the groom appeared in the main room and the wedding began.

Following the marriage ceremony came the wedding dinner, again held at the apartment and very extravagant. Cunhail paid for the dinner and did not spare any expenses. After this, the bride was normally escorted to her husband's house. This was the wedding procession. They decided to leave the apartment and process through the streets, making a loop and returning to their point of departure. The marriage hymn was sung and the groom took the bride with a show of force from Gainer's arms. Isolde, attended by three boys whose parents were both living, joined the procession. Two boys held her hands and one carried the wedding torch of hawthorn. Behind her walked Marsallas and someone carrying a distaff and spindle, emblems of domestic life. During the march, they sang songs. The crowds, noticing the procession, shouted the ancient marriage cry. The bride had three coins with her, one of which she dropped as an offering to the gods of the crossroads, another of which she later gave to the groom as an emblem of the dowry she brought him, and the third she offered to the Lares of his house. The groom scattered nuts, sweetmeats, and sesame cakes through the small crowd that had gathered along the route.

When they arrived back at the apartment, the bride wound the doorposts with bands of wool as a symbol of her future work as mistress of the household, and anointed the door with oil and fat, emblems of plenty. Getarix then lifted her carefully over the threshold. In the apartment, Getarix offered his new wife fire and water in token of the life they were to live together. The bride kindled the hearth with her marriage torch. The bride recited a prayer and was led to the wedding couch, and they were married.

That night, Gainer and Cunhail took rooms at the inn, leaving the newly married with their privacy.

XLVII

CONNECTING THREADS

Cunhail remained at the apartment for another week until his body had re-covered enough to travel again. This time he left in the morning and Gainer was his only traveling companion. Once they left, Getarix immediately went to work on sorting out his accommodations. With the apartment and marriage to Isolde, he no longer had a need for his room in the Praetorian Guard's lines.

Early the next morning, Jodoc was awoken by the noise below. By a strange co-incidence, he had had a slow night and had gone home early. He figured since he was now awake and without the customary hangover, he might as well go down and help clear out the room.

As he walked into the room, he saw something in the corner. "Hey Getarix, what's this?" He picked up the linen-wrapped bundle.

"It's that sword the senator gave me," Getarix said. He turned his back on Jodoc and began to fold his bedding. Upon hearing it was a weapon, Jodoc eagerly unwrapped it. Before long, he had it in his hands held high, testing it for balance.

"It's beautiful, Getarix," Jodoc said almost in a whisper.

"Do you like it?" Getarix was now attending to his personal kit spread all over his bed.

"Yes…" This time he was whispering.

"It's yours." Just then, Cullen walked in and froze at the sight of the sword in the hands of his friend. Jodoc was completely transfixed by now, busily fighting an imaginary battle. He was slowly swinging the sword through the air in what looked more like a dance, with an expression of ecstasy on his face. Cullen, looking at his face, had the disgusting feeling that this was how he must look when he was with one of his women.

"Getarix, where did you get that from?"

"Get what?"

"That sword. Jodoc, wake up, where did you get that?"

Jodoc came out of his pretend battle. "Hey Cullen, look at what Getarix just gave me."

"No he didn't."

"Yes he did."

"Yes, I did, Cullen."

"No, you didn't." Cullen grabbed the sword out Jodoc's hands.

"Hey, give that—"

Cullen gave him a look of hostility Jodoc had never seen before. The greater strength and determined demeanour of Cullen won the battle before it began. "Getarix, did you ever think of actually looking at this before you gave it away?"

"I did."

"With the wrapping off?"

Getarix finally stopped what he was doing on his bed and began to turn, saying. "Okay, what the hell are you going on…?" His eyes fell on the weapon. Getarix's face went white. Cullen was inspecting the hilt very closely. Jodoc stood there, lacking all understanding.

"A drunk? No…what you saw happens about once a year, if that…or happened, I guess." Julius gave a narrative of the sorry life of his friend Antonio, as far as he knew it. He talked about the humiliating way the senator treated all his slaves and the frequent beatings they were forced to endure. Upon hearing it, Getarix burned with shame that he had even considered the thought of turning Isolde over to the likes of such a monster. His self-chastisement was disrupted by Julius continuing his account. "Freedom…an impossible dream for all who slave for the senator." Getarix knew the senator did not sell his slaves, but not the senator's plans for them. Julius explained the retirement the senator had reserved for his slaves upon his own death. This made Getarix feel better in regards to the fate of Antonio. A quick public death that took an hour in front of the mob was still better than one much more painful, taking years, unnoticed and forgotten. He was also more determined than ever to hold on to Isolde, as he privately felt disgrace for ever going to the senator's home to sell her into the same hellish existence.

Julius continued, "Ever since he was won in battle, he has been an unwilling actor in his hellish play…maybe death will finally free him."

"Wait, what did you say?"

"Maybe death will finally free—"

"No, before that. How did he get Antonio? You said he was won in battle?"

"Yes."

"You mean Antonio was a soldier?"

"Of sorts."

"When did the Greeks rebel?"

"Greeks…what do you talk of? The Greeks rebelled plenty, but—"

"Antonio—he's Greek, is he not?"

"No."

"But people refer to him as a Greek."

"You don't understand anything. Here in Rome, anyone of undetermined foreign blood is called Greek…he's Celtic. Gaulish, I believe. He never talks about it. Too painful and with his master it's better forgotten."

"Why the Greek name? Antonio is a Greek name, is it not?

"Well, that's the senator again. Whenever the senator replaces a slave, he simply transfers the name of the dead slave unto the next one. That way he does not have to learn a new name."

"What is his name?"

"Not a clue. Antonio wouldn't tell me. Again, too painful, I guess."

"Is this how you keep a low profile?"

"Well, he attacked me and I just want to know when he gets his just dessert. I don't think the invitation still stands with the senator. I want to make sure I'm there to see it."

"By the gods you're a lousy liar."

"Yes, sir. I checked with the Circus Maximus Prison where he was first delivered, but he's not there and no one knows."

Marsallas looked at Getarix and resigned himself to help his new friend find out where and when the public execution was to take place. Marsallas gave him a look saying this would only lead to some sort of disaster.

"Come back after lunch." Marsallas had grown to appreciate his new soldiers, but he also knew they had a way of drawing adversaries. Later that day, he confirmed that Antonio was still alive and now owned by the gladiatorial school run by Thalamus the Greek.

They were housed in a dilapidated building in a rundown part of old Rome.

"Yes, I still have him. I'm training him to give a good show on the day of his execution. He will die for sure, but at least the crowds will be entertained." Thalamus laughed at the thought. It would not hurt his school if they could show that they could train an old domestic slave to hold his own in the ring.

"I wish to see him, please."

"You...what, Centurion?"

"I wish to talk to him."

"Okay, he is training now, but...I'll have him brought to you. Come, I'll show you to his cell." They walked out of the small private room Thalamus used as an office and bedroom. The school was in an extremely old ramshackle house that was mostly open courtyard. Getarix looked around and recognized that it was once a large home of a noble family. The centre of the house had been gutted, creating the large training ground. The walls of the courtyard boasted some of the most brilliant marble mosaic work Getarix had yet seen. He could see where the various rooms once sat by the wall decorations. These different themes were framed by deep scars where the wall had been unceremoniously removed. In the courtyard, Thalamus had placed a number of wooden posts wrapped with cloth, creating crude figures of men. These were used to practice basic sword work. Some of them turned on a base to train the gladiators to duck from the high timber jutting out from the turning post, or jump out of the way of the lower ones. The courtyard was a hive of activity where every post fully employed, and off to the side men paired in mock battle using the heavier wood sword Getarix had learned to hate shortly after joining the army. Getarix tried to spot Antonio but could not.

"This was the house of the noble family of the Brutia. That is, until they committed that dastardly murder of the great Caesar." That was all Thalamus volunteered. Before long, they were across the courtyard and in the holding cells, some with beautifully decorated marble floors and walls. The years of abuse showed, and a number of patches of mosaic decorations were missing. Getarix noticed that nowhere could he see a complete picture. Closer up, he could not help noticing the outstanding quality of the work. The idea of destroying the work of an artist simply because the occupants did wrong bothered him.

"Wait here, sir." Getarix kept himself busy examining the broken pictures that once decorated what looked like a *tricinium* room, which literally meant three couches. This room was one of the most splendidly decorated rooms of any house. It was here that the master of the home would entertain guests. This room would have also been used for smaller intimate dinner parties. The back wall had a beautiful mosaic of a forest scene with a river running down through the trees. His eyes followed the scene to where an inner wall once met the existing outside wall. He knew that the scene would have carried itself throughout the room, following around, meeting where the door had once been. The floor exposed the scars of the inner walls. There were two cells where once a single room stood.

"Here you are, Centurion." Getarix turned around to face the defiant stare of Antonio. "Do not worry, this maggot knows that if he tries anything on you I will personally whip him within two fingers of his death, only to bring him back to do it again…and again. Is that understood, slave?" Thalamus hissed in his ears.

"Yes, sir," Antonio spat with ardent hate.

"Just holler when you need to be let out, Centurion."

Antonio remained in the same flavour. "What gives me the honour of your visit?" He looked directly into the younger man's eyes. Antonio had changed deeply. Too many years of cowering at the hands of his master had created resentment he could not conceal anymore. Thalamus had put a sword back into his hands and with that a measure of his dignity had returned. In spite of his coming death, these months had been the best in his life since his capture. He was a man again. Antonio was alive once more. From within the demoralized, cowering creature had risen up a new man with a determination never to tremble at the feet of another. His life was over, that much he knew. There was nothing to be saved by cowering. Antonio would walk tall and fight as he never fought before. The one thing the senator gave him to his advantage was physical strength. Even though he was a domestic slave, hard labour was still his daily lot. It was his responsibility to do the hard work in the garden. Not only had it kept his muscles toned, it had helped him work out his frustration. Without it, he would not have survived the senator. He hoped the strength would give him an advantage in the ring. The routine beatings taught him to work through the pain, to put it aside and carry on. He possessed strength few did and to that, the senator got the credit.

Getarix looked at this mysterious man before him, not knowing what to ask. Antonio stood waiting to be addressed, until he lost his patience. "Did you just come here to look at me? If so, move out of the way; you're standing in front of my bed and if you're just going to stare I'll be sitting for that honour." He did not wait for a response and began to move for the couch that lined the wall. Getarix got out of the way, letting him get comfortable. Then Antonio began the interview.

"Where did you get them?"

"Get what?"

"Don't trifle with me, boy. Where did you get the gold?"

"You're awfully brave for a dead man."

"That's right, I'm already dead. Now where did you get the gold, boy?"

"The gold? Oh, the arm torques? They're mine."

"They are not." Antonio looked him straight in the face. "I have an idea. Why don't you come in the ring with me? You can do my execution. You can feed the blood-thirsty mob with my blood. Eh, what do you think of that, boy?"

"I'd kill you within two swings."

"You would try." He kept his eyes on the young centurion. Getarix got an uncomfortable feeling as this slave intimidated him. "I plan on winning, you know?"

"I would hope so. Where do you come from?"

"None of your business. My question first!"

"Listen, you, you're the slave and I'm a cent—"

"And I'm about to die so take your questions and go to hell." They remained in silence for a while, just staring at each other.

Getarix knew that if he wanted the information he sought he must back down. "They were given to me by my mother. They were my father's, and his before, and before that."

"You lie. They are yours, that is true, and maybe your father's, but not his—"

"Now my question. Where do you come from? I think you knew my father. He died in battle."

"Good and may you do the same."

"What have I ever done to you to earn your loathing?"

"You Romans never get it, do you?"

"Roman, I'm not Roman. My father died fighting them."

"But here you are in their uniform."

"I had no choice. Besides, that's my story. It's my father's story I seek."

"What was his name?"

"Kailen."

Antonio swung his head up and looked into Getarix's eyes. "No it's not, that I can guarantee you. Besides, those things were taken by a Roman in battle."

"They were." Getarix began to wonder.

"Then what are you doing with them?"

"Like I said, my mother, the wife of Kailen, gave them to me."

"You lie, Roman!" Antonio stood face to face with the taller Getarix.

"I'm not Roman," Getarix yelled back in Celtic.

"You probably lie about that too…but I know you're not the son of Kailen!" Antonio was yelling at the top of his lungs, drawing the guards to their cell. When they saw all was safe, they thought better not to intervene.

Getarix asked with a shaking voice, "Why am I not the son of Kailen and Aigneis?"

"Because I'm Kailen the husband of Aigneis and I have only one son—and you're not him." Antonio fell to the couch and said weakly, "Too young."

Getarix felt the world swept away from him. His knees lost all their ability to hold him. He fell on the couch next to Antonio.

Antonio sat looking down at the floor, at a complete loss. Getarix could not believe what he had just heard. "Cunorix is my older brother. No, you cannot be…Kailen died…in battle, Astnicx said so."

Hearing so many names that haunted his past, Antonio began to shake. He looked to Getarix and asked, "Who are you, boy?" Getarix noticed the left hand of the slave. It was crippled with scars and showed evidence of being crushed badly. Getarix remembered the crushed boss of the shield that still held the blood of his father.

"Your hand…that happened there…the boss of the shield crushed it."

"How do you know this, boy? How do you know any of this?"

"The shield with the crushed boss. It was recovered by Astnicx with the rest of the things that once belonged to the Great Vercingetorix," Getarix said.

Antonio felt overwhelmed and leaned against the wall. "Not everything."

"The sword?"

"It hangs on the wall of the senator's house."

"Not anymore."

"Where is it?"

"He tried to bribe me with it."

"Bribe you for what?"

"That doesn't matter now. But it was the sword that brought me here, to you. I thought you knew my father…but you are my father. Astnicx said you died…"

"I almost did. But you are still not my son." Antonio went quiet, tears welling up in his eyes. Quietly he muttered, "Aigneis, how could you…I've been so faithful, my footprints still in the dust and you..." He could not verbalise what he feared the most.

Getarix was confronted by feelings he had never known, and with tears burning his own cheeks, he said something he never thought he ever could. "Father."

"My boy, you have been deceived. How old are you?"

"No, Father, your wife has been faithful all these years. I'm only now twenty. When you went to battle, I was there. You lay with your wife the night before. You planted your seed then."

"And so I did...has it been twenty years?"

"It has."

"And the dagger...?"

"Mother gave them to me on my sixteenth birthday. She said they were from 'your father and I,'" Getarix said with tears streaming down his face.

"And so they are."

They sat for half an hour in stunned silence, both just trying to absorb their new discovery.

XLIIX

TRAINING

"That's impossible…no, not possible." Cullen got up, circling his cot.

"But it is, I tell you, it's the only explanation." Getarix remained seated on a small wooden bench, the only other piece of furniture in the tiny room.

"No! My father saw…" Cullen sat heavily on his cot.

"Your father sees lots of things."

"No, Getarix, you don't get it, everything about that day—every minute, every movement, even the smells—he relives, like he is still there. Even in his sleep they come, unbidden, unwelcome…but accurate. He has no control over them, but they are accurate. That's why he drinks…or drank…to silence the battle in his mind. My father had more faults than good, but I will swear my life on his memory of that day."

"Fair enough, Cullen, but what do you remember about your father's narrative?"

"That your father was dead and remained in Gaul."

"No, the details."

"My father reported that Kailen fell in battle."

"Okay, but did he see him fall? Where did he get the shield from, the one that hangs in my mother's home?"

"He found it abandoned on the battlefield. He later recovered the dagger and belt off a dead Roman. He said it was probably the Roman who killed Kailen."

"But he never saw him. It was *probably* the Roman who killed him, right? The shield was recovered, abandoned. My father's body was not beside it. He did not see him die, nor did he see him dead."

"He saw him with the other injured, and later father saw all the wounded dead."

"But not my father. He did not see him fall. He only assumed he died, but he didn't. Your father might have detailed memories of that day, but he was wrong about his conclusions on my father's fate because he never witnessed it. His memories are exact but his conclusions are not."

"I never thought of it like that. I guess you're right. What do we do now? You finally get a father, only to watch him die."

"I'm going to do the only thing I can." Without elaborating further, Getarix got up and was out of Cullen's barrack room, heading down the stairs.

"I cannot sell him to you, Centurion."

"But you own him, do you not?"

"Yes, but for the reason of execution only. He's lucky he won't be bound together with other prisoners and devoured by the beasts in the ring. Normally that's what would happen, but there are going to be three months of games, nonstop, and Rome is short of gladiators. Some of the better prisoners charged with lesser crimes are being prepared for battle. That being said, their main purpose in entering the ring is still to die. The only difference is he's meant to entertain us more on his death, but death nonetheless."

"What if he wins in the ring?"

"Then I guess I still own him."

"But not for the purpose of execution?"

"No, just a simple slave. If he were a freeman, winning would mean freedom, but he's a slave and a slave he remains."

"But your slave?"

"Yes, what are you getting at?"

"If he wins, would you sell him to me?"

"I guess."

"Deal. When is he scheduled to fight?"

"Middle of the second month of games. What's your interest? Oh, I get it, you two are lovers. You had a lovers' quarrel and now you're here to fix it. He will die and you will be alone with only your guilt as a companion, eh?"

"Nothing like that at all. You Romans," Getarix said with irritation. "As it turns out...he is my father."

"Father! Him, the father of a Roman centurion, the finder of the eagle standard? Not likely. And besides, don't call me Roman. I'm not Roman, I'm Greek, a real one."

"He is my father. I know it's not likely, but it's true. We thought him dead twenty years ago. But he lives...and it's my intention to keep it that way."

"He won't win, you know. He's not a gladiator, nor even a soldier."

"Not yet, would you allow me and some of my men to help in his training?"

"There's nothing you can teach that we can't." Thalamus chuckled. "Okay, if you wish, but you're wasting your time. That I promise you."

"We will be here, and we will also bring extra food to help strengthen him up. That barley porridge won't do it."

"As a slave, he is only entitled to barley, but do whatever you want. However, don't just feed him meat. Gladiators need a lot of greens."

"Okay, it'll be done."

"Now, what theme do you want him to be?"

"Theme?"

"You don't go to the games, do you?"

"No, I'm a soldier, I don't do blood for sport."

"Yeah, well, every gladiator takes on a theme. They might have a short sword like the one you have, the gladius, and a large shield with heavy armour, and represent the Roman Soldiers. Other combinations represent Rome's enemies. Some have a long sword with a small shield, or a trident and a net and so on. All are balanced so that they are about equal in the ring."

"Unless you're an untrained slave."

"He is meant to die."

"We will see about that. I'll get back to you on this theme."

Later that day, Getarix regretted telling him about Antonio being his father, but it was too late. He would just have to trust him and trust the bag of money he gave Thalamus to keep up the story of them being lovers.

Cullen and Jodoc needed little persuasion to help. Over the next month and a half, one of the three were at the gladiatorial school, training Antonio during their off hours.

Cullen stressed strength training. When he was there, they did mostly weight training to build up Antonio's muscles. Jodoc, on the other hand, taught aggressiveness. "Antonio, fear in your opponent could be your greatest weapon. If you intimidate him and he fills his drawers, all you have to do is finish him off."

Getarix taught strategy and accuracy. "It does not matter how strong or fierce you are, Father, if you cannot hit the mark." He took soot from an extinguished torch mounted on the wall and made two small dots on the head of the turning dummy. "Now, aim for those dots. They represent the eyes. Even a soft jab in the eye socket will take the strongest man down."

As the weeks progressed, Antonio improved his skill and strength at an amazing rate. Thalamus still believed that Antonio would not make it out of the ring alive, but he would put up a good show and Thalamus would get the credit. Only good could come of that.

"Well, I must admit, he is doing extremely well. Better than I ever thought."

"He's training for his life," Getarix said as he sat in a chair Thalamus provided, his feet up on the desk like his host.

"There's no point, you know. He is expected to die."

"He may surprise you."

"Not likely, but if he does he'll still be a slave and I will likely use him as a gladiator, so he will be no further ahead."

"Wait, we had a deal."

"No, we had a conversation."

Getarix thought he could sort this out later and returned to the subject. "Who do you have fighting against him?"

"Me? I have no one. I don't choose the opponents."

"Who does?"

"For his fight, it will be Aufidius. He has a small school outside the city. He will choose your father's—I mean your lover's opponent."

"Aufidius, eh?"

"Need I remind you?" Getarix waited for a response. Thalamus grunted one. "If he survives this fight, I'm buying him from you."

"Forget it. He's meant to die and die he will."

"Nonetheless, if he wins I'll buy him. We already agreed months ago."

"That was in jest."

"This is in all seriousness."

"I won't consider it, because he won't live. Sorry, friend. Ho, by the way, what theme do you want him to be?"

"Theme? How about a Celtic raider?"

"Cullen, how much money do you have?"

"All of it."

"All of it? What do you mean all of it?"

"If you have not noticed I don't spend my money on anything."

"Other than food."

"Other than food and the odd bowl of wine, and most of that I get through the army." It was then Getarix finally clued in to how frugal his friend actually was.

"What do you plan on doing with this money, you cheap bugger?"

"Retirement. Some day we will, ya know."

"Mmm. Well, I have need of it, brother."

"How much?"

"All of it."

"All...wh—"

"Don't ask."

"Don't ask...I'm going to hate myself for this. Or better yet, you."

The day of the fight came upon them. It was late spring and the sun at midday could be searing. Getarix had dropped off his Celtic-style checked pants he had managed to keep over the years. They were the ones lovingly make by his mother in the early spring before his departure. Getarix had held onto them as one of his most treasured possessions. Antonio's hair had grown long enough to work into two short braids. Not in a truly Celtic fashion, but braids nonetheless.

"It's not long enough to look proper, son," Antonio said.

"Trust me, Father, I'm sure no one in Rome is an expert in Celtic fashion. It's good enough for this crowd." The braids complete, he took animal fat and pulled the hair on top of Antonio's head straight up into spikes, making him look fierce indeed.

When Getarix handed him the pants, he explained about their creator. Antonio held them firmly to his face, closing his eyes tight. He breathed as much as he could, in hope of inhaling some of Agenais with the air. He paused and wept for a second before recovering. Getarix stood in silence and respect until Antonio had composed himself.

Antonio was supplied with a round shield similar to the shield that still hung in their home in Britannia, however this one was significantly smaller and strapped to his forearm. Antonio had never felt so fit in his life. He stood in his cell, naked, about to put the pants that his wife lovingly made for her son, when Jodoc disturbed the proceedings.

"Wait up, there," he called, carrying a pail of blue paint the colour of the late summer sky.

"What are you going to do with that?" Antonio asked with a touch of fear.

"I'm about to paint you, old man."

"The hell you are...we never—"

"You're about to. Listen, you want to scare the courage right out of them, right?"

"Right."

"Well this is how you do it."

"Alright..."

"And if I know Rome, which I do, you will be a crowd-pleaser." Jodoc began to paint zigzag lines starting at his forehead going right over his eyes and down his cheeks to his neck.

"Jodoc, damn you, you're getting that stuff in my eyes."

"Then close your eyes, old man."

"Don't call me old man."

Jodoc ignored him and continued to paint lines across his chest and arms in a design reminiscent of warriors of old. Once the paint had dried and Antonio was dressed in only the checked pants, he paraded barefoot with the other gladiators through the streets of Rome to the Circus Maximus. Crowds of cheering citizens and slaves alike lined the streets. It was a heady experience for the heroes of the day. For a moment, Antonio forgot that by the day's end many of these men would be dead or dying, and for no greater purpose than to entertain a bloodthirsty crowd.

They arrived at the service entrance of the Circus Maximus. It led directly to the holding cells below the seats. Getarix was there to meet his father.

"Well, how do you feel, Father?"

"For a man about to die, not bad." He chuckled.

"I have something here for you." Getarix went to the corner and got an old weathered leather bag that had seen many repairs. He dug his hands into it and brought out the dagger and belt Antonio had worn in battle a lifetime ago. After the belt was secured, Getarix presented the arm torques and helped his father get them on his upper arms.

"Why is part of this one missing?"

"I'll explain after your victory."

"You are confident."

Getarix stood back to see the entire picture. He could not help but notice the tears flowing from his father's eyes across the blue paint.

"I don't know what to say, Son."

By this time, Cullen and Jodoc were standing silently at the open cell door.

"Umm, I have one more thing." Getarix went to the corner and unwrapped their grandkin's sword.

"So, here it is, from my master's wall? How did you get it?" Antonio held it, remembering his youth.

"He is not your master any longer or ever again. Like I told you, he gave it to me as a bribe. But in doing so, I finally made a connection with you. I...we recognized the work of the artisan and even though I had never set eyes on it, I knew, the second I saw it, that it belonged to the dagger and the dagger belonged to whoever held that sword and he had to be connected to my father. I never dreamed..."

"Unfortunately, not for long. Even if I survive this fight, I will live a life in the ring and as on old man that would be a short life indeed."

"Not so, Father. I just got paid and I bought you this morning. The deal is, if you die, you die as Thalamus', and if you live you live as mine—you live free."

"Nothing like putting fire in ones belly, eh? I will fight and fight well, and even if I die, I will at least die well."

"You shall not die, Father...not today, that I'm sure. Remember the eyes."

"I will, Son." Their conversation was disrupted by one of the guards calling for Antonio to get ready to enter the ring. It was almost noon. The late-morning sun was hot and the crowd was restless. Six weeks into the games, the people were getting bored and wanted something different. The other prisoner-gladiators had not held up well and the crowd was hard to please.

When Antonio entered the ring, the crowd was not so sure about this blue Celtic warrior.

Getarix, Cullen, and Jodoc stood behind the bars of the gate where Antonio entered the ring.

"So Getarix, I thought you were to sit with the senator?"

"Funny how that invitation never came through." Getarix smiled.

"So, the bet with Thalamus the Greek is what you used my money for? At least if he does not come out we have not lost our money, eh?"

"Wrong on both accounts, Cullen. I used my own money to buy my father and I had to pay in full for him. The deal is, if he lives he is mine and if he dies he is still mine. I lose it all. That was the only way Thalamus would accept any deal."

"But you told your father—"

"He did not need that burden added to him just now."

"Tough deal, especially with the game stacked against your father."

"It's not."

"What?"

"What do you think I spent your money on?" Getarix turned to Cullen with a smile.

XLIX

THE FIGHT

The first thing that struck Antonio was the deafening noise from all sides. He looked up at the crowd and noticed that wooden stands built a third of the way down one end of the Circus Maximus created a horseshoe-shaped amphitheatre. The Circus Maximus was essentially a racetrack with stone seats running its length—a long, rectangular shape. In order to hold the fights they had needed a smaller, compact space. Even though there was plenty of talk about the need for a proper amphitheatre, Rome still did not have one.

The sun was hot and Antonio began to perspire under his paint. This caused him to itch all over. He used his crippled left hand to bring relief to his belly. The shield strapped to his left arm was so small it did not even cover his hand. He noticed that the paint was beginning to melt. He wondered if it had been such a good idea. A door opposite him opened, taking his mind from that. When his opponent appeared in the arena, he was announced and the crowd went wild as the large, heavily armoured figure carrying a full-length shield strode forward. He looked like a fanciful figure of a Roman soldier. As the crowd roared, he strode in a circle, holding his shield aloft, acknowledging their cheers. The only other men on the field of battle were the announcer and the referee. Gladiators were expensive and it was the referee's job to keep the fight fair and prevent unnecessary or unsporting deaths. Antonio had the feeling it would do him little good in this fight.

As the crowd cheered their hero, the announcer waited for silence. As the announcer introduced Antonio, the crowd booed him as vigorously as they had cheered his armoured foe, expecting another lame attempt from a prisoner fighting a trained gladiator.

Antonio looked all around him and noticed to his left a grand balcony built within the wooden stands. He turned and approached the stand, as instructed by Thalamus. There in the middle sat Tiberius, Emperor of Rome, and behind him, unmistakably the immense bulk of Antonio's former owner. He could see the senator's irritated reaction to the costume worn by his errant slave. By this time, both fighters were standing opposite the wooden stand to salute the emperor. Antonio could see the senator enjoying the booing for his former slave; nonetheless, he held his grandfather's sword high, looking not at the emperor but defiantly into the eyes of his former owner. The sun sparkled off the now highly polished gold Celtic rope design that decorated his recovered sword. The senator lost his look of arrogant victory as he recognized the sword of Vercingetorix the Great in the hands of the condemned, the very hands that had brought the sword to battle twenty years prior, and the sword that had hung victoriously on his wall for those twenty years. He almost stood up in agitation. He leaned to the emperor to say something, but Tiberius brushed him away like a pesky fly. At this, Antonio smiled wildly, boldly looking straight at the senator. Antonio felt a great victory and was at peace for the moment. He could now accept his fate, whatever it would be. This rebellion was not lost on the senator.

After their oath to fight bravely and fairly, the warriors turned to face each other. Antonio sized up his opponent. He looked tall and strong—a fighter. Antonio was glad he was not armoured like his opponent. It was hot and the paint was uncomfortable enough. Antonio could not see any of his adversary, whose armour covered him completely. Even his helmet covered the entirety of his face. Unlike the soldier's helmet, the only exposed portions were two small holes for his eyes, about the size of a man's thumbs. His advantage of armour was balanced by the weight he carried and the loss of vision and speed.

Nonetheless, Antonio muttered to himself, "So, it's here I shall die." He expected the gladiator to attack him immediately, but he simply held his defensive stance. The crowd cheered him on but he did not move. Antonio finally concluded that if this fight was to begin, he must be the one to start it. He lunged at his armoured opponent, who stepped backward. Antonio swung his sword wildly and struck the armour, creating a terrific noise, but the blow slid off him harmlessly.

The crowd did not know what to think of their hero as he continued to step back whenever Antonio lunged forward. The Celt was making a mess of his opponent's armour, but doing the wearer no harm. The crowd began to cheer for the condemned. Getarix peered to his left through the barred gate up onto the wooden stands to get a glance of the senator. He could tell his face was red. He was standing, until Tiberius in front of him got irritated and gestured to him to sit down.

Back on the field, Antonio could tell the crowd was now cheering for him and not the gladiator. He also noticed that the fight was wearing on him. He began to stumble, as Jodoc's aggressiveness had won the crowd but done little damage to his opponent. The cost of this aggressiveness was exhaustion. He was thankful for the work of Cullen in his strength training. He realized he would have been spent by this time without it. After about ten minutes, he began to really stumble. His vision became impaired as the blue paint on his forehead began to flow into his eyes. They burned violently and he knew he had to clean them out. He tried to shake his head to no avail. He brought his crippled hand to his face, blocking what little vision he had left. The tall gladiator saw his one opportunity and lunged, driving his gladius for his stomach. Antonio saw this movement from the small noontime shadow and instantly brought his left arm down where he caught sight of the blade just before his appointed death. He arched his back, falling away. The gladius continued its trajectory, but instead of driving deep into the body of its intended victim and up under the ribcage, it stayed outside, slicing a long cut from the left of his stomach up to his right collarbone. It was not deep enough to loose the contents of his body, but cut in enough to cause a flow of blood, giving the impression that he was wearing a deep red sash over a blue coat.

He lost his balance and fell backward. The crowd went wild at his survival. When he fell to the ground, his opponent did not take up his advantage. He stood there, allowing Antonio to get up and clear his eyes. Antonio knew he was spent. With the shock of the newly earned cut, he felt like someone had drained what energy he had left. His one advantage he still had was given to him by the senator. Over the twenty years of abuse, Antonio had been expected to perform no matter how many times he was whipped. This gave him unusual endurance. Adding to his determination was the thought of the senator having the final victory.

This was all he needed to tap into his final reserves. As he stumbled, his opponent attacked again. This time Antonio deflected the gladius with his sword not once but three times. The battle was fierce and the crowd reacted with greater enthusiasm than they had for weeks.

The fighters parted, breathing heavily. Antonio noticed that his opponent was at the point of exhaustion from wearing the armour in the heat. Antonio attacked again and again, only scratching the outside shell. They both were stumbling, having spent the last of their last strength. Antonio paused, realizing he was doing no harm to the wearer. He looked into the eyes of his opponent.

What he saw shocked him.

His opponent was not wisely wearing him out. Antonio saw genuine fear. It was then he heard the voice of Jodoc: *Fear in your opponent could be your greatest weapon.* Gulping deep breaths, he looked at the gladiator's helmet with the small eyeholes and his son's training finally made sense. *Remember the eyes. It does not matter how strong or fierce you are, Father, if you cannot hit the mark.*

The eyes, the eyes!

Antonio raised his grandfather's sword. The storied weapon had become increasingly heavy during their battle. His one good arm strained at the weight, tired from so many ineffective strikes. He had enough strength left to muster one last attack. He stared into the eyes of his opponent again. He saw exhaustion and eyes filled with perspiration. Antonio saw him close his eyes. It was the opportunity he needed. He thrust his grandfather's sword upward, concentrating on directing the narrow tip into the right eyehole.

He hit his mark. Not deeply, but deep enough to pierce the eye and beyond. The gladiator dropped like a sack of barley and laid there without moving. Antonio just stood, spent and bleeding. As much as he wanted to collapse beside his opponent, he needed his strength in order to have the triumph of standing before the emperor and the senator as the victor and champion of the crowd.

As he walked toward the dais, the cheers of the crowd almost carried him to his appointed spot. He felt lighter than air. Tired and spent, he held the sword of Vercingetorix the Great victoriously above his head before the emperor with all of Rome's wild approval. Finally, he had the victory he sought when he crossed the sea twenty years prior. Finally, he owned his own dignity again. Once again he was a man.

Once again, he was Kailen.

EPILOGUE

RESTORATION

After more years than he wished to count as a slave, Kailen stood victoriously before the emperor. The thunder of the crowd closed in on him like a blanket. When he had entered the temporary stadium, they had booed him as a hopeless slave and criminal. Now they cheered wildly, imploring Tiberius to grant him pardon. Kailen was in a daze, partially due to blood loss from the long cut dealt him by his fallen opponent. His blood still seeped from the wound, a blood-red sash to contrast the Celtic blue paint now melting off his body. Even the loss of blood did not tire him as much as the sheer exhaustion from the protracted fight. He found it difficult to remain standing. If it were not for the cheering of the crowd that propped him, he surely would have collapsed. He had not looked up at the crowd since the beginning of the fight. Now, in victory, he took in the spectacle of a thousand lives all cheering for him in the presence of the fat bulk of his former owner.

He looked into the wooden stands and spotted the emperor. The senator behind him was shaking like a clay pot on a stove, about to explode.

Damianus Aurelia Marius Gius, Senator of Rome, gazed in disbelief as Tiberius returned the salute from the victorious slave. The crowd went wild. A slave that a few short months ago was his possession to have, to whip, to use as he saw fit. A possession he destined to have executed in the ring.

To receive such a salute was a true honour for any warrior. It was a rare thing to receive from the first man of the empire, especially this first man of Rome. For Kailen, this meant legal exoneration for his crime. This, the senator knew. What he was not aware of was the deal made between Getarix and Thalamus the Greek. Kailen, knowing his freedom was assured, dared to look straight into the eyes of his cruel onetime owner.

Damianus glared back, attempting to intimidate without success. His only comfort was visualizing beating this slave to his death once he had bought him back from the gladiatorial school. The self-importance in the eyes of this slave painted in that ridiculous blue was more than he could endure. He glanced to the emperor for support, but Tiberius looked like he was enjoying the moment as much as the slave below. In a mix of disgust and defeat, Damianus Aurelia Marius Gaius, the great senator of Rome, stormed out of the Circus Maximus in a flaming retreat.

Kailen tempered his feelings of triumph with the knowledge that tonight some hapless slave owned by the senator would pay and pay dearly for his victory—probably the young slave Marcus.

"Drink up, everyone. This party is on me," Jodoc said. They were lounging comfortably in the apartment's main room around a large table brought up for the occasion. The table, now filled to overflowing with food, sat the guest of honour, the newly returned Kailen. Next to him on his right sat his recently discovered son, Getarix. On the other side sat his greatest discovery, his brand new daughter, Isolde. Across the table sat Cullen in a happy, wine-induced haze, and Jodoc with a yet-unnamed date. Nobody was concerned about getting to know her, because as everyone suspected she was there by the hour.

The party ebbed and flowed until the sun rose. Kailen was overwhelmed with the innumerable feelings of his newfound freedom and the knowledge that this little party would not be broken up by the tirades of his ex-master. A hard concept to grasp. Throughout the night, he was struck with the unbelievable fact that he was free. Free, and surrounded by those who loved him, and those he now loved. People he was free to love. *Free to love.* In these moments, he would experience a twinge of melancholy about his other family still in the grips of his old master.

Still awake at dawn, Kailen noticed the morning sun working its way through the slats of the window shutters. Rising from the table, he painfully discovered that his now-mended cut was swollen stiff and extremely sensitive to the touch. As he weakly stood, he noticed that the party had run its course. Getarix and

Isolde had retired to their bed. Cullen was snoring loudly in the corner. Jodoc was on his back, lost to the world, hugging an empty amphora, his true love, his date long paid off and on her way. As he turned to the window, Kailen opened the shutters and watched the sun crest the rooftops. This brought him back to the many times he'd done this just to regain his peace of mind. Seeing the sunrise helped him recover a thread of self, a self so tattered by the endless humiliation meted out at the hand of senator. He got peace from knowing that in Britannia, Aigneis might be watching the same sunrise. *Aigneis, oh Aigneis, how I long for you, to touch you, to hear your voice...to see your face. Has it been twenty years since I lost my freedom, my son, and worst of all you? To think you were carrying my second child when I went off to fight the Romans, a son I never knew until now.* Kailen fought back tears. Until he had met his new son, he hadn't known if Aigneis still lived. Not only had his bride and Cunorix survived his disappearance, but she had kept herself for him these twenty years, or at least for his memory. His eyes filled with tears as he remembers his early days with his new bride. The memories faded as newer events crowded into his consciousness. Many scenes ran through his mind: the beatings, the hate, the continual humiliation. At times, he had trouble shaking these memories from playing their narrative. Some scenes he could not bear to think of without trembling in a mix of horror and hatred for his former master.

He often wondered what ever happened to that child in the German inn who had suffered at the hands of the senator, until tonight. It had become his custom every morning to pray to whoever would listen to somehow help her. He had wrestled with guilt of being so close to her back in Germania yet unable to help. Many times the thoughts of her had chased sleep away. Even when he reminded himself that he had known nothing of the senator's actions that night until Centurion Cornelius told him the next day, he had still felt helpless to the guilt.

Now he prayed again, but this time in deep gratitude that she was safe, and in complete wonder that he could be one of those sent to protect her. It had filled him with unspeakable joy to have her sit next to him all evening, and for Isolde to call him father.

As he mulled over and wrestled with the many thoughts that raced through his mind, the sun wrapped its warmth around him. He had to close his eyes to its brightness, but let his face soak in its caressing. He thought of his love and the growing hope of someday returning to his home and bride. These thoughts were too much. He began to weep and deeply so. He wept for almost a half hour.

He wept for his loss, he wept for what he had gained. He wept at the thought of all the suffering he had been forced to endure and witness. Most of all, he wept for the close scrapes. The thought that he should not only be alive, but free and healthy with a family of his own, overwhelmed him. For that, he wept tears of joy.

AIDE MEMOIR*

Vercingetorix the Great is a real historical folk hero. He is famous in France today. He fought Caesar and won, only to later lose in the battle of Alesia in the autumn of 52 BC. In this story, he is the great-grandfather of Getarix and Cunorix.

Getarix, short for Vercingetorix, the main character of our story.

Cullen, lifelong friend of Getarix.

Jodoc, cavalry soldier and friend of Cullen and Getarix.

The Trinovantes, or Trinobantes, were one of the Celtic tribes of pre-Roman Britain. Their territory was on the north side of the Thames estuary in current Essex and Suffolk, and included lands now located in Greater London. They were bordered to the north by the Iceni and to the west by the Catuvellauni. In the book, there is a very tense relationship between the two tribes of the Trinovantes and the Iceni.

---

* Memory Aid

The Icenian was a British tribe to the north of the Trinovantes in the area of modern East Anglia corresponding roughly to the modern-day county of Norfolk between the 1st century BC and the 1st century AD. They were bordered by the Corieltauvi to the west, and the Catuvellauni and Trinovantes to the south. In the story, it is the tribe that the family of Vercingetorix settled shortly after the battle of Alesia.

Prasutagix, pronounced *Pra sue ta gix*, the frail aging chief Druid priest for the village.

Cunorix, brother of Getarix. Eleven years his senior and now the patriarch of the family, responsible for their religious and temporal affairs.

Aigneis, pronounced *I jn es,* mother of Getarix and Cunorix.

Kailen, father of Getarix and Cunorix. He went off on a raid to Roman Gaul before Getarix was born and was never see again.

Astnicx, pronounced *asst nick,* father of Cullen. He fought the Romans alongside Kailen. He cannot rid himself of memories from the war.

Cunhail, brother of Aigneis. He is a wealthy merchant who buys from the British and sells to the Romans.
Epona, Getarix's horse. Epona is Celtic for horse.

Caballo, the horse given to Getarix by his uncle Cunhail. Caballo is Latin for horse.

Marbod, the village chief and a veteran of the war that took Kailen's life.
Eppillius, pronounced *Ep pil li us,* captain and owner of the Black Rose, a merchant ship.

Damianus Aurelia Marius Gius, Senator of Rome, known as Damianus, pronounced *Dami an us.*

Antonio, the senator's chief household slave.

Centurion Cornelius Faustus Aeolos Pricus, Cornelius pronounced *Cor nil lius*, the senator's military aide appointed for a two-year term. He is based on a historical person.

Phalera, large, round disks approximately five inches in diameter, mounted on leather straps and worn over the chest armour of the soldier. Awarded for bravery similar to modern medals of honour. Made of either gold, silver, or bronze, awarded according to the merit of the act of bravery. Could also be very elaborately decorated, with glass figures or the faces of deities, emperors and such.

Teutoburger Wald, a great historical battle in AD 9, where Arminius, the German leader, soundly beat the Romans led by Publius Quinctilius Varus. The Germans destroyed three whole legions. It is believed that about 15,000–20,000 Roman soldiers died in the conflict.

Arminius (18/17 BC–AD 21), also known as Armin or Hermann. Arminius is the Latin version of Herman, which means hammer. He was a chief of the German tribe Cherusci. He defeated Varus in the Battle of the Teutoburg Forest. Through his political skill, he held an allied coalition of Germanic tribes together until defeats by the Roman general Germanicus. Afterwards, his influence waned and Arminius was assassinated on the orders of rival Germanic chiefs. Arminius's victory against the Roman legions in the Teutoburg forest had a far-reaching effect on the subsequent history of both the ancient Germanic peoples and on the Roman Empire. The Romans were to make no more concerted attempts to conquer and permanently hold German lands beyond the river Rhine. Arminius is a great folk hero to the Germans, as Vercingetorix is for the French.

Günter, innkeeper and owner of the Boar's Head Inn.

Freya, wife of the innkeeper, Günter.

Fritz, son of the innkeeper and Freya.
Isolde, daughter of the innkeeper and Freya.

Pathius, pronounced *Pa thee us*, a skinny older crewmember of the Black Rose. Called a Greek because in Ancient Rome if you were not sure of someone's ethnic origins, you designated them Greek.

Duka, a large African crewmember of the Black Rose, hails from Ethiopia, Africa.

Duplicarius, pronounced *Dup lee car ee us*, a Roman rank similar to a sergeant today. See table on Roman rank system, next page.

Duplicarius Gullis, a senior non-commissioned officer, training to be a doctor.

Miles Aquilla and Cassius, junior non-commissioned officers who train soldiers at the local Fort.

Belgica, a province in Roman Gaul, from which the modern county Belgium gets its name.

Portius Itius, a small port city later called Gesoriacum and then Bonobia, now part of France where the city of Boulogne is today, not far from Dunkirk in the area of modern Calais.

Amphora, a type of red clay (terra cotta) container with a pointed bottom. It was used to transport wine, oil, and fish sauce.

Alesia, a great battle in history where Caesar fought and beat Vercingetorix. It essentially spelt the end to any organized opposition to Roman rule of what is today France and Belgium.

Centurion Secundus Lucius Martialis, known as Martialis, the course officer for the infantry course Cullen and Getarix started.

Centurion Appius Valerius Domitus, known as Domitus, a senior centurion, commanding officer of the small training base just outside Portius Itius.

Oppidum Batavorum, the historical Roman military settlement near modern Nijmegan Holland.

Ansgar, a fellow infantry soldier in training, a strong but cocky fellow.

Ortwin, another recruit, from just west of the Rhine River. A weak soldier.

Augustus, Emperor of Rome. Born September 19, 63 B.C. Gaius Octavius. Octavius is what our month of October is named after. In the year 27 B.C., Octavius was known as Imperator Caesar Augustus. He became ruler of Rome that same year and by the end of his life, the leaders of Rome were known as emperors. He died in AD 14. Augustus is what our month of August is named after.

Antonius, the fort physician.

Centurion Sergius Vincens Faustus, the cavalry course officer who features during the German campaign.

Centurion Lucilius, based on a historical figure known for his cruelty. Upon the death of Augustus, the soldiers mutinied based on his treatment.

Esquiline Hill, one of the seven hills of Rome, and one of the best neighbourhoods to live in.

Subura, part of Rome that still exists today. It is in the Vertus Creek Valley. At the time of ancient Rome, a rough neighbourhood. Unlike the rest of Rome, Subura still had dirt roads and lacked even the basic amenities.

Rufus, real name Gwalchmai. A fellow cavalry soldier training at Portius Itius.

Beaudin, daughter of the local smith, serves tables at fort inn.

Gainer, a displaced Britannia captured in the village. A slave.
Koran, another auxiliary soldier.

Caecina, the historical adjutant of Germanicus.

Segestes, a historical character. He was a noble of the Germanic tribe of the Cherusci. He was an ally of Rome during the reign of Roman Emperor Augustus and supported Rome's attempts to conquer northern Germany. He was the father of Thusnelda, the wife of Arminius. In 21 AD, Segestes and other members of his family murdered Arminius. Segestes was eventually given a residence by Germanicus somewhere in the Roman provinces west of the Rhine.

Thusnelda, a historical figure and the wife of Arminius, the Cheruscan noble and military leader. He married Thusnelda, Segestes' daughter, against her father's will and there was ill feeling between them. She was captured and it is believed she died in Roman custody.

Segimundus, son of Segestes and brother of Thusnelda. He is a historical figure but little is known of him.

Adulfus, a spy for Rome.
The Marsi, a small Germanic tribe (German: *Marser*) settled between the Rhine, Rur, and Lippe rivers in northwest Germany. Tacitus mentions them repeatedly, in particular in the context of the wars of Germanicus. They had been part of the tribal coalition of Arminius that in 9 AD that annihilated the three Roman legions in the Battle of Teutoburg Forest. Germanicus, seeking revenge for this defeat, invaded the lands of the Marsi in 14 AD with 12,000 legionnaires, 26 cohorts of auxiliaries and eight cavalry squadrons. Celebrating the feast of their goddess Tanfana, the Marsi were too drunk to respond effectively to the Roman surprise attack and were massacred. According to Tacitus (*Annals* 1, 51), an area of 50 Roman miles was laid to waste with fire and sword: "No sex, no age found pity." A legion eagle was recovered, in the book it is the XIX. Enraged by this and other similar bloodbaths, the frequently quarrelling tribes united once again to fend back the Roman invaders. After two more years of warfare, Rome finally abandoned its efforts to push its boundaries eastward to the Weser river, and retreated permanently behind the Rhine.

The Chatti, an ancient Germanic tribe near the upper Weser, settled in central and northern Hesse and southern Lower Saxony, along the upper reaches of the Weser River and in the valleys and mountains of the Eder, Fulda and Weser River regions, a district approximately corresponding to Hesse-Kassel. According to Tacitus, among them were the Batavians, until an internal quarrel drove them out, to take up new lands at the mouth of the Rhine.

The Cherusci, a Germanic tribe that inhabited parts of the northern Rhine valley and the plains and forests of northwestern Germany, in the area between present-day Osnabrück and Hanover, during the 1st century BC and 1st century AD. Subsequently, they were absorbed into the tribal confederations of the Franks and Saxons.

The Bructeri, a Germanic tribe located in northwestern Germany (Soester Börde), between the Lippe and Ems rivers south of the Teutoburg Forest, in present-day North Rhine-Westphalia, around 100 BC through 350 AD.
They formed an alliance with the other tribes under the leadership of Arminius that defeated the Romans at the Battle of Teutoburg Forest in 9 AD. Six years later, one of the generals serving under Germanicus, L. Stertinius, defeated the Bructeri and devastated their lands. Among the booty captured by Stertinius was the eagle standard of Legion XIX that had been lost at Teutoburg Forest. Refusing to bow to Roman rule, the Bructeri in 69–70 participated in the Batavian rebellion.

The Bructeri, eventually absorbed into the larger Frankish (Ripuarians) community. A large bronze and granite monument to Arminius (colloquially known as "Hermann the German") was erected near Detmold in the 19th century and portrays a romantic interpretation with a winged helmet, his short sword held aloft in victory, and a Roman standard ground beneath his foot.

River Amisia, properly known as the Ems River in German, called Eems in Dutch and Low German, runs 371 kilometres, all of it in Germany and the Netherlands.

Broiiox, Chief of the Trinovantes.

Silius, one of Germanicus' generals.

Lucius Stertinius, a historical person. He was one of Germanicus' colonels assigned to Caecina. According to Tacitus, it was one of his soldiers who found the missing Eagle Standard of the Legion XIX.

Lucius Caius Asinius, Senator Damianus' new aid.

Centurion Gius Velius Marsallas, a century commander cohort of the Praetorian Guard.

Thalamus the Greek, a gladiator school owner. In Rome, they used the games as an opportunity to execute their criminals while gaining entertainment value out of them.

Caracalla, a consul, a minor government bureaucrat.

ROMAN RANKS

Aquilifer – The soldier who carried the eagle standard of a legion.

Alaris – A cavalryman who is a non-citizen serving in an ala, an auxiliary unit.

Ballistarius – A soldier who operates artillery pieces.

Beneficiarius – A soldier performing an extraordinary task such as military policing or another assignment outside the norm.

Capsarior – A soldier assigned to the surgeon as a medical orderly.

Centurion – The backbone of the officer corps, it means in charge of century or 100 men, but actually a century was 80 men. Similar to the modern rank of Captain.

Clinicus – A medic.

Draconarius – A Roman soldier assigned as a cavalry standard-bearer.

Decurion or Decion – A junior rank similar to a section commander, a commander legionary tent group (8 men) or a troop of cavalry (14-30 men). Paid the same as the rank Miles.

Duplicarius – A rank similar to today's Sergeant. The name means two times the pay. It was sometimes given to a soldier without the rank as an award.

Hastiliarius – A weapons instructor.

Miles or Miles Gregarius – The basic private-level foot soldier.

Optio or Optie – A Roman rank for a senior non-commissioned officer. One per century as second-in-command to the centurion. They were often soldiers who could read and write. They performed the role of administration clerks or other special tasks due to individual skills. Optie was often a stepping-stone rank just before centurion.

Praefectus Castrorum – camp prefect or camp commander.

Principales – A group of ranks, including aquilifer, signifer, optio and tesserarius. Similar to modern NCOs.

Legionaries – The heavy infantry that was the basic military unit of the ancient Roman army in the period of the late Roman Republic and the Roman Empire.

Quaestionarius – A soldier assigned the job of an interrogator or torturer.

Retentus – A soldier kept in service after serving his required term. This was one of the problems with the army at the death of Augustus. Many of the soldiers who rebelled were held over.

Signifer – Standard-bearer of the Roman Legion.

Tribuni militum angusticlavii – Military tribune. Often rich young men would do a tour with the army as part of their formation preparing them for a life of politics.

Tribunus militum laticlavius – Military tribune of senatorial rank. They were given second-in-command of a legion.